LOST

JAMES PATTERSON

& JAMES O. BORN

arrow books

1 3 5 7 9 10 8 6 4 2

Arrow Books
20 Vauxhall Bridge Road
London SW1V 2SA

Arrow Books is part of the Penguin Random House group of companies
whose addresses can be found at global.penguinrandomhouse.com

Penguin
Random House
UK

First published in Great Britain by Century in 2019
Paperback edition published in Great Britain by Arrow Books in 2020

www.penguin.co.uk

A CIP catalogue record for this book is available from the British Library

ISBN 9781787461932
ISBN 9781787461949 (export edition)

Printed and bound in Great Britain by Clays Ltd, Elcograf S.p.A.

MIX
Paper from
responsible sources
FSC
www.fsc.org FSC® C018179

Penguin Random House is committed to a
sustainable future for our business, our readers
and our planet. This book is made from Forest
Stewardship Council® certified paper.

LOST

CHAPTER 1

MIAMI INTERNATIONAL AIRPORT isn't exactly a tranquil space on a normal day—if there's such a thing as a normal day at MIA. Now, as I watched a human trafficker strolling toward the immigration portal with six kids in tow, it felt like a hurricane was about to hit indoors. An ill-tempered Customs supervisor from the Department of Homeland Security fidgeted next to me.

The supervisor's pudgy fingers beat on the tan veneer counter, thumping out a rhythm I almost recognized. The only thing Customs supervisors hated worse than a Miami cop asking for help was a Miami cop on an FBI task force asking for help.

The man stopped tapping out "Jingle Bells"—hey, I got it—and shifted to rubbing his gut, which was hanging over his belt despite the extra holes he'd punched in it. He looked up at me and said, "So what kind of task force is this?"

"International crime."

"Who from Customs is on it? There's no way you can have an international crimes task force without Customs."

He was right, but I ignored the question to concentrate on the operation.

We were acting on a serious tip we'd gotten from the Dutch national police. They were looking at a smuggling group associated with the Rostoff crime organization, and I was now looking right at the suspect, Hans Nobler.

The Dutch national was about fifty years old and dressed like he was trying to impress twenty-year-olds. In his skinny jeans and leather bracelets, the dude was more creepy than stylish. He wore a blue and orange Dutch World Cup jacket with the swagger of someone who'd played, but the colors were too close to the University of Florida's for it to seem genuine. I had at least eighty pounds on him; he didn't worry me.

I turned my attention to the children Nobler was herding, four girls and two boys. The two teenage girls looked scared. The two younger girls, a blonde and a brunette with olive skin, were striking; they couldn't have been more than ten or eleven years old. When the creepy Dutchman caressed the face of the blond girl, I almost snapped.

But part of police work is patience. Besides, I was in charge of this operation, and it looks bad for the boss to break the law during an arrest. I didn't want other members of the task force telling the FBI that I was some sort of lunatic.

The Dutchman steered all the kids to the same line for entry. Why that line? There were seven lines open, and others were shorter or moving faster. Had to be significance to that choice.

The inspector was alert and moving people along reasonably quickly. I checked the roster and saw his name was Vacile. Vacile waved the four older kids through with barely a glance;

next up was Nobler with the two younger children. Nobler casually draped his hand over the little blond girl's shoulders and played with her hair.

My stomach knotted. This wasn't my usual assignment, some shitty dope deal in the city between lowlifes I didn't really care about. I desperately wanted to get these kids out of here safely—and, to an extent that surprised me, I wanted this task force to succeed.

I phoned Stephanie Hall. As she answered, I felt a tap on my shoulder.

I flinched and turned quickly to see Stephanie herself. She said, "Are you jumpy, Tom Moon? Let's grab this shithead and call it a day. What else do you need to know about this guy? Remember, curiosity killed the cat. And will make me late."

I said, "I want to see how he accounts for the kids." My mind ran through scenarios of what could happen once we made our move. Crowds of tourists, kids in danger—the complications made me shudder.

The other two members of our task force—Anthony Chilleo, who worked for the Bureau of Alcohol, Tobacco, Firearms, and Explosives (ATF), and Lorena Perez, a Florida Department of Law Enforcement (FDLE) agent—were also lurking in the area. I used my police radio to urge everyone to be alert and gave a detailed description of the suspect.

Stephanie said in a singsong voice, "Sounds like you're trying to impress someone."

"You're the only one I ever try to impress." That made her smile, which seemed to brighten the whole room.

CHAPTER 2

AFTER I MADE detective, I realized that different law enforcement agencies always talk shit about one another. Here's the first joke I heard an FBI agent tell: "What's blue and white and sleeps four? A Miami police patrol cruiser." (Made me laugh, if I'm being honest.)

But sometimes the suspicion among agencies came from genuine issues, like the one I was having now with Customs. These agents at the airport had their own little fiefdom; they didn't care about how we gathered evidence for different crimes. They liked things quick and simple: *You're smuggling contraband; we seize it; you plead guilty; case closed.*

I tried to keep things pleasant. I turned to the Customs man and said, "Someone from the task force needs to lay hands on him before you guys."

"Ah, politics. I guess I shouldn't be shocked the FBI wants to get some publicity from this." The supervisor gave me a dirty look, yanked a radio from his belt, and said, "Raoul, pull the guy with the two kids out of line three. The guy who looks like a reject from some half-assed *American Bandstand*, the one wearing the wannabe Gators jacket."

I guess he showed me.

I looked out over the crowd. At least I had a good view of the room. There were only a few people as tall as me, and we all stuck out like giraffes. There were Europeans eager to get out in the sun, Americans returning from vacations in Europe. And rising heat in a room where too many people had been pushed in too quickly.

I watched as a lanky Customs officer in a rumpled blue uniform—Raoul—stepped away from a back wall.

I followed him. A guy my size can usually cut through a crowd, but these were people escaping U.S. Customs. Before I could even squeeze past the first heavyset tourist coming to visit America's most exotic city, the Customs agent was already making contact with the suspect, waving him over. It looked casual, at best. Raoul clearly didn't know the circumstances of the crime.

The Dutch suspect had the children behind him when he stepped up to the Customs agent. Without telegraphing his intentions, Nobler headbutted Raoul. Soccer moves to match the jacket! Then he punched the stunned Customs man in the throat and drove his whole body into Raoul's long, lanky frame. As I stood helplessly watching, Nobler somehow managed to get a hand on Raoul's pistol. He had it out of his holster before the Customs agent flopped onto the cracked tile floor, gasping for air.

I turned to the supervisor and said, "I think your man just made my point for me. Now this asshole is armed. Cover the exits, quick."

Nobler frantically searched for a way out of the crowded

room, then pointed the semiautomatic pistol into the air and fired twice. The rounds sounded like bombs in the enclosed space. The smell of gunpowder quickly reached my nose.

When my hearing returned to normal after the gunshots, I heard the higher pitch of screams as the shocked crowd realized what was happening. Soon the whole place sounded like a police siren wailing.

People scurried in every direction without regard for where the danger was coming from. I'd seen it a hundred times; panic caused more panic, and few people used common sense.

I broke free of the lines entering passport control, Steph Hall right behind me. We both sprinted, trying to catch the suspect, who knocked down about four people as he fled. The sight of the armed man made everyone panic even more, and the crowd parted in a wave to get away from the guy holding the gun.

I caught a glimpse of Nobler just in time to see him find an open access door and disappear through it.

CHAPTER 3

THERE'S AN OLD police saying: Only rookies jump into a foot chase. My own philosophy was that only an idiot chased an armed suspect on foot. But sometimes, you have no other choice. I ran like a sprinter—albeit a sprinter who weighed 240 pounds—gripping my pistol in my right hand. I had an equal match in Stephanie Hall, who stayed neck and neck with me as we kept the suspect in sight. Steph ran gracefully; I was just plain determined. There was no way this jerk-off was going to get away, even if he was considerably faster than I'd anticipated. The skinny jeans alone should've slowed him down.

The last guy we'd chased together was a murder suspect who had shoved our colleague Lorena Perez. It was embarrassing to check a prisoner with black eyes into the jail, but I had never even touched the man. No one noticed Steph Hall's bruised knuckles. I'd hate to be this guy if she caught him first.

Nobler didn't look back as he sprinted across the rough concrete floor, his longish hair streaming behind him.

Ahead of us, a black Delta baggage handler who looked like he could wrestle professionally took in the sight of the man running in his direction with the police right behind him. He moved into position to block the suspect. I appreciated it. Cops didn't see that kind of help much anymore.

Then the Dutchman raised his pistol and fired once on the run. The sound of the shot echoing through the cavernous area made the well-built baggage handler dive behind a stack of luggage.

Unexpectedly, the Dutchman spun, raised the semiautomatic pistol, and fired two rounds at me. One of the bullets pinged off the floor a foot to my right. Jesus Christ!

I dived to one side and Steph to the other. We both took cover behind concrete pillars. My heart raced and I had to take a gulp of air. Then I leaned around the solid barrier to squeeze off a shot at the suspect.

When I peeked around the pillar again, he was back to running as hard as he could. It had been a good use of a couple of his bullets; it pinned us down and gave him time to put some distance between us. I hate smart criminals.

We sprang back into the chase. The suspect was still keeping up the pace, and I was starting to get frustrated. He looked over his shoulder and saw that Steph and I were not about to give up. He changed course slightly, zigging and zagging through stacks of luggage like a striker weaving through defenders, then dived headfirst down a steel baggage chute. As he did, he dropped the pistol, and it clattered onto the concrete floor.

I scooped it up on the fly as I hit the same chute, hoping to catch up to this moron before he reached the bottom. Steph took the stairs to cut Nobler off.

He did a pretty good roll at the end of the chute, landed on his feet, and went back into an all-out sprint. That pissed me off even more. When I hit the bottom of the chute, I was gasping for air.

I stood up and started running again. Now Steph was in front of me and I could just barely see the Dutch suspect. He was making for a far door on this lower level of maintenance and storage.

A large black woman with an MIA Services jacket was the only thing between the suspect and his freedom. At least he didn't have a gun anymore.

Nobler skidded to a stop in front of the airport worker as she leaned against a souped-up golf cart that looked like it could climb a mountain. He tried to slip past her to get into the cart. When she resisted, the man took a swing at her.

She dodged the punch and lifted her knee hard into his groin. He was stunned. Then she drove an elbow right into his face.

I could hear the cartilage in his nose crunch from twenty feet away. It made *me* wince.

He tumbled onto the concrete floor, wheezing and gurgling.

As Steph and I pounced on the fallen man, I heard the woman say, "I finally got to use my Krav Maga classes."

I put cuffs on the idiot Dutchman quickly, looked at Stephanie, and said, "I love Miami."

CHAPTER 4

STEPH HALL AND I walked back through the terminal with our prisoner in tow. He didn't want to talk, but the scam was easy to figure out. He held the passports for the kids. He'd brought the kids to the U.S. after someone had paid for their transport. Paid a lot. The kids were expected to work off the cost of their transport—usually in the sex trade. It pissed me off just thinking about it.

The other two task-force members, Lorena Perez and Anthony "Chill" Chilleo, fell in next to us. The whole team marched past the corpulent Customs supervisor. Not to show off, of course, but I hoped he'd take notice; these were the cops who'd passed the FBI requirements to join the task force on international crime.

A uniformed Miami-Dade cop took our Dutch prisoner to the tiny holding cell at the airport until we were ready to transport him to Miami MCC. The federal detention center never seemed to fill up the way it should.

Anthony Chilleo had a tough aura about him, forged by fifteen years in the ATF and five before that as a Tampa cop.

Lorena, as usual, looked like she'd just stepped out of a fashion magazine. Even after running through the terminal after us, she wasn't flustered and her clothes weren't disheveled.

She said, "You okay?"

"Yeah. Do I look that bad?"

"Your hand is wrapped in a paper towel and dripping blood, your shirt's ripped, and you're sweating like you're in detox. Didn't you play football in college?"

I was about to make a snappy comeback when a man wearing a nice polo shirt and madras shorts stepped in front of me. He was only an inch or two shorter than me and had a little muscle as well.

He didn't waste any time on pleasantries. "My name is Randall Stone, and I'm an attorney here in Miami. Let me tell you something—that was some of the most careless, stupid police work I've ever seen. You put people at risk to stop someone who's just trying to get into the country. Let me guess—he insulted the TSA? Or maybe it's just another arrest to pad your statistics."

The lawyer made sure he said this loud enough for everyone in the immediate vicinity to hear. Then a woman trying to comfort her little boy stood up and walked over to me. She didn't say anything as everybody stared at us. Then, without warning, she slapped me. Kinda hard.

The slap brought Steph Hall over. Moving fast, she grabbed the woman by the shoulders. Steph was mad and I didn't want this to get any more out of control. As the boss, I had to set the tone. I'd been slapped before. Punched, bitten, and stabbed as well. This was Miami, not Disney World.

The woman said, in a strong Brooklyn accent, "My son

was almost crushed by the panic you caused. You should be ashamed of yourself."

I stood there silently, staring at the woman. I wanted to point out that it was the suspect who'd fired a pistol and run, but years of experience had taught me to let this go. In fact, from an early age, I'd learned to let most things go—my lack of achievement on the University of Miami football field, my failed love life, and even parts of my family life.

Lorena said to the lawyer and the woman who'd slapped me, "How can you people be so stupid?" Then she glared at the attorney and said, "I understand an ambulance chaser like you trying to stir up a crowd, but this lady is way out of line. You have no idea what was going on."

I cut her off and waved at the team to start walking again, away from the crowd. "It's okay, Lorena. 'The only true wisdom is in knowing you know nothing.'"

Lorena said, "Socrates."

I turned and smiled at her. "Very good. That's impressive."

She laughed and said, "You rotate between Plato, Socrates, and politicians. I took a shot. You're right—no matter how much we explain, assholes like that lawyer hate whatever the police do."

I even avoided bumping into the attorney as we took our walk of triumph.

Everything in police work depended on experience. I wanted to lead everyone away from these loudmouths before someone said or did something stupid. Lorena had a temper, something she'd have to learn to control. Maybe my example could serve as a lesson; I figured it was easier than some of the teaching methods I'd seen at local police departments.

When I was a rookie, I'd arrested a local crack dealer. The narcotics detectives set up to interrogate him and made a big deal out of allowing me, a new patrol officer, to watch it over a closed-circuit TV in the next office. I had to lock up my service weapon and promise that I wouldn't make any noise or tell anyone I was allowed to watch the interrogation.

I sat there quietly with an older narcotics detective and watched as two of the better-known narcotics detectives sat across a small table from the thin, antsy crack dealer. One of the detectives wore a shoulder holster.

Less than a minute into the interview, the crack dealer started to shout, and then, without warning, he reached across the small table and grabbed the pistol in the shoulder holster.

It happened so fast I didn't react until he was standing behind the table with the gun raised at the two detectives. Then he pulled the trigger. I still remember seeing the flashes on the fuzzy TV. *Bang, bang,* and both detectives were on the floor.

Holy shit.

I sprang out of my seat, burst through the door into the hallway, and yanked open the door to the interrogation room. That's when I got one of the biggest surprises of my life: the two detectives were sitting on the table laughing, and the crack dealer was laughing right next to them.

The crack dealer was one of their regular informants and they'd put blanks in the gun. The idea was to have a laugh at the expense of a rookie and teach him two important lessons, both of which I have never forgotten: don't wear a shoulder holster, because it's tactically unsound, and don't take a gun into an interrogation with a prisoner in the first place.

I also learned that a person could literally have the piss scared out of him from a prank like that.

Today, I'd learned never to underestimate the speed of a skinny guy. And Lorena had learned that it never paid to argue with an idiot.

CHAPTER 5

ABOUT AN HOUR after the airport worker had used her martial arts skills to disable our Dutch suspect, I found myself sitting at a long table in a Department of Homeland Security conference room with all six of the children Nobler had brought over. We looked like the weirdest corporate board meeting in history.

I said, "My name is Tom Moon. You can call me Tom."

The kids and I started chatting. At eighteen, Joseph from Poland was the oldest. His accent was thick, but he spoke decent English. We talked sports. He said, "Real football players are the best athletes, both in skill and endurance."

"I still prefer American football."

Joseph gave me a sly grin and said, "I would too if I were as big as you."

The two youngest kids didn't speak much English, but I doubt they would have said a lot even if they'd understood what was going on. They were shy and quiet. Considering what had just happened to them, I got it.

Michele, a little blond girl, was only nine years old. She was not ready to talk about how she'd ended up in this situation. She spoke only French. Our office was trying to find her parents or guardians, who were somewhere outside of Paris.

The other little girl, Olivia, was eleven years old. She was from Madrid and thought she was on some kind of field trip. I still wasn't clear on the details of how the traffickers had tricked her into coming, and I didn't know if she had family back in Spain, but we had no problem finding a translator for her. More than 70 percent of the population of Miami–Dade County was fluent in Spanish. Even *my* Spanish was good enough to just chat.

I asked her, in Spanish, "What do you like to do when you're not in school?"

"I have Rollerblades and roller skates. I'm faster than anyone in my apartment building." Her eyes positively shone as she boasted of her skill.

"I bet you are." I couldn't hide my smile.

Monnie, the teenage girl from Kenya, turned to fifteen-year-old Jacques from Belgium and whispered in his ear. They both giggled. I smiled to let them know it was okay to speak, but they were happy in their private joke.

I looked over at the Finnish girl, fourteen-year-old Annika, and said, *"Hei, kuinka voit."*

Her blue eyes opened wide and she hit me with a slew of Finnish.

I held up my hands. "Whoa, sorry. 'Hello, how are you,' is all I know in Finnish."

She smiled and switched to English. "Where did you learn to say that?"

I said, "'If you talk to a man in a language he understands, that goes to his head. If you talk to him in his language, that goes to his heart.'" The quote covered the fact that I didn't remember where I'd learned the Finnish phrase.

"What's that mean?"

"It's a famous quote."

"Who said it?"

"Nelson Mandela."

"Who's he?"

"A smart man who changed the world."

Joseph said, "Aren't you a policeman? How do you know things like that?"

"A policeman can read and go to college," I told him. I turned back to Annika and said, "What kind of music do you listen to?"

She fixed her blue eyes on me and said, "Mostly I like Top Forty pop. But sometimes I listen to classical music like Brahms or Mozart." She looked at Joseph and said, "Joseph played me a Mozart sonata on the piano before we left Amsterdam. He's really good."

I said, "My mom plays piano."

Annika asked, "Did she teach you to play?"

I let out a laugh. "She tried, but in South Florida, there are an awful lot of things for a boy to do that are more interesting than playing piano."

"Is she a piano teacher?"

"She ..." I decided to let that one go.

A short while later, a dark-skinned man wearing a jacket that said DEPARTMENT OF HOMELAND SECURITY INVESTIGATIONS stepped into the room and announced, "Time to get your stuff together, kids. It's a little bit of a drive to the place where you'll be housed."

I looked at the man and said, "Where is that?"

"Krome Detention Center."

"These kids are *victims* of a crime, not suspects. You dumb-asses let the damn suspect run. *We* caught him. Can't you find a better place than Krome for them?"

The man gave me a hard stare for a moment, then said, "Look, pal, there are certain procedures we follow, and that's where I'm taking them."

As soon as the DHS agent stepped out of the room, I gathered everyone together. Joseph looked at me with big brown eyes and said, "What are we doing?"

I smiled and said, "We're making a break for it."

CHAPTER 6

IT WAS A little bit of a challenge to fit all six kids in my unmarked FBI-issued Ford Explorer, which was made less spacious by the steel box bolted to the floor in the back. It held an MP5 machine gun, a few hundred rounds of ammunition, and a ballistic vest.

In the eight months I'd been on the new task force, I hadn't needed the extra firepower. It still amazed me how much money the federal government had to spend on international crime investigations. It was the hot new flavor of the month, and the FBI wanted all of us to look and act the part.

Even the way they'd selected us was unique. There were actual tryouts for the unit that included a fitness test, reviews by the applicant's bosses, and a breakdown of his or her three biggest cases. I'd liked the whole challenge, even the fitness test, which was held in the middle of a hot afternoon, maybe to see if anyone complained.

I'd known about half the cops there. One of them was Alvin

Teague, a Miami detective like me. The thirty-year-old Florida A and M graduate who never seemed to have a hair out of place and whose wardrobe looked like it would have bankrupted a Wall Street broker had been talking shit to everyone, trying to get in the other candidates' heads. It looked like it was working on some of them. He called me by my street name, "Anti." The name the Miami residents had given me was a source of pride.

I said, "Hello, Smooth Jazz." He was a good enough cop to have earned a street name. His was a nod to how he spoke— like an announcer on a late-night jazz station.

Steph Hall, whom I didn't know at the time, asked, "How'd you end up with a street name like 'Anti'? What are you opposed to?"

Before I could answer, Teague looked at the group and said, "Only one other brother and he's on the stout side. I'll smoke you all like cheap cigars."

The heavyset Fort Lauderdale cop looked offended as he glanced down at his stomach. Then he looked up, smiled, and shrugged.

Steph Hall stepped up and said, "I'm black. Did you overlook me because I'm a woman?"

Teague didn't miss a beat. "I couldn't overlook someone as beautiful as you. But I ran track in high school. I was the all-county champion in the four hundred meters. There's no way someone here beats me."

That's when Lorena Perez said, "Sounds like you're worried about the other parts of the tryout. Didn't you have any good cases to go over? You run your mouth so much, I don't see how you would ever hear anyone offer you a decent case."

"I recognize you. You're that financial-crimes genius from

FDLE." He didn't hide the fact that he admired Lorena's curves.

"And you're the Miami cop that I'm going to bet ten bucks can't beat my girl Steph here."

It was a great afternoon and gave me some insight into my new partners. It also gave me a good laugh. I may not have been the fastest one on the track, but I finished the one-and-a-half-mile run within the twelve-minute time limit and I had a great view as Steph Hall's long, graceful strides wore down Alvin Teague. She crossed the finish line a full ten seconds before he did.

Alvin didn't have to be reminded that he owed Lorena ten bucks. Being a resourceful detective, he used it to his advantage. He started to hand the ten-dollar bill to Lorena, then snatched it back and said, "Any chance I could pay off the bet with a nice dinner?"

"You can eat all the nice dinners you want. As long as I have your ten dollars to get a pizza later."

Everyone roared with laughter, even Alvin Teague. He was a loudmouth and a braggart, but he wasn't a bad guy, and everyone recognized he was one hell of a cop.

But he didn't get chosen for the task force.

Now, as I ushered the kids through the halls of the Miami Police Department headquarters, I was hoping to avoid Teague and any other cop I knew. I stashed the kids in an interview room with a dispatcher who I knew could handle them.

As I slipped out of the room, the dispatcher said, "Anti, you know you owe me a big favor after this."

"Anything you want, Tosha."

I raced up the stairs, wondering if witness services could help me find a place for the kids for the night, and ran into the one person I'd most wanted to avoid.

Alvin Teague, wearing a starched shirt and a blue Vineyard Vines tie with a sailboat design, stood in the middle of the staircase. He gave me a smug smile and said, "Hey, Anti, you still holding my spot on the task force?"

I just stared at him. I didn't have time to trade burns.

"I'm not joking," he said. "I'll be there one day. I hear that if you don't keep making arrests, you're rotated off."

"That's what they say."

"That's what I say too. I wish every unit was so strict. Maybe we'd get rid of some of the deadweight."

"You can have my spot when the Dolphins win a Super Bowl."

Teague let out a laugh. "Look at the philosopher making jokes. I thought your only joke was your football career."

It was pretty much the same shit I heard everywhere in Miami. It didn't faze me.

"By the way, is that fine Agent Perez still on the task force?"

I said, "She's still on the task force, but I doubt she'd give you the time of day."

"Lesbian?"

"Good taste."

Teague laughed again and waved as he brushed past me on the stairs. He called over his shoulder, "Stay safe, Anti."

"You too, Smooth Jazz."

That interaction went better than my conversation with the witness advocates. They told me the only place they could house that many kids together was Krome. I had already decided that wouldn't happen. Now I had to make another decision.

CHAPTER 7

I DROVE OUT of Miami slowly so the kids could get a decent look around. They marveled at the speeding, swerving cars, and I explained that in South Florida, hitting your brakes is considered a display of fear. It's best to avoid it.

I mentioned a few historical facts so the trip would be educational. For instance, I told them the city's name had come from the native word *mayaimi*, which meant "big lake." (No one cared.) And that Al Capone had lived here in the 1930s. (No one knew who Al Capone was.) I grew a little desperate and dredged up the legends of Blackbeard and Jean Lafitte, pirates who, it was said, used to visit the area and hide treasure on the coastal islands and the mainland.

Joseph said, "Can we look for treasure?"

"Maybe. It's not common to find it anymore, but we can go to the beach and try." That seemed to satisfy everyone.

We stopped to pick up three gigantic pizzas from Pizza Brew, and by the time we reached our destination, everyone was hungry and tired. Each kid carried a small suitcase or backpack; I balanced the three pizzas like a Ringling Brothers act and opened the front door.

When the kids stepped into the cool, wide room, they all asked some version of the same question: Where are we?

I still had some explaining to do. I'd been avoiding phone calls from my FBI supervisor that I was sure were related to me taking the kids. He was a stickler for rules, and I was fairly certain the FBI had a rule about not kidnapping minors. I wasn't worried. I intended to return them once I was certain they'd be treated right.

Jacques, the Belgian boy, stared through a sliding glass door at the patio with the pool wedged into the backyard. He turned to me and smiled. "I am a good swimmer."

I patted him on the head and said, "We'll put that boast to the test after dinner."

All of the children turned and looked at the hallway on the far side of the room. I let them stare in silence for a moment at the two women standing there like ghosts. They didn't move and both happened to be dressed in light clothes. The effect was perfect. I wasn't sure how this would play out, but the time had come to see how good my decision-making abilities were.

I cleared my throat, raised my voice slightly, and said, "Hey, guys, let me introduce you to some people." I waited as the children all gathered around me. "This is my mother and my sister. You can call them Mrs. Moon and Lila." I turned to my mom and sister. "Mom, Lila, this is Michele from France, Olivia from Spain, Joseph from Poland, Annika from Finland, Monnie from Kenya, and Jacques from Belgium. They're going to be our guests tonight."

My whole body tensed as I waited to hear what would come

out of my mom's mouth. The longer the silence stretched, the worse I felt. Then a smile spread across my mother's face and she said, "It'll be so nice to have kids around the house for a change." I glanced at my sister, who just winked.

The relief I felt was incredible. I knew I should've called first, but I'd been afraid that if my mom was having a bad day, I would've lost my nerve and changed my mind about breaking the kids out of the Department of Homeland Security.

My mom looked at me and said, "Thomas August Moon, this is the best surprise you could've brought me."

My mom was the only one who ever used my middle name, August, and she did it only for emphasis. My little sister's middle name is June. We called her Junie for a while when she was a baby, but my dad put a stop to it. He wasn't on board with my mom's semi-flower-child love of odd names.

My mom walked across the room to greet the kids. To little Michele from France, she said in perfect French, *"Bonjour, Michele. N'est-ce pas jolie?"*

The little girl grinned like a Texan holding a gun.

My sister, Lila, leaned in to me and said, "You got lucky. How'd you know she was having a good day?"

"I didn't. It was a calculated risk. Immigration wanted to hold these poor kids at the Krome Detention Center. I just couldn't let that happen." I didn't comment on the alcohol I'd just smelled on Lila's breath.

Lila was a vivacious twenty-four-year-old who partied a little on the hard side, but she never missed a day of work and took good care of our mom. I sometimes felt like my mother and I were stealing part of her youth.

"That's my big brother." She slapped me on the back. "Have you started throwing all those quotes at them? You know that's annoying, right?"

"Maybe a couple of quotes. It's one of the few skills I can show off."

"I can tell the kids already trust you. Sounds like tonight will be lots of fun. Sorry I'm gonna miss it."

"Why? Can't you cancel whatever you're doing?"

"Nope—I've got a date. You're on your own tonight with both Mom and the kids. Are you okay with that?"

"It depends on who you're going out with. If it's Blake, the idiot PE teacher from your school, then no, I'm not okay with it. He has a man-bun. If it's Melvin the accountant, I'm reasonably okay with it."

My sister cocked her head and gave me the same look she'd been giving me since she was a kid. "Funny. But if it were either of those two, I wouldn't have told you I was going on a date. I don't want to hear shit about dating Blake just because you think he's a slacker. And I don't want to be encouraged to date Melvin just because he's got a good job. Besides, last time Melvin was here, all you guys did was talk about the University of Miami and Florida State."

"Our alma maters. At least we have college degrees."

"And Melvin even uses his degree in his job."

"Ouch. That hurt."

Lila smiled and said, "I think having the kids around will be good for Mom. At least for one night. Where'd they come from?"

"I already told you. From all over the world."

"You're an ass."

"That's the word on the street. Hey, what did the doctor say this afternoon?"

Lila shrugged and brushed her light brown hair away from her pretty face. "Nothing new. He gave me a little notebook to keep track of when Mom loses her grip on reality. He told me to cherish the days that she's lucid. Big help, huh?"

"He obviously didn't go to the University of Miami's med school. He probably went to Florida's." I looked over at my mother, who I loved so much and missed at the same time. She was talking with the kids, who'd gathered around her like she was giving away candy.

I saw my mother smile, and suddenly all the problems I'd had today just faded away.

CHAPTER 8

Amsterdam

HANNA GREETE LOOKED out the wide bay window of the apartment she'd converted into an office. She and her twelve-year-old daughter, Josie, lived in the apartment next door. She'd spent a small fortune to purchase both apartments and have a door installed between them so that she could go from one to the other easily.

She stared down at the tourists rushing around on the street below. Hanna liked living in the De Wallen District of Amsterdam, the old town quarter, because of the nice apartment buildings and safe streets. Tourists loved to tell people back home that they'd wandered through the red-light district and looked at the canal from Oudezijds Voorburgwal, just below her window. There were even organized tours of the red-light district, with guides and everything. The guides always said how great the young girls in the brothels had it. How they chose their own hours. Took only the customers they wanted. Didn't mind showing off their bodies in the windows. The charade made Hanna sick. She knew what these girls really went through. There was no glamour in prostitution. Not unless you controlled a whole stable of prostitutes.

But the tourists ate it up. They'd take photographs around the sex shops and tell their friends back home about how they'd seen real-life prostitutes. Big deal. Amsterdam was a city that had historic sites in every form, but all the tourists wanted to talk about was legalized marijuana and prostitution.

Hanna had just finished speaking to someone in the United States. She made a quick calculation in her head and realized the six kids she'd been trying to smuggle into the U.S. had cost her about eleven thousand euros so far, and that wasn't even factoring in Hans's expenses and salary. She didn't like letting him sit in jail in Miami, but she wasn't in a position to bail him out. She hoped he'd understand.

There were other issues with the failed operation, the load. She'd borrowed money to cover expenses and then had essentially gone into business with Emile Rostoff, a local Russian gangster who had more than fifty thugs working for him in and around Amsterdam. But Hanna had heard that was a fraction of the men Emile's older brother, Roman, employed in Miami. The two were known as the Blood Brothers for reasons Hanna preferred not to think about. She had seen what happened to people who disagreed with the Rostoffs—missing ears, severed fingers, and scars from beatings. The local criminal population was a walking advertisement for why you shouldn't cross the Russian gang.

One of the worst punishments Hanna had seen was meted out to a young woman who hadn't paid her "tribute" to the Rostoffs to sell heroin to tourists and who'd mocked a Rostoff lieutenant. Now she had Emile Rostoff's initials carved in her cheeks, one letter on each side, and the end of her nose was missing. The girl was a tourist attraction all by herself.

Now Hanna had to explain to these same people why she couldn't make a payment on her loan.

Hanna turned and saw the three young women she employed as administrative assistants staring at her. She understood the fear in their eyes. The loss of the kids was a major blunder. Someone on her staff was responsible. Someone had talked too much.

She knew it wasn't Janine, who had been with her the longest. And it wasn't Janine's sister, Tasi, who was an airhead and therefore not given much responsibility. That left Lisbeth.

Hanna could tell by the way Lisbeth's eyes darted around that she knew she was the focus of Hanna's rage. Lisbeth had made all the flight arrangements, so this was her fault. Now she was going to learn a lesson about owning up to one's mistakes. Hanna had rescued Lisbeth from prostitution, taught her some basic clerical skills, and given her a life without strange men accosting her every night. But Lisbeth had screwed up somehow, and Hanna couldn't have that.

At thirty-five, Hanna was a lot older than these girls. Sometimes, she felt almost like their mother, and occasionally, parents had to punish their kids. She started slowly. She held Lisbeth's gaze as she started walking across the hardwood floor of the enormous room to where the twenty-one-year old sat.

Hanna said, "Lisbeth, did you hear about the cockup in Miami?"

The young woman shivered and nodded. The expression on her pixie face showed her fight against tears. "I know Hans was arrested. I don't really know anything else." Lisbeth brushed her blue-streaked brown hair out of her eyes.

"Don't I pay you to know what's going on?" Hanna kept advancing.

"I made the flight arrangements and ensured the kids had all the right paperwork."

"And spent plenty of my money doing it. Now that's all gone. We have nothing to show for it. This is a business. We need cash flow. Especially now. How do you think I should handle this?"

"I . . . I . . . I mean, I'm not sure what you're talking about."

Hanna reached down, snatched the girl's long multicolored hair, and jerked her out of the seat. The rolling office chair spun from the force of it. Hanna dragged her across the floor to the balcony.

Lisbeth said over and over, "Please, I didn't do anything wrong."

Hanna released her when they were both on the balcony. She said, "Who did you tell about the trip?"

"No one, I swear."

Hanna repeated the question slowly. "Who did you tell?"

The girl started to cry.

The tears made Hanna snap. She grabbed Lisbeth by the shoulders and shoved her so that she was dangling over the brass railing of the balcony. Hanna held on to her belt, leaving the girl suspended upside down six stories above the cobblestone sidewalk.

Hanna said again, "Who did you tell about the trip? Was it the Russians? Did you speak to the police? You'd better start talking or the last sound out of you will be a scream on your short trip to the ground." She relaxed her grip so the girl slipped a little bit more.

Lisbeth was crying and screaming now. "I swear I didn't tell anyone!" She begged for mercy, then mumbled several Hail Marys and another short prayer some priest had probably told her would protect her. He was wrong.

CHAPTER 9

HANNA LOOKED DOWN at the terrified girl dangling off her balcony. She wasn't sure what to do with Lisbeth, but at least she was getting her message across. Her other two assistants would be much more careful in the future.

Hanna heard the chime that told her the inside door between the apartments was open. That meant her daughter, Josie, was home from school. With some effort, she pulled Lisbeth back onto the balcony. She straightened the girl up and brushed her hair out of her face. Lisbeth kept sobbing.

Hanna said, "Shut up, you stupid cow. Don't let my daughter see you upset."

Lisbeth nodded nervously and wiped her nose with her bare hand.

Hanna pulled the girl close and said, "I was going to drop you, but I changed my mind. Maybe you aren't completely useless." She kissed Lisbeth on the forehead. "You know I love you girls. Now go get cleaned up."

Lisbeth scurried off to the powder room as Josie and Hanna's brother, Albert, who often walked Josie home from school, came in.

Josie trotted out to the balcony. Hanna gave her a quick hug and told her to do her homework before they went out to dinner. She watched as the twelve-year-old scampered back to their apartment, high-fiving her uncle on the way.

Hanna had needed to see a little gesture like that to calm her down. Thank God her brother was such a help.

He joined her on the balcony, where she explained the disaster in Miami.

Albert shrugged his broad shoulders and said, "Just the cost of doing business."

"I know you're not involved in the finances of the business, but the money I was going to make from those six kids would have covered a lot of our debt to the Russians."

"I told you not to borrow money from the Russian mob. Emile Rostoff doesn't fool around. He and his brother are big on messages. He sent one to the guys in Aalsmeer who were making their own meth instead of buying from him. Two of them were skinned and then dumped on the sidewalk in front of the apartment where they were cooking the meth. They were still alive and screamed for five minutes until paramedics arrived. It was a mercy they died on the way to the hospital. There's still a bloody outline of their bodies on the sidewalk. *That's* a serious message."

Hanna had heard the story but insisted that she'd had to borrow the money. "If we hadn't gotten that money last year, we'd be living on an abandoned farm somewhere down in the south. Josie's idea of culture would be American TV. Besides, what's done is done. We have to pay them back soon."

Albert ran a hand over his neatly trimmed goatee. "You

always seem to have something in the works. Are you telling me you don't have any plans now?"

Hanna gave him a faint smile. "I've been trying to put together a big load for a month. At least twenty people. Right now, I'm still waiting for two more to come from Germany. I have them stashed all over the city."

"And the diamonds? How long do you intend to hold them?"

"Not much longer. I need you to buy an electronic tracker, one we can put in a backpack. I'm going to hide the diamonds in the pack, then give it to one of the people in the next load bound for Miami."

Albert looked at his sister and said, "You're not worried about Customs finding it when they go through the airport?"

"They won't be going through the airport. Twenty is too many people to fly. This time we'll send them by ship. And when it's all over, we'll be debt-free with cash in hand. That's all any business owner could ask for."

CHAPTER 10

HANNA AND HER brother, Albert, spent much of the rest of the afternoon visiting various contacts around Amsterdam. They hoped someone could tell them something about what had happened in Miami. There was no way Hanna was going to lose that much money without getting some kind of explanation.

But so far, they hadn't gotten much information. The longer this went on, the more frustrated Hanna became. And if Hanna was frustrated, Albert was on the verge of fury.

They crossed into the Noord District by way of the Coentunnel and walked until they were a couple of blocks from the city office on Buikslotermeerplein. Their contact would meet them near the bronze statue of children playing.

At the edge of the park, Albert nudged his sister and pointed to a young woman and a man huddled in conversation.

Hanna said, "What about them?" Then the woman looked up and Hanna saw her clearly. It was the girl who'd had

Emile Rostoff's initials carved in her face, an *E* on her right cheek and an *R* on her left. Each scar covered almost the entire cheek.

The missing end of her nose was also jarring, but in a different way. It took a moment to recognize the blunted tip of an otherwise normal nose.

The man next to her was missing the fingers on his right hand.

The image of the two sent a shudder through Hanna, just as it was intended to. That was one of the reasons Emile Rostoff could live in a waterfront penthouse without anyone ever touching him: everyone was terrified of him.

Hanna and Albert had spent most of their lives in Amsterdam. They hadn't heard of this kind of violence until the Russians arrived en masse and took control of much of the city's criminal enterprises.

Hanna looked away from the Rostoff victims and spotted Heinrich, her contact from the city office, a corpulent little bald man who'd been bleeding her dry for years by claiming to have connections in law enforcement worldwide.

She saw a smile spread across the man's face as he watched her approach the bench he sat on. She'd never really liked the way Heinrich looked at her. Hanna knew his preference was for young girls because she'd provided him with some over the years, but the grubby, forty-five-year-old civil servant didn't impress her as being particularly discriminating when it came to women.

Hanna did like the way Heinrich's smile faded instantly when he noticed Albert walking a few feet behind her. Her big brother had looked out for her ever since they were kids.

A light breeze blew the man's thinning hair into odd angles.

Even though temperatures were mild now in the late summer, he had sweat stains blossoming under his arms.

She wasted no time on small talk. "I'm quite bothered about losing an entire load in Miami."

Heinrich hesitated, then said, "Is that why your brother is with you?"

Hanna said, "Don't worry about Albert. I just need a few answers."

"I would prefer to speak with you alone."

Albert stepped closer; he towered above the seated man. "What's wrong, Heinrich? You got something to hide?" He didn't wait for an answer. Albert plopped down on the bench right next to him. He pulled a long survival knife from under his light jacket. Then he made a show out of using it to clean his fingernails.

Hanna stayed on her feet. She looked down at Heinrich with her hands on her hips like a schoolmarm. "No games. Do you know anything about it or not?"

"The American FBI got the tip from the Dutch national police about your man with the kids," Heinrich told her.

"You know who gave the tip?"

He shook his head, but Hanna couldn't tell if it was a nervous gesture or if he was saying no.

Albert slammed the point of the knife into the bench's wooden seat less than an inch from Heinrich's leg. That made him jump. Albert said, "C'mon, Heinrich, it's not like someone from the Dutch police will cut off a body part if you tell us who called the tip in to the Americans."

Heinrich said, "I think you both know who it was."

Albert said, "Tell us."

"I thought we were business associates. I don't appreciate being threatened," Heinrich said.

Albert jerked the knife out of the bench and swung it like a tennis racket toward the civil servant's face. He froze it just as the edge of the blade touched Heinrich's throat.

Both men sat perfectly still, like statues. A thin trickle of blood dripped from the tiny cut Albert's knife had made.

Even Hanna flinched at the suddenness of the action and the sight of blood. But she held steady as Heinrich whimpered.

Albert acted as if nothing had happened and smiled as he said, "A name?" He lowered the knife.

Heinrich hyperventilated as he lifted his left hand to feel his neck. He mumbled, "Detective Marie Meijer."

Albert said, "That wasn't so hard, was it?"

CHAPTER 11

HANNA CALLED FOR a cab, then turned to her brother and said, "Was that really necessary?"

Albert put on an innocent look. "What? You mean the shave I gave to fat boy? People are beginning to take advantage of us. They no longer fear us. Something's got to change."

"You have a point. But threatening a public official, no matter how petty or corrupt, could come back to haunt us."

"If you weren't with me, I would've sliced off one of his fingers or an ear. Just to show that we mean business."

"That doesn't change the fact that we're facing scrutiny by the national police as well as the Koninklijke Marechaussee. We have to be careful."

Albert said, "I trained with the Koninklijke Marechaussee when I was in the army. They're mostly muscle. They don't really investigate. This all has to do with that one detective, Marie Meijer. She has it in for us."

Hanna nodded. He was right.

"I have no idea what we ever did to her," Albert said. "Maybe we should offer her a cut of our profits."

"I don't think so. She's a true believer. A bribe won't work this time."

"I could deal with her. Permanently. I could even make it look like an accident, although that's more work and less fun. Drop her in the Markermeer."

"No. Bodies always wash up on the shore eventually. Besides, cops never give up chasing someone who's killed another cop."

Albert looked down the road at the approaching cab and pouted like a little boy. "You don't let me have any fun at all."

CHAPTER 12

Miami

THE TASK FORCE was officially called Operation Guardian, mostly because when it was known as International Criminal Investigations, ICI, everyone referred to it as "Icky." Now we had an okay name and office space in North Miami Beach, a few miles from the main FBI office.

No one outside of law enforcement seemed to understand that Interpol didn't make arrests. Interpol was just a global organization that shared information. For instance, if there was a jewelry heist in Paris that was somehow connected to Miami, a French detective would fly to Florida and work with either the FBI or the Miami police.

That was one of the rationales for taking the best investigators from the most active agencies—now there was a single unit that took on the biggest international crimes. And we had to make a name for ourselves. Make a big splash.

The problem with an active unit, though, was that the office was always busy. It was hard to find a space where six kids could hang out.

I'd moved my laptop into the conference room so that I could work at the end of the table and also keep an eye on my new posse. No one in the office had shown much interest in helping me babysit.

The kids were a distraction, but only because they seemed like they were having fun and I didn't want to be left out. I abandoned my report to play the Monopoly game someone had brought in to keep them occupied.

Monnie said, "I've never seen this game before."

Jacques was amazed. "It's old. I saw a TV show where they said the British POWs in World War Two played it."

Olivia said to me in Spanish, "Can I play?"

I hugged her. "Of course. We're all a team. We all play or no one plays."

And that's how one of my best days started.

Forty minutes later, while I was considering putting houses on Ventnor Avenue, Anthony Chilleo stepped into the room. Sometimes, dealing with Chill was like dealing with a wild animal; he might disappear or he might eat out of your hand. I hadn't quite figured out the quiet ATF agent yet.

Chill was about average size, but he was solid. He also had a certain intensity to him that made everything he said seem vital. I hated to generalize, but that was a characteristic I'd noticed in all the ATF agents I'd worked with—they brought this intensity to everything they did. I figured it was one of the reasons they had such a high conviction rate. And I guess if I worked for a small, underfunded agency whose main task was getting illegal guns off the street, I'd develop the same kind of determination.

He placed a black camera bag at the end of the table. All he said was "This is for you."

As he started to leave the room I called out, "Whoa, Chill, what are you trying to give me? That doesn't look like a gift."

The wiry forty-five-year-old ATF agent said, "It's a bag of electronic-surveillance shit. As the second in charge of the unit, you're supposed to keep it in your car in case we need it in the field. A couple of recorders, a camera, and a tracker. Usual stuff."

He hesitated like he had something else to say, then motioned me out of the room so the kids wouldn't hear us. He said, "I heard something that might be related to your new case."

"What's that?"

"Roman Rostoff was part of the group trafficking the kids."

"Rostoff? I thought he was more of a drugs/extortion/pimp kind of gangster. Now he's involved in human trafficking?" Roman Rostoff tried to present himself as a legitimate business-man who had a ton of political influence from his donations, but most cops knew he was the Godfather of Miami.

"He's involved in anything that'll make money. I'm looking at him for exporting guns to Syria."

"You got any snitches into him?"

Chill shook his head. "It's tough to get someone close enough. He only has other Russians near him. They're the ones that talk to people outside the organization. He's a shifty one. I hear things through the grapevine. And I heard he's pissed. He had plans right away for the girls in your new little family."

I shuddered at that thought.

I said, "Do you think he could cause trouble?"

"He can always cause trouble. The question is if it's worth it for him. If he thinks losing these kids reflects badly on him, he might do something. I just have no idea what."

"I thought you said he only cares about what makes money."

"Yeah, but Rostoff thinks ahead. If he believes losing a load of people hurts business later, he might do something crazy. I'll keep my ears open."

"Thanks, Chill."

And just like that, he was gone. Chill didn't like wasting time in idle chitchat. He wanted to get things done right away. That's probably why he'd joined the ATF instead of the FBI.

CHAPTER 13

A FEW MINUTES after Chill left, Stephanie Hall popped her head into the conference room and greeted us; she addressed each kid by name and in his or her native language. Maybe what people said about the education you get at Ivy League schools like Brown, Steph's alma mater, was accurate. I could barely pronounce some of their surnames.

Steph pulled me out of the conference room to give me a quick heads-up. "I've heard that the bosses are annoyed you took the kids without anyone's approval. Be ready if the skipper calls you into his office."

She must've seen the concern on my face because she added, "Don't worry. You handle him really well. We're all glad you're the second in command so we don't have to talk to him."

I said, "Does he always start off with the 'I have two years before I retire' speech?"

"He does it more during stressful situations. I think it's a mantra he uses to keep calm. By telling someone else about his retirement, he's reassuring himself."

Right on cue, after my conversation with Steph, I got a text saying the boss wanted to see me, and I didn't waste any time getting to the office of the FBI supervisory special agent in charge of our unit. He seemed like a decent guy, but I'd heard his background as an accountant made him risk-averse. He weighed every decision and tried to anticipate every possible outcome, even though any cop out of the academy knew you couldn't plan for everything. Shit turned bad at a moment's notice and you had to improvise.

One thing my mom had taught me was not to overthink things. Make a decision and go with it. I had helped my mom since my dad left, when I was fifteen and Lila was only seven. That's why I chose a college so close to home. While my friends went to far-off Florida State in Tallahassee, almost five hundred miles away, at the University of Miami, I was never more than forty minutes from home. Some of my teammates used to call me a mama's boy. If being raised by a strong, decisive woman made me a mama's boy, I was not offended at all.

I was still getting used to having a friendly, measured boss. Police department supervisors are much more straightforward than FBI bosses, and they don't have too much regard for your feelings. I always knew when a Miami PD captain was mad at me because he or she would yell and maybe even throw something. I liked that directness. No fuss, no muss. Get it out in the open, know where you stand, and move on.

The FBI didn't seem to work like that, but they liked the fact that I had done well at UM and knew how to talk to people. And this time, when I sat down, my FBI supervisor was direct and to the point.

"Next time you intend to kidnap a group of kids, give me a call first. DHS is all bent out of shape. They're being a pain in the ass about getting the kids back to Amsterdam."

"What? When did you intend to send them back?" I asked.

"I'm sorry, did you want to play board games with them a little while longer? We need to get them home as soon as possible."

"Fine, let *me* escort them home. That way I can confer with the Dutch authorities and maybe gather some more evidence on this shithead we locked up yesterday."

"You have any idea how much that would cost?"

"You sound like it's your money. Someone is gonna have to fly back with them. Why not me?"

"What if something happens here while you're gone?"

"Steph Hall can handle anything that pops up. I thought that was why we had a whole task force to work with. You can't imagine what these kids have been through. And it happens to kids every day. We've got to make a case on the entire ring smuggling people into the U.S. That might make a difference. I can't do that if I let my best witnesses disappear."

I studied the supervisor's face. He didn't look worried. He was thinking. Thinking this through to see how it might affect him over the next two years.

Finally, he sighed.

That was usually a good sign.

"Make the arrangements and be on your way in the next two days."

CHAPTER 14

AT LUNCHTIME, I took all the kids out. No one seemed sorry to see us leave the office. Maybe I was already used to how much noise my new posse made. They were kids; what were you going to do? Maybe they were a little rambunctious. After all, most of them hadn't had much parental supervision for a while. But God, I enjoyed spending time with them.

As we hustled out the door, Monnie said, "Where are we going?"

I said, "You can't visit Miami and not have a little fun. We're going to do some sightseeing and have a *lot* of fun." I didn't tell them that I also wanted to be away from the office in case my supervisor changed his mind and sent them back to Amsterdam with a DHS representative.

I drove through the city, giving the kids more fun facts, like how it was the only major city in the United States founded by a woman.

Annika asked, "Who was she and what'd she do?"

"Her name was Julia Tuttle. She did it by sending an orange to a railroad magnate named Henry Flagler. It was after a frost, and everyone thought the Florida orange crop was destroyed. She convinced Flagler to extend his railroad all the way to where Miami sits today."

I glanced around the car and realized they needed a different form of fun.

We visited the Miami Seaquarium, where I had a contact who let us in for free. It's amazing that a couple of University of Miami football tickets twelve years ago still got me free shit around the city. This city loved its team, warts and all.

The kids thought they were at SeaWorld. I explained to them that SeaWorld was two hundred and fifty miles north and this was a local attraction everyone loved.

Once they saw the sharks, they thought the Seaquarium might be the greatest place in the world. I agreed. I remembered my dad taking me here when I was a kid. I didn't care if the other kids thought it was lame; I was with my dad. It was cool.

Monnie pointed to a flock of parrots noisily fighting in a tree. "I didn't know there were parrots in the U.S."

I smiled. "There weren't, originally. People brought them to Miami as pets and let them go. Without natural predators, they multiplied fast. Now they're everywhere."

Finally, the kids were appreciating my Miami trivia.

After a couple of hours of fun, we got back in the car and started to make our way north toward my house. Joseph and I got into a deep debate about the merits of soccer versus American football. The next thing I knew, I'd bought a football at a local Walmart and we were in a park next to the Pompano Beach airport.

I explained the basic rules, which they seemed to have a

hard time understanding. We tried some simple plays with me as a quarterback and each kid taking a turn as receiver. I told Joseph, "Run a pattern along the sideline, then cut to the middle, and I'll drop a pass right over Michele into your hands."

I called out a fake signal and Jacques hiked me the ball. I watched as Joseph ran in a random manner, went past Michele, then ran back toward me. I tossed the ball a few feet and he caught it.

When he was done, I said, "Why didn't you run the pattern I suggested?"

He looked at me like a kid explaining something obvious to a parent and said, "I didn't understand anything you said after *Run.*"

That made me laugh. Hard and loud.

After we were once more in the car and headed back to my house, Annika said in her elegant accent, "Did you play football in school?"

"I did. I even got a scholarship to play football at the University of Miami."

Jacques was excited. "Did you play professionally after that?"

I chuckled. "No, I never got close to the NFL. I barely played at the University of Miami. My position coach reminded me often that I had run the slowest forty-yard dash of any tight end ever at the school."

Olivia said, "What's a tight end?"

That made the older kids laugh.

I said, "It's a receiver who also blocks. Usually they're bigger than wide receivers."

Annika said, "You're really big."

I laughed. "Back then, I lifted a lot of weights, and I was thirty pounds heavier than I am now."

"Did you like playing?"

"I did. It also paid for my schooling, and then, when I went back for law school, they gave me a huge discount. I'm pretty happy with my limited football career, even if I never did go pro."

Joseph said, "Did you have a nickname? Like 'the Rocket' or 'the Greatest'?"

After I finished laughing, I thought about how happy I was that no one from my old team had heard the question. Then I told them all my current nickname, "Anti."

Annika said, "Like someone's aunt?"

"No, like you're against something or the opposite of something. Like anti-government means you're against the government."

"What are you against?"

I hesitated. "In this case, it's a name people in the neighbor-hood gave me. They say that Ray Lewis is the greatest defensive player who ever came out of the U, so the real nickname they gave me was 'Anti-Ray' because I was the opposite of him. They were saying I was the *worst* offensive player to come out of the U. Over time everyone shortened it to just 'Anti.'"

"Isn't that an insult?"

"Yes and no. The local residents wouldn't give me a street name unless they knew me and trusted me. I like to be called Anti by people in Liberty City. It means I made some kind of impact."

Joseph said, "Should we call you Anti?"

"Not unless you want me to make up a mean nickname for you."

CHAPTER 15

WE MADE IT back to my house in Coral Springs late in the afternoon. Lila met me at the door and said, "Tough day."

That meant my mom wasn't herself. Or, more accurately, that she was herself at a different time and place.

I followed the piano music, which was always great no matter what kind of day my mother was having. When I stepped into the small parlor, she looked up and said, "Hey, Chuck."

Ugh. Chuck was my dad. He'd divorced my mom sixteen years ago, and that was where she'd flashed back to when she'd checked out for the day. I suppose that was a time when everything seemed to be going well. I had given up trying to understand this goddamned disease a long time ago. I just wanted my mom to be happy. I didn't care what the doctors called the disorder; whether it was dementia or Alzheimer's, she was just as lost to me. I felt like one of the pillars of my life was gone.

I pulled Lila into the kitchen and told her about my pending trip to Amsterdam with the kids. My sister poured her heart into working with special-needs children every day, and she still managed to deal with my mom without complaint. I felt guilty piling more on her.

She said, "I can probably take care of Mom on my own, but it's a scary prospect. I thought the reason you went with the Miami Police Department instead of a federal agency was so that you could help me."

"You're right. If you really think I need to stay, I'll work it out."

She thought about it for a moment, then said, "I can handle it. I think it's great you want to take these kids home personally."

"I'm glad somebody thinks it's great."

Lila cocked her head and said, "I've never heard Mom play Beethoven before. She's more of a show-tune-and-pop-music kind of gal."

We walked back into the parlor and I was surprised to see Joseph sitting next to my mother on the bench playing Beethoven's Piano Sonata no. 4. It was the first time my college music-appreciation class had come in handy. It was haunting.

All of the kids stood around the piano, and my mother looked positively thrilled.

And that made me positively happy.

CHAPTER 16

I WAS GROGGY the next morning as I pulled over by the park in Hallandale Beach, right next to the county line. It was so early that the presence of police cars and a crime scene still hadn't attracted many onlookers.

Hallandale's South City Beach Park used to be referred to as "Needle Junction" and "Body Drop Park." It had been cleaned up a lot since then, but there was still room to do shit without anyone seeing you.

The phone call from Anthony Chilleo at 5:15 that morning had startled me out of a sound sleep. I'd raced over here from my house, twenty-five miles to the northwest.

I held up my badge to the young patrol officer who was maintaining security around the perimeter of the crime scene. She seemed like a kid to me even though she was probably in her midtwenties. That's what six years of police work in Miami can do to you.

I followed her directions and carefully walked along the path marked by tiny flags. Crime scene people were busy combing the area on both sides of the path, and I could see Chill talking with a Broward County Sheriff's Office homicide detective.

Chill made the introductions, and the homicide detective reminded me that we'd met once in a class on money laundering.

After the small talk, I asked, "So did you think I needed to come down to the beach so early?" I said it with a smile, even though I was confused.

Chill said, "I told you about the rumors of Roman Rostoff being involved in everything, including human trafficking."

"I remember."

"I think he's showing his displeasure with how we interrupted his shipment of kids being smuggled into Miami International." He pointed to a set of screens hiding something that a crime scene technician was photographing.

I stepped over to the screens and looked behind them. I knew there was going to be a body. There wouldn't be this much commotion over cocaine that washed up on the beach or some recovered stolen property. But the image shocked me, and I knew it would haunt me for a long time.

The young woman, a teenager, lay sprawled on the sand, naked. She had blond hair and a beautiful girl-next-door face. Her blue eyes were still open and staring straight up at the sky.

There was a neat slit in her throat with dried blood on both sides leading to the sandy ground. I squatted down to make it look like I was getting a better view, but in fact the scene disturbed me. I needed to wrap my head around this nasty business. She reminded me of some of the girls I'd rescued from the Miami airport.

Chill squatted down next to me and held up a plastic evidence bag.

I struggled to see past the spatters of blood on the inside of the bag. "What am I looking at, Chill?"

"Someone stuck her Florida driver's license as well as her ID from Serbia into the wound on her throat. We've already done some quick background on her. She was a dancer at one of Roman Rostoff's clubs. The two IDs and a talk with a coworker indicate that she was smuggled into the United States. Rostoff wants us to know that if we screw with his business, someone is going to get hurt."

I looked down at her pretty, lifeless face. Somehow I felt responsible. At the same time, I was pissed. Who did this asshole think he was?

I stood up and backed away from the body. I looked at Chill and said, "How do you feel about doing something the FBI wouldn't approve of?"

"To tell you the truth, I do that every day. Just on principle."

I smiled. The ATF agent didn't say much, but I was getting the idea that he'd be useful in an insurrection. People like that are hard to find.

CHAPTER 17

A FEW HOURS later, I found myself on Biscayne Boulevard in front of a beautiful skyscraper overlooking the bay. It housed the headquarters of AEI Enterprises, and I cringed when I realized that it also housed the law offices of Robert Gould, the man who was now married to my ex-fiancée.

Chill met me in the lobby. He'd thrown on a sports coat and looked remarkably professional. I was still wearing my 5.11 Tactical pants with my gun on my hip. We were in the city of Miami now. This was my territory.

Chill said, "I worked a case in front of here once."

"The Che Guevara shirt?"

He smiled. "Exactly. You were on it too?"

I hadn't been, but I remembered it well. A Cuban immigrant had taken deadly offense to a tourist's Che Guevara T-shirt. "I had just come on the PD and was working patrol," I said. "When I heard someone had been shot in this area, I was curious. I guess that hipster from Chicago learned his lesson the hard way; even *I* knew you didn't praise Castro or Che in Miami."

Chill nodded. "People who don't understand shit like that shouldn't be allowed to leave home. I was surprised the jury even convicted the Cuban shooter."

"Of manslaughter, not murder. He was a hero in the city when he came home three years later. I heard he never has to pay for a meal on Calle Ocho."

I glanced around the opulent lobby and said to Chill, "What does *AEI* stand for?"

"American Entertainment and Investment. It's Rostoff's supposedly legitimate business, the one that handles his nightclubs, alcohol-distribution companies, and foreign investments. He's listed as the president, and there are half a dozen other Russians in the top corporate spots."

"Hiding in plain sight."

"Roman Rostoff doesn't even try to hide. He just donates truckloads of money to the county and city commissions. One of the state senators in the area has stepped in four different times to help him out with business licenses and real estate issues. He's an old-time gangster who brings in money from a dozen ventures and understands that he needs politicians in his pocket to keep going. They're giving him some kind of award in Miami Beach soon."

We rode the elevator up to the forty-first floor. All of the offices here were occupied by AEI Enterprises. A sharp-looking receptionist who wore superthin glasses, probably as a fashion statement, asked if she could help us.

I said, "We'd like to speak with Mr. Rostoff."

She looked us over, and we clearly didn't pass the test. "I'm sorry, Mr. Rostoff's schedule is quite filled today."

"When does he have some time?"

She glanced at her computer, hit a few keys, then smiled and said, "Unless you have an appointment that he's agreed to, his next free time is in April of next year." She smiled again and somehow made it seem sincere.

That was my cue to walk past her. If you're not making some kind of effort, I don't have time to deal with you.

Chill let out a low chuckle as he followed me to the giant double doors that I assumed led to Rostoff's office. I opened both doors to make our entrance seem more spectacular. But our entrance couldn't compare to the incredible view of Biscayne Bay, South Beach, and the Atlantic Ocean beyond. It might have been the best view I'd ever seen in Miami.

That pissed me off a little bit more.

We walked toward a man in a blue Joseph Abboud suit sitting behind a carved oak desk. He looked to be about fifty-five years old. Before we'd gotten three steps, two other men sprang into action. The tall, muscular one turned to me; an older guy in a suit moved toward Chill.

I held up my ID quickly and said, "This is a police matter."

The man near Chill said, "I know. It's called criminal trespass. And you're going to get arrested for it."

CHAPTER 18

I APPRECIATED THE quick comeback by the jerk in the suit.

The tall man closer to me didn't say anything, which meant he was the one who was going to take action first. He was about an inch taller than me. I'm not used to men with a longer reach than I have, but he didn't try to punch me. He reached out with both hands to grab me by the shirt. It was like a drill we used to do on the practice fields—someone grabs your jersey, you knock his hands away. In this case, I put my weight into it, and after I knocked his hands away, I gave him an open-handed slap on the back of his head. That is one of the most disorienting blows you can suffer, the good old Gerber slap. It might not cause much damage, but for a couple of seconds you're knocked stupid.

He stumbled forward, fell onto an expensive Asian carpet, then slid into the decorative baseboard.

I reached for my gun, and the man near Chill started to reach into his suit jacket. This was turning ugly fast.

Just as everyone was about to pull a gun, Roman Rostoff yelled, "Enough!" We all froze. Rostoff said, "Billy, help Tibor up." He looked at Chill and said, "What can I do for you, Agent Chilleo?"

Chill said, "I'm impressed you know who I am."

"I always learn the names of people trying to hurt me or my business. But who have you brought with you? He looks more like a professional wrestler than a cop," Rostoff said. He had almost no Russian accent. I was surprised that he was neither intimidated nor flustered. That was a disappointment. I'd been hoping to scare him a little bit, but mostly I'd just wanted him to know we were watching.

I said, "My name is Tom Moon. I'm a detective with the Miami PD working on an FBI task force."

"What kind of task force, Detective?"

"International crime. Right now we're looking into human trafficking."

Rostoff clucked his tongue and said, "Is there such a thing as human trafficking? There are so many people that wish to come to America, how could there be human trafficking here?"

I knew his smile was designed to annoy me. It worked. I took a moment to size up the other men. The one named Billy looked like he was in good shape. He had dark, thinning hair and a goatee with a blue tinge to it. I guessed he was trying to look younger, but no hipster I'd ever met wore a thousand-dollar Brooks Brothers suit or had hands that looked like they could crush granite.

The other guy was standing now and trying to look tough even though I had just smacked his ass onto the floor. He was younger than the other one and had long hair tied in a pony-tail and the sides of his head shaved. A tattoo of a blossoming branch came from under his collar up his neck to the right side of his face. It looked a little like the van Gogh painting of almond branches. I was willing to bet each white blossom represented something, like a person he'd killed. None of these ass-wipes had tattoos for the hell of it.

I said, "Wasn't the girl found murdered on Hallandale Beach trafficked? Poor Serbian girl was brought to the U.S., thinking she was going to live the dream. Instead, she ends up working at one of your shitty clubs."

Rostoff kept his smile. "Who are you talking about?"

"Valentina Cerdic."

He shrugged and said, "Don't know her."

Chill said, "She worked at Club Wild." He looked at the man with the dyed goatee. "That's one of the places you run, right, Billy? You're the guy people call Billy the Blade."

Billy gave him a smile and then looked over to his boss.

Rostoff turned his attention to the ATF agent. "Did you enjoy watching this dead girl dance?"

Chill was far too cool and collected to let a comment like that get to him. Cops who bite at that kind of bait never get much done.

Rostoff said, "Now, why did you gentlemen really come up here? Was it just for the view? Perhaps to practice your martial arts on my associates?"

I said, "I wanted to get a look at what kind of shit-heel murders a girl and stuffs her ID into a hole in her neck."

"Then I suggest you start searching for the killer."

"We already are." I looked at the well-dressed, fit man who had confronted Chill. I said, "Billy, is it? What kind of Russian name is Billy?"

The man lost his smile and said, "One you should remember."

"No need to worry about that. I remember almost everything. Plus we'll be keeping a close watch on you."

Rostoff clapped his hands together. "Excellent. You can never be too safe. Tell me, Detective Moon, do you think you're safe? Being a police officer is a terribly dangerous job."

I stepped a little closer and said, "You think you're smart. Beyond our reach. Let me assure you that you're wrong. This isn't a seventies NYPD movie. No one is untouchable. Especially if the FBI is after your ass. You should have learned that from Al Capone. Another Miami resident."

"We shall see."

I turned to leave. "We'll be in touch."

As we stepped through the door, I heard Billy mumble, "So will we."

CHAPTER 19

I SPENT A long, tiring day making sure everything was in order to take the kids back to Amsterdam.

Virtually everything in the police world ran on favors. The more help you gave, the more help you got. So even though I was crazy-busy, when a homicide detective asked me to swing by the PD to help him interview a witness, I couldn't refuse.

The witness, Hazel Branch, was an elderly woman who lived off Miami Avenue and had known me since my first days on patrol. She was an eyewitness to a drive-by shooting and she said she'd only talk to me.

I had to help, but it wasn't because of the detective's request. It was because Miss Hazel had helped me out once. When I was on patrol as a rookie, she'd warned me about a gang-initiation ambush. Two beefy young men with baseball bats were planning to break my legs when I walked through the apartment complex. Thanks to Miss Hazel, I changed my route and walked up behind those two young men while they were waiting for me. I said, "Can I help you fellas?"

They both jumped and turned quickly. One of the men inadvertently whacked the other in the arm with the bat. That started an argument between them, which led to some good swings, and each man took some lumps.

I didn't make an arrest. I couldn't risk tipping them off to Miss Hazel. Besides, it was fun watching those two punish each other more than any judge would have. And I never forgot what I owed her. I always came when she called.

I stepped into the comfortable interview room. Miss Hazel, who wore a simple, dignified dress, as she always did, looked up and said, "Hello, Thomas. Would you explain to this young man that I don't need trouble with any of the local gangs?"

I sat down in the chair across from the elderly woman. "Miss Hazel, he's just trying to figure out who killed that young man in front of your apartment. I know you said you heard the gunfire, but do you know what time? Did you happen to glance at the clock?"

"Thomas, if I looked at the clock every time I heard gunfire in my neighborhood, I'd never get any sleep."

I tried not to laugh—I didn't even know if she was trying to be funny—but I couldn't help it; the detective and I both broke up. After some casual chatting, I finally got something worthwhile from Miss Hazel. I asked, "Do you have any idea who shot him?"

She smiled slyly. "Now, that's a good question. The youngest Gratny boy shot him."

"How do you know that?"

"Because I heard him tell Bean Pole, who lives in the apartment next to me."

I glanced up at the detective to see if he knew who Bean

Pole was. He nodded, looked at Miss Hazel, and said, "Why didn't you say that at the beginning of our interview?"

She said, "I don't know you from the pope. But I know Thomas. He won't tell anyone what I told you. And he wouldn't have asked the question in front of you if he thought you'd tell anyone."

Now the homicide detective owed *me* a big favor.

CHAPTER 20

THAT EVENING, LILA slipped out again with some friends, this time to go dancing in Fort Lauderdale. Looking after both my mom and the kids that day had sapped my last bit of strength.

Which was why I was sleeping so hard when Lila called in the middle of the night.

"Hey, are you okay?" I asked.

"I am great, big brother," she slurred. "Come down to the beach and join me. That way you can give me a ride home when I'm done."

"It sounds like you're already done. How much have you had to drink?"

"Just a few vodka-and-cranberries and some champagne."

I heard someone say something behind her and caught snatches of music. I figured she was in the ladies' room or maybe outside one of the clubs.

Lila added, "Oh, and we had a few shots too."

Ever since men started realizing my little sister was a beauty, I'd told her that if she had too much to drink she should call me and I'd come pick her up, no questions asked. I didn't mind missing a little sleep if it meant my sister didn't accept a ride from a stranger.

I said, "Where are you?"

"Beach Rockets, between Sunrise Boulevard and Las Olas."

"Isn't that the new place for spring-breakers? I thought it had a young crowd."

"I'm only twenty-four! Just because I act like an old person around you and Mom doesn't mean I'm not young. It's a fun dance club and tonight was ladies' night."

"Okay, I'll be there in twenty minutes."

I slipped through the house quietly. There were kids sleeping on couches and air mattresses everywhere. At least, that's how it felt. I checked to make sure my mom was asleep.

I was a little nervous about leaving, but I had no choice. I didn't want to wake up six kids and drive them twenty minutes to wait outside a bar. Everyone had my phone number, and they all knew how to use the house phone. Kids in the U.S. might not know what a landline was, but these kids did.

When I pulled up to trendy Beach Rockets, I could feel the music pulsing through the walls even from my car. The bright colors and decorative rockets near the door covered up the fact that the place had been a dive bar six months ago. Of course Lila wasn't waiting outside for me, and she wasn't answering her phone. I could hear the beat of the bass through the thick concrete walls, so there was no way she could hear her phone inside the club.

It'd been a while since I'd had to pass a bouncer and a uniformed cop working the door to get into a dance club in Fort Lauderdale. Or anywhere else, for that matter.

The place wasn't all that big, but I didn't see Lila. I stood there for a few minutes, hoping she'd walk by. Then someone said, "Are you waiting for your sister?"

I was about to say yes, but then I turned and saw who had asked me the question: Rostoff's man Billy. Billy the Blade. His blue goatee seemed to make his teeth glow in the low light of the club. And standing at the bar right behind him, wearing a goofy smile, was Tibor, the tall Russian I'd smacked. Even in the dark, I saw the flowering tattoo running up to his face.

CHAPTER 21

I STARED AT the two Russians casually drinking Budweisers at the end of the bar. My right hand involuntarily moved toward the department-issued Glock that was stuck in my waistband with my shirt hanging over it.

It was one of the few times I was at a complete loss for words. I wanted to just pull my pistol and put a bullet in the face of each of these lowlifes.

Billy, as friendly as ever, said, "Lila was here just a minute ago. I'm sure she'll be right back."

The other Russian, Tibor, winked at me.

I don't know what he thought would happen. I don't know who they were used to dealing with. But it didn't matter. I brought my hand up to his crotch and used the strength I'd been working on since the coach had told me I needed a better grip on the football twenty years ago. I felt Tibor's testicles mash in the palm of my hand.

He gasped and his eyes rolled back in his head as I

maintained my hold and pushed him against the bar. No one saw what was going on except for his friend Billy.

I turned to Billy and calmly said, "My next move will be to rip his balls right off him. I doubt he wants that to happen. What do you think?"

Billy struggled to maintain his composure and said, "I think you just committed felony assault. I think you need to release him right now. We're part owners of this club and there's a Fort Lauderdale police officer working the front door."

"Why don't you go get him? I've got a few questions to ask him myself. And if I don't see my sister in the next thirty seconds, your buddy here isn't going to have any kids and you're going to have a pistol stuck halfway down your throat. Is that what you want to happen in your nice little club here?"

Then I heard Lila from the other end of the bar. "Hey, Tommy, I see you met my friends."

I turned to see my little sister wobbling toward me with a stunning young woman whose arm was draped around her shoulder.

I released Tibor's balls. He stumbled back and plopped onto a barstool without a word.

I turned to Billy and said, "This is not cool."

"What do you mean? Your sister making new friends? I thought it was very cool."

Lila came up to me, unaware of any potential violence, and said, "This is Nadia, Billy, and"—she looked at the man I had nearly castrated—"and their friend."

I took her by the arm and started to drag her out of the club.

Lila tried to yank her arm away from me and said, "Hey, what the hell are you doing? I thought you were okay with me calling you for a ride now and then."

We burst out of the club into the warm night air of South Florida. No one paid any attention to us.

This wasn't the time to explain things to her. As soon as we were both in my Explorer, I pulled out of the spot and rolled past the club.

Billy stood just outside the door and gave me a friendly smile and a wave.

CHAPTER 22

THE TALK WITH Lila went about like I'd expected it would. She said I was too suspicious; I told her she was too naive. In the end, she agreed not to go back to that club or any of the other ones Rostoff owned. She also promised she'd check in with Anthony Chilleo every couple of days while I was away.

Chill told me that he'd keep an eye on things. When a guy like Anthony Chilleo tells you he'll take care of something, you can be confident it will be taken care of.

Two days later, the kids and I were all on a KLM flight from Miami International to Amsterdam. The two youngest girls were next to me, and the other four kids were across the aisle spread out over two rows in front of me. The man across from me asked if we were on some sort of school field trip. Some of the passengers looked relieved I wasn't sitting beside them. No one wants to be stuck next to a big guy in economy for eleven hours.

The kids were not excited about going back to Amsterdam. Annika from Finland had told me she lived there with her mother, but her mother's drug problem had gotten so bad that she could no longer function. Once Annika's mother had gotten into the social services network of Holland, Annika had lost touch with her completely. Two months ago, she'd learned her mother had died, and she'd decided to start fresh in the United States. She met a woman who promised to get her to America and said Annika could work off the debt once she got there. She had no other choice at that point.

Joseph's story affected me deeply, maybe because I was so close to my sister. He had left Gdańsk, Poland, with his sister, Magda. While traveling through Germany, they were caught up in a protest of the European Union's refugee policy. They'd gotten separated in the crowd just as the police arrived. Joseph waited four days in Berlin, avoiding social services, hoping to find his sister. He hadn't had any success. Now she was all he thought about.

The younger girls, Olivia and Michele, had essentially been tricked into coming to the United States. I didn't even want to think what someone had had in store for them.

I noticed Jacques fidget in his seat, then lower his head. I went over and knelt down by the fifteen-year-old Belgian boy and said quietly, "You okay, Jacques?"

"It's embarrassing."

"More embarrassing than me admitting I was the worst football player on my college team?"

That made him smile. Finally, he said, "I'm a little scared. This is only my second flight. This waiting is making me nervous. I wish we'd just take off."

I glanced around, then said to Jacques, "Close your eyes and take a deep breath."

He did as I asked.

I said, "Now think about the most exciting thing you can. Feel the excitement."

A smile slipped across the boy's face.

"What are you thinking of?"

"A girl."

I laughed. "A pretty one, I assume."

"Beautiful. She's nice too."

"Oh, is this a real person? Not some fantasy?"

"She's real."

"Who is it?"

He didn't answer. Then he blushed.

"Jacques, you can tell me."

"You won't tell anyone or get mad?"

"Of course not. Who are you thinking about?"

"Your sister."

"Lila? She's ten years older than you."

"Nine."

"Are you crazy, telling me that?"

"You said you wouldn't get mad."

I smiled and snapped my fingers. "Foiled by a loophole." That made Jacques giggle.

The flight attendant announced we were about to take off.

I said to Jacques, "You okay now?"

He nodded.

"By the way, my sister can be a handful. You might've dodged a bullet by leaving town."

He liked that.

As I went back to my seat, I looked at the smiling Michele and Olivia and pulled a deck of cards out of my back pocket.

"How would you guys like to learn a counting game? It's going to be hard because of our language differences, but I think you'll like it."

Olivia managed to say, "What game?"

I smiled and said, "It's called blackjack."

CHAPTER 23

Amsterdam

WE ARRIVED AT Amsterdam's Schiphol Airport about midmorning. The children had slept during most of the interminable flight, but I'd stayed awake. I felt like the kids were too vulnerable. I didn't want to risk taking my eyes off them.

This airport was either a lot less busy or a lot more organized than Miami International because walking through it seemed like taking a quiet stroll. The airport even had its own shopping mall. I held Olivia's and Michele's hands and let the boys fight over who would push the little cart with everyone's luggage.

A tall woman wearing a tailored blue dress approached us before we reached the police substation where I was supposed to contact my Dutch counterpart. She wasn't walking so much as marching. A few feet in front of me, she stopped and said, "Detective Moon?"

I gave her my best smile and said, "You must be psychic."

"I'm hardly psychic. I was told to look for an American over one hundred and ninety centimeters tall who looked like he played professional rugby and who was accompanied by six children." She held out her hand and said, "My name is Marie Meijer. I'm your liaison with the Dutch national police."

She had an elegant accent, graceful movements, and a grip that could crack a walnut. I wouldn't want to be on the wrong side of her.

Marie leaned down and spoke French to little Michele, then greeted each of the kids by name.

"Wow, you learned everyone's names before we arrived. You're quite thorough."

"I've been working on this ring of human traffickers for more than a year. I finally have someone to feed me information, so I'm hoping we make some serious arrests soon."

Olivia was either scared or bashful. She hid behind my right leg, peeking out like a puppy. The other kids had gravitated behind me too, and we now faced this woman as a single group.

Marie smiled and said, "I'm happy to see the kids trust you. That must mean you're trustworthy. Kids and dogs are rarely wrong about such things." She focused her blue eyes on me and said, "Shall we get to work?"

After being at the FBI for the last eight months, I liked that attitude.

A few minutes later, we were in front of the airport looking at a long white Mercedes passenger van. A blue VW hatchback with an official police emblem on the dashboard was parked behind it. Marie directed the kids into the van, then turned to me and said, "You can say your goodbyes. I'll drive you in my car."

I almost didn't understand. I saw the stunned expressions on the kids' faces. I said, "If you don't mind, I'd like to ride with my posse. I want to see where they're staying and what the conditions are like."

Marie didn't miss a beat. "Of course."

I watched her walk toward her car. Jacques looked up at me and said, "I wouldn't mind riding in her car."

I laughed as I playfully shoved the Belgian teenager toward the van.

About twenty minutes later we arrived at an apartment building. I'd been relieved to see that the Dutch drove on the right side of the road. And so far, aside from about three thousand bicyclists, traffic didn't look all that much different from what you'd see in a big city in the U.S.

Marie showed great patience as I checked out the rooms, questioned the two social workers, and made sure the children were all settled with their bags next to their own beds. I'd friended them all on Facebook and gotten their e-mail addresses, and they all had my e-mail address and my cell phone number.

I couldn't believe how upset I was to say goodbye to them. I promised I'd see them again before I flew back to Miami. Everyone wanted a hug.

I couldn't meet Marie's gaze as we walked out of the facility because I was trying to keep the tears out of my eyes. I hate that kind of shit.

CHAPTER 24

AFTER I'D HAD a sandwich accompanied by an eight-ounce Coca-Cola in a glass bottle that made me feel like a giant, Marie gave me a quick tour of Amsterdam. I didn't want to explain that I'd been up all night on an airplane and that my circadian rhythms were all screwed up. I just tried to take in the sights and listen to what this sharp detective had to say.

"I heard you had to chase the man bringing the kids into Miami. Do you have many foot chases?" Marie asked.

I shrugged. "Some. I guess it depends on how badly you want to make the arrest."

"Do you get angry at runners?"

"No. I learned early in my career to keep it in perspective."

"What happened?"

"I was a rookie in uniform and saw a young man selling crack on Miami Avenue, right in the center of the city. When he ran, I chased. As I ran, I kept screaming, 'Police, stop,' like that might help.

"Finally, near a highway underpass, I tackled him. I was mad and yelled, 'Why'd you run from me?'

"The crack dealer kept calm and said, 'It's my job to run. It's *your* job to catch me.' I had tackled a philosopher. He was right and I've kept it in mind for every chase I've ever been in."

I liked that Marie found the story funny. She had a beautiful smile and an engaging laugh. I noticed now that her left eyelid looked heavy, half closed over her dazzling blue eye. But her creamy skin was flawless. I was finding her more and more interesting.

Marie said, "This is the De Wallen District of Amsterdam. It's the largest of the red-light districts, although it's almost nothing more than a tourist attraction now. No one wants to risk a tourist getting hurt, so everyone makes sure the streets are safe."

"Is this where most of the human trafficking occurs?"

"The whole city is used as a hub to traffic people, mainly to the U.S. The Amsterdam police joke that we should be classified as an official rest stop for Russians in transit. The local Russian mob is constantly running people through Amsterdam."

I said, "I wondered if they were causing problems here like they do in the U.S. The northern part of Miami–Dade County has seen a huge influx of Russians over the past few years."

"Do the Russians in Miami organize in groups to commit crimes as much as they do in Europe? I know the criminal justice system is different in the States."

"No. They're like any other immigrant group—they tend to keep to themselves. The problem is the criminals prey on other Russians, and the crimes are difficult to investigate. One crime lord in particular, Roman Rostoff, is engaged in some human trafficking as well as a long list of other crimes."

"I'm familiar with Rostoff, unfortunately. His brother, Emile, has a smaller operation here in Amsterdam."

"Is he as big an asshole as Roman?"

Marie smiled and said, "I'm glad we both view the family the same way. But from what I hear, Roman is much more brutal. Emile is vicious, but he tries to keep things quiet. We don't have the same level of violence as you do in the U.S."

"But somehow every country has organized crime and people like the Rostoffs who screw things up for everyone else."

Marie pulled over on a block with a lot of pedestrians. I had to unwedge myself from her VW. We walked down the street to a series of four-story apartment buildings that looked like they'd been there a long time. I stared at a line of people that stretched around the block. "Is this a place where you find a lot of human smuggling?"

She smiled and shook her head. "No, this is the building where Anne Frank lived in hiding. I thought you might like to see some of the history of the city."

I felt like a moron. I didn't want to tell her I was too tired to see anything like this, so I just followed along.

I had no idea the day would stretch into the evening. The detective took me through the Heineken factory and on a drive along the IJmeer coastline. She also showed me several dilapidated buildings where the police suspected human traffickers kept people on a regular basis.

"For a party city, I don't see anyone walking with a beer in their hands like they do in New Orleans," I said.

"No beer allowed on the street, just in pubs. Alcohol makes people aggressive."

"Let me get this straight. You can smoke a joint in the red-light district and no one will bother you, but you can't drink a beer on the street?"

She smiled. "When was the last time you saw a person high on pot punch someone?"

She had a point.

I noticed something on the glass of a decorative street lamp. I stopped to look closer at the image of a man with a guitar. It was remarkably detailed and lifelike.

Marie chuckled and said, "This is a rare treat. Usually when he puts those up, people steal them quickly. The artist is Max Zorn. He makes these incredible images using nothing but packing tape and a razor."

I studied the figure illuminated by the lamp. It was extraordinary. I murmured, "'The purpose of art is washing the dust of daily life off our souls.'"

She said, "Excuse me?"

I turned to her. "Picasso said that."

She smiled. "You are not at all what I expected of an American police officer."

"Is that good or bad?"

"Just surprising." She started to stroll down the street and added, "I like surprises."

As we continued on, I couldn't stifle a yawn. Marie said, "Is a big, tough American police officer like you getting sleepy?"

Her mocking tone made me smile. She sounded like Stephanie Hall or my sister. That meant she was okay. It also meant she was giving me some kind of a test. She might have wanted to see if I would take offense or show me how tough she could be by outlasting me. I didn't need any convincing.

When I saw the Hilton sign in the Noord District, I knew salvation was at hand.

CHAPTER 25

IT WAS LATE in Amsterdam, but it was a good time to call home. I wanted to check on my mother and Lila, though I knew my mom didn't like that I worried so much about her; she always said I needed to get a life.

Lila picked up the home phone on the second ring. The first thing I did was get Lila to talk a bit so I could listen to her speech and make sure she was sober. Then I ran through our regular checklist of concerns: Did Mom have any doctor appointments coming up? Was she getting exercise? Was she staying occupied? That was a big one; we'd learned that her dementia was worse when she wasn't busy. When she focused on the piano or crochet, she tended to stay grounded. Even reading helped quite a bit.

One thing I'd noticed recently was that my mom tended to read the same books over and over. I thought she was just a huge Brad Meltzer fan until I realized she had read the same book of his, *The President's Shadow*, at least four times in a row.

It was tough to deal with my mom's issues, but I could never put them out of my head. It was part of my upbringing; I'd been raised a good Lutheran and still attended services with my mom. I still believed. But like most humans, I had questions. That's what had attracted me to philosophy in the first place. That whole notion of the search for truth.

Philosophy came down to opinions. It wasn't science. It was one man's or woman's idea of what life should be. So far, I hadn't found any answers that would solve all my problems.

I'd read what Plato and Schopenhauer and various other philosophers had said about adversity, but it was former president Bill Clinton who'd said it best: "If you live long enough, you'll make mistakes. But if you learn from them, you'll be a better person. It's how you handle adversity, not how it affects you. The main thing is never quit, never quit, never quit."

It was that quote that kept me going sometimes. In football, in police work, and especially in dealing with my mother.

Everything at home was fine, and after the call, I conked out almost immediately. In fact, when my room phone started ringing at seven forty-five the next morning, I was still lying on top of the covers in the khakis and blue button-down oxford I had been wearing the day before.

It wasn't a good idea for a guy my size to cram himself into a tiny airplane seat for a transatlantic flight and then spend the next twenty-four hours walking around town. As I reached for the phone, I heard creaks in my joints that reminded me of every time I'd caught a football and then been knocked to the ground by some defensive back.

"Good morning, Detective Moon," Marie Meijer said

cheerfully. "Are you ready for another day of excitement in Europe's most interesting city?"

I know I made a sound like a groan before I said, "Please call me Tom, and please call me again in two hours."

She laughed and said, "I'll meet half your demands. I'll be in the lobby waiting for you in about ten minutes, Tom."

Before I could object, she hung up.

CHAPTER 26

SOMEHOW, TEN MINUTES later, I was in the lobby wearing clean clothes and searching desperately for a cup of coffee.

Marie bounced into the hotel as if she'd just gotten back from vacation. She greeted the doorman by name and then we hopped in her official VW hatchback.

It seemed like every third building was some sort of museum. When they talked history in Amsterdam, the topics were events that had occurred before the U.S. was a going concern. In South Florida, *history* meant the Cuban migration or Jackie Gleason living there in the seventies.

It wasn't all sightseeing; there was a purpose behind it. Marie explained how the city was laid out and told me where different crimes were most common. She also showed me potential safe houses for the Russian mob. At one point, we stopped by a building next to a canal.

Marie said, "These apartments are often used to house people before they're smuggled to their next destination. There's going to be an operation to make some arrests tonight. I wanted to bring you so you can see what it's like. There are some legal prostitution houses in this block as well," she added.

I was genuinely curious. "Did you find that legalizing prostitution had much of an effect on crime?"

"There's never an easy answer to things like that. Even if you legalize something, there's still a black market. People think that decriminalization eliminates black markets, but those are people who don't experience life on the streets. For customers who want to avoid taxes or identification, there's always a market that the government can't control. Legalizing prostitution has made Amsterdam a destination for desperate people, and that provides an avenue for human traffickers. They convince runaways or young people with drug problems that if they can just get to somewhere else, everything will be all right. It's basically the same scam every criminal has used for the past two hundred years."

In the early evening we stopped at a café. I'd expected to throw down half a gallon of coffee to perk up, but as soon as we settled into a small table in the corner, I realized this was no ordinary café. This was one of the coffeehouses Amsterdam was famous for, the kind where they served pot along with coffee.

It was not dark or dank. The different strains of marijuana were proudly displayed in glass containers. The conversations in the small coffeehouse were muted and private. A light shone on a poster of the Rolling Stones at Altamont. Except for the odor of pot in the air, it could've been any hipster hangout in the States. Commercial cigarettes and alcohol were both strictly forbidden in the coffeehouse.

When I told Marie I knew what was up, she gave me a

sly smile. "It's completely legal here. At least, inside a place like this."

I glanced around at people enjoying pot-infused pastries or smoking joints or hookahs.

Marie said, "Would you like to try marijuana legally?"

"Just because it's legal here doesn't mean I'm allowed to try it."

Marie said, "Have you ever tried pot?"

I laughed. "I went to the University of Miami. Of course I've tried it."

She ordered in Dutch. Before long, I had a cup of coffee and a lovely-looking pastry in front of me. Marie had the same. She also had a single, perfectly rolled joint.

I said, "Knocking off early today, are we?"

"No. Just breaking all kinds of rules."

I watched as she lit the joint with a plastic lighter and took a single puff. She handed it to me. I thought about it for a moment, then copied her single, light puff. If it was a test, I'd passed it. She put out the joint by crushing it under the edge of her coffee cup.

Marie said, "I was hoping you weren't one of those by-the-book cops who are so insufferable."

I let out a laugh and said, "I can be insufferable even while breaking the rules."

We chatted about differences between the U.S. and Europe. It was as nice an evening as I'd had in years. The pot seemed to hit me in waves. At first, it was just some ringing in my ears, but before I knew it, I felt the full effects.

This shit was so much stronger than anything I'd ever tried in college. Of course, I hadn't smoked a lot back then, and the few times I had, it was to fit in or impress a girl.

I guess things hadn't changed much.

Marie asked me about the task force and I felt like I was

slurring my words as I told her about it. Finally, I said, "No one realizes that Interpol is basically a series of databases with no real arrest powers."

"Isn't it funny how people assume they know all about police work from movies?" Marie said. "My father always asks me if I have a CSI team with me. He watches reruns of the American show."

"I get that all the time. Especially with my size, people assume I'm duking it out with bad guys every day."

Marie laughed. "It's true that much of our view of Miami police work comes from reruns of *Miami Vice*."

"It's a good show, but it's about as realistic as *Game of Thrones*."

"Another favorite. I prefer a good fantasy to some of the horror we have to face in real life."

I raised my coffee cup and said, "Amen, sister."

It might have been the pot, but we both laughed for a really long time.

CHAPTER 27

HANNA GREETE LOOKED across the small table at the two men she'd been chatting with for the past half hour. The older of the two men, Alexi, worked directly for Emile Rostoff. She said, "Can't you talk to someone on my behalf?"

Her overriding feeling was relief that she had not brought Albert with her.

Alexi acted as if he was trying to help her. But she knew that, with the Russians, it was all about business. They wanted her to pay them back, and she couldn't pay them back if they killed her. That's why she'd left Albert at home with Josie. Her brother would have stirred up even more trouble. He didn't handle threats well.

Alexi said, "We're not a bank. You can't pay in tiny installments. You owe us almost five hundred thousand euros. We want at least half in the next month."

"Five hundred thousand? That's crazy. We borrowed three hundred thousand less than six months ago."

"Money is a commodity. Right now, the value of money is up."

"Not according to the European Union or any reasonable banks. Their interest rates are all hovering around one percent."

Alexi was not impressed with that reasoning. "You are most welcome to take out a loan to pay us back. One of the advantages would be that banks aren't going to break your leg or follow your daughter home from school if you miss a payment. Why don't you try for a loan?"

That comment made the younger man with Alexi snicker. He was clearly Alexi's answer to Albert—in his thirties, tall, well built, unshaven. He looked like a movie thug.

Hanna said, "No, I don't think I'll get a loan from a bank. I have some money coming in soon and I'll use it all to pay you off."

Alexi sat back and smiled. He had scars on his face that seemed to brighten when he smiled. They were like a map of his professional life. He had clearly been an enforcer when he was younger, and now he ran the operation for Rostoff out of the Noord District. Of course, Emile Rostoff ran the whole city. No one dealt directly with Emile, but if you did something to displease him, the results were almost always disastrous.

Alexi said, "Everyone knows about the diamonds you bought. We'd be willing to cancel a hundred thousand of your debt for five nice diamonds. We don't care where they came from."

Hanna had to be careful about how she played this. "If, hypothetically, I had any diamonds, they would be worth the full five hundred thousand." She knew her estimate was about right, and she would jump at the opportunity if Alexi agreed.

Instead, he shook his head and said, "I don't deal in

hypotheticals. And I don't pay retail for diamonds. I hope your next load goes better for you so we can get paid. Mr. Rostoff's man in Miami will help set everyone up with jobs. That will go a long way toward paying down your debt. But you're going to have to do more. We are starting to lose patience."

The other man, whose English was much more accented than Alexi's, said, "Tell your crazy brother not to do anything stupid."

Hanna looked hard at the younger man. "I can control my brother only so much. I can tell you're afraid of him. That means you're a little smarter than I thought."

She walked away before he could respond.

CHAPTER 28

THE NEXT DAY, Hanna and Albert went to check out the port at Rotterdam. She'd decided it was too dangerous to move the load out of Amsterdam. Between the police and the Russians, someone would cause headaches.

In the late afternoon, they arrived back in Amsterdam to the apartment that held half a dozen of the younger people going on this trip. She had two older Indian men and several women at another apartment across town.

The Indian men had paid for the trip up front. They just wanted a fast way into the U.S. Hanna used their money to pay for everyone else's expenses.

In addition, she had six girls divided among two apartments. The apartments held people going on other shipments with other groups. Hanna and her brother felt it was a way to minimize exposure and keep traffickers from turning other smugglers in to the police.

She and Albert visited an apartment near the Emperor's

Canal. One of the teenage girls she'd stashed there stepped into the main room wearing tiny shorts and a T-shirt that looked like it was made for a little kid.

Hanna greeted the girl and pulled her close to sniff her hair. "Where'd you get shampoo that smells like that?"

The girl just shrugged and said, "The lady that works for you, Janine, bought it for us."

Hanna said, "Where's Gregor?"

The girl said, "He's taking a walk with Freda."

Hanna grabbed Albert and pulled him out the door. As they walked down the hallway, she said, "First thing I want to do is scream at Janine for buying luxury items for these girls. They don't need to worry about expensive shampoo until they're in the U.S. getting ready for a job. And second, I told that prick of a landlord, Gregor, not to fraternize with the girls. Now, when I need to talk to him, he's out touring the city with one of them."

They stepped outside the main entrance to the building and saw Gregor with his arm around the shoulder of the teenage girl. Albert said, "I'm guessing someone is about to be yelled at. If you need me to do anything more than that, just nod."

Hanna wasted no time walking up to the squat, middle-aged landlord. She poked him right in the chest until he took his arm away from the girl. "I told you not to have any social contact with these girls," she said.

Gregor backed away, raising his hands. Dark hair bristled on his forearms.

Hanna glared at Freda and said, "Get back to the apartment now." The girl ran into the building.

The landlord said, "I'm not making any money housing these girls. All I want is a little bit of fun. It would be easy for me to go to the police and explain what you're forcing me to do."

That was over the line. Hanna turned to her brother and nodded. Albert didn't disappoint. He pulled out his favorite survival knife and let it dangle from his hand right in front of the landlord.

Gregor stared at the knife for a moment.

Hanna said, "This is a critical time. You will not tell anyone about what we're doing. Not the police, not your friends, no one. And in case you don't understand, Albert is going to make it clear for you."

She had no idea what her brother had planned, but she watched with great interest.

Albert was very casual. He simply leaned forward slightly and flicked the knife up between the landlord's legs. The sharpened tip was enough to pierce the man's off-brand blue jeans and catch him right in the testicles.

The landlord grunted, grabbed his groin, and dropped to his knees.

Albert said, "And that was for even *thinking* about going to the police. Imagine what will happen if you really do."

As the siblings walked away, Hanna said, "I'll admit that sometimes you're more articulate than me." She waited until they were at the end of the block and said, "This will be our last dealing with Gregor. Once the girls are on their way, make sure he doesn't talk to anyone."

Albert just smiled.

CHAPTER 29

AFTER THE EFFECTS of my single puff of marijuana had worn off and Marie and I had had a decent dinner, she brought me back to the apartment complex she'd shown me earlier. We were at the edge of the Nieuwmarkt neighborhood in the Centrum-Amsterdam borough.

Marie said, "I've tried to give you a good overview of the city's criminal issues. The information I get on the group that tried to smuggle the kids into Miami comes from a couple of sources. The woman who runs the group is named Hanna Greete. She's managed to keep a relatively low profile, but she deals with Russians, and Russians always talk about their competition among themselves."

I said, "It's been my experience they don't hesitate to talk about their competition to the police too."

"I haven't been able to conduct decent surveillance on Hanna's group because of a lack of resources. All anyone seems to care about anymore is terrorism. Human trafficking has taken a back seat. That's why I work closely with our paramilitary agency, the Koninklijke Marechaussee. And that's why I brought you here tonight."

I noticed the activity at the far end of the block. "You're taking me on a police raid for our first date?"

She smiled. "No, on our first date I dragged you all around the city after you had traveled for twelve hours. This is our second date. And things will only get more exciting from here."

"Are these guys going to arrest Hanna Greete?"

"This apartment is used by several different smuggling groups. I got this specific tip from some Russians, which means they're not holding any people here themselves. We don't have a lot of information, but we know that the man who owns the apartment building tends to like younger girls. It's very common among these safe-house owners. And that's not something our friends in tactical gear down the block appreciate."

I felt a twinge of excitement. This was a big deal. It also meant that Marie trusted me. She'd gone out of her way to involve me in this. After spending time with the kids we'd rescued from Miami International, I had a genuine interest in watching human traffickers taken down. I wanted to see a whole group rounded up. I wasn't satisfied with the skinny Dutchman I'd grabbed at the airport.

It was a swiftly evolving, complicated crime, but it didn't capture the public's attention as much as terrorism or narcotics did. I'd learned in the short time I was involved with this case how dangerous these human traffickers could be.

Obviously, the Dutch police felt the same way. They were taking no chances. I watched as two different groups of men dressed in black tactical clothes with body armor and carrying

MP5 machine guns hustled along the street in the shadows. They looked like a SWAT team from any major U.S. city. This was getting interesting fast.

I said a silent prayer for the poor people in the building who were trying to get to the States. They might not have realized the danger they were in from these scumbags who viewed them only as a source of income.

CHAPTER 30

I WATCHED AS the SWAT team lined up outside the wide, decorative wooden door that had probably been handcrafted three hundred years ago. They were all precise and quiet, the definition of a good SWAT team.

TV shows make SWAT teams look sexy and glamorous. In real life, it is a tough, physical job with endless training. Critics call them *militaristic* or *threatening* without ever considering the decisions SWAT members must make in a split second. And just the sight of a team has saved lives; that alone has made barricaded suspects surrender and dangerous crowds disperse. A SWAT team is the big dog you don't always have to let off the leash.

At the end of the block, the support officers were pulling into position. They would be the ones to enter the building after it was secured.

This was one of the most dangerous activities for any SWAT team. When noncombatants or victims are inside a house with the suspects, tactics change. Like most cops, I don't know how I could live with myself if I accidentally hurt an innocent, like a child, while executing a search warrant.

I felt nervous for the team about to enter the apartment building. You never know; the next entry might be your last. Marie listened on a radio. I couldn't understand any of the Dutch being spoken, but I recognized the tone. They were getting ready to breach the main door. I'd bet there was another team that would make entry from some other point.

An older apartment building like this would have several doors. Most would crumple under a strike from a battering ram.

Marie Meijer said something into the radio, then turned to me and said, "If someone runs from the building in this direction, we're the ones designated to stop them. Is that okay with you?"

I smiled. This was a lot more action than I'd expected. I no longer felt tired.

Then the SWAT team swung into action. Even from our position, I could hear the pounding on the door and the officer yelling in Dutch. I suspected he was saying something along the lines of "Search warrant. Open the door."

A team member came up from the back of the line with a one-person battering ram. He swung and hit the solid wood door twice, and the booming thumps echoed in the ancient street like explosions. On the second strike, the lock gave way. The door flew open wide, with only the lower hinge keeping it attached to the frame. The team was inside in an instant.

My heart raced as I watched the raid commence. I was worried about the cops, worried about the victims, and bothered that I had no role in it.

I could hear a woman's wailing scream like a fire alarm, then two flash-bangs—distraction devices that we also used in Miami to shock and blind. The loud *boom, boom* echoed through the apartment complex like thunder. Even at this distance, standing just outside Marie's car, I could feel the vibration.

CHAPTER 31

THE NEXT SOUNDS I heard were not flash-bangs but gunshots. *Holy shit.* I could see the muzzle flashes in the windows. Frozen to the spot, I couldn't think about anything but the poor captives, running in fear.

I heard return fire from the automatic MP5s. It was controlled and disciplined, short bursts of two or three shots. I just hoped it was disciplined enough.

Suddenly, people started spilling out of the apartment building, a few tripping and piling up right in the doorway. Once they were cleared, more people poured out onto the street. A lot of people. I realized that the people waiting to be smuggled didn't want to deal with the police either.

Most of them just stopped in the street. But two men tried a different tactic to escape: blending into the shadows. Unknowingly, they ran directly toward us.

Both were young men and ran with an easy gait. The man closest to me was small and muscular, like a gymnast.

I squinted in the dark, trying to see if they had anything in their hands.

Next to the car, Marie never flinched. "Let them get closer. And stay on your side of the car unless I call for you." She was calm and quiet. That's how any good cop talked in the face of a disastrous raid. You didn't want to get others excited or distracted.

The men continued to race up the street toward us, no one following them. They must have imagined they were in the clear.

Marie stepped in front of the car with something in her right hand. The men started to slow, looking over their shoulders at the apartment building. Marie called out, "Politie, stoppen."

Both men skidded to a halt about six feet in front of her. I'm not sure they even noticed me standing on the other side of the car. I fought the urge to race out and help her, a cop's natural instinct for backup.

One man said something to Marie in Dutch while the other tried to slip between her and the car.

Marie gave them another command; I assumed she was telling them to stand still and raise their hands. The man closest to her laughed and then lunged toward her.

That's when I realized what she was holding in her right hand. It was an expandable baton. We usually called it an ASP, the name of one of the baton's manufacturers.

Marie swung up so swiftly that the baton extended during the motion. She caught the man hard under his extended arm. She spun in a complete circle with the ASP still in her hand. This time, she caught the man on the opposite arm.

I winced at the motion and the sickening sound the ASP made when it struck the man's flesh. I'd been in too many training sessions and seen too many people hit with an ASP not to know that the pain was always excruciating.

The man froze as he tried to decide which arm hurt more. Finally, cradling both arms, he crumpled to the ground.

The man who had been trying to slip past Marie turned to see if he could help his partner.

Marie didn't hesitate. This time, needing a little more reach, she took a quick step and lifted her foot off the ground as she swung the baton. It caught the man across his chin and sent him into the side of the car.

He was smaller and in better shape than the other suspect. Apparently, he was also smarter. When he staggered to his feet, he knew he wanted nothing to do with Marie. He turned and broke into an all-out sprint.

I heard Marie mutter, "Damn." She couldn't leave the suspect she'd brought down.

Now it was my turn.

CHAPTER 32

I RAN AFTER the smaller man as fast as I could. Growing up, I was never the quickest kid on the playground; God had decided to make me too big for that. Way too big. So my whole life, I had compensated by thinking races—or chases—through to the end.

I paced myself. I watched as the man darted down an alley to the left. I took that turn, and I saw him slow considerably as he went around another corner. I tried to fix my position in my mind so I wouldn't get lost. It wouldn't be a good look for American law enforcement if I had to call out for help on an empty street with no idea where anyone else was.

When I turned the next corner, the suspect was down to a fast walk. He approached a section of the block under construction. The sidewalk was roped off, and lightweight scaffolding rose along the side of the building.

I kept my easy pace, trying not to make any noise. Even

with all my chases in Miami, I'd never gotten used to running in long pants.

Maybe the man heard me coming, or maybe it was chance, but just as I was about to pounce on the suspect, he looked over his shoulder. He immediately sprang up into the air.

The move took me completely by surprise. Then I realized he had grasped a low bar on the scaffolding and pulled himself up like a monkey. The whole structure shook. It wasn't secured to the building yet.

I called for him to come down.

Shockingly, he ignored me.

I watched as he climbed higher, hoping he'd come to his senses. The scaffolding wobbled more and more.

Then it happened—he lost his grip and slipped off the scaffolding. I wanted to say, *I told you so,* but I didn't have the language skills. *Oh, shit,* I thought, *that fall could kill him.*

I watched him drop the twenty or so feet through the cool night air. Some instinct kicked in and I moved to stand underneath him with my hands outstretched.

He landed in them like a toddler.

His left elbow hit me in my right eye, but the sound he made as he landed told me the blow was unintentional. He was more shocked than I was.

I stood there with a grown man in my arms. After a moment, he said something in Dutch. I let his feet touch the ground gently. He spoke again. I said, "I'm sorry, I don't speak Dutch."

The man nodded and said, "English, good. I wish to thank you. You saved me from falling."

"Actually, I saved you from hitting the ground. You were falling no matter what."

"I am in your debt."

"And now we're going to calmly walk back to where your friend is under arrest. And you're not gonna do something stupid like try to get away again."

The man was in his late twenties, I could see now. He looked me up and down, then said, "If I had realized how big you were, I probably would not have run."

I turned him in the direction I wanted to walk and draped my arm across his narrow shoulders like we were friends. "Let's enjoy this stroll back."

"Do I have a choice?"

"Everyone's got a choice. But your other options in this situation would have you limping for at least a year."

I returned to Marie with the man still at my side. I was impressed that she already had her suspect handcuffed and in the back of her car.

She turned and smiled as soon as she saw me. "I was starting to get worried."

"You told me not to let anyone get away." As I stepped from the shadows into the street, she noticed my eye, which I could feel was swelling shut.

Marie said, "Now we have matching eyes."

CHAPTER 33

A FEW MINUTES later, Marie and I led our two prisoners back toward the apartment building. I wasn't prepared for what I saw. I stepped past the battered door, still hanging at an angle, and got my first good look at an apartment that held large groups of people. Human smuggling made real.

These dazed and scared people, some of them near starving, stared up at us with no hope in their eyes. One young woman looked too exhausted to cry. Her blond hair was a tangled mess and her ribs were showing under a translucent nightgown.

Inside, it got worse. The stench of urine and unwashed bodies assaulted my senses. Add the sharp smell of gunpowder from the flash-bangs and gunfire, and it was brutal. The odor seemed to have a life of its own. It made my eyes water.

No one should ever have to live like this. I was angry at myself for not acting fast enough. It was frustrating that something as terrible as human smuggling was so widespread. I was also angry at my bosses for not taking it seriously enough. Most of all, I was angry at the smugglers.

Three teenage girls in oversize T-shirts wept on a couch. A young female police officer tried to comfort them. I felt like I was invading their privacy just by glimpsing them in this condition.

Marie was clearly respected among the cops. SWAT team members stepped out of her way immediately. One young uniformed officer who had taken part in the raid escorted both of us upstairs.

Marie looked over her shoulder as we walked. "You can see that this was a relatively big operation. There were twenty-six people housed here and five men running the place. The two we caught are known drug runners from the Rotterdam area. But there were two fatalities in the raid."

We stopped on the third floor. Several uniformed officers stood around the corpse of a pudgy, middle-aged man. He had four bullet holes in his chest and one in his right cheek. A World War II Walther P38 with the slide locked back sat on a table next to him.

The blood from his chest wounds had pooled to a sticky puddle on the hardwood floor. His brown eyes were still wide open. His Nirvana T-shirt looked to be original; it had faded lettering and a few tears in it.

It was hard for me to muster much sympathy for a modern-day slaver.

Marie said, "He fired six rounds. They fired sixteen." Then she led me farther into the room. I felt a wave of sorrow looking down at the next body.

It was a young woman sprawled across a velvet couch. Someone had placed a blanket over her body, but her face was exposed. She was young, nineteen or so. Blood still trickled from the corner of her mouth.

Marie said, "For some reason, the man shot her in the chest before he opened fire on the arrest team. They think she might have run for the door to get away just as he started shooting. In any case, it's a tragedy."

None of the cops could even look at the dead girl. I knew what they were thinking—that they had failed her.

I felt the same way. I'd seen my share of bodies in Miami, but most of them were criminals involved in the drug trade or in gangs. Somehow, those deaths didn't affect me nearly as much as seeing this one, a young woman whose only crime was wanting to get out of Europe.

In the United States, the media doesn't care much about gang violence in places like Chicago and Miami until a by-stander is killed. But the subsequent outrage rarely lasts long enough to galvanize the public into helping the police.

I thought of all the things this young woman might have done with her life. She might have had children eventually. A death like this can ripple through eternity.

After a minute, I stepped over to the edge of the room and sat on a folding chair. My legs felt shaky. Marie pulled another chair close to me and sat down too. "Now you see why I am so obsessed with the smuggling rings. With your help, we can really hurt them."

I looked at her and said, "Hurt them? I want to crush them."

CHAPTER 34

HANNA GREETE SAT with her brother at Mata Hari, a little restaurant on Oudezijds Achterburgwal, right on the canal. She liked the food, but even more, she liked how quiet it was.

Albert bitched about it being too fancy. She knew his real complaint was that they didn't sell pot, although he had already smoked a joint with a pretty Canadian tourist earlier. The three beers he'd downed here had only made him mellower. This was the best time to talk to Albert.

He put a hand on Hanna's and said, "We only lost two girls from our load. Some groups lost as many as ten. We should feel lucky they hit that place instead of the one Gregor runs. Not only would we have lost most of our load, but you know that fat little turd wouldn't have hesitated to flip on us to the police."

It took Hanna a moment to realize her brother was actually

making sense. He was a loose cannon and a hothead, but no one had ever accused Albert of being stupid. In fact, if he hadn't been thrown out of school for sleeping with his teacher, he might have had a fine academic career.

Hanna sighed and shook her head. She still couldn't speak.

Albert said, "She's getting to you. That policewoman, Marie Meijer. Are you bothered that she has made it her business to cripple our business?"

Hanna slapped the flat of her hand on the table, startling her brother, and said, "Yes, that's exactly what's bothering me. It's what's been bothering me for months. That smug detective. All we hear from our contacts is that she's leading the charge against our industry."

She looked at Albert. She noticed for the first time a gray streak running through his goatee.

Albert said, "It's easy to focus on Marie Meijer, but we have plenty of other problems to address."

Hanna glared at her brother. "Not until we deal with her. I don't even want to hear her name again. If you need to refer to her, call her Funky-Eyed Bitch or Snake Plissken."

A broad smile spread across Albert's face.

Hanna said, "What is it?"

"First, I like the fact that you can see a little humor in this. Second, you know *Escape from New York* is my favorite movie, and now, every time I see Kurt Russell, I'll smile, thinking about the one night when I was the reasonable sibling."

Hanna said, "It just starts to be overwhelming. You try to make a better life for your family, but there's always someone looking to stop you—the Russians, the police, or someone on your own payroll."

Albert said, "Then let's deal with the detective." He paused, then said, "No, let's deal with Funky-Eyed Bitch first. That should be relatively easy."

"When do you want to do it?"

"We can do a little surveillance tonight. Let's see what happens. But I promise, by the time you're ready to ship those people to Miami, she won't be a problem anymore."

CHAPTER 35

TWO HOURS LATER, Hanna and Albert stood on a street corner in Haarlem, about twenty kilometers outside of Amsterdam.

Albert glanced down the slowly sloping hill to a redbrick road that led to a pleasant-looking three-story apartment complex.

Albert turned to Hanna and said, "How on earth did you find exactly where she lived?"

"Heinrich got the information for me. And he's still quite upset that you threatened him with a knife. I had to pay him more than double what I normally do."

Albert grinned. "Usually the knife gives me a discount. Maybe next time I can make my point more clearly."

Hanna said, "He even found out that she lives with two cats. It sounds like he knows someone at the national police headquarters. Say what you want about Heinrich, he can be subtle and inconspicuous."

Albert pulled his survival knife from under his sports coat. In the lamplight, his eyes seemed to glow. He said, "I can go down there and finish this right this minute."

Hanna shook her head. "We need to wait. We can't do it anywhere around this apartment complex. The cops would be all over us. And I don't want to risk anyone finding out that I have ears everywhere. If we did something like this, there's no way Heinrich would ever give us information again. And there's no guarantee he'd keep his mouth shut."

She turned and looked down at the building. The apartment was on the second floor, and several lights burned. The Funky Eyed Bitch was home.

"We need to do this in the street somewhere," Hanna said. "That way it won't be traced back to us. With any luck, it could be written off as some kind of random act of violence. Maybe they'll believe some refugee went crazy and stabbed her. I'm just not sure how we might find her later."

Albert said, "I have an idea." He reached into the outer pocket of his sports coat and pulled out a case about the size of a deck of cards.

"What's that?"

"The tracker you told me to buy. I was going to test it to make sure I understood it. This will work perfectly." Without waiting for a reply, Albert started walking toward the parking lot on the side of the apartment building. The very first car in the lot was a Volkswagen Golf hatchback with a police emblem on the dashboard.

He was already on his knees checking the batteries in the store-bought tracker when his sister caught up to him.

"Do you know how to use it? Can it be traced back to us?"

"No, it can't. And we need to practice with this gadget. Once we have the diamonds, we'll want to be sure we know how to track them accurately."

Hanna heard a door shut. She glanced around the corner of the building to see Detective Marie Meijer strolling down the sidewalk toward the parking lot.

Hanna barked in a harsh whisper, "Hurry up. She's coming."

Albert smiled and said, "Last chance. I can kill her right here, right now."

Hanna shook her head.

Albert said, "Got it. Let's get out of here."

Hanna was surprised by the rush she got from doing something as simple as this. Her heart was racing, perspiration forming on her forehead. They stepped onto the sidewalk with their backs to the detective, and Hanna put her arm around Albert's waist as if they were a couple on a date.

She heard the car door open and shut, then the pinging sound of an underpowered engine as the detective pulled away from the parking lot.

Albert brought up his phone and opened an app. He said, "We got her. Let's see where she's headed."

CHAPTER 36

THERE WAS A different vibe between Marie Meijer and me the next evening. The swelling in my eye from the suspect's elbow had receded during the night, but I was still disturbed by what I'd seen after the raid by the Koninklijke Marechaussee. The image of the dead girl stuck in my head. Her pretty face would never smile again.

It's easy for a cop to pretend he's seen it all and nothing bothers him. The reality is that if you see too much, there's nothing anyone can do to save you.

So on the job, I never minimized the tragedy I saw. It kept me human. Connected. I embraced the fact that I could still be shocked. I tried to stay positive, and I genuinely liked people. Most people. Even knowing what I knew, I gave people the benefit of the doubt. Like my dad used to say, people do what they have to do. Of course, he was using that as an excuse for why he was leaving my mother, but I could see how it made sense.

Now we were back in De Wallen, the largest of the red-light districts, and Marie was showing me the building where she believed the human-trafficking ring operated. We walked because it was faster than sitting in traffic, no matter what kind of car you had.

I didn't like seeing the young women in bikinis behind windows. I knew what a hard life prostitutes had, sanctioned by the government or not. The girls in the booths with red lights worked twenty-two hours a day. The booths were closed from six to eight in the morning, then opened again for the businessmen to stop for a quickie on the way to work.

I was surprised at the number of tourists, some with children, casually walking down the district's narrow streets. We slipped into a café for a quick break.

Marie took a sip of coffee and stretched her arms. She seemed more relaxed in this setting. She said, "What's your social life like back at home?"

"Dull to nonexistent."

She smiled and said, "I doubt that. A tall, handsome police officer in a city like Miami? I bet you're busy every night."

We'd shared a lot over the past couple of days, but I wasn't quite ready to get into my home life with her. At least, not the details about my mom. We sat quietly for a while longer, then I finally had to ask her about her eye.

She focused both eyes on me and said, "It's a birth defect. Why? Am I not pretty? Would I be a freak in Miami?"

I held up my hands. "I'm so sorry. I didn't mean to touch a nerve. It's just that you're so confident and your eye doesn't seem to bother you. You even made a joke about our eyes matching. I was just curious."

Marie waved off my apology and said, "I try not to be self-conscious about it. The doctor said the eyelid droops slightly because of damage to a nerve. I used to wear nonprescription eyeglasses to hide it, but when I turned thirty, I realized anyone who was bothered by my eye was not someone I wanted in my life."

I said, "'Think of all the beauty still left around you and be happy.'"

Marie gave me a dazzling smile. "Okay, I'll bite. Who said that?"

I couldn't hide my own smile. "Anne Frank."

"So you have a quote for every situation."

I laughed. "I picked that one up reading about Anne Frank last night."

"Why did you learn all these quotes?"

"My bachelor's degree is in philosophy. I noticed that it freaked out my coaches at the University of Miami when I spouted quotes. No one expects a big tight end to go to class, let alone study. I knew there was no way I was going to go pro, so I studied hard."

Marie gave a dainty laugh. "What does one do with a degree in philosophy?"

"Go to law school."

"And how does someone who went to law school become a police officer?"

That, I was not about to get into. There were too many complicated elements involved. I could've told her that I wanted to make a difference in the world or that I liked the excitement. Instead, I just shrugged and said, "I like my job."

She got that I didn't want to talk about it. "Do you live alone? I bet you have a fancy apartment on South Beach."

"That's almost exactly right. Except that I live fifty miles northwest of South Beach in a house with my mom and my sister."

Marie paused, then said, "That's sweet. I think."

"Sweet, weird—it's a matter of perspective. The fact is they're good roommates and I can trust them. I haven't always had that kind of success in my other living arrangements."

Clearly wanting to move on and not make me uncomfortable, Marie said, "Why don't we take a look at some other neighborhoods?"

It was like police work anywhere. Gather as much intelligence as possible before you act. I felt at home.

CHAPTER 37

IT WAS EARLY evening when Hanna and Albert started following Marie Meijer. Hanna wanted Albert to practice with the tracker. The signal had faded in and out a couple of times during the day, but he was learning how to follow the display on his iPhone.

Albert put his hand on her arm as they turned a corner in central Amsterdam. He pointed across a busy street and said, "She's just leaving that café and her car is parked out front."

Hanna said, "Who's that with her? It looks like a cop."

"He's either a cop or some kind of wrestler. He'd be a handful."

"It's too crowded here. Let's see where they head next. I'd prefer to get Funky-Eyed Bitch by herself." Albert had given Hanna a Browning nine-millimeter pistol. He carried the Makarov nine-millimeter he'd bought at a military-surplus show. He'd had to pay the man extra to buy a working pistol, not just a museum item.

They tracked the couple into the Oost District and found the car parked near Molukkenstraat, a block from the canal.

Hanna said, "Why would they be over here?"

"Does it matter? This is perfect. With all the crazy shit that goes on around here, no one would be surprised by a shooting." He glanced around, hoping to see Meijer. "Remember, your gun is just for extra security. Let me do the shooting. We'll do it when there are no witnesses."

"Are you going to shoot the man too?"

"If he's with her, I have to shoot him. There can't be any witnesses. But I'm pretty good with this thing. I might be able to do it from down the block."

Hanna didn't like the idea of murder, but she could only deal with so many problems at once. Marie Meijer was the driving force of human-smuggling investigations. With her gone, Hanna could focus on the Russians. Just today, they had threatened her again, after Albert had stabbed one of their flunkies in the shoulder. She'd tried to explain that it was a personal argument in a bar, nothing to do with business.

That's all Russians cared about.

CHAPTER 38

WE PARKED THE car on a side street in the Oost District, and I noticed that this area catered to a younger, more vibrant crowd. There didn't seem to be many tourists here, judging by how clean and serene the district felt.

I was so comfortable with Marie now that it felt like I'd known her for years. She had a quick sense of humor, and, more important, she could let things go. She showed no resentment for my question about her eye earlier.

When she took me to a charming place called the Volkshotel, I wondered what she was up to. One of the desk clerks waved to Marie as we entered.

Marie looked over her left shoulder and said, "There's a bar on the roof, Canvas. It'll give us a nice view, and they have several beers that are outstanding."

I had given up trying to decipher the menus, so when we got there, I left my order up to Marie and she didn't let me down.

The IPA was from Belgium and the name unpronounceable. It had to be close to 10 percent alcohol. But it went down easy. Very easy. If this beer had been available in Miami when I was younger, I might not have graduated.

Marie looked over and said, "Do you feel like being honest with me for a few minutes? Have I earned your trust enough?"

I lifted my beer and said, "Fire away."

"How's a smart, good-looking guy like you not married? You wouldn't be able to stay single for ten days on the streets of Amsterdam."

I'd been prepared for a question about my mother. I was even ready to tell her all about the dementia that had stolen Mom from me and Lila a little bit at a time. It was the biggest, most difficult thing in my life. But this question hit home in a different way.

I took a long pull on the beer and said, "It's not a big deal."

That made Marie laugh. "I'm sorry, but when anyone begins a discussion with 'It's not a big deal,' it's usually a pretty big deal."

She was right. "What I meant to say was there's not a good explanation. There's just an old story." I paused to take another sip of beer and choose my words.

"Basically, I was engaged to a girl in law school. I took an internship with a local attorney in Miami, and the flashy son of a bitch stole my fiancée. That's why I'm not married."

Marie was quite serious when she said, "I'm sorry the woman didn't have enough sense to recognize she was with a good guy." She paused, then added, "I was engaged once myself."

"What happened?"

"Who knows? He got scared, I got scared. It just didn't work out."

I said, "At least my way, you end up with an interesting story."

I enjoyed making Marie laugh.

I said, "The worst of it is that I see the son of a bitch around town all the time. And he's married to my ex-fiancée. If the fact that he's still alive doesn't show how much restraint I have, nothing will."

She smiled, patted my hand, and said, "Poor baby."

She meant it, and I felt better. Not a bad evening.

CHAPTER 39

HANNA WATCHED AS Albert jogged across the street to her. Generally, in their business, she handled all the details about shipments and money, and her brother acted as an enforcer. But lately, she was concerned she'd given him too long a leash, and she had been accompanying him on some of his jobs to ensure that he didn't go overboard.

Now he trotted back to her position and said, "They're sitting up in that rooftop bar, Canvas, having a beer. Their car is a few blocks the other way. They'll come out the front and probably take the alley back to the car. We could wait and catch them then."

Hanna said, "And you still don't know who the man is?"

"No. I don't care how big he is—a bullet in the face should keep him pretty quiet."

Soon, just as Albert had predicted, the Dutch detective and her big male friend came out of the hotel and started walking toward her car, stopping periodically to look at things on the walls.

Hanna and Albert fell in behind their two targets, and Hanna wondered what they were looking at. It took her a few minutes to realize they were reading some of the historical plaques on the buildings. The man had to be some kind of tourist.

A few blocks from the car, Albert turned to Hanna excitedly and said, "This is perfect. There's no one around. It's dark. They've slowed down. This is so easy, it's embarrassing."

Hanna said, "Can you do it from a distance? Even with just a handgun?"

"We can stay right here behind this Mini Cooper, and I'll hit both of them. If it doesn't do the trick, I can walk down there and finish them. But this should be no problem at all."

He knelt down next to the British car. There was a blank space where the Cooper emblem should have been. He pulled the Makarov semiautomatic pistol from the back of his waistband and steadied it on the edge of the car.

Hanna crouched behind him and saw that his barrel was pointing at the Dutch detective. Good. Marie Meijer was the main target. Hanna didn't really care if they got the big man or not. He wouldn't be able to identify them anyway.

She could hear Albert steady his breathing and sight down his extended arm.

This was one less problem Hanna would have to worry about.

CHAPTER 40

IN FRONT OF a small brick building, I studied a little bronze plaque that informed me the structure had been built in 1790.

I mumbled, "Holy shit. The oldest house in my neighborhood was built in 1963."

Marie said, "Perhaps you can come back when you have more time. I could show you a lot more than just the criminal aspects of Amsterdam—there's art and history here as well. The Rijksmuseum and the van Gogh museum are fabulous."

I let out a laugh. "Art and history? Are you crazy? I'm from Florida. I want to see sports and pretty girls."

A smile slid across Marie's face. She reached up and gently touched my black eye. "We have soccer, and there's a rugby club on Saturdays that would love to have someone like you. As for pretty girls, that's a matter of your perspective."

I said, "I'm impressed with Amsterdam so far. Who knows,

you and I might make some key arrests, and then we can visit every museum in the city."

She paused for a moment, then said, "I hope we can sort out the information I'm getting now about another load of people bound for the United States. We think the traffickers will try Miami again. That's where their contacts are."

"Now *you've* got some pretty good contacts in Miami as well. We'll do whatever we can to stop these criminals." I was serious. Aside from the fact that she'd shown me a good time here in Amsterdam, Marie was a hell of a cop, and she was working a really big case. A case that could shut down a human-trafficking operation. She had intel and a witness who was feeding her tips; that's how we'd saved the kids in Miami, and that's how we'd stop the traffickers. There was no way anyone could pull me off it now.

I heard the gunshot. Then two more. Instinctively, Marie and I both crouched behind a concrete planter for cover.

Amsterdam was starting to feel more like home.

CHAPTER 41

HANNA WATCHED HER brother line up the shot. Yes, this was business, but it was also clearly personal, and killing Marie felt necessary. The detective was too interested in Hanna's operation. The Funky-Eyed Bitch had made it personal first.

Hanna was crouched low behind the Mini Cooper, watching the spot where the detective had taken cover, when a movement near her left shoulder caught her attention.

Albert looked ready to shoot when Hanna whispered, "Wait."

Albert whispered back, "What's wrong?"

"Someone's behind us."

Just as Albert started to turn, Hanna heard a gunshot, and the rear window of the Mini Cooper shattered. Albert grabbed his sister and shoved her away from the car, across the sidewalk, and into the entryway of a small shop.

There were two more shots. The bullets pinged off the bricks surrounding the entryway. A fleck of debris hit Hanna in the eye. She was confused and fighting panic. What the hell was this? Who was shooting at them?

Albert kept low with his gun up, scanning the dark buildings around them.

Hanna said, "Who's shooting?"

He continued to scan for targets. "I'll give you one guess."

"The Russians," Hanna answered. "But why?"

"Take your pick: The money we owe them. The fact that I had to get rough with one of them in a bar. Or that we're competition for them."

"I meant, why *now*?"

Albert was silent.

Hanna had to ask. "Is there something you're not telling me?"

Albert hesitated, then said, "Remember the pretty Canadian tourist I got high with yesterday?"

"Yeah?"

"What if I told you she wasn't Canadian, but Russian? And that after we got high, we fooled around at my apartment. Oh yeah, and that her husband is an enforcer for the Russian mob."

Hanna shook her head. "You're an ass, but at least that makes a little more sense. Now I get why the Russians are trying to kill you."

Albert fired two rounds that looked like wild shots to Hanna. A streetlight across the road shattered, making it suddenly darker. Then two men scurried out of the shadows.

Albert fired three more shots. One of the men fell onto the hard brick road and dropped a pistol as he hit the ground. Albert immediately jumped up and ran toward the fleeing man.

Hanna was impressed by her brother's abilities, but he soon gave up the chase. The escaping man had had a solid head start. Albert turned and walked slowly back toward her. As he passed the Russian lying in the road, Albert extended his right arm and pumped another bullet into the man's back.

Hanna flinched at the sound and at the sight of the man spasming on the ground. Albert's expression never changed as he walked past her and said, "C'mon, we need to get out of here."

CHAPTER 42

MARIE AND I huddled behind the heavy planter, listening to the gunshots. As a Miami police detective, I'd heard plenty of gunfights. I once saw two separate gunfights converge, gang members opening up on people they didn't know or care about.

We stayed in position for a while after the shots ended and the sound of running footsteps receded. When I heard one last shot long after all the others, I knew someone had executed a coup de grâce.

Marie had her pistol drawn, but we both felt secure behind the planter. She had called for help, so it was hopefully on the way. But we couldn't just sit by if innocent bystanders had been injured or if someone was in danger.

Marie said, "I don't think those shots were meant for us."

"Let's not risk it. I heard at least two different calibers and it sounded like people were trading shots. At least until the end."

Marie stood up and said, "You can come with me or wait here."

That really wasn't a choice. I trotted alongside her to the main street. We paused at the corner to scan for any other gunmen. A crowd had started to huddle around someone lying in the street. That told us the fight was over.

Marie bowled into the group with her badge out. She checked the man's pulse, then looked at his face closely. She turned to me and said, "I know this man. He's an enforcer for Emile Rostoff's organization. Or, rather, he *was* an enforcer for Rostoff."

I said, "Any idea who'd tangle with him like this?"

"The better question is whether the Russian interrupted someone. Maybe someone with a gun looking for us."

"What makes you say that?"

"Just a hunch. Don't you ever have an intuition about something?"

"I do. Maybe this means you're really getting to the traffickers."

Marie said, "In that case, it's time to turn up the heat."

I looked at her, now fully convinced that Marie was the total package.

CHAPTER 43

MARIE WAS SUPPOSED to drive me to the airport, but I convinced her to let me see the kids first, since I'd promised them I'd say goodbye before I left. She knew me well enough by now to have built in time for the stop. We parked in front of the main administration building at the child-services facility.

Marie stayed by the car to make a phone call as I rushed inside. I realized in my haste just how anxious I was to see them.

A middle-aged man at the front desk looked over his reading glasses and said something to me in Dutch. I didn't speak the language, but I could understand snotty when I heard it.

I said, "My name is Tom Moon. I brought the kids from Miami."

The man nodded and said, "Ah, Mr. Moon, of course. The children are in class, but if you can wait a couple of hours, they can slip out and say hello."

"I'm sorry, I'm on my way to the airport now."

"No, *I'm* sorry. Shouldn't you have scheduled this better? At the moment, as I said, the children are busy."

I just ignored him and walked straight ahead through the unlocked double doors. The man almost fell off his stool trying to get to his feet and stop me. He followed me down the hallway, yammering at me as we walked. "Don't make me call the police," he said.

I looked over my shoulder and smiled. "I'll save you the trouble. Step outside your front door. There's a cop standing right out there. See if she'll do anything."

Before we could further cement our friendship, I heard a child yell, "Tom, Tom!"

At the end of the corridor, beautiful little Michele stood staring at me. She had a wide grin on her tiny face. She ran down the hall and leaped into my arms.

A moment later, Olivia darted from another room and jumped into the hug without a word. That caused a stir of excitement, and before I knew it, all six of the kids were involved. I felt like I was in a friendly rugby scrum.

After a few minutes of all of us hugging, one of the teachers gave me permission to talk with them in a classroom. *That should please the officious little prick at the front desk*, I thought.

Most of the kids had some piece of hopeful news. Joseph from Poland was very excited that the police had finally talked to him about his missing sister. One of Jacques's relatives from Belgium had invited him to live with their family.

The only one without an update was the Finnish girl, Annika, who was quiet. She looked down, her long blond hair hanging into her face.

I put my arm around her and pulled her close. That earned me a smile.

Annika said, "My mother was my only living relative. The social worker says she'll find a family for me to live with. I'll be okay."

I said, "You'll be better than okay. You're smart and beautiful. You're going to do special things."

"You really think so?"

"Absolutely. You can always call me if you need someone to talk to. And Marie will still be here in Amsterdam."

That brought a broad smile. I felt better. The kids were safe, and that's what mattered. When I had to leave, we had another group hug.

I had to take a quick break to compose myself before I stepped out to join Marie. This goodbye had been harder than I'd expected it to be.

CHAPTER 44

FORTY MINUTES LATER, Marie and I stood facing each other in front of my plane's gate. She checked the crowds moving around us every few seconds. You can't take the vigilance out of a good cop.

She said, "I look forward to hearing from you."

"I'll stay in close touch with you about everything."

She smiled and said, "I promise to check on the kids until all of them are back where they're supposed to be."

"Especially Annika?"

"Especially Annika."

"Thank you." I wanted to kiss her. I wanted to show her how I felt. I swept a strand of hair away from her face and carefully tucked it behind her ear. I knew we had a connection.

I sprang back to reality and said, "We'll probably see each other again soon. This case is going to heat up in more ways than we can imagine. If they do try to run a load of people to

Miami, just call me and I'll take care of everything. Maybe we can even scam a trip for you."

"I'd love to see Miami. I'd also like to meet your mother and sister. They sound wonderful."

"My mom's wonderful. I'm reserving judgment on my sister."

Marie smiled again and said, "I hope this visit didn't give you the wrong idea about Amsterdam, considering you caught a fleeing felon and almost stumbled into a fatal gunfight with the Russian mob. We really are a friendly city. Writers say we are a tribute to the ordinary man. You just got to see the worst part of ordinary men."

I said, "There's nothing about Amsterdam I didn't enjoy. Even our crazy first and second dates. And I never thought I'd say this, but I have to get back to the relative safety of Miami."

The man at the ticket counter called over to me. "You're the last one. You need to hurry, sir."

Marie patted me on the chest, then pushed me away. "Hurry, you don't want to miss your plane."

CHAPTER

Miami

SOMEHOW, THE PLANE ride back to the U.S. didn't wear me out like the flight to Amsterdam had. Probably because I was able to sleep better when I wasn't worried about six kids.

That doesn't mean I wasn't tired when I fumbled with the key to get into my house in Coral Springs. When I stepped inside, my mom saw me, and a smile washed over her face. I was glad to see her, and she was happy to see me too. She said, "Hey, Chuck." It was casual and friendly. But Chuck was my dad's name. This was not a good sign.

"How was work today?" Mom continued. "We really should have a family dinner because there's so much to catch up on. Tommy has decided to go to the University of Miami, and Lila is the top student in the fourth grade."

I wasn't sure how to handle this. Usually, Mom didn't go into this kind of detail when she slipped into the past. I just stood there, stuck. I was hurt. It hurt every time this funny, intelligent woman who raised me slipped out of reality.

My mom walked toward me with a big smile on her face. "Well, what do you think? Aren't you proud of your kids?"

I hesitated. "Yes, I am." I waited a moment. "Mom, it's me, Tom. Tommy. Your son."

She looked at me. Confusion swept over her face. She wiped a tear away from her cheek, and I wrapped her up in a hug. Even when I was twelve years old, I was bigger than anyone else in the house, and my mom used to say my hugs were like bear hugs. Now she felt particularly tiny as she wrapped her arms around my waist. She said, "I'm sorry, Tom. I don't know what came over me." She slipped away and hurried into her bedroom.

A few seconds earlier, my sister had walked in from the patio. She was wearing a tank top and shorts, and sweat dripped off her; she'd been doing some kind of exercise outside. "Hey, Tom. Welcome back."

I looked at her and said, "That was weird, right? I mean, even for Mom."

Lila shrugged. She said, "You handled that just right. The doctor says we should try to ground her in reality, that we shouldn't play along if she gets confused about who we are or what year it is."

I shook my head, then looked toward my mom's bedroom.

Lila clapped her hands together and said, "So, how was Amsterdam?"

"You know it was just part of the job."

"Really? No fun at all?"

"I didn't say that." I couldn't help smiling a little, thinking of Marie.

A grin crept across my sister's pretty face. "A girl? Did my brother finally start to chase women again?"

"If I was chasing, I didn't catch. But I did meet an interesting woman."

"Pretty?"

"Beautiful."

"Then you shouldn't let something like the Atlantic Ocean get in the way of seeing her. You deserve it. You're a great guy, and between Mom and your job, you don't have nearly enough fun."

It was the nicest thing my sister had ever said to me.

CHAPTER 46

THE NEXT DAY, I slipped into the task force offices early I said a few quick hellos and settled at my desk to get my shit in order. I wanted to hit the ground running, and I started by calling some of my contacts in the Department of Homeland Security. They'd help me keep an eye on ships coming into the South Florida area.

Steph Hall stepped into my small office and gave me a playful little slap on the back of my head. She plopped into the chair by my desk and said, "Rough trip? You look like shit."

"You don't look so sharp yourself," I said. But that wasn't true. She always looked sharp, if a little tired today. This was just how we busted on each other.

"That noticeable, huh?"

I immediately apologized. "I was just kidding."

Steph said, "I'm not. I'm exhausted. My mom came down from Riviera Beach to watch the baby."

I said, "Baby up late? Is she sick? And what about Chaz?"

She waved off my questions. "You know the DEA. If they wanted you to have a family, they'd issue you one. Besides, he's not the most attentive father in the world."

I had to wonder what she saw in the conceited DEA agent she'd been living with for two years. "What about his parents? Don't they ever help out?"

She shrugged. "They're still coming to grips with the fact that their precious only child is shacked up with a black woman. They're a little old-fashioned."

"You mean racist."

"Either way, they're no help."

I knew Steph wanted to marry the bozo, but the guy couldn't see the gold that was right in front of his face. That was enough to convince me that Chaz was an idiot. The fact that he wouldn't help out with his own kid sealed it for me.

Steph said, "I'm glad you're back. The boss tends to focus on me when you're not here. He had me running around doing all kinds of stupid shit that I'd much rather you would do." Her laugh positively lifted my spirits. She stood up and said, "What do you think about lunch today?"

I nodded and smiled as she walked out of my office.

Two minutes after Steph left, a new visitor surprised me. I heard someone say, "What's happening, Anti?" and I looked up to see Alvin Teague's grinning face.

"What the hell are you doing here, Smooth Jazz?"

"Just checking out the office I intend to move into once I replace you." Then he straightened his tie and added, "I was also hoping to run into Lorena Perez."

That explained it. "Look, Jazz, the only way she'd talk to you is if you literally ran into her with your car."

"Since when do you know so much about women?"

That was a good question. I pivoted. "I know about smart

women, and smart women aren't impressed by a Brooks Brothers suit—"

"Armani."

"Or that shit you call flirting."

Teague looked unfazed. "Tell that beauty I was looking for her and that I said hello." He winked and was gone.

CHAPTER 47

I NEVER LIKED doing briefings in front of my own squad. Cops tend to ignore any information that comes from someone they know. That's why a lot of agencies use outside trainers. To paraphrase Jesus, you can't be a prophet in your own hometown.

A few years ago, I was in a briefing for a narcotics warrant where an undercover detective, Willie Hodge, went on too long about what a little apartment looked like on the inside. That's all it took for Willie to earn the nickname "Cameron"— as in James Cameron, director of movies that run way too long, like *Titanic* and *Avatar*. One slip-up and you could be stuck with a nickname for your entire career. I still call Willie "Cameron." And he answers to it.

Studying philosophy occasionally gives me insights into why people react to certain things the way they do. But philosophy doesn't help me connect to high-achieving cops who are anxious to get out and work.

Now I wanted to find a way to make each of these experienced cops understand how important this case was to me, even if I had to begin with an educational seminar. Human trafficking is not a crime commonly investigated by U.S. authorities, and our laws and understanding of the crime are evolving. Too many cops still equate human trafficking with prostitution. There are overlapping elements, but human trafficking encompasses all kinds of exploitation. And it's not confined to faraway, impoverished places; it's a growing blot on wealthy countries.

I wanted to make sure everyone on the task force realized that human trafficking was all I would focus on until we wrapped up this smuggling ring. I recapped everything that had happened to me in Amsterdam. (Almost everything. I might've left out a detail or two, like smoking pot.)

I could tell it would be a hard sell when the smartest member of the task force, our resident CPA, Lorena Perez, said, "Isn't it mostly just prostitution?"

"I gotta tell you, Lorena, a month ago I might've said yes. We all know how dirty a business prostitution is, how some of the girls work for rough pimps and make almost no money. Prostitution is not a career most people choose if they can avoid it.

"But human trafficking is bigger and ten times worse. Essentially, traffickers are taking people, both male and female, and turning them into slaves. The victims earn almost no money while they're trying to pay off what they think their debt is. Pretty girls are often forced to become sex slaves. Someone's got to do something about this."

To her credit, Lorena nodded and said, "I guess that's why every strip club in Miami-Dade now has only Russian dancers."

"It's one of the reasons. Chill and I had a talk with Roman Rostoff before I left. He's wrapped up in human trafficking, as well as all the other shit he's into. We may end up tangling with his organization."

That got everyone's attention. Good.

Lorena Perez said, "What are you going to need from us, Tom?" She flipped her dark hair; it looked like she'd spent hours styling it.

"Lots of surveillance until we can interdict the next load of people being smuggled in. I'm in close contact with the Dutch national police. They have a couple of sources giving them information."

After the meeting broke up, Steph Hall caught up to me before I made it back to my office.

"You have such a good grasp of the issues we're facing," Steph said. "But maybe try acting a bit more fun-loving. Not so intense. I've seen you outside of work; I know how you joke with your sister and how you take care of your mom. We could use that guy around the task force a little more."

All I could say was "Understood and noted." I thought about it for a moment, then added, "Thanks. Not everyone is so honest."

"There is something you could do for me to show your appreciation."

I looked at Steph and said, "Anything you want."

"Explain to me how you got the nickname Anti."

It bothered Steph to no end that I'd never given her the backstory on my street name, and it tickled me that it frustrated her not to know. Still, I was almost about to say something when our supervisor asked me to come into his office. I smiled at the look on Steph's face, shrugged, and said, "Sorry, some other time. Duty calls."

CHAPTER 48

I WAS CONCENTRATING so hard that when the phone on my desk rang, it startled me. As soon as I heard Marie Meijer's voice on the other end of the line, a goofy grin spread across my face.

After some small talk, Marie said, "I visited the kids at their facility. Monnie was reunited with her father and they're leaving for Nairobi in two days."

I didn't tell her that Monnie had already sent me a message on Facebook about it.

Marie went on. "They've also made contact with Olivia's mother. She's been frantically searching for the little girl for the past four months. The Spanish authorities thought it was some kind of custody dispute with her ex-husband and never took the matter too seriously. The others are all fine and living like a little family. It's really quite sweet. They're just missing their giant, dim-witted father." She let out a great laugh after delivering her little dig.

I said, "I'm setting things up on this end in case another load of people comes in."

"One of my sources said they're getting ready to move any day. I have surveillance on the Amsterdam and Rotterdam ports. We're also monitoring all the airports in Western Europe with flights to Miami. My source thinks that's where they're headed again."

I said, "Have you heard any more specifics about the time of arrival or method of travel? Just like you, we have limited resources. There's no way I can cover all the ports in South Florida and all the airports."

"I think it's too many people to ride on a single commercial airliner. It would be too expensive. From what I hear, there are more than twenty people ready to be moved. That means it's got to be by boat. We're trying to figure out where and hopefully rescue the people while they're still in Europe." Marie paused, then added, "There's something else."

"What's that?"

"Emile Rostoff is definitely involved. That means his brother in Miami will be too. My source says that the Russian we found in the street had been shot by Hanna's brother."

"Can you arrest him for it?"

"No. No evidence. But that means the Russians will be in no mood to fool around. I wouldn't be surprised if our case ends with the murder of Hanna and Albert Greete."

I let out a laugh. "Sorry. I guess I should sound more concerned. I've had narcotics cases end that way. We say they're 'exceptionally cleared.'"

"I like that term. Either way, it's crucial to find these people being smuggled."

"It sounds like you should come to Miami. We need to work this case together."

"I agree. I'm trying to figure out the details now."

We chatted for a few more minutes, then I stepped out of my office and ran into Steph. "Hi," I said.

"Why are you in such a giddy mood?" she asked.

"How can you tell what kind of mood I'm in from a quick hello in the hallway?"

Steph smiled and put her hands on her hips. "Really? I spend more time with you than anyone else in your life does. Besides, if you're not scowling, you're probably in a good mood. All I'm saying is, keep it up. It's a good look and good for the office."

I was getting the sense that maybe I wasn't as collegial as I could be at work. Thank God for honest people like Steph. Aside from my mom and sister, she might have been the only person in the world I could count on.

CHAPTER 49

WHEN I SAW Anthony Chilleo walking past my office, I grabbed him and pulled him inside.

After we talked for a minute about the task force and my trip, I got to my real concern. "Did anything happen with the Russians or my sister while I was gone? She claims that she didn't even go out during my entire trip."

Chill smiled. "She didn't leave the house after six on any of the days you were gone."

"Holy crap, you didn't do a full surveillance on her the whole time I was away, did you?"

He didn't say a word but pointed to the bag of technical equipment he had given me weeks before. It was still where he'd left it; I hadn't bothered to put it away yet. I knew it held several trackers and other devices.

"You put a tracker on my sister's car?"

"Yep."

I stared at him as I searched for the right words. Then I nodded and said, "Brilliant."

Chill just shrugged. He'd been around a long time and knew every possible trick. Why physically follow someone when you can just check your phone and see where her vehicle is?

But I didn't like to think about how close Lila had come to being a bargaining chip in this deadly game. We were going to have to have a serious chat soon.

I asked Chill, "Do you have anything new on Rostoff?"

"He's been holding off on a drug deal he was making with some Colombians. It must piss him off to know that someone is finally watching him. This is the first time he's ever had a problem he couldn't buy his way out of."

"That means he might get desperate and try to threaten us. Or worse."

Chill let out a snort. "Good luck with that."

I liked his attitude. I sensed that Chill didn't do anything in a half-assed way. Maybe that's why he had been married twice.

I looked at him. "Keep your eyes open. You should probably warn your ex-wife as well."

"It'd be a sad day for any Russians who bother her. A redneck from Ocala with a concealed-weapons permit? I think she'll be fine."

I believed him.

CHAPTER 50

Ostend, Belgium

HANNA GREETE HAD spent a lot of time on this load. Minors tended to listen well, but this group was mixed ages. Hanna had a few teenagers, several Eastern European women, and two Indian men. The total count was twenty-three.

Earlier, at her office, Hanna had supervised as one of her workers sewed the five blood diamonds Hanna intended to sell in the United States into a red Everest backpack. She'd already secured the tracking device in a pocket of the bag and had sewn the pocket shut. The woman had held up the backpack for inspection. Hanna ran her hands over the strap where the diamonds were hidden. Aside from a few bumps, there was no way to tell anything was concealed inside.

She'd touched the pocket holding the tracker. "It's bigger than I remembered."

Albert said, "It's the same as the one I stuck on Marie Meijer's car. I added a second battery pack so that it will work on the low setting for almost twenty days."

"Why is there a low and a high setting?"

"It has to do with how strong the signal is. We're losing some strength but gaining many extra days of use. I didn't think you wanted to trust our cargo to switch out batteries halfway through the trip."

Satisfied with that part of her plan, Hanna had to firm up the details that would mean the difference between earning half a million euros or hiding from the Russians for the rest of her life.

Hanna had noticed surveillance at the port in Rotterdam; she'd started looking at alternative ports. She'd finally settled on Ostend, Belgium, near Bruges

Her brother had put her in touch with the first mate of the *Scandinavian Queen*, a midsize freighter that operated under a Danish flag.

Now Hanna was meeting the first mate at a bar in Ostend. The place didn't even have a name. It was just "the bar near the port." The bare concrete floor showed stains of old fights. Other stains represented where patrons had puked up the thick Belgian beer.

She looked across the table at the tall, weather-beaten first mate. "My brother says you're reliable and will make sure everyone arrives safely," she said.

The fifty-year-old sailor nodded, then took another giant gulp of beer from an oversize mug. Albert had told her the man had been on the ship for the past seven years.

"For what I'm paying you, I expect reliability," Hanna added. "I should probably expect more than that for the cost."

The sailor put down his mug and looked across the table at her. "You came to me. Not the other way around. I know Albert and trust him, so I agreed. But taking shit from a skirt is not part of the price tag."

He seemed to think that he'd put her in her place, which bothered Hanna. She chose her next actions carefully. She stood up from the table and marched away. With every step, she expected the first mate to call out and stop her. She paused ever so slightly at the door, lifting her hand to the knob slowly.

Still silence.

She stepped through the doorway into the evening air of Ostend. A cool breeze blew from the water. She couldn't have people she paid talking to her like that. She'd have to find another way to move the load.

The specially built storage container she'd bought had already been moved to a facility just outside the port, and the plan was easy. Just before the ship was set to sail, she would have her cargo loaded. The extra-large container, with four air vents and a small toilet built into one corner, could be used over and over.

Apparently, the container would now have to be on a different ship.

As she reached her car, Hanna heard a man say, "Hold on." It was the sailor.

She opened the car door as if she hadn't heard him.

He raised his voice. "Perhaps I was a bit too blunt."

Hanna glanced at him. "Too *stupid* is more like it."

The man looked sheepish. Finally, he said, "I'll do it. I can check on the container every day and bring them extra food. If I do it late enough, when most of the crew is asleep, I can even let them out onto the deck."

Hanna thought about it, then said, "No. I'll hire someone else." She slid into the car.

The sailor stepped closer and said, "C'mon, I'll do a great job."

Hanna said, "For half the money."

"You mean half the money up front?"

"No, nothing up front and half of our original price when the load arrives safely. That's my only offer now. Consider it a tax on being reactionary and sexist."

The man stood there, mulling over the offer. Finally, he said, "Damn, I thought your brother was the tough one."

CHAPTER 51

Amsterdam

MAGDA ANDRUSKIEWICZ SAT on the edge of the bed. If she looked out the window, she could catch a glimpse of the moon. She'd turned sixteen a few months earlier, but to the other girls in the room with her, she was something like a mother.

Sitting next to her on the edge of the bed was a thirteen-year-old Belgian girl who couldn't stop crying. The only common language they had was English, but the other girl's accent was so thick it was difficult for Magda to follow what she was saying. As best she could tell, the girl was homesick. That didn't explain why she was trying to get to the United States, but it did explain why Magda's shoulder was soaking wet from the girl's tears.

Magda didn't know what else to do but put her arm around the girl and tell her everything would be all right. That approach had worked with the other girl crammed into the room with them. She was also sixteen and had been crying earlier, but Magda had gotten her to lie down quietly and close her eyes. The exhausted teenager had fallen asleep almost immediately.

Magda had left Poland with her older brother, intending to come to Amsterdam. They had met a nice man in Poland who'd said there was plenty of work in Amsterdam and easy transit to the U.S. from the Netherlands' largest city.

The trip was a series of bus rides and hostel stays until they reached Germany. There, in a chaotic Berlin station full of refugees from various nations, they'd been caught up in a crushing crowd, and she'd gotten separated from her brother. Magda didn't have any identification or a working mobile phone, and she was too scared to go to the police.

She waited in Berlin for three days, hoping to find her brother again, searching the streets; she'd even tried e-mailing him from an internet café.

Out of options, she had found a way to get to the United States, thinking she could get in touch with her brother from there. The lady who had set everything up, Hanna, had even given her a new backpack with clothes and a few other things. Hanna told Magda that she could get her into the United States and that all Magda would have to do was work for someone in Miami to pay off the expense. It sounded like a pretty good deal.

The girl Magda was comforting quieted down. After a few minutes, Magda realized she had fallen asleep in her arms. Magda looked through the window to see the moon one last time for the night.

She settled the younger girl on an air mattress, then lay down on her own thin mattress and stared up at the ceiling. It was only then, after trying to comfort the two other girls in the room for most of the evening, that she wanted to cry as well.

Magda wondered who would comfort her.

CHAPTER 52

Miami

I KNEW EVERYONE in Miami, and as more information came from Marie Meijer, that was really starting to pay off.

I had run down a dozen tips and confirmed some details, but we still didn't know exactly how the load of humans was going to come into the United States. And as much as I wanted to know everything about the case and get it done as quickly as possible, I had other responsibilities.

That's why at lunchtime I drove my FBI-issued Ford Explorer at incredibly unsafe speeds back to my home in Coral Springs. I was well aware of the FBI restrictions on vehicle use, but sometimes you just had to be efficient and flout the rules. In my case, *sometimes* was all the time. My sister claimed I had a complex about authority and enjoyed breaking rules. I could never admit to her that she was right, I *did* enjoy it. Breaking rules had become my hobby.

My mom had a doctor's appointment, and I'd decided to take her to it since my sister had already done a lot more than her share of looking after her. I was also starting to worry about Lila's drinking, but I was still working out a way to talk to her about it.

That's why I didn't mind taking my mother to the neurologist, just across the county line in Boca Raton.

My mom had been acting a little differently recently. I'd really noticed it since I'd gotten back to Miami. It wasn't just being in the moment versus living in the past; she had started to get confused about exactly *where* she was and she wasn't shy about expressing that confusion.

In the car on the way to the doctor's office, my mom asked, "Are you going to bring those kids by the house again? It was wonderful having young people around."

"I don't think so, Mom. They were just visiting."

"I don't suppose you'll be supplying me with grandchildren anytime soon?"

"Not unless I kidnap them. If I go the normal route, it could take a while. First I have to find a woman that I'm attracted to. Then we have to date and fall in love. We should share the same goals with regards to kids. And then, finally, we'd start the process of having one. I wouldn't hold my breath."

"Nonsense. A tall, handsome, educated man like you should have his pick of women."

"Says his mom."

She laughed at that. The laugh lines that formed around her eyes made me smile. It was just like when I was younger, when I could talk to her about anything.

We got to the doctor's office and I checked us in while my mom took a seat in the lobby. There were a few people there, the usual assortment of elderly men accompanied by concerned wives or children. I had seen it all before in the three-year odyssey of my mother's disease.

While we were sitting there waiting, out of the blue my mom said very loudly, "Where are we?"

"At Dr. Spirazza's office."

"Who? Why aren't we at Dr. Goldman's office? I like her."

"Because Dr. Spirazza is a neurologist. He might be able to give us some tips on how to manage your issues."

My mom said, "What issues?" Her voice got louder; it was starting to make me nervous. "The only issue I have now is that I'm not seeing Dr. Goldman."

I could see in her posture and movements that she was getting agitated. I had no real response to it. The man sitting next to her slid over another seat. A woman who was accompanying her father gave me an understanding look. But my mom became more upset.

I held her hand and stroked her arm, but it had no effect. I kept my cool and finally thought of something. I looked at my mother and said, "What's the difference between a jellyfish and a lawyer?"

The question immediately caught her attention and she calmed down. She was intrigued as she considered the options. Finally, she asked me, "What's the difference?"

"One is a spineless, poisonous blob. The other is a form of marine life." It was an old joke, but it made her laugh hard. And then, for no apparent reason, she went back to normal and started quietly flipping through an AARP magazine.

The woman with the older man smiled and said, "You're a pro, aren't you?"

"You can catch my show nightly at the Improv."

Even my mom chuckled at that one.

CHAPTER 53

NO ONE EXPECTS a philosophy major to be terribly organized. And by FBI standards, I was not. That didn't stop me from being effective, but still, sometimes the mess got to me.

It took me an hour to get my office just the way I wanted it. Stacks of papers that had been sitting on the credenza behind the desk were now in either the shred basket or the filing cabinet. The stuff pinned to my bulletin board was updated. I recognized that some of the previous reminders, like a to-do list from two and a half years ago that I'd carried with me from the Miami Police Department, were probably no longer useful.

I'd even used the tiny vacuum cleaner someone had brought in to give the carpet a good once-over.

Steph Hall stepped into the doorway and said, "Wow, I didn't know you had so much room. What's the occasion?"

"No occasion. It was just getting a little messy."

"We all assumed that was the natural order of things with

you. The office looks about the same as it did right after you moved in. What are you going to do for an encore this afternoon? Maybe wash your Explorer?"

"Did it last night. It smells like a new car."

"Okay, what the heck is going on? Do you know something I don't?"

"I don't know how busy I'll be once this case gets off the ground. I thought it was a good time to clean things up."

"Uh-huh. And when does the Dutch detective come to Miami?"

"This afternoon." I tried to sound casual, but Steph knew me too well.

"I'm starting to suspect that you and this detective have more in common than the case."

"It's not like that."

Steph raised an eyebrow and said, "With guys, it's always like that. Men have one-track minds. So tell me, is she pretty?"

"Beautiful." I didn't even bother to hide my smile. I checked the clock on my desk and realized I had to head out to the airport soon.

Steph said, "Can I help with anything?"

"You've already done too much. You're the best." I stood and gathered my things.

She said, "Have I done enough to learn why your street name is Anti?"

"I don't know if I'd go that far."

She playfully slapped me on the arm. "Don't be a shit. I could just ask a Miami cop."

"Where's the fun in that?"

Steph bowed her head. "You're right. I'll figure it out. Or I'll get you to spill one day."

"Good luck with that." I let her hear me snicker as I left.

An hour later, I used my connections at Miami International to get right to the gate as passengers disembarked from the Amsterdam plane.

I didn't want to go overboard, but I had gotten a haircut. I wore a simple sports coat. Marie spotted me as soon as she stepped off the Jetway. I liked the smile that spread across her face.

I reached in for a hug and she put out her hand and we were caught in the awkward no-man's-land between a hug and a handshake. She put one arm around my shoulders and gave me a squeeze.

After we retrieved her single bag, we walked to my car. Marie said, "The newest information I have came from my best informant, who told me that a ship left from somewhere in Northern Europe about a week ago and should be here in the next few days."

"And you can't narrow that down at all?"

"I might be able to once we're closer to the day the ship arrives."

"Just like they can trick you by leaving from any one of the ports in Europe, they could come into the port of Miami, Port Everglades in Fort Lauderdale, or even Palm Beach."

Marie said, "I understand. I just want to make the best case possible."

"I'd like to get a little press on the arrests so that people can see how serious human trafficking really is. Media coverage would probably help the task force as well."

Marie agreed. As we made our way to my car, she said, "What do we do now?"

"I'm going to get you something to eat. You set the standard in Amsterdam for hospitality."

I loved her smile.

CHAPTER 54

IT WAS LATE in the afternoon by the time I got Marie settled in her downtown hotel room. I had planned to take her to the office and introduce her around, but to be honest, I liked my alternative plan better.

She was hungry, so I'd stopped my Explorer near a food truck that was always on Eighth Street just west of the interstate, before the street turns into Calle Ocho, famous for restaurants visited by presidents and the Cuban culture on display.

Marie looked at the truck with the neon letters on the side that said SANDWICHES. She said, "You're only taking me to the nicest places, I see."

The owner, Luis, waved to me as we stepped up to the truck's window. I smiled and held up two fingers. He nodded.

"I don't want you to fill up too much before dinner. Besides, these are the best Cuban sandwiches in the city. He's usually sold out by this time of day."

"What other kinds of sandwiches does he sell?"

"There are no other sandwiches recognized by Miami residents. Try one."

Marie said, "Don't we get a choice of what's on it?"

"No. In Miami, a Cuban sandwich is ham, pork, pickles, mustard, and a little mayo. Otherwise it's not a Cuban sandwich, and most places won't sell it."

When I tried to pay, Luis held up his hands. "Never from you."

I thanked him and stuffed a ten in the tip jar.

As we sat in the air-conditioning of my car, Marie said, "Did he not charge you because you're with the police?"

"Sort of. Years ago, he was robbed and his teenage daughter was pistol-whipped by the robber. There was no way to ID the suspect and Luis was too scared to give us many details. His daughter was a mess. She had two surgeries. It pissed me off," I said. "So I put an offer out on the street for information about the guy."

"What kind of offer?"

"I let the best snitches know that I'd give them a walk on their next crack-possession charge if they came up with the name."

"And did they?"

"The next day I had Ronald Jerris in custody for robbery and assault. It was his fifth arrest that year."

Marie thought about it and said, "An offer to ignore possession of crack? I'd never be allowed to do that at home."

"I'm not supposed to do it here either. But letting a brutal robber get away with beating a teenage girl isn't right. Given the choice between what's legal and what's right, I chose right."

"And now you get free sandwiches."

"Which I'd like to pay for, but it would hurt his pride. But better than a free lunch is that his daughter is entering her third year at the University of Central Florida."

We finished our sandwiches and got on our way. As I drove, Marie sat in the passenger seat and took in all the sights of South Florida. "What city is this?" she asked at one point.

"It's called Coral Springs. This is where people who work in Miami live. At least, people who work in public service."

Marie turned to me. "Are we going to your house?"

"I thought you might like to eat a home-cooked meal and see what an average American family made up of only adults is like." I was taking a risk; I wasn't sure how she'd react to this.

She gave me a broad smile and said, "Will your mom and sister be there?"

"They're busy making our dinner as we speak."

All Marie said was "Excellent."

CHAPTER 55

I TOOK MARIE to my house, despite the fact that I had some concerns. My mom had been pretty good since the incident at the doctor's office a few days ago, but the likelihood of her having an episode increased as time went on, and I was afraid we were due for a bad night.

My apprehension grew as I turned into my driveway and parked the Explorer. I didn't know whether I should warn Marie or just roll the dice and see what happened. "Marie, I probably need to tell you something," I said.

She turned in the seat to give me her full attention. "Of course."

I thought about how to phrase it, but there'd be no point in telling her if my mom was doing well. Finally, I chickened out and said, "I'm really glad you got a chance to come to Florida. My mom and sister are going to love you."

I appreciated the smile she gave me.

I felt like I was about to make entry on a search warrant as we ambled up the walkway. As soon as the door opened and I caught a whiff of the Italian food, I felt better.

My little sister popped out of the kitchen immediately, walked right up to Marie, and extended her hand. "You must be Marie. I'm sorry you have to put up with my bonehead brother. He said you took great care of him in Amsterdam, so we hope to do the same for you."

I stepped next to my sister and gave her a hug. My primary purpose was to gauge the amount of alcohol on her breath. It was tolerable.

Lila took Marie by the arm and walked her toward the kitchen. Lila casually looked over her shoulder and winked at me. That meant everything was okay. At least for now.

I don't know why, but my mom had become something of a gourmet cook since her diagnosis of dementia. As kids, Lila and I got only the basics. We were well fed, but no one would've considered our house a culinary mecca. Now something had clicked, and my mom seemed to understand much more about seasoning; she'd begun making astonishing dishes. I'd asked the doctor about it. He'd just shrugged and said, "I wish I could tell you if it was related to the dementia. The truth is, we have very little idea of what things are triggered by this disease."

Tonight, I was happy and relieved to see that Mom was as gracious and charming as she normally was. Or at least, as she used to be. She ushered the three of us out to the patio, where she had a pitcher of mojitos ready. We settled in for a drink, Marie sitting between me and my sister, and my mom said, "I tried a new lasagna recipe tonight, and we'll start with a salad of arugula, strawberries, and walnuts."

I clapped my hands and said, "That sounds delicious."

My mom touched my arm and said, "Thanks, Chuck."

My heart skipped a beat.

After my mom had wandered back into the kitchen, Marie leaned over and asked, "Why did she call you Chuck? Is that your middle name?"

I decided it was time to explain things. I wasn't embarrassed; I just never knew how to tell people that my mom sometimes lived in a different time and place.

CHAPTER 56

Amsterdam

HANNA GREETE HAD raced around Amsterdam for several days taking care of various tasks so that she could leave for the United States with a clear schedule. She'd planned to fly to Miami to be at the dock when the *Scandinavian Queen* arrived, but now she had to waste time meeting with her Russian contact Alexi at his favorite little pub in the Oost District.

At least in a pub she'd only have to put up with alcohol, not the constant odor of pot.

She tried to be friendly as well as professional when dealing with the Russians, as there was no way to completely avoid them in this business. Today, though, she didn't have the patience for pretense, and as soon as she sat at the small table and faced Alexi, she got right to the point. "I hope this is important. I have never been busier in my whole life," she said.

Alexi was as calm and cool as always. He took a sip of his

beer, wiped his mouth with a napkin, and asked, "Are you about to go to Miami?"

"Yes. Yes, I am. And the people I'm delivering there should go a long way toward covering any debts I have with Mr. Rostoff."

Alexi nodded and smiled. "I'm sure it will. But Mr. Rostoff is a little nervous that you're leaving the country. We're going to need some collateral before you depart."

"Collateral? You already loaned me the money. The only way I can pay it back is to go on this trip. You should've asked for collateral when you offered me the loan."

"But we didn't, which is why we're asking for it now."

"What kind of collateral did you have in mind?"

"We were thinking about the diamonds that everyone knows you possess."

Hanna gave him a flat stare and said, "No."

That didn't faze Alexi. He said, "Perhaps we could baby-sit your daughter. She would be safe and we would have the collateral we need."

Hanna looked at the well-dressed, middle-aged man, trying to assess if he was joking. Finally, she said, "Are you insane? Why would I ever leave my daughter with you? I'm afraid the entire concept of collateral is not going to work out."

"What about your brother, Albert?"

"You're not listening to me. There will be no collateral. Besides, I heard some of your people are very angry at Albert."

"He did kill one of our enforcers. It was most impressive. And we understand that our man was not without some culpability. But this is business. We would guarantee your brother's safety until you returned and a payment was made."

Hanna tried to appear as if she were considering the offer. That was probably her best option to get out of this pub safely.

She said, "Let me speak to Albert. I'll see what we can work out. I won't be leaving for almost a week anyway." That little lie should buy her some breathing room.

"We have contacts in Miami waiting to help you. Your success is our success. But there needs to be some trust between us."

"In our business, trust is a rare commodity. Just like collateral, it's difficult to come up with, and no one has much."

Alexi flexed his fingers and said, "I'm the one who stood up for you when you needed money. I saw that you ran a reasonable operation and had the potential to supply us with a lot of people in the Miami area. We are always needing more people in the organization. At least, the kind that you supply. Please don't mistake my faith in you for foolishness. I do not like to be jerked around."

Hanna nodded as she stood up. "Nor do I. This load will go through. My debt to you will be paid and I don't expect any trouble while I'm gone." She had nothing more to say, so she simply turned on her heel and left.

CHAPTER 57

HANNA WAS COMPOSED as she walked away from the infuriatingly calm Alexi, but as soon as he was out of sight, she rushed back to her office. She was not about to risk the Russians deciding they were going to *take* collateral whether she offered it or not.

Janine, Tasi, and Lisbeth—the young women who worked for Hanna—could tell just by her stride what kind of pressure their boss was under. As soon as she burst through the door, all three of them jumped up to see how they could help.

Hanna took a moment and looked at the three young women. She might be tough on them occasionally, but she couldn't put them at risk. There was no telling what the Russians would do while she was gone. She said, "We might be facing some challenges from the Russians. I understand if anyone wants to quit." She looked from girl to girl. "Let me know now. I'll even throw in a full month's pay as severance."

None of the girls spoke up.

"No one wants to jump ship?"

They all shook their heads with varying degrees of decisiveness.

"That may be a lack of judgment, but I'm proud of you all," Hanna said, a catch in her voice. This was loyalty.

Janine spoke up. "What do you need us to do?"

Hanna thought about it. "What I really need you and Lisbeth to do is nothing. Just lay low for the couple of weeks I'll be out of town. Don't come here, no matter what. I'll call you and let you know when it's safe."

Janine's younger sister, Tasi, who didn't have her sister's organizational skills or street smarts but who was as pretty as any twenty-year-old in the city, said, "What about me? Am I okay to work here?"

Hanna looked at the poor, silly girl who didn't have the common sense to know when her life was in danger. "No, Tasi, I'm going to need you to come with me."

"To the United States?" It was clear the girl thought this might be a joke.

Hanna nodded.

The young woman smiled, revealing perfectly straight white teeth. "You need me to help you on your trip?" Tasi couldn't hide her excitement.

Hanna said, "I've decided to take Josie with me. You'll be an excellent nanny."

It all seemed to make sense to the young woman at that point. She bounced up and down for a moment, clapping her hands. All Hanna could think was that Tasi was too naive to stay here alone. And she certainly didn't believe Tasi was capable of keeping her daughter safe. That's why she was going to bring Albert too.

Hanna found her brother in the back room. She said, "I've decided to take Josie and you with me on the trip to Miami."

Albert looked up from the magazine he was reading and said, "I thought you said there'd be nothing for me to do in Miami. This sounds fishy to me."

"Alexi has asked for collateral if I'm leaving the country. He made some veiled threats against you and Josie."

"Take Josie. That's perfect. Besides, if I don't have to worry about you two, I can eliminate a lot of our problems here in Amsterdam."

Hanna liked his optimism, but she wasn't about to let her crazy brother go running around Amsterdam murdering Russians.

Before an argument developed, Josie walked into the room. Albert adjusted immediately. He was always careful not to let his niece overhear anything about their business.

Hanna looked at her daughter and said, "How would you like to go on holiday?"

The young girl widened her eyes and asked, "Where?"

"Miami, Florida, in the United States."

"Is that near Disney World?"

"How big can Florida be? When we're done in Miami, we'll go to Disney World."

Josie turned to her uncle and said, "Mom won't go on some of the wild rides."

Albert said, "I know, she's not much fun." He winked at his sister, then looked back at Josie. "But I'll take you on any ride you want."

Josie said, "Do you think we'll be able to see an alligator in Florida?"

"I guarantee it. They have whole farms of alligators there. Some of them even do tricks."

Josie tilted her head and said, "That's not true, is it?"

Albert raised his right hand and said, "I swear."

At that, the girl excitedly bounded out of the room.

Hanna looked at her brother. "I guess that means you're coming. I should get Josie to ask you to do things more often."

CHAPTER 58

HANNA DIDN'T WANT to take any chances, so she decided to leave for Miami out of Paris. She, Albert, Josie, and Tasi took the train to France. The entire trip, Albert conducted his version of countersurveillance by roaming through the cars, making certain no one was following them on the train.

Hanna, Albert, and Josie had fake passports that identified them by different names. Tasi used her regular passport. No one would recognize her name or suspect her of anything.

Hanna wanted to let down her guard for just a moment and enjoy the train ride. She wanted to appreciate the scenery and think about the future. She was starting to believe they had a future. But she just couldn't relax.

Josie and Tasi were oblivious as they searched their phones for information on Florida and Disney World. It made Hanna smile, seeing Josie so excited. It was a childhood Hanna would've liked. All that mattered to her was Josie's happiness.

Albert came back to the car.

Hanna snapped, "Sit down. You're making me nervous."

"Rostoff won't be happy we slipped away from Amsterdam."

"All will be forgotten when we pay him. The Russians will help us in Miami because they need our load. It will all work out. So just sit down and relax."

He plopped into the seat facing the girls and Hanna felt like they were a little family.

Fifteen minutes later, two young men came into the car and sat near the door. They smiled and nodded when Hanna and Albert looked up at them, the only other people in the car. One of the men lowered the wide window, and the noise of the train boomed through the car. Cool air rushed in.

Albert gave Hanna a look.

She said, "No, relax. They're just passengers."

Albert sat for a minute more, then stood up and casually strolled down the aisle. The girls, who were facing forward, were still engrossed in their phones. They couldn't see the new passengers without turning around.

Albert headed toward the loo at the far end of the car. As he passed the men, he said, in Dutch, "How's it going?"

The thinner of the two, a man about twenty-five years old, answered, "Good, and you?"

Hanna heard the slight Russian accent in the greeting. Damn. Albert was onto something.

Her brother turned just as the man stood and popped open a switchblade.

Albert moved like lightning as he parried a blow, then threw his elbow into the young man's clean-shaven jaw.

His head twisted, and a tooth flew out of his mouth and bounced off the seat. A line of spittle with blood in it streaked across the clean tan wall.

Somehow, Albert ended up with the knife in his hand.

Hanna watched, stunned, wondering how she could help. The girls were still in their own little world, and the sound from the open window had drowned out the commotion.

Albert moved again before the second man could draw a weapon. He put the point of the switchblade to the man's bearded throat and took a small automatic pistol from him. Albert turned to his sister, winked, and smiled.

The young man's eyes were wide. The neatly trimmed beard made him look like a boy pretending to be a man. So did the ease with which Albert had disarmed him.

Albert put the pistol to the man's head and gave him an order in a low voice.

The bearded man helped his dazed Russian friend up and Albert escorted the two of them to an electrical and maintenance closet wedged next to the restroom. Albert said something else, opened the locked closet door with the first man's knife, and forced the two inside.

Thirty seconds later, he flopped, exhausted, into the seat next to Hanna.

She said, "How do you know they won't scream for help?"

Albert tapped the pistol in his waistband. "I explained that if they didn't keep quiet until I told them they could come out, there would be plenty of air holes in the door. Young pretty boys aren't used to people fighting back. We'll be fine."

Hanna had known her brother was tough, but this was spectacular. He looked like a movie spy. How could she *not* feel safe traveling with him?

CHAPTER 59

Miami

I'D BEEN BURNING up my contacts trying to keep an eye on everything that came through the ports in Florida. The problem was that Florida, being a long peninsula, had a lot of damn ports. I didn't even bother to consider what would happen if the ship came into a port outside of Florida.

It was easy to get overwhelmed with data and details, and this was where my background in sports came in handy. If I viewed major cases the way I used to view football games, I kept a better attitude and was able to manage each task that popped up a little more easily.

This wasn't a game, but that's how cops have to look at major cases. Every cop has some form of psychological trick to help cope with the stress that gets piled on us from all sides by the administration, the public, and our own natural desire to make arrests in every case. Not to mention the stress that comes from department infighting, though in my experience, the hardworking cops who want to solve cases don't care much about promotions or office politics.

Still, it didn't pay to ignore them completely. As Plato said, "One of the penalties for refusing to participate in politics is that you end up being governed by your inferiors." That's especially true in police work, and I was experiencing it on the task force. Luckily, our supervisor left decisions about assignments up to my discretion.

Chill, Steph Hall, and Lorena Perez were all looking at the Rostoff connection. It bugged me that the smug son of a bitch Roman Rostoff thought he could sit in his fancy office and count his money without facing any consequences for his illegal activities. Maybe that's how it worked in Moscow, but it wouldn't fly in Miami. I didn't care how many Russians lived here.

Now Marie Meijer and I were in my FBI-issued Explorer heading to Port Everglades in Fort Lauderdale. The way Marie took in everything that flashed past as we drove made me feel like I'd brought her to an alien world.

"It's all so green," she said.

"It's the subtropics. That's what happens. Wait until summer and you'll understand why things are green—they get watered every single afternoon."

"Why don't they call this the port of Fort Lauderdale instead of Port Everglades?"

I shrugged. "No one consulted me when they were naming it. It's a big port with the second-busiest cruise terminal in the world."

"Where is the busiest cruise terminal?"

"Miami. Where else? That's part of what's making everything so difficult. There are so many ships coming into the ports daily, not even counting the cruise ships, and it's impossible to investigate them all."

I drove into the port off Seventeenth Street so that Marie

could get an idea of the size of it. Even the county convention center was at the port. The cruise terminal was bustling as I eased past a security checkpoint and inched toward the cargo terminal. While not as elaborate as the cruise terminal, this area sprawled over acres of the port.

There were oil and natural-gas storage containers on the property between the port and US 1. I had visited them once during a class on terrorism, and I didn't like to consider the damage that would be done to downtown Fort Lauderdale if a terrorist managed to puncture one of the tanks and ignite the contents.

I didn't mention that to Marie. Tourists don't like to hear about potential terror threats.

I found a spot near the southernmost part of the port. This part of the port wasn't too busy today. In fact, it felt a little isolated. A few cars were parked haphazardly. One crane was working to unload a small freighter farther down the dock, and the sound of metal against metal echoed through the port.

We stepped out of my car and looked at the three ships that had docked since last night. None of them would have been confused with the *Queen Mary*.

The middle ship held about fifteen containers on the bow and dozens more amidships and on the stern. One of the containers caught my attention. A rail-thin man smoking a cigarette was playing with the lock on the front of it.

I nudged Marie and pointed at the ship.

Marie said, "I'm not sure what I'm looking at. It looks like a normal cargo ship to me. I don't see anything unusual."

"The container near the bow of the ship has air vents along the sides. We've got to get a better look."

IT'S HARD TO overestimate the importance of cell phones in modern police work. As I hustled down to the ship with Marie, all I could manage was a quick check with an FBI analyst on my phone; I gave her the ship's name and said that it was docked at Port Everglades. The analyst told me right away that the ship had left from Belgium and had made several other stops before arriving in Florida, and she was working on the registration as I reached the gangplank.

It wasn't a particularly large ship. I guessed it had about fifteen crew members. It wouldn't have drawn my attention if I hadn't noticed that one container; I'd seen enough containers to know they usually didn't have air vents.

As we approached, I slipped on a blue FBI windbreaker and draped a police badge on a chain around my neck so there would be no confusion that I was a cop.

A muscle-bound fortyish Hispanic man wearing a shirt with the shipping company's logo on it stepped onto the gangplank at the other end and walked forward. He raised his hand like a crossing guard and said, "The ship is not open to the public." He held his crossing-guard pose for a few seconds to show off his massive biceps, then added, "Step back. They're gonna unload."

I stared at the man for a moment. "What about this windbreaker makes you think we're part of the general public?" I asked. "And I don't see the crane down here ready to unload anything."

The man stood straight and flexed his chest muscles, a move a bouncer might make to intimidate someone. He said, "Look, *pendejo,* I don't give a shit who you are. You ain't coming on this ship."

"Are you a member of the crew?"

"I'm a security officer for the shipping company. Move away from the gangplank. I'm not going to tell you again."

"Listen, Paul Blart, Mall Cop, we just want to get a quick look at one container, then we'll be on our way. It'll take only a minute or two."

The muscle-head was a couple of inches shorter than me, and clearly not used to having to look up at someone. He pointed at my FBI jacket and said, "Why do you have an FBI jacket but a City of Miami badge?"

I shrugged. I wasn't in the mood to answer questions. I said, "I'm sorry to confuse you, but we're coming aboard, and I mean right now." I stepped onto the gangplank with Marie directly behind me. The man gave a few inches but didn't get out of the way.

He said, "Don't you need a warrant to search the ship?"

"Not for this. I have concerns about someone's safety. It's called *exigent circumstances.* And you'd be smart to step aside."

"What are you, a lawyer?"

"As a matter of fact, I am. But this is police business and someone's life might be in danger." I began marching forward, Marie right behind me. It wasn't until we reached the far side of the gangplank that the security officer offered any resistance. He braced himself at the end of the gangplank as if he thought his big chest and biceps would be enough to stop a determined cop who was six foot four and weighed 240 pounds.

He was wrong.

CHAPTER 61

ALL IT REALLY took was a slight body twist, just like a coach had taught me at the University of Miami. I quickly shifted everything to my left, and the security officer squirted past me. He fell face-first onto the gangplank. I never actually touched him. That was the best kind of confrontation.

I liked how Marie calmly stepped over the man without saying a word.

We wasted no time heading to the bow of the ship and the container with the air vents. I didn't want to think about what it would've been like to cross the Atlantic in something like this. I was scared to see what was inside.

The security officer picked himself up and caught up to us. Like an angry little kid, he said, "I called my supervisor. Only Customs can come on the ship at any time. You're not with Customs. That's about the only police-agency ID you don't have on you."

I said, "Did you call your supervisor over to the ship? I'd like to speak with him or her."

That brought the man up short. "No. She's not on-site. But she said you don't have permission to be on the ship."

All I said was "Noted," and we continued making our way to the bow of the ship.

Before we even reached the container, the thin sailor who I'd seen smoking a cigarette in front of it earlier turned to face me. He was wearing a faded red Def Leppard T-shirt with a frayed edge where the collar should have been. His laminated ID and port card were attached to his belt.

The man spoke to the security officer in English with a thick Dutch accent. "Hey, what's this? The captain said no one was to come aboard until the crane was ready to start unloading."

I pointed to the badge on my chest and said, "Police business. I'd like to look at this container more closely."

The crew member said, "And I'd like to get a blow job from a Hooters waitress. Both of us are going to be disappointed."

I scooted around the man, secretly hoping he'd make the mistake of putting his hands on me. I don't know if it was my size or my official position that gave him a little bit of common sense, but all he did was follow me, complaining in my ear the whole way.

"We can't open any of these containers," he said. "They have special locks. You're wasting your time. You're wasting my time."

Marie looked at the door and said, "This lock has been tampered with. It's not even an official transport lock."

I didn't hesitate to pull a rescue tool off the wall. It looked like a thick crowbar with a pointy end.

Now the crewman stood directly between me and the door to the container. He looked serious. I hoped I wouldn't have to fight him or, God forbid, go for my gun, although I would if he or the security officer drew a weapon.

We stood there in silence. Marie sensed the tension and, like a good partner, moved into position to take action if she had to. She was behind the men, neither of whom was paying any attention to her. I'd seen her in action and had no doubt she could stop these two idiots from doing anything stupid.

Sweat poured down the security officer's face. He was nervous. This was way outside his experience.

Finally, the crewman said, "The captain'll have something to say about this."

He looked toward the bow. I stepped past him to the shipping container, avoiding the security guard like I was a hockey player skating past a defender. No one had touched me and I still had the crowbar in my hand.

I paused at the door for a moment. I thought I heard something move inside the container. Marie knocked on the side of the container, and I heard more movement. My heart started to race. I prayed that we weren't too late to save everyone inside.

Then the security officer said, "What's that noise?" It was like a light bulb went on over his head. He realized what was going on and what was at stake. When the crewman started to move toward me, it was the security officer who stopped him.

I nodded my thanks to the security officer, then set the crowbar against the lock. It broke off with the right leverage and my full weight against it.

I pulled one side of the door open. The smell that hit us was ferocious. It turned my stomach and made my eyes water.

Behind me, I heard Marie mumble, "Oh my God."

CHAPTER 62

ASIDE FROM THE stench that was making my eyes water, the first thing I noticed was the strange light inside the container. There were two scratched Plexiglas panels across the top that allowed sunlight inside, but the light that came through the hazy plastic was yellow and gave the entire container a freaky look.

Something flashed out of the corner and made me duck my head to one side. Then a shriek tore the air. I was completely confused.

All at once, things came into focus, and I understood much more clearly. There were no people inside the container. It was filled with exotic parrots and macaws.

I stepped inside and saw feathers raining down from the birds in the top row of cages. A battery-operated light dangled from a cord. The man in the red T-shirt must have just been in to check on the birds.

I tried to get an idea of how many birds were crammed into

the container. At first, I thought it was dozens, then I realized it was more than a hundred, all of them extravagant, with lavish colors and powerful vocal cords, or whatever birds use to make noise.

Marie stood just outside the door, which was wise. She said, "These are all African. A number of different species. I'd say they're really, really valuable."

Here I'd been thinking we were about to set twenty or so people free. I turned to ask the thin man in the Def Leppard T-shirt about the container and cargo, but he was already racing for the gangplank.

I looked at the security officer and said, "Can you call someone to stop him?"

The muscle-bound man raised his hands and said, "My job is to make sure no one gets *on* the boat."

"Don't you have the sheriff's office or Customs on your radio somewhere?"

He shook his head. "They made me take their channel off my radio. They said I was too enthusiastic and made too many calls for assistance."

I looked at Marie.

She said, "Isn't this still a crime? I mean, he *is* a smuggler."

I wasn't happy about it, but I started to jog after the man. This day was not going the way I'd thought it would.

CHAPTER 63

BY THE TIME I was off the ship and on the dock, the thin man in the Def Leppard T-shirt was jogging west, away from the water. He headed toward the wide-open fields that housed the storage containers for gas and oil. This was not the kind of chase people saw on police shows or in the movies. Most criminals aren't in particularly good shape, and most cops avoid running after suspects unless they've committed a serious crime.

I kept the man in sight easily enough, but this was not an impressive foot chase. We weren't going terribly fast, and there were no obstacles or traffic. Just as real-life fistfights tend to be messy events, real-life foot chases generally aren't that exciting either. I could have just let him run—the guy lived on the ship, and he'd be easy to find. But secretly, I didn't want to disappoint Marie. This was the kind of story I'd have to embellish a few years down the road. Maybe I'd add a parrot sitting on his shoulder...

Then the chase got even less interesting. The man started to slow drastically, and by the time I was a dozen yards behind him, he was leaning over with his hands on his knees, gasping for air.

Before I could say anything to him, he vomited onto the grass. That made me jump back. I can put up with a lot of unpleasant things; I'd seen more nastiness in my few years working in Miami than most people see in a lifetime. But vomit always made me gag and want to vomit myself.

I did a moonwalk away from the man. He was downwind so I didn't smell it, but the second time he heaved, I almost lost my lunch.

Then the man looked up at me and said in a Dutch accent, "I can't believe you guys figured out what I was doing."

I just shrugged. "It's my job." I needed someone to see me as superior today.

The man started to ramble about how he'd gathered the birds over several months during a trip to the western coast of Africa. He had an agreement with the captain and first mate to split the money. That's how he'd been able to get back and forth to the container so easily. "We needed a big pay-day here in America," he said. "I already spoke to a pet-store owner in Miami and one in West Palm Beach. Between them, I was going to be able to sell almost my entire shipment." The man sounded wistful and depressed. I let him talk. I hadn't placed him under arrest, and these were voluntary statements. Although I kind of wished he'd shut up.

A few minutes later, an SUV with two U.S. Customs agents rolled up next to us. I identified myself, explained the situation, and told them about the man's confession. The older agent, a tubby man about fifty, said, "We appreciate getting good cases like this, but why the hell didn't a

Miami cop working on an FBI task force call us about these concerns beforehand?"

"I was afraid it was just a wild-goose chase. Excuse the pun."

The younger agent, a woman, said, "More like you didn't want to share the credit for any arrest on human trafficking."

Her partner said, "Why didn't you follow protocol? We don't bother you at your office."

I looked over at the scared Dutch sailor and said, "Looks like you don't bother people at *your* office either."

U.S. Customs was not amused.

CHAPTER 64

AFTER ARRIVING IN Miami and checking in at the Miami Gardens Inn, Hanna and Albert rushed downtown. They spoke with several jewelers in the Seybold Building, trying to find a buyer for the diamonds that would arrive in Miami with their load of human cargo. Albert also made inquiries into where he might find a gun quickly.

They were directed to a pawnshop on Seventh Avenue near Twenty-Fifth Street, just east of the airport. Jeff's Pawn and Gun was in a tiny strip mall with multiple vacant stores. The area looked like a ghost town.

Hanna checked the time. The sign on the shop said it was open until eight p.m. They still had half an hour.

Albert strutted into the place like he owned it. This was his area of expertise. Hanna thought it was only fair to give him some leeway in this side of their work, since he listened to her in business matters.

Albert smiled at the thin, older man behind the counter and said, "Howdy, partner. How are you this evening?"

The pawnshop clerk just stared at him over the frames of his glasses pushed to the end of his long nose. A pack of Camels sat in the front pocket of his plaid shirt. If this was Jeff, whatever money the store made was not due to the owner's sparkling personality.

"You're not on drugs, are you?" the man asked Albert.

Albert looked astonished and shook his head. "Just a visitor. I guess I'm a little too friendly. Sorry."

Maybe-Jeff said, "I can deal with friendly visitors. It's the drug addicts that traipse in and out of here all day that I have no patience with. What can I do for you?"

Albert looked into the glass case and pointed to a black semiautomatic pistol. "Could I take a look at that Beretta?"

The man retrieved the gun and racked the slide to be sure it was empty. "There's a three-day waiting period, and you'll have to show me ID." He looked at Hanna, then back at Albert. "Where the hell are you from, anyway?"

Albert didn't hesitate. "Belgium."

"Good. You don't look like it, but I wanted to make sure you wasn't one of them Muslim freaks always interested in blowing something up."

Albert chuckled and said, "Nope, not a Muslim. And anything I blew up, you would approve of."

That comment earned a quick cackle from the older man.

Albert handled the gun briefly, checking the barrel and the breech. Then he shook his head and said, "Wish I could buy this right now. I'm afraid we'll be on our way to Disney World in a few days. The only ID I have was issued in Europe."

The pawnbroker said, "Yeah, even if they call it a gun-free

zone, you hate to be unarmed when others are packing. More innocent people die in gun-free zones than anywhere else."

"Guess I'll be helpless too. Just want to protect my family." Albert watched the man closely.

Finally, he said, "I got nothing against Belgians. I hear you've loved Americans since the big war. You seem to know your guns pretty well. And I hate how the government is always interfering."

Albert muttered, "Me too."

"I have a way to get you a gun right now, but there's a premium."

"How much of a premium?"

"A hundred percent of the cost of the gun."

Albert held up the Beretta and said, "This gun?"

The pawnbroker nodded.

Albert smiled and said, "Done."

A few minutes later, they walked out of the store with the Beretta and two boxes of ammo. Albert turned to Hanna and said, "America really is the land of opportunity."

CHAPTER 65

HANNA DIDN'T WANT her brother to see the tremor in her hands. She was as nervous as she'd ever been. It was just before nine o'clock and they were sitting at a booth in a bar called Glow inside the massive Fontainebleau Hotel on Miami Beach. The luxury of the place was mind-boggling to Hanna. The bar was on an outdoor deck with a shimmering pool and view of the Atlantic. The people at the bar looked like movie stars. Every one of them, men and women, could have been a model or an actor.

From a business standpoint, it wasn't late, but from a parenting standpoint, it was getting there; she'd told Josie and Tasi they would be back to the hotel before eleven. Hanna didn't like breaking a promise. She tried to set a good example for her daughter.

Across from her in the booth was her Russian contact, a fit forty-year-old who looked more like a lifeguard than a gangster. He had a dyed-blue goatee that gave him an edgy vibe, but he was friendly enough. He spoke with a Russian accent, and he'd told them to call him Billy.

Albert had whispered, "Somehow I don't think that's his given name."

Hanna just gave her brother a stare.

Billy had ordered a round of Mojitos, but Hanna hadn't touched hers. She wanted to get to the meat of the conversation now that they'd gotten through the small talk.

Billy said, "I can take ten girls as long as they're not too ugly or old. My preference is for Europeans. I can make more money with them. The downside is they tend to form relationships with customers and make some of my men jealous." He looked at them from under his dark, thick eyebrows, but he got no response.

He added, "I might be able to take the rest off your hands, but at a discount. The cops have been bothering us recently and nothing is easy. But what I can offer should cover most of your debt to the Rostoff brothers."

Hanna saw what Billy was doing. She had spent five years in this business and knew all the negotiating ploys. Where others had failed or been murdered by the competition, she and her brother had built a decent business. If it hadn't been for some bad luck, she never would've had to borrow the money she was so desperate to pay back now.

Hanna said, "By my calculations, it will cover the whole debt."

Billy smiled. "Let's get the people in first, then we'll see where we are with money. There's a charge for using our contact in Customs, and there are a few other fees."

Hanna didn't want to ask what the other fees were.

Then Billy said, "I heard you might be interested in selling some high-quality diamonds."

That took Hanna by surprise. "How did you hear about the diamonds?"

Billy chuckled. "My dear, I speak with my partners in Amsterdam at least twice a week. If they know about it, I know about it. I also know that, late this afternoon, you visited three jewelers in the Seybold Building. Nothing remains a secret there. By tomorrow, every jeweler in the city will be interested in your diamonds. I was just hoping to beat the rush."

"Let's worry about dispersing my load of people first. Once that's settled, I'll be happy to talk about other issues."

"Where and when does the load come in?"

This time, Albert, who had been sitting quietly next to his sister in the booth, said, "That's not information we wish to share before they arrive. I'm sure you understand."

Billy flexed the muscles in his jaw. He understood, and that was the problem.

Hanna took control of the conversation again. "I need to arrange transportation and housing before I can do anything else."

Billy smiled and said, "If you want, you can call me directly as soon as they arrive. I can have transportation ready to take much of the load off your hands right away. That should keep your expenses down."

Hanna considered the offer. It would certainly be easier if someone else arranged for vans and hotel rooms. They were also running short on cash, and with that thought, she made her decision.

Hanna reached across the table and shook Billy's hand. "I will be calling you sometime in the next three days."

Billy gave her a charming smile and said, "I look forward to it."

CHAPTER

I SAT IN a conference room at the task-force offices with Marie Meijer and Steph Hall. Both of them looked fresh, while I looked like I hadn't slept much. Because I hadn't.

Marie's informant in Amsterdam had said to expect the ship to dock somewhere in the Southeast sometime tomorrow, but that was all the information available. Marie said, "It comes from a well-placed informant, but they say they're getting only bits and pieces. They pass the information on to me as soon as they get it."

Steph shook her head and said, "That rules out undertaking any kind of rescue on the high seas, which was a long shot in the first place. But we've got to free those people as quickly as possible. There's no telling what sort of conditions they're being held in."

That's why I liked working with Steph Hall—she understood what was important. All the arrest stats in the world didn't help someone who died while being trafficked.

Lorena Perez said, "I've been looking at some financial info we've gotten on Rostoff. Most of it appears legit. He donates a shitload of money to a Miami Beach councilman and charities associated with Miami Beach. He's getting a humanitarian award there next week."

I said, "Great. Everyone thinks he's a prince while in reality, he ruins lives."

Lorena said, "His main muscle, Billy the Blade, lives in Fort Lauderdale. He doesn't owe anything on his condo or his Corvette."

Lorena was matter-of-fact when she passed on information. She wasn't an accountant, but she knew how to figure out relationships by following the money. She was good on surveillance too. No one suspected that a beautiful woman with big hair and perfect makeup was actually a cop.

I stood up. "I hate to say it, but it's time I have a discussion with the boss about what we're going to do."

Steph said, "Good luck."

"You're not coming with me?"

"Oh, *hell* no. It's depressing to go in there. He sucks the life out of me. If I ever get that skittish, I hope someone shoots me."

"You'll be lucky if someone doesn't shoot you for other reasons long before that."

She tried to hide it, but she laughed. That gave me the courage I needed to march into the supervisor's office. Still, I felt like I was walking the green mile.

To me, the supervisor's office seemed antiseptic and fake. He had certificates and newspaper articles framed and hanging on the wall. Everything had a place. There was no mess on the desk. In police work, I considered that the mark of someone who was not doing enough. I don't care how OCD you are, if you're busy in law enforcement, shit gets messy. Both figuratively and literally.

I stood in the doorway until the supervisor looked up from the computer screen. I always got the impression he was a little annoyed when he had to speak to someone personally instead of reading a report.

He said from his desk, "Can I help you?"

It was hardly a warm invitation, but this had to get done. I stepped into the office and sat down in the chair directly across from his desk. I quickly explained the developing situation and finished up by saying, "All we have to do is identify the right ship, then make a tactical entry. Possibly get a search warrant to go through the containers as rapidly as possible. We don't want to risk the lives of the people being trafficked."

I sat in awkward and uncomfortable silence while my supervisor considered everything I'd said. After almost a minute he said, "So that's all we need to do. Just identify the right ship out of the hundreds that enter our Florida ports every day, go to a magistrate with this pile of info coming from God knows where, then risk the lives of FBI personnel as well as civilian port workers by assaulting the ship. If that's all we have to do, then I'm thrilled with your plan."

"When you say it like that, it sounds almost impossible."

"How should I say it? I'm the one responsible for everyone's safety on this task force. And everyone's actions."

"Are you saying we should do nothing?" I kept my voice under control. Just barely.

He shrugged. "For now, keep gathering more intel. The information coming from Holland is sketchy at best. You're talking about using multiple agents on surveillance for several days. Plus, I'm still clearing up some of your mess from that wild-goose chase down at Port Everglades. I've had more than a few calls from bigwigs at Customs who say you insulted their agents and agency. Is that true?"

"Insulted or enlightened. It's a matter of interpretation."

The supervisor said, "The Customs agents at Port Everglades would disagree with that."

"Sure they would. No one wants to admit that it was a Miami cop who discovered a whole container of illegal tropical birds. And that the smuggler ran halfway across port property before anyone from Customs even bothered to waddle out to a car and see what was going on."

The supervisor said, "So you see my point. Do more background and let's see how things shake out before we commit too many resources to this human-trafficking case. We already have the one arrest of the Dutch guy at the airport."

The lawyer in me was ready to debate the purpose of law enforcement in general and this task force in particular. Instead, I took a shortcut.

I said, "That's fine. No problem. I'll just call the Miami Police. Their SWAT team has a lot more experience than the FBI's anyway. They'll swoop in there and grab those people. That way we won't risk any resources from the task force." I had to fight to keep the smug smile off my face.

After considering this for ten seconds longer than I'd thought he would, he said, "Don't call the Miami police. I can justify this as part of the task-force activity. I was just worried because intercepting a ship can be tactically difficult. I don't want to risk lives unnecessarily."

"I don't know anyone who does. I'm sure we can handle it within the task force. Some surveillance, and we'll get a DHS agent on the case with us. Most important, we'll make sure to get some stats for the task force."

I could tell by his smile that stats were his real goal.

CHAPTER 67

WE DECIDED TO focus on the port of Miami. It was a risk, one that was tearing at my insides. I couldn't sleep. I barely ate. If we were wrong, there was no telling what would happen to the people on the ship.

Marie brought up an excellent point. "Hanna must have contacts in Miami, no? We know she had a contact here when she tried to smuggle the children through the airport. I have a stomach feeling she'll do it again."

"Gut feeling," I said.

"Isn't the gut the same as the stomach?"

I let it go.

As a Miami cop, I'd done a ton of surveillance at the port. Once, while waiting for a ship that was supposed to have a load of hash from Turkey, I witnessed a snatch-and-run. A young white guy grabbed a woman's purse and sprinted out of the port toward the American Airlines Arena. I was the only one around, and the ship I was waiting on hadn't docked yet, so I chased him.

Come to think of it, maybe I do chase after suspects more than your average cop. Probably an instinct carried over from my U M days on the field. He was fast at first, then lost some steam. I almost cornered him near Sixth Street, but he jumped over a fence and had a clean getaway in front of him. Then he stopped on the far side of the fence and turned back to me.

He said, "You're Moon, right?"

"Yeah."

He laughed. "Anti–Ray Lewis. I can see why the 'Canes never made a decent bowl while you were playing. See ya later." And he was gone.

Every time I'm at the port, I daydream about catching that guy. Even though he had a point.

I tried to imagine what it might be like to live in a shipping container for over a week. It gave me the willies. We had to get this right. I didn't want to see another dead girl someone had been trying to smuggle. I didn't care if I was kicked off the task force for not making arrests. Right now, I just wanted to find those people.

I never realized how many ships came and went out of the port. I had a DHS supervisor on call. I explained about a possible leak coming from Customs.

The DHS supervisor, a guy named Rick Morris, said, "You watch too much TV."

I chuckled and said, "I hope so. But I also work in Miami. Anything's possible."

With the trouble I'd had from Customs over the past few days, I thought it would be best not to call Rick until we had a hot prospect.

The waiting was killing me.

CHAPTER

THE SUN DIPPED in the west and all the lights in the port came on. You could argue that a full day of surveillance with no results was a bust, but all it really meant was that we'd be doing it over again tomorrow. That's the life of a cop.

Marie had found the day fascinating. She liked seeing how the port operated and hearing stories about police work in and around Miami.

She asked me, "How long will you stay on the task force?"

I shrugged. "Who knows? I have to produce or they'll just rotate me off. I know someone from the Miami PD who wants my spot."

"You need arrests to stay?"

"They don't keep me for my charming personality."

"What if we don't make arrests but are able to save the people being trafficked?"

"I'll be thrilled."

"Even if you get moved off the task force?"

"I'll still be a cop."

She smiled and squeezed my hand. She looked toward the water.

Two ships had just docked. I checked with my DHS contact and he said they had both sailed from ports in Europe. After a moment, he narrowed it down, said one had come from the Netherlands, the other from Belgium.

After I convinced him to come down to the port, I turned to my partners and said, "Let's walk down to the ships. The one on the left is from the Netherlands and the other one is from Belgium. These are the best prospects we've had."

We didn't want to blow the surveillance in case neither of these was the right ship, so we stood back from the dock looking at them both. Steph asked, "Is one of them more likely than the other?"

Marie said, "I haven't heard anything more specific from my informants. But both ships fit the profile we've been looking for."

I was torn. If we jumped on one of the ships, word would get out. Sailors talked, and now, with cell phones, they were in instant communication with one another all over the world. I didn't want to expose the surveillance early, but I couldn't risk leaving people locked in one of those shipping containers one minute longer than they had to be.

If we picked the wrong ship, the crew on the other ship could flee and we'd have no suspects. I felt a knot in my stomach as I worked through the different scenarios. I wasn't even factoring in the chance that someone aboard either ship might be armed and try to stop us.

There was no way we could do this without causing a major stir. It would throw the port into chaos for at least two hours and the news media would swoop down on it in minutes.

I looked around at the port crews and Customs people walking right past us about fifty yards from the two ships.

One Customs inspector with dark hair paused and checked his phone right in front of us. There was absolutely nothing remarkable about him—except his ID. His name was Vacile, which sounded familiar to me.

My eyes involuntarily followed the unremarkable Customs inspector.

Then it hit me. I remembered where I had seen his name. He was the inspector at the Miami airport. I'd noticed at the time how the trafficker purposely moved to Vacile's line for entry to the U.S. We'd just thought it was a case of a lazy inspector. DHS had said they'd follow up on it as a personnel matter.

This couldn't be a coincidence.

We had to risk it. I wasn't about to lose a load of people just to make some arrests. We had to do something, and now.

Whatever ship Vacile stepped onto was the ship we were going to search.

CHAPTER 69

I PULLED OUT a small pair of binoculars that generally saw action only during Miami Dolphins games and used them to track the Customs inspector named Vacile.

He spoke to a few people but kept moving, so no one was with him when he started poking around containers sitting at the front of the suspect ship.

My heart started to beat faster. This could be it. There was so much riding on what we did next that I felt a flutter of anxiety. I couldn't stop thinking about the people locked on board. We had to get to them.

By now, Lorena Perez, Anthony Chilleo, and Rick Morris, the DHS supervisor I'd been talking to on the phone, had gathered near the ship. I explained how I'd recognized Vacile from the airport. Morris, an in-shape, middle-aged man with a slightly graying crew cut, said, "That's a pretty thin story to ruin someone's reputation over."

I said, "Do you know this guy personally?"

"Never heard of him." He glanced down at his phone. "But I'm looking at his personnel file and he doesn't have any complaints. Coincidences happen all the time. That's why they're called *coincidences*. Like how it was a coincidence that I was the internal affairs supervisor on call when you said you needed help. If you had called the next day, then, by coincidence, I'd be at my college reunion right now instead of here. See what I mean about coincidences?"

He was right. It was a long shot. "'Coincidence is God's way of staying anonymous,'" I said.

Only Steph knew to ask, "Okay, who said that?"

"Albert Einstein."

The DHS agent said, "So your probable cause is based on a dead physicist's comments about God?"

I was losing my patience, and I raised my voice. "Look, Rick, people might die. This is a literal life-and-death situation. C'mon, don't be an administrative geek now. Be a cop. If we ignore this and do nothing and people wind up dying, we're responsible for the death of every one of them. Tell me, is that something you could live with?"

Rick shook his head and said, "Let's go."

CHAPTER 70

THE TIME HAD come. Hanna Greete felt like a bundle of exposed nerves. Everything was an assault on her senses. She tried to stay quiet as she and Albert waited near the port of Miami. All of her hard work came down to the next few hours. If anything happened and they weren't able to pay off their debts, all was lost. There was no other way to look at the situation.

They could see the ship they were waiting for, the *Scandinavian Queen*, docked next to another ship in the easternmost section of the port.

Two long passenger vans rumbled into the loading zone behind Hanna and Albert.

Hanna twisted on the bench and saw Billy, her Russian contact, pop out of the front passenger seat of the first van. He wore a dark suit and had his thinning hair slicked back. She hid her surprise.

He was his usual cheerful self. Billy clapped his hands

together as he walked toward them. "And how are my Dutch friends on this beautiful evening?" He had a wide grin.

Albert leaned in close to his sister and mumbled, "This can't be a good sign." He reached under his shirt. Hanna placed a hand on her brother's arm.

She said, "Wait. Let's hear what he has to say."

"Whatever he says, it will mean he's screwing us out of our money. This isn't the Vatican we're dealing with. These guys don't care about our troubles."

Hanna stepped forward and asked Billy, "How did you know it was time to come to the port?" Her aggressive tone didn't seem to bother the friendly Russian.

Billy held up his hands but kept a smile. "You're not serious, are you?" Billy said. His accent sounded almost elegant. "You don't think our mutual contact won't call us first? Surely you can't be that naive."

Hanna eyed the other Russians coming out of the vans. They all had hard edges, even the lone woman, who was tall, with straight dark hair. Serious expressions, alert eyes, and the quiet restlessness that came with expecting trouble.

Hanna said, "We're paying for the service; we expect to be the ones who get the benefit from it."

"Vacile may take money from you, but he's a loyal Russian. He texted me as he was about to enter the ship."

Hanna noticed the Russians near the vans were keeping a close eye on Albert. Her brother was aware of their interest.

She hoped this didn't turn into a bloody fight.

CHAPTER 71

THE FIRST THING I noticed as we carefully approached the ship we'd seen Vacile enter—the *Scandinavian Queen*—was a security guard standing at the top of the gangplank. The lanky young man looked from the ship to the dock. *Not this shit again*, I thought.

I slowed everyone down a little way from the ship and said, "I've had to deal with a shipping security agent once already this week. I'd rather we didn't have to muscle our way past this guy. Any ideas?" I looked around the group.

Without any hesitation, Steph Hall said, "I got this." She hid her badge, unbuttoned two buttons on her shirt, looked over her shoulder, and gave me a wink.

Lorena Perez said, "Really, you think that's gonna work?"

Steph said, "He's a dude under twenty-five. It'll work."

Chill said, "Probably would, but what if I try something else first?"

Steph looked annoyed for a moment, then said, "I'll defer to your experience." ATF agents went undercover on a regular basis.

I moved a little closer to the ship in case there was trouble. I was really doing this for the benefit of the young security officer on the boat. If he did something stupid, I didn't want Steph or Chill to break one of his legs and toss him in the water.

Chill made a little show of wandering around like he was lost. I liked how he stooped over slightly to give the impression he was older than he was.

He stopped by the gangplank and called up to get the security guard's attention. The guard looked down at Chill, who said something in a quiet voice.

The guard yelled back, "What was that? I can't hear you."

Chill leaned against the gangplank handrail and coughed like he'd been a lifelong pack-a-day smoker.

I was impressed. He sold me on the coughing fit even though I knew he was a runner.

Chill hacked a little louder and motioned to the young security guard to come close.

The man didn't hesitate. He scurried down the gangplank like a lab rat waiting to eat cancer-laced candy.

Chill looked over at us with a sly smile. There really wasn't any substitution for experience.

Once the guard was next to him, Chill composed himself and mumbled thanks. He straightened up a bit and said, "I'm okay now. Thanks for coming to help."

The young man beamed. "No problem. Are you sure you're okay?"

Now Chill began a subtle but effective interrogation of the security agent. First there was the usual stuff, like "What's your name? Where are you from?" Then he got to the real question: "How many people are on the ship right now?"

The young man did a double take and said, "Wait, what?"

It was like Chill had changed from a caterpillar to a butterfly. He slipped the badge he wore on a chain out from under his shirt and grasped the young man tightly by the upper arm. Chill changed his tone and said, "How many people are on board?"

"I—I—I don't really know."

Now Rick Morris, the Customs supervisor, stepped up to the young man and said, "Answer the question, jack-off."

Chill looked at him sharply and said, "I got this, Rick. Back off." He turned his attention back to the suddenly terrified security man. Chill put his hand on the young guard's shoulder and said, "Tell me who you *think* is on board."

The young man stuttered again and finally was able to blurt out, "The Customs inspector just came on, and the first mate is on board. I think a lot of the crew already slipped off for the evening."

Now our entire group gathered around the security guard. Chill slid the young man's radio out of its harness and said, "I'll give this back when we're done."

I stood in front of the young man and looked down at him. "You're gonna need to sit right here and not talk to anyone or call anyone until we come off the ship. Is this clearly understood?"

The young man nodded and sat down on the concrete bench near the ship.

We all carefully stepped onto the rickety gangplank, trying to limit the noise. Sounds echoed in the still night. I could hear a car horn out on Biscayne Boulevard. We fanned out near the bridge. I got a weird vibe from the almost empty ship, which reminded me of something from *The Walking Dead*.

The first thing Rick said was "That's weird. If there's a Customs inspector on board, there should be a Customs person at the gangplank and a couple in the wheelhouse. Something's not right."

Steph gave him a flat stare and said, "No shit."

CHAPTER 72

I WASTED NO time once we were on board. Every minute was vital; we had to get to the people in the storage container. I'd worry about arrests and charges afterward. If this Customs inspector, Vacile, was helping human traffickers, he was about to have the worst night of his life.

I just started marching toward the bow, cutting between the towering storage containers on the metal deck that showed signs of rust and wear. I felt like I was in Monument Valley

It was spooky. I didn't even *hear* anyone else on board. Stepping carefully, I minimized any sound. Everyone behind me was just as careful. My heart raced as I considered all the things that could go wrong. That's what I always did before any kind of operation, whether it was a search warrant, an interview, or something as important as this.

I heard muffled voices as we approached the front. A tall, older sailor, probably the first mate, was talking amiably with

Vacile. The Customs inspector was about forty-five years old; he had a potbelly, and his blue uniform didn't complement his shape. The two men stood in front of a single container. There were air vents along the top. It was obvious what we were looking at.

I stepped out of the shadows and came in full view of the two men.

The sailor barked at me, "No one is allowed on board."

I immediately recognized his accent as Dutch.

Marie stepped forward and spoke sharply to the man in Dutch, which caught him by surprise. It also tipped off Vacile that it was probably time to go.

He backed away slowly and bumped into Rick, our own Customs contact, who was clearly not happy.

Rick grabbed Vacile by the shoulders and said, "I'm Rick Morris. I'm an honest Customs supervisor, and you're not gonna move another inch until we've sorted this out." He calmly reached down and removed the inspector's service weapon from its holster.

I looked at the first mate and said, "Open this container." When he hesitated, I shouted, "Right now!" The man jumped but still made no move toward the lock.

The sailor said, "I don't have a key."

Acting on impulse, I reached over and banged the side of the container. There was a commotion from inside. I could hear shouting and people moving around.

Rick sprang forward with a passkey but couldn't get the container open. This was taking too long.

I looked around in desperation and saw another tool like the one on the ship with the smuggled parrots. I pulled it off the wall and shouted for Rick to move out of the way.

I swung the tool like a knight slaying a dragon, starting above my head and using my full 240 pounds to bring it down. The sound of the captive people yelling gave me strength.

I hit the lock perfectly on the first swing. The impact ran up my arm, but the door creaked open.

This time, I recognized the smell that hit me immediately. It was human waste. And something else.

CHAPTER 73

HANNA AND ALBERT glided along with Billy and his crew of tough-looking Russians. Hanna tried to speak to the lone female, the tall thirty-something woman with straight dark hair, but either the woman didn't speak English or she didn't want to engage with Hanna. Which was a bad sign for what might happen later.

Hanna glanced at her brother. Her concern was obvious to him; he was the person who had always looked after her. He smiled and nodded in an effort to calm her down. It was like when they were children; no matter what was going on, Albert would always say, "It'll all work out."

She wished she had his confidence. All she could think about was what would happen if they lost this load too.

Billy, the friendly Russian, looked over his shoulder at Hanna and said, "See, a nice quiet evening at the port. We'll walk out of here with everyone and no one will ever notice. You can't put a price on that kind of security."

Hanna sensed new fees coming her way. She cut her eyes over to Albert again. He had his hand near where his newly acquired pistol was concealed under his shirt. At least the Russians hadn't guessed that he was armed.

Hanna didn't like the wobbly gangplank or the loud noise their hard shoes made when they walked up the metal ramp. She was surprised no one came to investigate. The first mate she'd hired had done a good job.

Hanna realized the Russians had subtly changed positions to surround them; now she and Albert were in the middle of their group.

Thank God Albert was with her, Hanna thought.

Not even Billy was speaking anymore as they worked their way forward on the ship.

As she stepped between two shipping containers, Hanna saw a group of people standing around a familiar shape: the specially built container she'd bought.

Her heart stopped. She recognized Marie Meijer.

Before she could say anything, the tallest of the Russians drew a pistol from the back of his pants. Billy slipped away from the front and eased between other containers.

Albert inched to the rear of the group and drew his own pistol. No one but Hanna saw it in his hand.

CHAPTER 74

I STOOD BY the shipping container's open door and stared at the group of twenty or so pitiful people inside. Several girls were weeping. A couple of people darted out of the fetid container and onto the ship.

The scene inside the container shocked me, and that's saying something for a veteran of the Miami Police Department. Almost all cops reach a point when they think they've seen it all and can no longer be surprised by people's behavior or scenes of violence.

I'd witnessed children shot in the streets. I'd once held pressure on a wound in the abdomen of a nine-year-old girl in Liberty City, desperate to stop the blood that was pumping out. She had unwittingly stepped into a gunfight between two local gangs and caught a nine-millimeter round just below her rib cage.

I'd picked her up and carried her like a doll, keeping one

hand pressed down hard on the wound in her abdomen. I ran till I thought my heart might burst to where the paramedics said they'd meet me, a block away from the gunfire.

I rode with her in the ambulance because she didn't want me to leave her.

I stayed with her until she was taken into surgery, and then I waited at the hospital to explain to her stepfather what had happened.

I sat with my uniform covered in the little girl's blood. I could barely keep it together. Nurses offered me coffee and tried to talk to me as I waited.

Her stepfather finally showed up and asked me what the hell was going on.

I explained what had happened and told him that the surgeon was hopeful he could save the little girl.

All the man said to that was "This ain't gonna cost me nothing, is it?"

That whole situation had shocked and bothered me for weeks after. And it didn't touch what I was looking at now.

The stench of human waste and vomit coming from the shipping container made my eyes water. A rat scurried out of it. Before I could tell the people inside they were safe, I heard movement behind me. It caught everyone's attention.

I looked around to see a group of people I didn't know. I focused on a blued semiautomatic pistol in the hand of a tall guy wearing a dark sports coat.

Lorena Perez shouted, "Police, don't move!" and drew her department-issued Glock. But it had no effect on the man with the handgun. She let loose three quick rounds.

The sound of the gunfire among the containers was deafening and disorienting, like thunder inside a small room. The noise was everywhere, swarming my senses. I stumbled forward and tried to pull the container door shut to protect the people inside.

But that wasn't going to happen. There was no way those prisoners would let the door shut on them again, not even if people were shooting right in front of them. A mass of the people still inside the container slammed the door open.

I backed to the side of the container and drew my service pistol. People from the unknown group had guns up and were firing. Steph and Rick Morris were returning fire.

I needed to know Marie was safe. She was unarmed. What had I been thinking, bringing her here? I raised my pistol. There were no obvious targets, but a few shots crossed between the two groups.

My heart was pounding in my chest from the adrenaline rush and the shock of being shot at. I looked over my shoulder. There were a few people cowering inside the storage container and several others lying still on its nasty, garbage-covered floor.

Marie leaped forward and slammed her body into a man trying to get to the container. She knocked him back, but he quickly regained his balance and swung the butt of his pistol into Marie's face.

Her head snapped and twisted.

I needed to help her.

Two things happened quickly: three rounds pinged off the vent I was using for cover, forcing me back down, and Marie took another blow, this one a punch from the man's other hand.

I stared in horror as he brought his pistol up and pointed it at Marie. I raised my pistol for a tricky shot, hoping to at least distract the man.

But Marie was quicker. She kicked and darted to one side.

Her foot connected with the man's knee and he fell, and she followed that up with a kick to the man's head.

Teeth flew and blood painted a pattern on the side of the container.

A tall woman scooped up the injured man, and the two of them disappeared into the maze of containers.

There was one more rush of fire, then, like the aftermath of most gunfights, an eerie, all-encompassing quiet. Part of it had to do with my ears ringing from the sudden loud noises. Part of it was the fact that there was very little activity at this time of the evening in the port of Miami.

And part of it, I knew, was that there were people down on both sides of the fight.

CHAPTER 75

AS SOON AS she heard the first shots, Hanna realized exactly what Albert planned to do. He wanted to use this as cover to shoot Billy the Russian. He wasn't going to wait for a police officer to do it.

Hanna flinched as Albert shot one of the Russians in the back. The man just dropped. Nothing like in the movies. He just fell forward, silent and still in the midst of chaos.

Albert wasted no time. He grabbed Hanna by the wrist and tugged her along as they fled the shooting.

Albert managed to say, "I think that shit Billy is headed for the gangplank. We better not see him on the ship."

Hanna risked a quick glimpse over her shoulder. They'd already gotten far enough away that all she could see was a few flashes from pistols. It was amazing how much the sound of gunfire was reduced when you got a few dozen yards and a couple of shipping containers away from it.

Hanna recognized a couple of the younger women running

past them, headed for the front of the ship. They were girls she had housed in Amsterdam.

She'd thought these girls would've trusted her. It must be the gunfire. Hanna didn't like the idea that they would betray her and run when they knew they still had to work off the cost of their transportation. The people she transported usually wanted to trust someone. And they'd known the travel would be hard.

She planted her feet to stop Albert from dragging her along.

He looked at her, astonished. "Are you crazy? We've got to get out of here."

"We need the red backpack. Either Magda has the pack or it's back in the container."

"Back there, where all the gunfire is? Where the police are waiting for us? No, thanks. We need to keep running."

Hanna glanced over the side of the ship and saw the girl she was looking for. And she had the backpack over her shoulder. She yelled at Albert, "Right there. Magda's right there."

"And running faster than we could ever hope to," Albert pointed out. "Don't worry. The tracker is in the backpack. We'll let things settle down here and then we'll be able to find her easily. At least we can salvage the diamonds."

Hanna followed her brother off the ship. The chaos from the ship had spread to the docks. People were running in every direction. No one knew if this was a terrorist attack or a drug-gang shootout.

Hanna followed Albert's lead as he immediately slowed to a fast walk. They headed directly off the port grounds. She was going to take a serious financial hit on this fiasco.

CHAPTER 76

IT TOOK ONLY a moment for me to regain my senses and realize I had to act immediately. I wanted to chase the shooters, but there were too many people who needed help right in front of me.

I swept the area for gunmen. Once I determined it was clear, I holstered my pistol. Two men from the group that had confronted us were dead.

One of the men had been shot in the back, but I didn't know if it was an accident or if someone from his group had gotten tired of him. For safety reasons, I took the pistols from the bodies and secured them.

A moment later, I was at Marie's side. She was on the deck and bleeding badly from cuts on her face. I could barely recognize her under all the blood. It pooled and dripped off her nose like a cheap faucet.

She said, "I swear, it's not that bad. Some of the blood isn't mine. Check on the girls in the container."

A moment later I was in front of the storage container. The smell turned my stomach. A haze seemed to have settled over the few people still in the container. Piles of garbage filled the back corners. Junk-food wrappers, empty water bottles, and used toilet paper overflowed from one small garbage can to form a small mountain. Cockroaches scattered when I stepped inside.

A bucket used as a toilet was visible through a flimsy plastic curtain. I had a hard time imagining what the nine-day trip from Europe had been like for these poor souls.

Steph was checking the pulse of a man on the ground. He was ashen and his eyes looked up lifelessly at the rusty walls of the container. One leather loafer was missing from his left foot.

Steph looked up at me and shook her head.

I said, "Hit by a stray bullet?"

Steph said, "No. We have four dead in here. It looks like they all died from illness or heat exhaustion." She indicated another man on the ground and two girls against the rear wall. There were three young women, alive, huddling together near the door to the container. Steph went to comfort them.

I went over to the rear wall. The two girls looked like they had been dead a couple of days. They had been placed next to each other and covered with a plastic tarp.

Both the girls looked like young teenagers; they had long hair and pretty faces. Faces with eyes that would never see home or family again. It was heartbreaking.

I thought about how these poor people had lived for the last nine days and I got mad. Fury washed over me like a wave. I couldn't remember the last time I had been this pissed off. And I knew just who I could focus my anger on.

I stepped out of the container with my hand on my pistol and said, "Where is that goddamn Inspector Vacile?"

Lorena Perez just pointed.

Across the cluttered deck, our best source of information lay flat, half of his face missing. Blood had gushed from the gunshot wound on his left cheek. Based on where he'd landed, I guessed he'd been shot by the men who surprised us. I wondered if it was done on purpose to keep him from talking to us.

I stepped over to Lorena. She wasn't injured but she didn't look too good. Her hands were shaking and she was leaning back against a storage container.

I put my arm around her shoulder. "You saved our asses. You okay?"

She looked up and nodded but didn't say a word. I'd seen it before. The aftermath of police shooting could be devastating. She'd done her duty and proved she had talent.

Anthony Chilleo was holding pressure on the wound on Rick Morris's arm.

I said, "Chill, how bad is it?"

"I'll survive," the Customs supervisor said.

"We've got help on the way. Nothing we can do for the others," Chill said.

I searched the two dead men's pockets, found some ID, and said, "They're Russian."

Chill mumbled, "Shocker."

CHAPTER 77

HANNA SLAPPED THE wall in frustration. "Why can't we get a decent reading on the tracker?"

Albert didn't take his eyes off his phone as he tried again to refresh the location of the tracker sewn into the red backpack.

They'd spent two hours near the port looking for Magda with the red backpack.

During a quick break, sitting on the seawall in Bayside with the trendy shops behind them all closing down for the evening, Hanna turned to her brother and said, "Why did you shoot a Russian in the back?"

Albert looked at her as if she were speaking Martian. "What do you mean? Why *wouldn't* I shoot him? They were trying to rip us off. It was our best chance to rid ourselves of the Russians here in Miami."

"Did you see what happened to Billy?"

"No. It was too crazy. We're lucky we got out of there

alive." Albert focused on his phone as he tried to bring up the tracker again.

Hanna said, "It's getting late. Let's head back to the hotel."

As soon as the cab pulled into the Miami Gardens Inn, Hanna saw that the lights to their first-floor room were off. There was no way Josie and Tasi had gone to bed this early. There should have been a glow from the TV set, at the very least.

They rushed to the door, Albert with his pistol out.

Hanna fumbled with the key in the low light, then shoved the heavy door open and immediately flicked on a light so that Albert could scan the room.

The first thing she noticed was the blood spattered across the sheet on the foldout bed.

The second was a bloody handprint on the bathroom door.

Hanna's whole world started to spin as she tried to comprehend what had happened. She cried out, "Josie," praying to God she would get some kind of response.

There was just dead silence.

CHAPTER 78

HANNA FOUGHT THE urge to scream. Nothing had prepared her for the scene she was witnessing. She cried out again, "Josie!" Then she heard a sound coming from the bathroom.

She and Albert rushed to the bathroom door. The smell of vomit was overwhelming. She pushed the door open and found Tasi kneeling next to the toilet with blood pouring from her nose and lips. She had two puffy black eyes. Josie's babysitter had been beaten so badly, she was sick to her stomach.

Hanna didn't like to see the young woman in such distress, but she couldn't waste any time. "Where's Josie?"

Tasi started sobbing, then leaned over the toilet to throw up again. The retro pink toilet made the blood and vomit stand out more. Even the kitschy palm-tree wallpaper seemed ominous now.

Hanna gently took Tasi by the shoulders and made her turn from the toilet. She said, "Tasi, what happened? Where is

Josie?" She spoke slowly and clearly, as if she were talking to someone who didn't understand Dutch.

Tasi took in gulps of air. Haltingly, she said, "A man tapped on our front door. He said he was a maintenance worker. I opened the door just a crack." Tasi broke down and cried for a moment. "There was a woman there too, and she started kicking me in the stomach and the face. I was crying and couldn't see but I heard Josie yell as the man dragged her out of the room."

"When did this happen?"

"Less than an hour ago."

"What did the man and woman look like?" Albert asked.

Tasi coughed and spit some blood into the toilet. She collected her thoughts and said, "The woman was tall with dark hair. The man had a goatee. It was dyed blue."

Billy. Hanna would murder him right now if he were in front of her. She asked Albert, "How do you think they found us?"

Albert was silent for a moment, then said, "I know exactly how they found us."

Five minutes later, Albert and Hanna were in the cluttered reception area of the Miami Gardens Inn. Ancient magazines, paperbacks with torn covers, and old VHS movies lay haphazardly on a shaky bookshelf. The clerk who'd checked them in looked up and said, "Good evening." His Russian accent set Hanna on edge. Albert was already over the edge.

Without saying a word, Albert grabbed the young man by the shirt collar, dragged him over the counter, and threw him onto the hard floor. He'd stuck his pistol in the young man's ear before Hanna even realized he'd drawn it.

Albert spoke slowly and clearly in English. "I don't want you to make a mistake you'll regret the rest of your life." He shoved the pistol into the man's ear harder. "I'm going to ask you a question. If you lie, I'm going to put a bullet through your head. Do you understand me?"

The young man nodded vigorously.

Albert said, "Let me see your phone."

The clerk carefully reached into his pocket and pulled out a new iPhone. Albert made him open it, looked at a few numbers, and said, "Whose number is this?"

The young man hesitated and Albert pressed the gun harder into his ear. The man yelled, "Wait, wait, I don't know his name! He runs a lot of the strip clubs. He told me to keep an eye out for you guys. I just did like I was told."

Albert remained unnaturally calm and said, "Where did they take the girl?"

"I don't know I swear to God, I don't know." The clerk started to cry, and sweat poured down his forehead.

Albert said, "FaceTime him."

"What?"

Albert smacked his cheek with the barrel of the pistol. He didn't feel like explaining. The young man quickly hit Redial. After a couple of rings, an image came on the iPhone. It was Billy.

Friendly as always, Billy said, "Ah, Albert. I wondered what happened to you guys. Glad you made it away from the ship safely."

"Where's Josie?"

Billy kept smiling. He said something to someone else in the room.

Albert made sure the pistol in the clerk's ear was framed in the phone properly. "Tell me where my niece is or you'll be cleaning up this asshole's brains for a week."

Billy said, "The young man that works at that nasty little

hotel? I don't know him. Go ahead and shoot. I couldn't care less. But you might be able to use the five hundred dollars cash I gave him. Perhaps you should check his pockets. But shoot him if you want."

The young man sucked in some oxygen and started to shake.

Then Billy said, "If you'd like to be reasonable, I'm sure we could work out a simple trade. The diamonds for the girl. That's the only thing I'm interested in talking to you about."

Hanna grabbed the phone and said, "Is Josie okay?"

Billy chuckled and said, "Don't worry, mama bear. We're taking good care of your baby bear." He turned the camera briefly so Hanna could see Josie sitting in a chair with a Kleenex in her hand.

Billy said, "It's late. We'll talk some more tomorrow. It's a simple deal. Diamonds for the girl. It will make up for that disaster at the port." The image disappeared and the line went dead.

Albert gave the clerk a hard look, then he patted his pants pockets. He reached in the right pocket and pulled out the wad of cash.

Just as Hanna opened the door, Albert turned and screamed, "Bang!"

The young man flinched and then burst into tears.

CHAPTER 79

I SAT BY Marie's side at Jackson Memorial as a distressingly young ER doctor put nine stitches in her left cheek. She'd been right; most of the blood was not hers.

After Marie had been sewn up, she turned to me and asked, "How do I look?" Her sly smile broke the tension and I laughed.

"Beautiful." I wasn't kidding. But even with the scrapes and stitches, she was ready to get back to work. After the visit to Jackson Memorial, we searched the streets of Miami for the people who had fled from the ship. We managed to find six young women, two young men, and two older women. Most were wandering around the port area. Two were at a shelter.

Once back in the station, we began taking statements from the victims who spoke English. Their accounts of traveling over the Atlantic in the shipping container were harrowing.

About five days into the trip, they said, the older of the

two men from India had fallen asleep and never woke up. The younger women, who spoke the same language and appeared to be friends, said they believed that the younger Indian man had had some sort of cardiac event when he discovered the other man was dead.

The two dead girls, they said, were from somewhere in Belgium. One of them had started getting sick a few days earlier, and the other girl, who never spoke to anyone and whose name they didn't know, began throwing up as well. They had both died about a day ago.

It was heartbreaking. Marie, for all of her toughness, had a hard time dealing with it. She clearly felt like she had personally let them down.

I gave her a few minutes. She composed herself, but it wasn't easy. Cops aren't robots, and few civilians can comprehend what police officers see on a regular basis. It's a miracle that there aren't cops breaking down all the time.

I said, "It's not your fault. It's the traffickers and people like Rostoff. They don't care about anything but money."

"It's just so sad," Marie said. "Society has forgotten these people. I've seen it in Amsterdam. Young girls think they can make their fortune by coming here, but it's all lies. I wish we could do something to hurt predators like the Rostoff brothers. The death penalty would be too good for them."

I nodded and said, "We'll do something. I can't let Roman Rostoff sit up in that luxury office like he's an earl."

Marie took a moment to wipe her tears and blow her nose on a paper towel. Then she looked at me with bloodshot eyes and said, "Let's get back to work."

I don't even know what time I got home that night. When I woke up in the morning, after only a few hours' sleep, I was still exhausted. The smell of pancakes and bacon drew me out of bed. I felt like I was a character in a fairy tale wandering into a trap.

My sister, looking very professional in a dark, fitted dress, was in the hall, getting ready to head to the school where she worked as a speech pathologist. She tilted her head toward the kitchen and shrugged. That's when I realized it was my mother cooking. This was phenomenal; she almost never cooked in the morning.

My sister and I sat down at the small dining-room table and before we could say anything, my mom plopped down two plates piled with eggs, pancakes, and bacon. She looked like a waitress at a Denny's.

Why couldn't it be like this every morning?

I asked a few of my normal questions, trying to figure out if she was in our current reality or a former one. She seemed fine. She called me Tommy and asked Lila some specific questions about her job.

Finally, I had to say, "Mom, what's going on? What's with all the food?"

She eased down into the chair next to me and took a sip of her coffee. "You think I'm not aware of what's been happening, that I just live in my own little world and expect you guys to cater to my every need? It's terrifying. Not because I'm losing my grip on reality, but because of everything I'm putting you through."

Lila reached across the table and grasped my mother's hand. They both had tears in their eyes. I almost did the same, but I wanted to hear what else my mom had to say.

She flicked a tear off her cheek and said, "You both do so much for me, I just wanted to do a little something for you."

Lila stood up and hugged her. "We do it because we love you, Mom."

"And I'm doing this because I love you. No one realizes how much a mother loves her children. She really will do anything for them. I'm just sorry you have to do so much for me now."

I stood up and kissed her gently on the forehead. There was nothing else I could add to this conversation.

CHAPTER 80

BEFORE I PICKED Marie up at her hotel, I stopped by the Miami Police headquarters to put the word out about what had happened at the port. The oddly shaped five-story building on Second Avenue had seen its share of history. Over the years, Miami had witnessed all kinds of riots, shifting demographics, mass immigration from Cuba, and even a visit from the pope. Through it all, the police department—at least the building— never changed. And even the department's critics always knew they could run to us when things in the neighborhood got out of control.

Most people had no idea how things really worked on the streets. I remember a crack dealer named Walter Slates from back when I worked patrol just west of the downtown. He'd shoot a bird at me every time I drove past in my cruiser. He made fun of my record with the University of Miami's football team.

That's why, when he approached my patrol car one day, I was suspicious. He said, "I need help."

I took the bait and asked him what the problem was.

"The goddamn Colombians say they gonna kill me. Ain't nothing like the Cubans. The Cubans'll listen to you. The Cubans are reasonable. But these Colombians is crazy. I need protection."

"So all of a sudden you don't hate the police?"

"Never really hated the police. It's just fun to screw with you. Even if I did hate the police, I don't hate no more. Can you help me?"

We helped him. Walter Slates turned his life around. He now works for Florida Power and Light somewhere up near West Palm Beach. He made it a point to come by and thank me a few years ago.

I knew that by putting the word out at the station, I could count on tips from contacts on the street. The beat cops heard we hadn't found all the people who'd been in the container, and it took them only about an hour to round up the rest. Now we had almost all of them. Except one. A blond Polish girl named Magda who spoke some English.

Finding that girl was our only goal this morning.

Instead of hello, the first thing Marie had said to me when I met her in the lobby of the downtown Marriott was "I just got off the phone with my best informant. Hanna and Albert Greete are in Miami, looking for a girl who fled from the boat. She has a backpack with a fortune in diamonds hidden in it."

"Let me guess—it's the one girl we haven't found yet. Magda from Poland."

"Exactly."

"Does she know she has the diamonds?"

"I don't think so. I heard they're supposed to be sewn into the strap."

We got busy checking shelters and streets near the port and downtown.

Around midmorning, I grabbed a doorknob that turned out to be covered with grease. Someone had smeared the knob with goo as a joke or as a way to put people off, but in any case, I now had bicycle grease all over my right palm.

Marie was speaking with a woman who ran a homeless shelter and I was looking for a paper towel to wipe my hand when I noticed someone coming in my direction.

There are a lot of men wearing suits in Miami, but not many with goatees dyed blue. It was Billy the Blade, Rostoff's muscle. I immediately realized he was doing the same thing Marie and I were. He didn't know how many people we'd rescued from the ship and he was probably hoping to recover some of his investment right now.

I turned to face him, and after a few seconds, he looked up and noticed me. That's one of the benefits of my size—I can be very obvious when I want to be.

I'd obviously caught the Russian by surprise. It took him a moment to put on his usual smile. Then he strutted toward me in his expensive cream-colored Brooks Brothers suit.

Billy kept his broad smile as he said, "Detective, did you already get kicked off your task force? You have to work the streets of Miami again?"

I gave a little chuckle and said, "I think you overestimate your boss's influence."

"I'm not sure it's possible to overestimate Mr. Rostoff's influence."

"The better question is why *you're* working the streets of Miami."

"We're not far from my office. I just thought I'd go for a walk and get some fresh air. By the way, how's your lovely sister?"

He'd pushed the right buttons. I decided to keep my mouth shut.

Billy said, "We're not that different, you know."

I held up my left hand—the clean one—and said, "Hold it right there. We could not be *more* different. You're a predator, plain and simple. You're a dirtbag here just like you were in Russia. Leopards don't change their spots."

"Believe what you want, but the truth is that you'll die poor while I live near the beach in Fort Lauderdale."

"Maybe, but you'll die a lot younger than me."

"Is that a threat?"

"A fact. Go ahead and try to point out the old gangsters in Miami. There aren't any. Even the Colombians don't last much past fifty, and that's if they're lucky."

Billy shook his head and said, "Drugs are a dangerous and dirty business."

I leaned in a little closer. "Can I give you some friendly advice?"

"Sure, why not?"

I gently placed my right hand on his shoulder and said, "Your boss is going to go down. You don't have to be on the ship when it sinks."

Billy let out a laugh. "This isn't Russia. There are many rules the police must follow here. I don't think you can harass us for no reason."

I just smiled as I removed my hand. I admired the perfect grease handprint on his otherwise pristine cream suit. "You have a nice day, Billy."

"Same to you, Detective." He turned and left.

I could see my handprint on the suit even from a block away. I knew we had to find the missing girl before the Russians did.

CHAPTER 81

MAGDA ANDRUSKIEWICZ OPENED her eyes with a start. It wasn't until she glanced up and saw the blue sky past the rough metal roof that her body relaxed slightly. The long ride to the United States in the shipping container with the others had been horrifying. Especially when people started dying. Even the girl she'd worked so hard to comfort in Amsterdam had fallen sick and died the day before they'd arrived in Miami.

Magda wasn't sure if she'd ever be able to sleep indoors again. She'd fled the chaos around the ship where people were shooting and kept running. She'd run and run until she'd realized just how big the city was.

She'd tried to get into a homeless shelter, but it was full for the night. It was warm in Miami, though, and a woman there had told her that she could sleep in the alley behind the shelter. Then the woman had given her two turkey sandwiches. Magda had eaten one immediately and saved the other for the next day.

Now, after a few hours of snatched sleep, Magda had no idea what to do. When she'd waited in Amsterdam, the woman named Hanna had arranged everything. Here, she knew no one. And after the way they had traveled, Magda no longer trusted Hanna.

She had found herself a little nook between some boxes and a dumpster. After the stench in the container, the scent from the dumpster was like a forest in springtime. A metal roof covered her hiding spot and would keep her dry if it rained.

Several others had come and gone during the night, mostly older men. No one bothered her, which was both a surprise and a relief.

Just before she'd fled the ship, Magda had grabbed the red backpack by instinct, and she was now using it as a pillow. It held a change of clothes and a light jacket.

She sat up and began eating her second turkey sandwich. An older black man wearing a red beret leaned against a wall a few meters from her. He seemed to be staring at her. It made her nervous.

The man must have realized he was upsetting her because he said, "I'm sorry, I didn't mean to scare you. It's just that your sandwich looks good. I'm not allowed to go inside no more because they once caught me with alcohol. That's one of the big rules here. No alcohol and no weapons. I wish I'd paid more attention."

The man had a friendly quality to his round face. Magda liked his beret. Without thinking, she tore her sandwich in two and offered half to the man.

With a broad smile, he stepped over to her and took it, then held it up as if he were about to give a toast. The words PROPERTY OF THE AMERICAN AIRLINES ARENA were stenciled on his windbreaker.

The older man went to eat his sandwich, and she tucked herself farther into her nook. She was scared and tired. She prayed to the Blessed Virgin to keep her safe and help her find her brother. She was starting to doubt her own judgment. No way she should have traveled across the Atlantic in a nasty shipping container. She worried about the other people who'd been with her. Where had they all fled?

She finished her sandwich, then laid her head on the backpack, hoping to drift off to sleep for a while. She hummed a lullaby her mother used to sing to her and Joseph when they were little. It had been a long time since she'd felt safe and happy. She missed Joseph. They had been separated during the trip from Poland.

A few minutes later, she heard a new voice. It was louder than any of the others she had heard in the alley.

She peeked between the slats of a pallet next to her and saw a middle-aged homeless man with a white film over one eye speaking to a man in a fancy suit.

CHAPTER 82

MAGDA HAD A bad feeling about the man in the fancy clothes. When she looked more carefully at him, she saw that his goatee was dyed blue, and he had a grease smudge on the shoulder of his cream-colored suit. Just the way he scanned the alley made him seem like a predator. She thought he spoke with an accent, but her English wasn't good enough for her to identify where he was from.

He was talking to a homeless man who had spent the night in the alley using an empty milk carton as a pillow.

The man was smoking a cigarette and sitting on a pallet that had TROPICAL SHIPPING burned into its side. He rocked back and forth slowly, like he was on a ship.

Magda smelled the smoke from his cigarette. It barely masked the man's own body odor.

The man in the suit asked him, "Have you seen any young women around here? Not regulars. Some girls who would've shown up last night."

"Heh, heh, we all want young women," said the homeless man. He was balding, and the little hair he had on the sides of his head shot out in crazy patterns. He laughed. His foggy eye moved in unison with his good eye. The homeless man squinted. "Hey, I know you."

"I don't know how. I don't volunteer in this shithole."

"You work at the club over on Fourth Street." The ash on the homeless man's cigarette slowly grew. A seagull landed near him and pecked at a French fry on the ground.

The man in the suit said, "So what?"

The homeless man said, "You told me to get lost one night. You weren't very nice about it." His voice sounded scratchy, like an old record, but he got his point across: he was mad.

"Did you have the thirty-dollar cover charge?"

"I didn't try to get inside the club. I was just sitting on the sidewalk."

The man in the suit nodded and said, "Oh, panhandling."

"Working."

"Bums scare the customers. We have a certain image."

"You were nasty to me. Why should I help you now?"

The man in the suit reached into his pocket. "For the reward. You help me find some girls I lost last night and I give you a wad of cash."

The homeless man shook his head. "Bullshit. I don't trust you." He looked around at several of the other men; they were ignoring the whole conversation. "I don't think you'd ever pay. So now it's *you* who has to leave. This is *my* alley and I don't want you bothering me." The man stood on unsteady legs from the stacked pallets. He was much smaller than the other man.

The man in the suit just stared. He cut his eyes around the filthy alley to see if anyone intended to help the cocky homeless man.

Then the homeless man barked, "Go." He reached up with his left hand and shoved the man. The long ash from his cigarette broke off and floated down onto a crumpled McDonald's coffee cup.

The man in the suit seemed astonished that someone would speak to him like that, but he recovered quickly.

Magda watched silently as he punched the man with the bad eye. Everyone in the alley looked away. But Magda saw it all. And she knew the man in the suit was searching for her.

The man stayed on his wobbly feet and glared at his attacker. That set the man in the suit off again. He shoved the man onto the stacked pallets, then leaned in and slapped the homeless man hard across the face. "Who the hell do you think you are?" he screamed as he punched the man over and over.

Magda stared, terrified. She looked over and saw the friendly black man in the red beret. She hoped he wouldn't tell anyone she was there.

The man in the suit punched the poor homeless man six times in the face. Blood poured out of his nose and lips and, finally, one of his ears. It left a wild, dark pattern on the patched asphalt of the alley.

He slid off the pallets and lay on the garbage-covered ground, whimpering. Flies were already swarming around his bloody face. One fly stuck in the thick blood on the man's cheek.

The man in the suit cursed at him and kicked him in the ribs several times. When he was finished, he glared around the alley at the other men sitting on broken plastic chairs or stacked boxes. It was a challenge to see if anyone else wanted to cross him.

He disappeared around the corner, and a moment later Magda started to cry.

CHAPTER 83

AFTER MY RUN-IN with Billy, Marie and I continued searching downtown Miami. I had avoided the calls from my boss, but when Stephanie Hall called, I answered.

Stephanie said, "Are you working?"

"Downtown now."

"You've got to be crazy. Do you know how many policies you're violating by coming in the day after a shooting?"

"Miami PD policies or FBI policies?"

"You are the most infuriating man I have ever met."

"Are you telling me *you're* not working? Because if you say you're sitting at home, I won't believe you."

There was a pause. "Maybe I'm at the office with Chill. But we're keeping a low profile. We'll come down to you right now. I checked on Lorena a few minutes ago. She seems to be doing fine."

"I checked on her too. She's definitely doing better than the

Russian dude she plugged before he could massacre the rest of us. She better not catch any shit over this."

Steph said, "She won't. It's you I'm worried about."

"Why me?"

Steph said, "I heard the boss talking to some DHS bigwigs. They don't like you. Sounds like you've disrespected them several times in the past few weeks."

"Actually, it's only been this past week. Unless they want to count their screw-up at the airport."

"So you're not worried about it?"

"The only thing I can think about right now is making sure everyone from the shipping container is safe. I put the word out with all the Miami PD and every snitch I ran into on the street that we're still looking for a Polish girl named Magda."

When I finished the call, I turned to Marie, who was just ending a call on her own phone. She looked up at me and said, "My informant in Amsterdam who gets information from Miami says that Rostoff's Russians kidnapped Hanna Greete's daughter from their hotel here in Miami."

"It must have something to do with the way Hanna bungled the offload."

"And what happened with the diamonds."

I noticed excitement in her voice. She usually spoke English slowly and clearly, but now her Dutch accent was pronounced. Police were the same all over—they got excited when they thought they were about to make a decent arrest.

I said, "So the reason I ran into Billy was that he's looking for the diamonds."

"Yes."

"We've got to find that girl Magda first. No matter what."

Marie said, "My informant also says there may be a tracker in the bag. Even with it, Hanna hasn't been able to locate her."

"Then why haven't the others found her already?"

Marie shrugged.

I said, "Trackers can be finicky. If it's a cheap one, even a metal roof can block the signal." That gave me something to think about.

Around Third Street and Fourth Avenue, when we were checking another one of the homeless shelters, I ran into one of my earliest informants, a tall, lean black man named Titus Barrow, whom everyone called Bulldog.

I pointed him out to Marie and her first question was "Why do they call him Bulldog?"

"You'll figure it out when we talk to him."

Bulldog was standing at his regular corner. He generally sold pot to tourists and crack to his regular customers, although that wasn't a hard-and-fast rule; it was more of a guideline.

As soon as he noticed me, he straightened up and tossed a baggie into the scraggly bushes next to him.

I said, "Don't make me search those bushes, Bulldog."

He mumbled, "Shit, man." Then he turned and squatted to recover the plastic baggie. He handed it over to me without any more complaints.

I think that's when Marie realized how he'd gotten his street name. His lower jaw jutted out and his bottom teeth rested on his upper lip when his mouth was closed, and although he was a thin man, he had drooping jowls.

Bulldog said, "You in narcotics now, Anti?"

"Don't need to be a narcotics detective to spot a shitty dope dealer."

"What's this really about?"

I liked that he was smart enough to realize I didn't give two shits about a minor street dealer. I said, "If you want me to toss this baggie down a sewer, then help us find a missing girl."

Bulldog gave me an odd look.

I said, "The description we have is that she's about sixteen, white, pretty, and blond. She has a thick foreign accent. She's in a world of shit and I need your help."

"I'm your man. What neighborhood you think she in?"

"Maybe downtown near the port. You got my number."

"I'll get everyone I know in on this."

"I expect nothing less."

Now I had a small army helping me find the missing girl.

CHAPTER 84

HANNA WAS DESPERATE to find her daughter. She couldn't even think about what Josie might be going through. She didn't believe the Russians would hurt Josie as long as they thought Hanna was getting them what they wanted. She had to find the Polish girl and the backpack—today.

She and Albert had cruised the streets near the port in an expanding pattern. She just didn't have enough contacts in Miami to reach out for help.

Albert paced nervously next to her. His hand rarely left the butt of the pistol he'd bought. Near the interstate, in an area that clearly wasn't visited by tourists, they checked homeless shelters. They had just walked through a shelter for homeless youth. The woman who ran the place wasn't friendly, but she was efficient. She marched them through the nine rooms used to house young people, four of them per room. She spoke with a drawl that made it difficult for Hanna to understand her.

The woman said, "We get new kids most every day."

Hanna noted the grimy walls and small, thin mattresses laid on the bare floor. It was spare, but probably better than sleeping in the street.

The woman said, "We don't ask no questions. That's why kids come here."

Hanna thanked her, and she and Albert left.

Outside, a young man with tattoos around his neck and upper arms rushed up to them and said, "I heard you asking about a missing girl."

Hanna showed him a photo of Magda on her phone. "Where can we find her?"

"Is there a reward?"

"Yes. Cash."

"How much?"

Hanna rummaged in her small purse and thumbed through the wad of cash Albert had taken from the hotel clerk. She looked up at the young man and said, "Five hundred dollars."

The tattooed kid turned his head in one direction, then the other. He played with the metal stud sticking out of his lower lip. He reached in his pocket and paused.

When his hand came out of his pocket, it held a knife. He raised it to Hanna's face. As he moved, the young man said, "Give me the cash. Maybe I'll find the girl later."

Before Hanna could answer, Albert had his hand around the kid's throat. He mashed the barrel of his pistol hard against the young man's temple.

Without a word, the young man dropped the knife and took a step back. Albert faced him and said, "Tell me the truth. Have you seen the girl? Do you know where she is? Anything other than the truth will be the last thing you ever say. Understand?"

Albert pushed him against a wall. The young man was shaking. The pistol was still pressed against his temple.

The young man swallowed hard, then gathered the courage to say, "I swear to God, I never seen that girl before. I just needed money."

Albert said, "Then give me a reason not to blow your head off."

The kid said, "There are a bunch of other homeless shelters. That's where I'd look."

Albert pulled the pistol back to smack the would-be robber in the face, but Hanna caught his wrist and said, "We have other things to do. C'mon, Albert."

CHAPTER 85

THEY TOOK THE tattooed kid's advice and started searching south of the port. It was now stretching into the afternoon, but Hanna was far too panicked about her daughter to give up.

On almost every street, Albert constantly swiveled his head, looking in every direction. He was afraid they were being watched.

Hanna said, "Who would be watching us?"

"I don't know. The police. The Russians. This is not paranoia."

"You're right. It's gone past paranoia. I agree we can't trust anyone, but the police don't know we're here, and the Russians already have Josie." She hadn't meant to raise her voice so much, but she was losing patience with her brother.

Behind one homeless shelter in downtown Miami, they noticed an alley where several people were lying on blankets or sitting on pallets. Hanna couldn't pass it by. When she stepped into the alley, the first thing she saw was a man who had been savagely beaten recently. He was holding a bloody towel to his forehead. His nose looked like it had been broken. Both of his eyes had swollen almost shut. His lower lip was split and clearly needed stitches.

No one there seemed too concerned about the man's injuries.

Hanna looked down the wide alley at the makeshift beds and chairs lining the walls. A rat crossed the uneven asphalt with no fear of the humans. The smell of urine and alcohol washed over her. She gave an involuntary shudder. She looked up at the six-story building with cheap air conditioners jammed into its windows. This was not where the rich people of Miami lived.

A round-faced older black man wearing a red military beret with the emblem ripped off looked up at her from his seat.

She stepped over to him and said, "Excuse me, we're looking for a missing girl." She held up her phone with the picture of Magda.

The man studied the photo on the small phone, then nervously glanced over at the man with the bloody face. Then he looked up at Hanna and said, "Why are you looking for her?"

The question surprised Hanna.

Albert snapped, "Why are you asking? Have you seen her or not?"

The older man studied the photo for a moment, then said, "No young women come here. You might want to check over on Miami Avenue. That's where most of the runaways go."

Albert stared at the old man, trying to intimidate him.

The man in the beret gestured at the bloody man and said, "A nasty Russian dude has already been here looking for her. She's a popular young woman. Good luck."

Hanna nodded her thanks.

CHAPTER 86

MIAMI IS A compact city with an easy street-numbering system. It's not until you're looking for someone that it seems vast.

In the middle of the afternoon, my phone rang. The name that came up on my screen was BULLDOG.

I looked at Marie and nodded as I answered the phone. "Talk to me."

Bulldog said, "Meet me over on Biscayne between Fifth and Sixth where the hot-dog vendor in the bikini sits."

"Did you find her?"

"Toss that baggie now." He let out his signature laugh. It sounded like a small pig grunting.

Bulldog was there waiting for us when we got to the meeting point. When I saw him, I said, "If this is some kind of prank—"

Bulldog held up his hand. "I get it. You don't trust me much. I done you right this time."

"How'd you find her so fast?"

"I know people. Kinda like you, but I don't scare them shitless just by showing up."

"Where's the girl?"

Bulldog said, "Behind them pallets. She's safe and sound. My man Reggie, the older dude in the red beanie, looked after her. He said all kinds of people been by asking for her today. One of them was a nasty Russian who slapped around one of the other homeless guys."

Marie walked past us straight to the rear of the alley. She weaved between makeshift beds, old chairs, and broken furniture.

I waited with Bulldog so as not to scare the girl. It looked like Marie was coaxing a frightened cat out of a tree. It took a while before I saw a hand reach out and touch Marie's outstretched hand. A moment later, Marie couldn't restrain herself and gave the girl a hug.

Apparently, that was all this girl needed. She wrapped her arms around Marie and began to sob. The girl started to speak quickly in what I thought was Russian but then realized was Polish.

Marie calmed the girl down and brushed her blond hair out of her pretty face. The girl picked up a red backpack and walked toward me. Marie slipped an arm around the girl's shoulder.

Marie introduced us and I said, "Nice to meet you, Magda."

Magda turned to Bulldog's friend Reggie, who was sitting in a sketchy green plastic chair with one of the legs cracked. In heavily accented English she said, "Thank you for not telling Hanna I was hiding in the back of the alley."

The man said, "Thank you for the turkey sandwich." He looked over at me, then back to her. "Everyone knows who Anti is. He'll treat you right," he said.

That was the best compliment I'd ever gotten. I handed the man a twenty and said, "Thanks for looking after her."

CHAPTER 87

TEN MINUTES LATER, Magda was sprawled on a beanbag chair in the witness room at the Miami Police Department. No one had seen us bring her in, which was how I'd wanted it.

I wasn't going to let social services take this girl off to some cold facility. Unlike interview rooms, these rooms had a touch of home. There were photos on the walls here, pictures of people riding bikes or going to the beach. Each wall was a different, calming color, not the industrial white or tan found throughout the rest of the building.

A green couch someone had brought from home stretched across the back wall. Magda had gone straight for the beanbag, and Marie leaned in close from a standard hard wooden chair. Most of the pizza I'd bought was gone from the open box on the folding table.

We'd immediately connected Magda's surname, Andru-skiewicz, to Joseph, the young pianist in the group of children we'd rescued at the Miami airport.

The raw emotion on Magda's face when Marie told her she knew where her brother was made everything I had done in this case worthwhile. She started to cry and laugh at the same time. By now her eyes were bloodshot, but she kept smiling and asking about Joseph and the others who'd been in the container with her; they were like family to her now.

Marie assured Magda she'd be able to speak to her brother shortly. First, we needed to know more about her ordeal so we could construct a case around her statement.

Magda calmed down and talked to us through occasional sniffles. "When I saw the container, I got scared. It didn't look safe. Hanna kept leading more and more people inside. By then, it was too late to back out."

Marie interrupted with a few questions, looking for details.

Magda said, "I cried the first day in the container. A lot of us did. But toward the end, it got so much worse." She had to stop and blow her nose.

She identified Hanna Greete and her brother, Albert. That, along with some of the information Marie had gathered, was enough to make a decent case against them. But I was after bigger game.

I'd been careful not to inject myself into the interview too much so far. Now I asked, "Did you meet any Russians during all this?"

She shook her head. Then she said, "Perhaps. I'm not very good with English." She paused, gathered her thoughts, and said, "I'm not very good with *accents* in English. There was one man. He beat a homeless man. Beat him badly. Blood everywhere."

"What did the attacker look like?"

She gave a vague description, but when she mentioned the blue goatee, I knew who it was. I told her, "He'll get what he deserves soon enough. You're safe now. You'll be back with your brother before long."

Marie handed the teenager a cell phone and coaxed her to speak. Magda said, "Hello?" Then: "Joseph?" I heard the catch in her voice as she realized who she was talking to. She spoke rapidly in Polish, alternating between laughing, squealing, and weeping.

This was the kind of day I lived for.

CHAPTER

I HAD THE whole team meet me east of Biscayne Boulevard in the parking lot between a Holiday Inn and Bayfront Park. The H and I in the first word of the motel's sign had faded. It had been like that for so long, some of the street people called it the "Olday Inn." It was known for cheap rooms in an expensive city.

Stephanie and Chill pulled up about the same time and we met next to my car.

Neither of them wore completely civilian clothes. Tactical pants and polo shirts covering the guns on their hips would fool most of the public, but criminals, street people, and other cops could always spot a plainclothes cop.

Lorena Perez had had to sit this deal out. She was on a ten-day leave while the shooting on the ship was investigated, standard practice in most police agencies. I'd called her earlier in the day, and I could tell she wanted to be out here with us. I would've liked to have her. She'd proven how tough and tactically sound she was last night.

I remembered my first shooting. Shit, I still dreamed about it.

I'd pulled over a shitty, beat-up Dodge Charger for running a stop sign. That kind of stop, it's simple: You give a lecture and let 'em go, unless they have attitude. For attitude, you might give the guy a ticket, although it's not like anyone ever pays 'em. There's a competition in parts of Miami to see how many tickets a single person can rack up. (The current record, sixty-one, is held by a lawn-service worker in Allapattah.)

As I approached the Charger, I noticed how dark the windows were tinted. I couldn't see a thing in there. Before the alarm traveled to my brain, someone poked a TEC-9 out of a cracked-open window.

You've heard of an *Oh, shit* moment? I literally said, "Oh, shit," as I fell back, drawing my service weapon as I went down. I don't know how many times the asshole in the car fired. I'm not even sure how many times *I* fired. I just pulled the trigger on my way to the ground. Forensics later found three slugs in a parked car and one in a tree behind me.

The car squealed away, but three hours later, a twenty-two-year-old convicted carjacker showed up at Jackson Memorial with a bullet deep in his shoulder and a wounded left ear. The surgeon later told me it was almost a perfect circle in his lobe, like the wide-gauge ear-piercings kids have. The surgeon was amused. He'd seen a lot of bullet wounds, but this was the most entertaining.

Good for him, but personally, I've never found bullet wounds or gunfights entertaining.

I was on leave for only three days before I was cleared of the shooting, but it left me shaky. For almost six months after that, I was nervous whenever I approached a car. It didn't help when the shooter pleaded guilty and got only a year in the county jail. There are always side effects to a shooting for a cop. And the effects are cumulative.

I hoped Lorena snapped back quickly. Like any nice Cuban girl born in Miami, she had plenty of family around her. The same family that had begged her not to go into police work in the first place. I once met her father, a dermatologist who lived in Weston. He didn't seem like he would ever give up trying to convince his daughter that it wasn't too late for her to become an accountant.

I briefed Chill and Steph about finding Magda, now safe at the station with my friend Tosha watching her, and told them that Miami Police had located all the other people from the container.

Chill said, "What now?"

"We can make a case against the traffickers from Amsterdam, but it's the Russians I want to tie up in this mess. No way we can let them skate," I said.

"Can't let that prick Rostoff get away with shit like this."

I agreed with him.

"How do we find the Dutch traffickers?" Steph said. "They could be anywhere."

I smiled. "We make them come to us." I grabbed a backpack from inside my car and started walking toward the band shell in Bayfront Park.

I intended to let the cheap tracker and wide-open sky do some legwork for us.

CHAPTER 89

HANNA AND ALBERT brooded on a bench near Miami Dade College's downtown campus. Hanna had just checked on Tasi, who was recovering from her injuries at a hotel in Little Havana. Earlier in the morning, they had left her lying on a king-size bed with ice bags on her face.

Hanna had never seen her brother hang his head before, but right now, his head was drooping toward the sidewalk.

Hanna thought about Josie and started to cry. Her brother put his arm around her shoulder and pulled her tight to him. He said, "We'll get her back."

"How? We need that backpack."

"I have several plans ready. By the time I'm done with Billy and his friends, there won't be many people left in Miami who speak Russian."

Hanna shook her head. "I can't risk Josie. We're going to negotiate." She stared hard at her brother and said, "Understand?"

Albert nodded.

Hanna thought about her own teenage years, about the abuse she took from her father. Albert would always step between the two of them. She didn't know how many beatings her brother had taken for her, but it was more than she could ever pay back. And he was still willing to risk everything for her and her daughter.

This had all turned into a tremendous mess, and Hanna had no idea how to fix it. She decided that if she hadn't found Magda and the bag by tonight, she would meet Billy the Russian in person and see what she could give him in exchange for her daughter. It was a sobering and terrifying prospect.

Hanna wondered what she could offer Rostoff instead of the diamonds. They would probably take Albert, just so they could exact revenge. She wasn't going to sacrifice her brother. But she would sacrifice herself if need be.

She didn't like the idea. She'd go back to work as a prostitute, as she'd done in her early twenties, to pay off her debt to the Russians. She'd do it happily if it meant Josie was safe.

Hanna considered all the selling points she could make during the negotiation. If the Russians took her as payment, they'd have an experienced woman who could handle herself in different situations. Plus the Russians would eliminate their competition in Amsterdam. The Russians were always looking for an edge in business. She could make the argument that this would give it to them.

Albert perked up on the bench next to her. He nudged her and held up his phone. "Look, look. We're getting a clear signal." He held the iPhone out so they could both look at the tiny map with a flashing blue dot that had appeared on the screen.

Hanna sat up straight and said, "Is that the tracker? Where's the signal coming from?"

Albert said, "Close by." He raised his eyes and looked across the street, then north toward the American Airlines Arena. "She's real close. Maybe over in that park."

He stood up and started moving in that direction, holding the phone out in front of him.

For the first time in a couple of days, Hanna felt real hope.

CHAPTER 90

I SAT ALONE at a picnic table just in front of the park's concert band shell, Biscayne Bay behind me. Marie waited in my car because this was not the right time to have her in public and meeting people. I'd been careful to place my team in the right spots. I kept up a calm demeanor, but I had no illusions about what could go wrong. It wasn't just my safety—the whole team could be at risk. If the Russians showed up, we'd probably be outnumbered and outgunned.

A few cars rolled along Biscayne Boulevard. It was the perfect place to sit and watch for surprises. The red backpack sat on the table with nothing blocking the signal from the tracker. My pistol sat in my lap under the table, though I hoped it didn't come down to fast gunplay. I wanted to be ready just in case. This was all my plan, from start to finish. No one else could be blamed if it went wrong. That was exactly how I wanted it.

It was a beautiful Miami afternoon with a breeze off the ocean. The sun was starting to dip behind some of the taller buildings, and I thought I could see some buzzards roosting on the state building downtown. It was one of the more famous quirks of the Magic City; no one had ever explained why the buzzards preferred that building.

I felt a trickle of sweat run down my back. It was nerves, I knew. A good cop doesn't ignore little signs like perspiration. I took a breath and thought about how this might play out.

I'd never dealt with Dutch criminals before, but from what I'd heard about Albert Greete, he was a badass through and through. In Miami, I could usually spot badasses. They weren't the guys in muscle shirts with big biceps; those were the showy loudmouths. The truly dangerous people in Miami were quiet and watched everything. They noticed when other people were nervous or tried to signal partners. The quiet, dangerous people never gave you a second chance.

If this Dutch dude Albert and his sister, Hanna, were like that, I had plenty to worry about. And that's why I had kept Marie out of sight.

Then I spotted them. They weren't hiding their approach. A man and a woman in their thirties walking across the parking lot, weaving between the cars.

The woman, Hanna, was very attractive, with brown hair and a lean, athletic body.

Her brother looked exactly like I'd expected him to—jeans, a loose shirt to cover a gun, and eyes that were fixed on me. He was shorter than me but in good shape, with broad shoulders and thinning hair. He was not intimidated.

Behind them, casually waiting by parked cars, were my partners and Marie Meijer.

Now the brother and sister were absolutely focused on me. They saw the backpack in plain sight and clearly wanted to discuss it. That meant Albert wasn't checking his surroundings and didn't see Steph and Chill start to follow him at a distance.

Hanna appeared calm as she approached. Maybe it was because she realized I was waiting for them.

When they were five yards away, they stopped directly in front of me. There were no civilians anywhere in the park. Looking at it tactically and as a police officer, I'd say the setting was perfect.

Hanna said in accented English, "You're the man we saw with Marie Meijer in Amsterdam. So you're a cop too."

I waited in silence for a few moments, then said, "My name is Tom Moon. I'm a Miami police detective." I kept a close watch on her brother as he gave me the stink-eye. I could tell Albert was used to people crumbling under his stare. *Welcome to Miami, pal.*

Hanna said, "At least you don't work for the Rostoffs."

Her brother added, "Or do you?"

I let out a laugh. "I would gladly trade you two if I could arrest Roman Rostoff."

That seemed to satisfy them.

Hanna said, "So what do we do now?"

"Before you do anything stupid, I should probably point out that there are two armed federal agents behind you."

Albert's head snapped around as he swiveled to look behind him.

Chill smiled and waved with his left hand; his right hand held a Glock nine-millimeter.

Steph held her own Glock along the seam of her pants.

Albert turned so they could see his hand was on his gun too.

Just another day in Miami.

CHAPTER 91

I STARED AT the two Dutch human traffickers. I was not particularly shocked that everyone standing around me held a gun. I was holding one too, just not as obviously. On the bright side, no one had been shot yet. That was a plus.

A flutter of nerves ran through me. I had to look at my overall plan and take a few risks.

Hanna said, "No one would benefit from a gunfight. I have only one goal—to save my daughter."

Steph Hall said, "Then tell your brother to drop his pistol. Have him put down the gun and we'll talk."

I was glad we had Marie stashed in one of the cars for now.

Hanna looked around at each of us, trying to decide what to do, for what felt like an hour. Her brother, meanwhile, was sizing us up, assessing whom to shoot first and what would be his best escape route. There was something about Albert that set me on edge, though I guessed he would hold off on using the gun. I assumed he didn't want to risk his sister being shot.

I took a breath, trying to keep calm in case I had to start shooting. I gripped my pistol tighter; it was still hidden from view under the table. I calculated how long it would take me to raise it.

Both Chill and Steph showed great tactical sense by standing off to the side in case I did exactly that. It was just another example of our team starting to jell.

Albert raised his left hand and opened his fingers wide as he said, "What if we compromise?" He held his pistol in his right hand with only two fingers and slowly tucked it into the waistband of his jeans.

Normally, a cop would never let that kind of bullshit go. But this wasn't a normal situation and these weren't our typical Miami knuckleheads. I was sensing a possible inroad to the Rostoff organization if we played this right.

I kept the gun in my hand as I calmly said, "Tell me what happened to your daughter."

Hanna surprised me by stepping over to the picnic table. She sat on the bench directly across from me. She had a pretty face and piercing brown eyes.

She said, "My daughter, Josie, was kidnapped last night from a hotel near the airport. The kidnappers will exchange her for some diamonds that are in that pack. I don't think we have any other options. We couldn't get her back if we were on the run for killing three police officers. That is, if we even managed to walk away from a gunfight. You have to believe me—the only thing that matters to me is getting my daughter back."

I thought about that for a moment, then said, "Do you know the people who took your daughter?"

"The man I've been talking to is named Billy—"

I said, "Does he have a goatee that's dyed blue?"

Her face told me we were dealing with Billy the Blade.

CHAPTER 92

I LISTENED TO Hanna with an open mind. Steph Hall holstered her pistol.

Albert looked at Steph like Wile E. Coyote looked at the Road Runner. He had no interest in becoming friends.

Hanna finished explaining about the diamonds and her daughter and the Russians. We sat in silence for a few moments. Then I said, "We could help you get your daughter back."

"This man, Billy, is no fool. I know he'll kill her if he has any hint the police are involved. The only way to get her back is to trade the diamonds for her. If you let me do that, I will turn myself in, I'll testify against Billy, I'll do anything. But I have to get my daughter back first."

She was direct and to the point. It left me stumped. I wanted Hanna's daughter returned safely too. I hadn't forgotten that Hanna was a human trafficker who'd ruined the lives of dozens of people and allowed at least four of them to die, but that didn't mean her daughter had to die as well.

I thought about it, and I was thankful no one felt the need to fill the silence with useless chatter. But I kept an eye on Albert. He was a wild card who might be a little crazy.

I looked from Steph to Chill. I bet they were great poker players, because they didn't give me a hint of what they were thinking.

Finally, I slid the backpack across the table to Hanna. The look on her face told me how shocked she was.

She wasn't the only one.

Steph said, "Wait a minute."

"Take it and go," I told Hanna. "Get your daughter back."

I tried not to chuckle at the confused expression on Albert's face. A hard-core criminal like him wasn't used to a helping hand from the police.

I sat in silence as we watched the brother and sister walk west across the parking lot, the backpack slung over Hanna's left shoulder.

I knew the conversation with my partners was going to be interesting.

CHAPTER 93

STEPH HALL PLOPPED onto the bench across from me. Outrage was written across her face. "Are you insane?" she practically shouted.

I shrugged and said, "Possibly. I'd have to blame it on my DNA."

Chill, standing in front of me, said, "Not cool, Anti. We worked hard for that arrest. We deserved it."

"You know as well as I do that Billy the Blade is not gonna fool around. He wouldn't think twice about slitting that girl's throat. Hell, I've seen his handiwork over on Hallandale Beach." I looked at Steph and Chill as I let them think about what might happen to that girl. "I had to let Hanna leave with the backpack. I'm sorry, but the FBI would only screw up the rescue. None of you can tell me a girl's life is worth a few diamonds."

Steph regained her composure and said, "You don't have

the authority to give away evidence and let human traffickers leave."

"And yet that's what I just did."

Chill said, "It's not even legal."

I shook my head and said, "No, it's not necessarily legal, but it's the right thing to do."

I motioned for Chill to join us at the picnic table. Now I had my annoyed coworkers sitting around me. They were not in the mood to hear me explain my reasoning, but I guessed I'd earned enough credit for them to let me speak.

I said, "Everything is going according to plan."

Steph said, "Your plan was to give away a fortune in evidence and let our main suspects go?"

I said, "How did they know to come to the park to find the bag? Because they have a tracker sewn into the backpack." I pulled out my iPhone and brought up a display. "Do you think that's the only tracker in the world? Chill gave me a bag of electronics that included trackers a few weeks ago." I held up my phone to show them the little map with the flashing signal. I said, "Looks like they're still on foot. The tracker should lead us directly to the Russians. We might be able to wrap this whole thing up after they get the girl back."

Steph stood up quickly and said, "We have to start following them. It'll take a few minutes to get the surveillance organized."

I unclipped the compact Miami police radio from my belt, mashed the button, and said, "Smooth Jazz, do you have eyes on the target?"

Alvin Teague's voice came over the radio. "They're about to get into a blue Chevy rental car and I have the tracker on my phone. I have detectives in each direction on Biscayne. This'll be the easiest surveillance in history."

I looked up at Steph, who was staring at me with an open mouth. All I could say was "Teague may be a pompous ass, but he's one hell of a good cop."

I would enjoy the memory of that look on her face for the rest of my life.

CHAPTER 94

HANNA GREETE WAS still in shock that the big cop had handed over the backpack without even asking for a bribe. Albert checked to make sure the diamonds were still in place. The police hadn't even bothered to open up the strap. The diamonds were still there, a ridge under the fabric.

Hanna had only one goal—to get Josie back safely.

Now she and Albert sat in La Carreta, a Cuban restaurant on Eighth Street in Little Havana. Albert had eaten some kind of ham sandwich. She had picked at chips that looked like they were made out of bananas and stared at her phone.

Finally, she called Billy, afraid of what he might say.

Billy answered the phone with his usual exuberance, shouting, "Hello, Hanna!"

"How quickly can you meet us?" Hanna asked.

"Do you have the diamonds?"

"Is Josie safe?"

"How could you think I would do anything to this sweet little girl? But don't forget, I know I can live without the diamonds. Can you live without your daughter?"

Hanna didn't mean for there to be silence on the line, but she had no response. Just the way he'd said that sent a chill through her body.

Billy said, "I can meet you in one hour in South Beach. On the sidewalk across from the Clevelander Hotel, near the beach."

"Put Josie on the phone. I have to know that she's safe," Hanna said.

"You won't take my word for it?"

"Put her on the phone." Hanna purposely kept her tone even and spoke very slowly so there would be no misunderstanding. After a long silence, Hanna heard a whimper on the other end of the phone. "Josie? Is that you, sweetheart?"

"Mama?" Then there was a bout of sobbing.

"Are you okay, Josie?" Hanna waited while someone spoke to her daughter away from the phone.

Josie came back on, sniffled, and said, "Help me, Mama. The man with the blue beard says he'll use his knife on my throat if you don't meet him." She started to say something else but the phone was snatched from her.

Hanna gasped, trying not to picture what Billy might do to her daughter.

Billy came back on the line and said, "I look forward to seeing you in an hour."

"Bring Josie."

"Of course. I wouldn't deny a mother the chance to watch her daughter's throat slit if things don't go exactly as planned.

If the diamonds aren't in my hand in one hour, you'll never see your precious daughter again."

He said goodbye, never dropping his friendly tone.

Hanna hung up and looked at her brother. "We have one hour to meet them over on South Beach."

She couldn't read the look in Albert's eyes.

CHAPTER 95

HANNA ALMOST LEFT her brother in Little Havana.

She said, "I need to know you won't do anything crazy, Albert."

"Define *crazy*."

She growled in frustration.

South Beach was only a few miles from downtown Miami, but it felt like a different world. The crowds of pedestrians along Ocean Drive seemed much younger than the people along Brickell or Bayshore Drive.

The Clevelander Hotel sat on the corner of Tenth and Ocean Drive in the Miami Art Deco District. Hanna had heard of the old five-story hotel, but she'd just read an article in the Miami paper that said the only thing the Clevelander was known for now was loud music by the pool and a TV sports show called *Highly Questionable* that was taped in the hotel every afternoon.

Albert drove past the hotel so they could both get a look

at the area, but there were too many people to see much, so Hanna told him to drop her near the Clevelander.

"Albert, I'm not kidding, I want you to stay in the car. I'm not going to risk Josie."

Albert said, "And I'm not going to risk both of you. If something goes wrong, I have to be close enough to act."

Hanna knew it was useless to argue with her hardheaded brother, and she appreciated how much he worried about her. She started to slip out of the car, then paused, leaned across the console, and kissed Albert on the cheek. "You're a good brother and a good man. Josie and I both love you."

She was out of the car before Albert could say anything. She didn't want to make it sound like she was saying goodbye, but, just in case, she was.

The backpack rested over her left shoulder. She could feel the diamonds sewn into the strap.

Hanna darted through a break in traffic on Ocean Drive. A red Ferrari swerved to avoid her. Groups of young partyers just starting out their night laughed and shouted as they passed her. She wondered if it was this loud all the time. If you were looking west, away from the ocean, this could be a sunnier, wider Amsterdam.

She twisted her head, scanning in every direction, but she didn't see Billy or any of his henchmen. There were still a number of people sitting on the beach as the sun set over the city behind them.

She cut down a path and saw, through a gap between the bushes and the sand, Billy sitting at a picnic table. Hanna couldn't help looking over her shoulder to make sure Albert hadn't followed her. She caught a glimpse of him across the street, still sitting in the rental car.

He was watching her every step.

She approached the picnic table and Billy. As she got closer, her heart soared at the sight of her daughter, Josie, sitting next to Billy. Josie's hands were folded on the table and her eyes were cast down. But she appeared unharmed.

The smile Billy gave her made her angry. When they'd first met, Hanna had liked his easygoing style. Now she realized it just masked a sociopath. When this was all over and she had Josie safely in her arms, she might let Albert kill this Russian son of a bitch.

CHAPTER 96

I KNEW ALVIN Teague would be able to conduct a quiet surveillance of Hanna Greete and her brother. I had my own issues to deal with.

Marie had a ton of questions, so I filled her in on everything. She looked at the road and said, "I might have been a complication at a meeting like that."

As soon as I'd crossed the MacArthur Causeway to Miami Beach, following the general path of the tracker I'd put in the red backpack, my phone rang—my office. No way that was good news. I decided I couldn't avoid my supervisor any longer. Hopefully, if I walked him through this carefully, he wouldn't get too nervous. I answered the phone with a friendly "Hey, boss."

The voice on the other end did not belong to the FBI supervisor in charge of the international crimes task force. That was clear.

The first thing I heard was a man with a harsh Brooklyn

accent almost screaming, "Don't give me that 'Hey, boss,' bull-shit. This is Martin Lobbeler, assistant special agent in charge of the FBI. I'm your supervisor's boss. The asshole who has to listen to your presentations and local-cop view of events. You know, the presentations I usually ignore."

"Yes, sir. What can I do for you?" I needed to keep this professional.

"One thing I don't need is a cowboy like you coming in and working after a shooting. Do you know how it looks for the Bureau to have to hold a press conference about a shooting? You've pulled a lot of shit, including not keeping your super-visory special agent in the loop. And I don't need a local cop stirring up shit with other federal agencies."

"Like which agencies, sir?"

"Like DHS."

"Sir, I'd like—"

"I thought you were supposed to be smart. They told me you had a law degree from the University of Miami, but you're not acting smart. I'm going to be talking to your chief tomorrow. You'll be back in uniform writing tickets."

I couldn't help myself. "In that case, be prepared for a shitload of parking tickets on your car." So much for profes-sionalism. "I'm trying to make a good arrest and I'm sure not getting much support from jerk-offs like you."

I was about to hang up when my supervisor's voice came on the line. He spoke quietly, probably trying to keep the ASAC from hearing. "Calm down, Tom."

"But that idiot ASAC just told me I'm off the task force right when we're in the middle of an operation."

"He said he'd talk to your chief *tomorrow*. Today you're still a member of the task force and a sworn Miami police officer. I expect you to use your best judgment the rest of the day. Do what you think is right, and we'll see what your chief has to say tomorrow. Am I understood?"

I sat in my car, silent. Had my meek and mild supervisor just given me a green light to move forward on this operation? That was sure what it sounded like to me.

Carefully I said, "I hear what you're saying. I'll call you when we resolve the current situation. I think you'll be happy with the progress we've made on the case."

My supervisor said, "You mean the human-trafficking case that I will attribute to Steph Hall if necessary?"

"That's exactly the case I mean." This guy was full of surprises. He already had a way of accounting for the arrests even if I got fired from the task force. That's all I wanted right now. Just a little leeway to do the right thing.

I could always practice law if I had to.

CHAPTER 97

I MET UP with the others in a parking lot behind the Regal Cinema on Lincoln Road. I kept quiet for a minute. I was surprised at how much the angry ASAC's threat bothered me. I really did love working on this task force. But there was no question that the only thing I cared about now was saving Hanna's daughter from the Russians and dropping a big net on as many human traffickers as possible.

An FBI ASAC was not usually involved in operations. For the most part, the ASACs were administrators, and like all administrators, they could be a help or a hindrance. I didn't like him saying that I was a cowboy. Just because I didn't follow the FBI rules didn't mean I was a cowboy. I didn't risk my partners' lives and I always made clean cases that held up in court.

Steph and Chill came up to my car as I was on the radio with Alvin Teague. "Do you have eyes on the target, Smooth Jazz?"

"Ten-four. There's no one we can't follow in the city."

"Especially when you have a tracker on them."

"I barely even looked at it."

"Right. And I was a great football player in college." I purposely said it over the radio so anyone who was helping me would get a good laugh. Now I got more serious and turned to my partners in front of me.

"As soon as Hanna has the girl, we'll swoop in. Smooth Jazz and the other Miami cops know to look after the girl and her mother. That leaves us able to focus on the Russians."

I looked at Marie. "You don't have tactical gear or a gun. I don't want to risk—"

She held up a hand. "I know, I'm a civilian here. Just like you were in Amsterdam. Yet, by chance, you still got involved in our operation when the suspects ran. I'll use common sense. I'll help with the daughter if I'm needed."

I nodded. She'd made it easy for me.

Chill had a half smile on his face. I knew the ATF agent liked the idea of the three of us going against the Russians. I knew he had an ax to grind with Rostoff. I just hoped he didn't do anything crazy.

On the radio, Smooth Jazz said, "The woman is out of the car and crossing Ocean Drive almost in front of the Clevelander. It looks like the male driver is staying with the rental car. She's looking for someone on the beach side of the road."

I grabbed the radio. "Be there in two minutes. Can you keep eyes on the female? She's the one who'll meet the Russians."

Alvin Teague said, "You forget who you're talking to? I can keep eyes on anyone."

I needed to hear that confidence about now.

CHAPTER 98

HANNA GREETE'S LEGS trembled as she headed down the gentle slope of the green area between the street and the beach to the picnic table where Josie was sitting quietly next to Billy the Russian.

Mosquitoes buzzed around her as she approached. She caught a glimpse of couples on the beach gazing out at the Atlantic. This would be a lovely place if it weren't for these crazy Russians.

She had no qualms about giving up the backpack and the diamonds in exchange for her daughter. Her human-trafficking endeavor might not have gone the way she'd planned, but right now all she wanted was Josie safe.

Billy stood up like a gentleman when she reached the picnic table. He held out his hand to show Hanna he wanted her to sit on the bench across from them. He was also telling her not to do anything stupid.

Hanna fought the urge to embrace Josie and forced herself to sit down across from the smiling Russian. She didn't look at Josie because she didn't want to reveal the wave of emotions swirling through her. Her baby was safe. At least for now.

Billy sat and stroked his blue goatee while his brown eyes assessed her. They sat in silence for a few moments. A Mustang revved its engine along Ocean Drive. The occasional sound of the band around the pool at the Clevelander Hotel floated in the humid air.

Billy said, "Hanna, so happy you could join us."

Hanna didn't say a word. She was terrified. She kept her hands in her lap so the Russian wouldn't see them shake. It was all she could do not to break down and scream. She had to stay calm for her daughter. She glanced at Josie, and the look in her eyes told Hanna she was traumatized. It was the first time ever that Hanna had wished she had a gun. If she'd had one, she would've shot Billy in the face.

Her eyes flicked up quickly to where Albert sat in the car. She had been right not to let him come with her to this meeting. But she had to admit there was a certain degree of security in knowing he was close by.

The short strip of greenery here, with the bushes and a few palm trees, changed the atmosphere from up on the strip. In other circumstances, it would be calming. The waves gently rolled onto the beach, making a steady noise that competed with the band at the Clevelander.

Billy smiled at Josie and ran the back of his fingers along her cheek. It made Hanna's skin crawl.

Billy said, "Do you have what I want?"

Hanna just nodded.

"With you?"

She hesitated. If he knew the diamonds were in the backpack she'd carefully set on the ground behind her, he might decide to eliminate both witnesses right there. Now she wondered if she'd made a mistake by coming here without Albert.

Billy's response to her silence was to yank Josie closer to him. He laid an open Buck knife on the table and smiled.

Hanna said, "There's no need for violence. The diamonds are in the backpack."

Billy laughed and clapped his hands. "You've given us quite the runaround."

Hanna didn't answer. She saw two men in suits step off the sidewalk and head toward them. Two more men appeared from behind her, and then a fifth man in a black suit started walking toward them. Billy's loud clap had signaled them.

The man in the black suit was a little older than Billy, about forty-five. He didn't show the deference to him the others did, and he came right up to the table. He addressed Billy in Russian and they argued briefly about something. Then the man marched away toward the beach like a sulking child.

Hanna said, "You annoy everyone, not just me."

Billy turned to Hanna and said, "You'll thank God if all I do is annoy you."

He was hard to fluster.

Billy said, "Give me the backpack."

"Give me my daughter."

Now Billy lost his good humor and leaned forward. "What have I done to make you think this is a negotiation? That knife could be in her eye before you say, 'Don't do it.'"

Hanna reached behind her and lifted the pack. Even under the weight of it, her hand shook wildly. She tossed it onto the picnic table.

Billy stared, a grin on his face.

Hanna ran her finger along the ridge of diamonds to show him they were in the strap.

Billy mumbled, "Clever." He looked up at his men, then at the backpack again.

Hanna said, "Josie, let's go." She stood up to emphasize that she was done talking.

Billy held up one hand and said, "I'm sorry, you can't leave just yet."

Hanna slowly sat back down. "Why? I have nothing left to give you."

"We need your brother."

That caught her by surprise. She just stared at the handsome Russian. Finally she said, "Albert? He's not part of this. I had the diamonds and I just gave them to you. Our deal was that you would give me my daughter for the diamonds."

Billy cut his eyes to the man standing behind Hanna. He shook his head and said, "No, I just said I had to have the diamonds or you wouldn't *see* your daughter again. You can see her. She's safe. If you want her back, I need your brother in her place."

"You can't expect me to sacrifice my brother."

Billy shrugged. "You can sacrifice your daughter if you prefer. Your choice." He gave a quick laugh and said, "Too bad your name's not Sophie."

Hanna said, "He won't come after you if you let us go. I swear to God."

"I'm not worried about your brother coming after me. I'm untouchable here in the U.S. But he's caused all kinds of problems in Amsterdam. We're one big organization. Roman and Emile Rostoff are brothers. You didn't really think we'd let Albert return to Amsterdam, did you?"

Hanna shot him a nasty look. "This was your plan all along."

"Part of it, yes. I knew we'd have to deal with your brother."

Her mind raced, searching for options. For the first time since this whole ordeal started, she realized she had none.

CHAPTER 99

HANNA FELT THE panic rise in her throat. This man wanted to ruin her life. He was going to murder her brother or her daughter. How was it possible that he had her in this position? He wasn't some sort of feudal lord. He was a Russian gangster.

Billy was looking at Hanna as if he expected her to cry. He couldn't have been more wrong. She wasn't sad; she was furious. Furious and scared for her daughter. There was no combination more potent for a mother.

Hanna said, "You won't let us go, even though you have the diamonds?" It was hard to say the words in such an even tone.

Billy said, "I am quite sorry. I wish it could be different. Until your brother shows up, you and your daughter will remain my guests."

"I don't want to leave here with you."

"What you want is of no concern to me. Your failed attempt to smuggle people not only didn't pay off your previous debt,

301

it cost us additional resources *and* our most valuable law enforcement contact. Your debt to us is now quite significant."

"Even with the diamonds? That's nonsense."

Billy didn't smile when he looked Hanna in the eye and said, "Speak to me that way again and your daughter will go through life without a left ear."

Hanna couldn't keep her eyes from drifting down to the knife Billy had set on the table. Suddenly, she felt like she had no control over her own actions. There was no conscious thought as she moved.

She reached down and grabbed the open folding knife on the table. The blade looked nasty, all sharp angles and gleaming steel. She brought the blade up and swung it at Billy's face as fast as she could.

The muscular Russian was quick. He jerked his head back, and the blade missed him by an inch.

Hanna swung at him again, but the result was the same. A smile spread across his face. That stupid, infuriating smile.

Hanna couldn't stop herself—she drove the sharp blade into the top of his left hand. She felt the steel pass through his flesh and tendons and then stick firm in the wooden table. Blood spurted up from the wound like a tiny oil-well gusher.

Billy's eyes bulged and he let out a wail. It hurt Hanna's ears, but it was satisfying to know she had hurt him so deliberately.

The two men closest to Billy rushed to his aid.

Hanna shouted in Dutch, "Run, Josie! Run!"

Her daughter didn't need to be told twice. She jumped off the bench and turned to run.

One of the dark-haired young men moved from Billy and grabbed Josie. She didn't make it three steps.

That's when Hanna heard the first gunshots.

CHAPTER 100

THIS WAS LIKE a lot of operations I'd run in my career. We were making the most of our limited resources and I was working with the local police without telling my supervisor. Everything was going about like I'd expected it to.

Rolling down Ocean Drive in my Explorer, I strained to see where Hanna had gone with the backpack. That was what the Russians wanted, or at least the diamonds inside it. That's what I was looking for. That's where I'd find the Russians.

The last I heard, Hanna's brother was still sitting in the rental car somewhere near the Clevelander Hotel. I could hear bits and pieces of music from the band around the Clevelander pool. Everything in South Beach picked up near dark.

Marie pointed to the road and shouted, "There!"

I saw him. Running across the street was Albert Greete with a pistol in his hand that he was aiming toward the beach. I heard gunshots. *Holy shit.* This crazy Dutchman was running through traffic shooting at someone.

I mashed the brakes and felt the car behind me crash into my bumper. That was the least of my problems. I popped on the blue lights and bailed out of the car.

Marie came out of the car with me but had the sense to wait by the vehicle.

Just as I pulled my service weapon, panic set in among the pedestrians. It started as a low rumble, then progressed to screams. Vehicles screeched to a halt and I heard the unmistakable thuds of cars smashing into other cars. A BMW swerved into a light pole.

A family with two little kids coming off the beach stepped right into the line of fire. My heart stopped when I saw the little girl's face. The beefy father grabbed the kids and fell to the ground, covering the children. That was some good tactical sense. He had to be a Miami native.

People on the beach were running as well, topless women and buff men who had no idea where they were going. It looked like a disaster movie, but only I knew all the terrible things that could really happen in this story.

When I got closer to the beach, I saw Albert exchanging fire with big men dressed in suits—Russians, I assumed. I couldn't see Hanna, but I knew where I was headed.

I dodged a Land Rover as I came off the street and cut across the sidewalk. I intended to intercept Albert.

It was showtime.

CHAPTER 101

HANNA DIDN'T CARE what happened to her; she just wanted to buy enough time to get her daughter away. The sound of gunfire had frozen everyone in place momentarily. Even the man who grabbed Josie had stopped midstride to look over his shoulder.

Billy had quit wailing and was now staring at the knife sticking through his left hand. Blood was still pouring out of the wound, but it wasn't shooting up in the air like it had been a moment before.

The young man just to the side of Billy, dressed in a slick gray pin-striped suit, started to pull the knife out of Billy's hand.

That's when the man's head exploded. Like a bomb. Blood spattered over everything near him. Billy was suddenly covered in brains and blood. The combination of the knife stuck through his hand and the blood everywhere briefly stunned him.

Somehow, he managed to grab the knife in his mutilated hand with his uninjured hand. It took three good tugs before the knife came free of the table and released him.

Billy reached across the table for the backpack.

Hanna snatched it away. Why not? Things couldn't go any worse for this deal. She spun away from the picnic table holding the bag. Albert was only about twenty feet ahead, just crossing the sidewalk.

He fired almost point-blank into a big Russian thug in a blue suit. Even five quick shots to the stomach didn't stop the man; he took another step and grabbed Albert by the neck.

Albert struggled with him for a moment, then broke free, took a step back, and fired a bullet into each of the man's knees. Finally the man dropped to the ground. So much blood was coming out of the wounds that the sand couldn't absorb it all, and it spread around his body.

Hanna needed to get Albert, grab Josie, and disappear with them. There wasn't much else to do at this point.

As she started to run to her brother, Hanna heard someone shout, "Police, don't move!" She looked toward the street and saw the big Miami cop, Tom Moon, rushing down the slope toward the picnic table. She hoped Billy would be the first person he grabbed. She looked over her shoulder for the bloodied Russian but didn't see him.

She turned back to Albert, who was aiming his gun at another Russian. Then she saw a blur as someone came from the side and knocked into her brother.

It was Billy.

Albert rolled and came up on his feet to face Billy. That's when the Russian brought the knife in a wide arc right across Albert's throat.

Albert stood there for a moment, motionless. Then the gash on his throat opened wide, and he reached for it with his left hand. A moment later, he toppled into the sand.

The gun he'd bought here in Miami was still in his right hand.

Billy held the bloody knife and turned toward Hanna. He didn't ask for the backpack.

She knew exactly what he intended to do.

CHAPTER 102

I TRIED TO control my breathing while scanning for the closest threat. Tourists and partyers from the Clevelander were scampering in every direction. I'd managed to block out the clamor of screams, car horns, and approaching sirens. My hand holding the Glock in front of me was steady.

I rushed toward the last place I'd seen Hanna. I knew that anyone in a suit was a threat. One man was already down by the picnic table with the majority of his head missing. Blood and brain matter covered the table and one of the benches.

There were two other Russians near the beach, but I saw Steph Hall and Chill rushing toward them shouting, "Police, don't move!"

I trusted them to handle the two Russians. I turned to the next target. Even though it was hard to see his face because of the blood streaked across it, I knew it was Billy. His build and stupid blue goatee gave him away.

The body next to him wasn't dressed in a suit. I saw it was Hanna's brother, Albert.

In almost the same instant, I realized Billy had a knife in his hand and intended to use it on Hanna.

I didn't have a clear shot at Billy, not with Hanna between us. She was dodging back and forth. I raised my pistol, then lowered it, looking for the right angle. Finally, I realized there was only one way to do this.

I lowered my head and charged forward, hoping my size and the element of surprise would win the day.

I took one step to the right to avoid Hanna, then crashed into Billy like a pickup truck. My left hand reached out to hold his right wrist and keep the knife away from me.

The sound he made when I careened into him told me I'd knocked the breath out of him. We tumbled into the sand and I managed to lose my pistol. This close together, it didn't matter. I held on to his right hand with all of my strength. I grabbed his left hand; it felt odd and slick. Then I realized it was covered in blood, and more blood was pumping out of a wound in the middle of his hand.

He rolled and slipped away from me. We both jumped into a crouch and faced each other. The look in his eyes told me he was scared. He'd lost some blood and had seen his deal go to hell, and now he was probably thinking about what he'd have to tell Roman Rostoff.

I might be able to use that fear.

I scanned the beach around me, searching for my pistol. As I glanced to my left, I took a hard punch to the right side of my face. It made me stagger. Blood started pouring from my nose.

Before I had my full senses back, Billy kicked me hard in the stomach. Now we were both short of breath. I stumbled back and caught a glimpse of Billy running straight at me. With his goatee, the blood on his face, and his eyes open wide, he looked like some kind of demon.

Just as he hit me, I fell backward on purpose and rolled with it. It was the first time in my whole life that that little move worked. He ended up rolling right over the top of me and landed with a hard thump on some sea oats in the sand.

I sprang to my feet, and when Billy got up on his knees, I pretended his head was a football and punted him as hard as I could. The top of my foot connected with his blue goatee. His head snapped up hard. A tooth flew up in the air and disappeared into the sea oats.

Billy grunted as he flopped over onto his back. All the fight had gone out of him. Quickly, I fell on top of him and patted him down for more weapons. He didn't even carry a gun. I guess that's how he'd gotten the nickname Billy the Blade.

It took me only a few seconds to handcuff him and retrieve my pistol.

Chill and Steph were holding their prisoners on the sidewalk about fifty feet from me. I shot Steph a quick thumbs-up to let her know I was okay.

Hanna was sitting next to her dead brother, weeping.

I pulled Billy to his feet so he was standing right next to me, a shell of the well-dressed confident jerk I had dealt with before. His face and suit were covered with blood. His hair was no longer neatly slicked back but stuck up in every direction, revealing his scalp. His face was caked with blood and sand, and his left hand needed immediate medical attention.

I said, "You're done. Kidnapping, murder, human trafficking—your days of living near the beach are over. I might die poor, but I guarantee you'll die in prison."

Billy said, "Wait, can't we work this out?" He spit blood and fragments of teeth into the sand.

"Billy, are you trying to bribe me? I don't mind being poor."

I thought the muscular Russian was going to cry. It was oddly satisfying.

CHAPTER 103

I HELD A shaken Billy upright. His whole world had just collapsed. I needed to give him time to understand that. I needed *him*. He could sink the entire Rostoff organization. I felt the tremor of fear as I held his arm.

Billy said, "I can't go to prison. That's why I fled Russia. I'm sure we can work something out."

I had him. "The only way we can work anything out is if you give up your boss. You make a statement right now to me about Roman Rostoff and maybe I can help you."

"I can transfer any amount of money into any account. Immediately," Billy said.

I snorted. "This isn't the movies. It's not Russia either. That shit doesn't usually work here. That's why I didn't say you could walk, only that I might be able to help you."

Billy considered it and finally said, "How can you help me?"

"Tell us all about the Rostoff organization. I know I can get a prosecutor to work with us. You'll do time, but it'll be in some country-club federal lockup, not a hellhole state prison like Raiford."

Billy stared at me with an unreadable expression. Blood seeped from a dozen places on his face. He was a beaten, broken man. Finally, he mumbled, "Mr. Rostoff will kill me."

I had to think fast. "Unless we arrest him first. We have ways to protect you."

Billy looked down at the ground. I wondered how many people he had killed to protect his boss. This wasn't an easy decision for him, but it was the best time to hit him with the proposal.

I just stood there in silence, letting him consider his options. It took longer than I'd thought it would. He started to speak a couple of times, then stopped. At last he nodded and said, "Okay."

I felt like I had just found a hoard of gold. I finally had a chance to land the big fish: Rostoff.

I heard Steph Hall shout, shaking me out of my daydream. I turned my attention away from Billy. Steph aimed her pistol at someone coming from the beach.

It was another Russian asshole in a black suit. He must've heard Billy and me speaking from the other side of the sea oats. My right hand moved quickly while I held on to Billy's arm with my left hand. He raised a pistol and at the same time I drew my Glock; we were like gunfighters in the Old West.

The man in the black suit got off three rounds before Steph opened fire on him. I popped off two more rounds. Between the two of us, we caught him in the center mass of the chest, and he went down onto the sand in a heap.

I felt Billy pull away from me, and for a moment I thought he was trying to escape. Then I realized the man's shots hadn't been directed at me—Billy had three holes in his chest. He sank onto the beach.

My best shot at taking down Roman Rostoff was gone.

CHAPTER 104

AFTER THE INCIDENT on the beach, it was a crazy few days. I was suspended while the FBI investigated the shooting. All the Russians had been armed, and the media painted law enforcement in the best possible light for a change.

I remember the relief I felt when Alvin Teague walked back to the scene with Hanna's daughter, Josie. Marie was with them. She had been instrumental in protecting Josie and calming her down. Once she'd spoken Dutch to the girl, Josie realized she was safe.

Teague had managed to cover the surveillance, help save the girl, and make it sound like a normal day at the Miami PD. Like I said, Smooth Jazz might've been a pompous ass, but he was a hell of a cop.

I attended Hanna Greete's first court appearance. I was still suspended, but there was no law that said I couldn't follow the proceedings closely as a civilian. The judge was a former federal prosecutor named Alice Jackson, someone I had dealt with a few times. She gave me a quick smile when I stepped into the back of the courtroom.

Hanna looked much different in the simple tan correctional scrubs she wore to face the judge. Her public defender, Chad Laine, asked for bail. I thought Judge Jackson might laugh out loud.

The judge looked over some paperwork and finally said, "Based on the crimes you're charged with, your lack of residency, and your lack of ties to the community, there will be no bail at this time."

Laine, a tall charmer in a cheap suit with a Florida Gator pin on his lapel, stood and said, "If I personally vouched for my client, would that influence the court?"

Judge Jackson smiled and said, "Yes, it would. It would make me think you were a good attorney who really cared about his client."

"What about in regard to bond for Ms. Greete?"

"Don't be ridiculous. She's a citizen of the Netherlands who appears to have entered this country only for a criminal endeavor. In addition, the indictment details the deaths of four people smuggled into the port of Miami."

The attorney hung his head.

Judge Jackson said, "Good effort, Counselor. I'd like to help out a fellow Gator, but I have no choice in this matter."

Josie had been allowed to return to Amsterdam in the custody of her babysitter, Tasi.

When the hearing was over, I stood at the rail between the public seats and the prosecutor's table. I said hello to the prosecutor and thanked her for her hard work.

The deputy U.S. marshals started to lead Hanna back to the holding cell. As they passed me, she looked up and said, "Thank you for letting us save my daughter."

That's not what I'd expected after such a demanding investigation. Now I felt like the Amsterdam connection on this case was closed. That didn't mean we were done. Though it did mean that Marie Meijer would be going back to Amsterdam, accompanying Magda so she could be reunited with her brother, Joseph.

Three days later, I found myself at the Miami International Airport with Steph Hall saying goodbye to Marie.

Marie had been chatty on the way to the airport, updating me about what she'd been hearing from the kids. Even the children still at the facility in Amsterdam seemed to be adapting well, though Marie said they all asked about me.

We were quiet a moment. I said, "Did this investigation work out the way you'd hoped?"

"We broke up Hanna's smuggling group. That's all I wanted. I'm sure I'll get onto the scent of another group soon." She looked at me closely. "What about you? Did the case work out for you?"

I smiled. "We saved some kids. That's all I ever want to think about."

Marie and I stood close together near the gate while Steph spoke with Magda a dozen feet away. Marie surprised me when she hooked her finger around mine and leaned in closer. "I hope this isn't a permanent goodbye," she said.

I smiled. "No way."

"Are they letting you stay on the task force?"

"Looks like it. It's tough to discipline someone who the *Miami Herald* calls a 'hero cop.'"

"Why do you say it like that? You *are* a hero."

"I'm lucky, that's all. So many things could've gone wrong. Or, I should say, even more wrong. But the FBI liked the press, so I'm still on the task force."

"Will you find another case connected to Amsterdam?"

"Probably. I'll try."

"I'm glad."

Then she surprised me again by taking my face in her hands and kissing me long and deep. When we stopped, the smiles on our faces said it all.

That was it. There was nothing I could say that would top that kiss. The last call for boarding came over the speaker. Magda joined Marie and they got on the plane.

I turned to Steph, who was grinning at me. I said, "We're just friends." I winked and started walking. I could hear Steph snicker as she followed.

CHAPTER

THAT EVENING, I was trying to figure out my life. It had been hard watching Marie leave. But I knew I'd see her again soon.

My home life had improved. Sure, I still took a step close to my sister to smell her breath for alcohol every evening when I came home, but my mom had started taking a couple of new prescriptions, and her condition had improved. She was much more in the moment and called me by my real name most of the time.

I finished eating a meat loaf my mom had made as we chatted about her hobbies. Mom was quite animated for a change. Then the conversation turned to my romantic life, like it always seemed to.

My mom said, "Are you going to see that lovely girl Marie again?"

"I hope so. You know she had to go back to Amsterdam."

"Too bad. She was smart and beautiful. That's a combination

that's hard to find anywhere." She looked over at my sister, who was in the kitchen, and then back at me and added, "Except in this family."

I laughed. I appreciated my mother's keen sense of humor, these precious times when she was lucid and in the moment. I said, "Did you do anything interesting today?"

"I played piano for Chuck."

Oh no! My heart sank. I cut my eyes over to my sister in the kitchen. We'd lost her again. I didn't understand the broad smile Lila had on her face.

My mom said, "Then Chuck showed me some stretches and sat with me until Lila got home from work."

Lila was still smiling. I excused myself from the table and stepped into the kitchen. "What's with the grin? You look like the Cheshire cat."

Lila giggled and said, "I've been waiting for this conversation for a couple of days."

"Why is that?"

"The nursing company has been sending a new aide over in the afternoons, a young guy named Chuck." She laughed.

I mumbled, "'The only thing I know is that I know nothing.'"

Lila said, "Jean-Paul Sartre?"

"Socrates, but at least you're playing the game now." I smiled.

"After years of your quotes, I had to pick up some of it. I even quoted Plato on the playground at school the other day."

"Oh yeah? What quote?"

"Something like 'You can discover more about a person in play than conversation.'"

"Close enough. I'm impressed." For the first time I noticed Lila was dressed up. "What're you up to tonight?"

"Going out with some friends. I'll save you the trouble of spying on me—it's three girls, you know them all, we're not going to any of the clubs you told me to stay away from, and I have to work tomorrow so I won't be drinking much. Happy?"

"Not as happy as I'd be if I could direct your entire life, but it's a start."

My sister kissed me on the cheek, then kissed my mom good night. When she got to the door, she turned and said, "You're being surprisingly reasonable about this."

"You're an adult. I trust you. Just use your head." I wasn't worried, although I couldn't help but touch the phone in my pocket. The tracker Chill had put on her car was still there. I didn't intend to use the tracker. Unless I had to.

I did more than enjoy the quiet evening with my mother. I *appreciated* it. She was interested in what I was working on and what the next steps in my career were going to be. It wasn't until I talked to her about the task force that I realized how much I wanted to stay on it. It was where I was meant to be.

I had one more item to take care of on our human-smuggling case. It was something I was looking forward to. Nothing I would bother my mom with, but the idea of it made me smile.

CHAPTER 106

IT WAS EIGHT fifteen in the evening, and I had timed our arrival perfectly. Steph and I were dressed in professional clothes, nothing flashy. This ballroom at the Fontainebleau in Miami Beach held two hundred of the area's wealthiest and best-connected residents. Rich people liked to show off their clothes and be seen at charity and award events like this one. Even though everyone knew it was all bullshit.

I slipped in the rear door with Steph Hall. A Miami Beach lieutenant, wearing his dress uniform, did a double take when he saw me. He got up from his table in the back and came over.

The tall lieutenant, who was a little older than me, said in a low voice, "Anti, what brings you here to civilization?"

"Business. What's going on with you, Sauce?"

"Usual." He looked up at the stage, where Roman Rostoff was behind a podium delivering his prepared comments in reasonably good English at a slow clip. "Some people don't look too closely at people's backgrounds when they give out awards."

I turned and said, "Steph Hall, this is Lieutenant William Stein. Sauce, this is my partner at the FBI task force."

The lieutenant said, "The task force that brought Miami-style violence to South Beach last week?"

I took a little bow and said, "The same."

We all chuckled.

Steph said, "How'd you get the nickname 'Sauce'?"

The good-looking lieutenant gave a charming chortle and said, "That's a secret you have to learn over time." Then the lieutenant realized my business might have to do with Roman Rostoff. "Anti, are you here to stir up shit?"

I just smiled.

He glanced at the stage again and said, "Anything you can do to that ass-wipe is good for all of us. I'll just pretend I never saw you. I've got three more years before I can pull the plug. I don't want to answer any uncomfortable questions about why I let you roam through here."

"You got it, Sauce."

Steph and I were careful not to be obtrusive as we walked along the side of the cavernous ballroom.

At the front of the room, I stepped behind some partitions. They hid me from the audience, but I could see the entire stage. I reached in my coat pocket and pulled out some papers. That's when a tall young guy with a ponytail, the one who'd run with Billy the Blade, stepped right in front of me. The last time I'd seen him, he'd made veiled threats about my sister, and I'd crushed his testicles in my hand. It looked like he thought he was going to get some revenge.

I stared at the tattoos going up his neck and could have

sworn he had another bud on the end of the tattooed vine that spread onto his cheek.

I said, "I'm sorry, what was your name again?"

He growled, "Tibor."

"Right, sorry. So, asshole, want to get out of my way? I have business with your boss. Official business."

"And it's my business to keep my employer safe," Tibor said.

"'Fortune truly helps those who are of good judgment.'"

"What?" He screwed up his face in a way that made me smile.

"A man named Euripides said that about four hundred years before Christ was born, and yet it applies to you tonight. Use good judgment and step out of the way."

"Or else what?"

"My cold-blooded partner will deal with you." I liked the look on his face as Steph came up and put the stun gun on his bare neck.

I said, "Move, and she zaps you with thirty thousand volts." I stood and enjoyed his silence. I needed to enjoy more things in life. This was a good start.

I stepped around him as Steph ordered him to lie on the ground. She took the gun from his holster.

I strutted right across the stage in front of everyone. Roman Rostoff was forced to stop midsentence. He stared at me. I enjoyed the way he looked past me to see how I'd gotten by his bodyguard.

I gave him a smile and a wink as I joined him at the podium and patted him on the back like I was proud of him. The people in the audience had no idea what was going on. They just stared at the big guy who couldn't afford a designer suit.

I handed the sheaf of papers to Rostoff.

He looked at me and muttered, "What?"

I made sure to speak clearly so that the microphone would

pick up everything. "This is a federal subpoena for records related to all of your businesses and bank accounts." I stood for a moment while he just held the papers and stared at me. "For a change, there are plenty of witnesses to the service of this subpoena. The subpoena requires you to personally appear at the FBI office with the records requested."

Everyone in the entire room was silent. Including Rostoff.

I leaned into the microphone and said, "That's right. Your Humanitarian of the Year is being investigated for money laundering, human trafficking, and his role in the shootout on Miami Beach last week. Also for about a thousand business violations relating to tax fraud and licensing issues." I let that hang in the silent room for about five seconds, then said, "Enjoy the rest of your evening."

I stepped off the stage and headed toward the exit. Stephanie Hall joined me, allowing Tibor, the bodyguard, to stand up. She dropped his pistol in a garbage can as we walked out the door.

Yeah, I was going to enjoy that one for a very long time.

EPILOGUE

Amsterdam

JANINE, ONE OF Hanna Greete's former assistants, sat at a desk in a small office in Amsterdam. The cramped office in a warehouse wasn't nearly as nice as the apartment they'd worked out of when Hanna was in charge. But Hanna was in jail in the United States now, and Albert was dead.

Janine had made the most of the opportunity. She knew all of Hanna's contacts. She and her sister, Tasi, simply moved to Oostpoort, away from the city center and tourists. Janine had kept the business going, albeit on a much smaller scale. But if she kept expenses down and only had to worry about Tasi and herself, she could make a fine living.

She doubted the police paid much attention to small operations like hers. And that detective with the national police, Marie Meijer, was probably so happy to have caught Hanna that she'd taken a vacation.

Since Janine had passed so much information on to Marie, the police had dropped fraud charges against her after she'd been arrested in Zaadam. Janine's information had led to Hanna's arrest. Now she was taking over Hanna's former life.

Sitting in the small office still made Janine feel like a queen. She answered her ringing phone and heard the voice of Bertram Hellot; he owned an apartment building that housed girls she was planning to move to the U.S. He told her that one of the girls had gone out and not come back. That wasn't supposed to happen.

Janine didn't mince words. "Find that girl by tonight or I'll have Max cut off your balls and I'll wear them as a necklace. Is that understood?"

"Yes. I'm looking for her right now."

Janine smiled at the former gang member's frantic tone. As it turned out, she had learned a lot more from Hanna than she had realized. Now she understood why Hanna had enjoyed bossing people around.

A knock on the thick wooden door startled her. No doubt the landlord looking for rent, as it was the beginning of the month. Sometimes, when she was short on cash, Janine would send her sister to answer the door. Tasi would flirt with the landlord to distract him. Tasi was there in the office, but today Janine had the cash.

She opened the door with a smile. It faded instantly when she saw Marie Meijer standing there with four uniformed police officers.

The detective with the national police nudged Janine back and barged into the office.

Marie said, "Did you really think the information you gave me on Hanna's operation granted you immunity for all crimes? Even after we dropped your cheap check-fraud charge?"

Janine said, "I don't know what you're talking about."

Marie smiled. Her drooping eyelid lifted up ever so slightly.

"That sounds convincing, except that we found your safe house in Diemen. Bertram Hellot has been working with us."

Janine said, "But I helped you!"

Marie said, "To avoid jail. I never agreed to let you ruin more lives by continuing to traffic in people."

Janine thought about that, then said, "What do you want?"

"Do you know Emile Rostoff?"

"No. Not personally."

Marie nodded. "Too bad. That was your only chance." She turned to a uniformed officer and said, "Take them both."

Janine started to cry as she and Tasi were handcuffed and led out of the office.

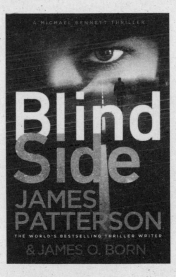

CHAPTER 1

I DID EVERYTHING I could to distract Lucille Evans from noticing the bloody footprint. A responding patrol officer had tracked the blood into the hallway. One look at the scene inside and the veteran needed to run into the street. I didn't blame him one bit.

The forensics people were in the small, two-bedroom apartment on the third floor of this building on 146th Street near Willis Avenue in the Bronx. The scene was so horrendous that the local detectives had called me to help even though it wasn't technically considered part of Manhattan North Homicide's usual territory. Two of the local detectives had lost it. It happens. It's happened to me over the years. I lost it once at the scene of a murdered girl. Her stepfather had bashed her head in for crying because she was hungry. She reminded me of my own Shawna, staring up through blood splatters. When I heard her stepfather in the other room, talking with detectives, I snapped. It almost felt like another being possessed me. I burst into the room, ready to kill. Only the fact that my partner at the time, Gail Nodding, was as tough as nails and shoved me back out the door had kept me from killing the creep.

Now I considered this bloody scene. Who wouldn't be affected by the sight of two bodies with bullet wounds in their heads? Large-caliber wounds. Not the usual .38s or 9mms used in the city. The bodies frozen in time. A mother trying to shield her little girl. I wanted to bolt home and hug my own children. But I had work to do.

I had my hands full with the sixty-five-year-old woman who merely wanted to say good-bye to her daughter and granddaughter.

Mrs. Evans tried to push past me to open the simple wooden door with the number 9 hanging upside down. The threadbare industrial carpet didn't give my feet much traction. My semi-dress Skechers were more for walking comfort than for wrestling.

Mrs. Evans said, "Let me pass, young man. I have to see my babies." She wasn't loud. She wasn't hysterical. She was determined.

So was I.

I said, "Ma'am, I'm not in charge. But I do have kids. I know loss. You don't want what you see inside that apartment to be your final memory of your daughter and granddaughter. Please, I swear to God, you'll get your chance to say good-bye."

She stared me down as hard as any drug dealer ever had. But I was resolute. I'd already seen the horror behind the door. I wasn't about to let this elegant, retired teacher see it, too. Her daughter, still in her nurse's uniform from the Bronx-Lebanon Hospital. The left side of her face missing from a single, devastating gunshot. Lying over her daughter. A nine-year-old with a hole in the side of her head. This time, too, the girl reminded me of my Shawna.

The whole scene had shaken me to the core. Never believe a cop when he or she tells you they've seen it all. Nobody ever sees it all.

Mrs. Evans cracked. Tears started to flow. It'd finally hit her with full force. Two of her greatest treasures had been taken from her. Her watery eyes looked up at me again. She simply asked, "Why?"

She started to weep. I put a tentative arm around her. She fell into me and I hugged her. I remembered how I'd felt when Maeve, my wife, died. That was a slow death from cancer. It still tore me to pieces.

This poor woman had been blindsided.

I eased her onto one of the cheap plastic chairs a detective had set up in the apartment's hallway. A little African American girl peeked out of one of the doorways down the hall. The light at the end of the hall near the stairs flickered.

Why would someone shoot a nurse and her little girl? Why did someone like Mrs. Evans have to suffer through this? How would I hold it all together?

I had to. It was my job.

CHAPTER 2

THE UNIFORMED CAPTAIN from the Fortieth Precinct erupted into the hallway from the stairs. I knew the tall captain from my days on patrol. He yelled down the hall to the NYPD officers working diligently, "Let's move this along, shall we, people?" Then he saw me.

I had just gotten Mrs. Evans seated. A young patrol officer stepped over and offered her a cup of cold water. She was starting to get that glazed look family members have after a murder.

The captain marched toward me and said, "This ain't Manhattan North. What are you doing here? Trying to steal a stat?"

Sometimes cops embarrass me. Yeah, it's a job, but it involves people. People with feelings. I kept it professional and said, "Just helping out, Captain Ramirez."

The captain was almost as tall as me. He wore his dark hair slicked tightly against his scalp. There were definite cliques inside the NYPD. Divisions happen in all large organizations. The simple old Irish-versus-Italian rivalry had given way to a much more complicated system. Ramirez identified strongly with the Hispanic clique and didn't give a crap if I was Irish, Italian, or black. I wasn't Hispanic so he didn't cut me any slack.

The captain barked, "Then help clear this scene. We got shit breaking all over the Bronx. There's a goddamn protest about the price of housing. In New York. You think they'd realize housing prices are going to be crazy."

I motioned toward Mrs. Evans, hoping this moron would get the hint. It was a foolish hope.

The captain said, "How much longer will this take?"

I eased us away from Mrs. Evans. When I leaned in close to the captain, I said, "This lady's daughter and granddaughter are in that apartment. It'll take as long as it takes. We gotta grab the asshole who did this. Don't you agree?" I'd spoken very slowly so nothing I said could be misunderstood.

The old-school captain locked me in his gaze. It was nothing compared to Mrs. Evans's stare down. Then he said, "Okay, hotshot. I'll get the manpower from somewhere else."

When I stepped back to Mrs. Evans, she said, "Oh, dear Lord. I have to tell my sons."

I decided to walk her the two blocks to where they lived. I needed the break.

CHAPTER 3

IN A SIMILAR apartment to that of their sister and niece, I helped Mrs. Evans break the news to her two adult sons, who both worked for the city and seemed like sharp young men. They took the news like anyone would. They were shocked.

The larger of the men, a good six feet five inches and close to three hundred pounds, started to wail and put his head on his mother's shoulder. She stroked his neck and spoke to him like she would to a toddler, in a soft, soothing voice. A mom's power never really diminishes, no matter how big a child grows.

I told them the lead detective would be down to talk to them at some point. They'd have questions about why someone might do this.

The older of the two brothers, a bus mechanic, said, "This is not a bad neighborhood. Not *too* bad. Who would do something like this?" He had the distant stare of a man in over his head.

That's the way it should be. No one should be used to tragedy like this. Not even a cop.

I gave them a card in case they needed anything. I felt confident Mrs. Evans would be most comfortable if she stayed here with them tonight.

The clear, cloudless skies and afternoon sun did little to lift my spirits. I barely noticed passing cars or the other normal rhythms of the city. I walked with a measured pace, trying to give myself a little time before I went back to the crime scene. All I could see in my head was a mother lying on top of her little girl. The left side of her face a massive hole leaking blood. The apartment a shambles.

No witnesses. No suspects. No hope.

I looked up at the sky and spoke to Maeve. I did that quite a bit. This time I said, "I hate that you saw stuff like this, too. A nurse's job is harder than a cop's in some respects. I miss you, Maeve."

Sometimes I swear I can hear a faint answer. It's easy and convenient to claim it was the wind or a distant radio. But it happens occasionally. Today I thought I heard, "Love you." And no one can tell me I didn't hear it.

I swung into a bodega and grabbed an ice-cold grape Gatorade. I'd briefly considered buying a beer, but they still needed me at the apartment. The radio behind the counter was broadcasting a news brief about the murders. That would attract more curious onlookers. The day was not getting any better.

The clerk looked at me and said, "Tough day?"

"Does it show?"

"Gatorade is on me."

I thanked him, more for a quick jolt of humanity. Then

9

dropped two dollars on the scarred and nicked counter before I headed back out.

I was still a block away from the apartment building and the growing crowd of onlookers. I had parked my city-issued Impala over here in case I needed to get away quickly. Experience has taught me that if you park too close to a scene, you can get boxed in.

Suddenly I had an uncontrollable urge to speak to Mary Catherine and the kids. As many of them as I could get on the phone. They were what kept me sane. If I ever needed a connection to my real life, it was right now.

Leaning against my car, I took a swig of the Gatorade and set it on the roof. I fumbled with my phone.

While I considered whether I should call Mary Catherine's cell or the home phone, someone said, "Let's make this quick."

I looked up into the barrel of a pistol.

CHAPTER 4

THE YOUNG BLACK man's hand trembled ever so slightly. There was no doubt the barrel was still pointed at my face. But he was new to this kind of stuff. That made him more dangerous. He had no idea what could happen.

He repeated, "Let's make this quick."

I didn't hesitate. I immediately reached into my sport coat for my personal wallet. My police ID was in my back pocket. At the moment, he thought I was just a citizen out for a stroll. I'd be happy to let him keep thinking that.

I can't count the number of times I've heard the wife of a murdered robbery victim say, "A lousy wallet wasn't worth his life." No way I was going to put Mary Catherine in that position.

I held up my wallet to show it to him and said, "Here, it's yours." I'd seen enough bloodshed today. I just wanted him to walk away. A few bucks and some credit cards aren't worth anyone's life. I figured this was over. There was no one on the street near us. He had no reason to hang around. Everyone could have another day on Earth.

Then I heard a second voice from across the narrow street. A tall, skinny man came out of an alley between an empty storefront and a ninety-nine-cent store. He wore a crazy heavy jacket with an odd, fur-trimmed collar. The man had an angry tinge to his voice when he said, "What chu doin', RJ?" He glanced at me. "You finally joinin' up? Good man."

The second man was about thirty. His pupils were black circles covering most of his eyes. But drugs were the least of his issues. His head swung in wide arcs as he glanced in every direction. His left hand had a constant, jittery movement. His tongue played with the gold grill across his front teeth. He was a walking advertisement for one of the antipsychotic pharmaceuticals advertised on news channels and ESPN.

The man said, "Lookee here, dressy." He stayed in the street, on the driver's side of the car. He stared straight at me and said, "You going out, Pops? Nice jacket. Not too hot, nice dark blue. Too bad you're too wide. Jacket would never fit me."

Why did he have to come and stir shit up?

The younger man, RJ, who still held me at gunpoint, turned to his friend and said, "I got his wallet. Let's go."

The man in the fur-trimmed coat said, "Somethin's not right about him. He's taller than us. That's enough to shoot his ass right there."

RJ said, "I got money, cards. It's cool."

"It ain't cool, RJ. It's a lot of things, but it ain't cool. He don't care nothin' about us. And he don't *mean* nothin' *to* us. Go ahead, show him how little he means to us."

RJ was torn. I could see it in his face. He wanted to leave. But this new guy, he wanted to see something happen. He wanted some excitement on a weekday afternoon.

The new man stepped to the front of the car and let his coat fall open. I could see the Colt stuck in his waistband. I thought about the head wounds at the crime scene I was just at. It was a big caliber. Probably a .45. That was not a common gun in the Bronx. I wanted to fix his face in my brain.

The man snapped, "What chu starin' at?"

I didn't answer. I did a quick scan to see if I could find any blood spatter on the cuffs or collar of the heavy coat he was wearing.

But that was the least of my worries at the moment. Now the man leaned in close to RJ and said, "Shoot this cracker in the face. You feel me, RJ?"

The younger man kept his eyes on me. He raised the gun slightly so he could sight more accurately. He mumbled, "Okay, Tight, okay. Give me a second."

I felt the shift in the young man. He was scared of his friend. I would be, too. The man was giving him almost no choice but to pull the trigger. At that point, I knew if RJ didn't shoot, I'd be facing that .45.

The man told RJ, "You own his ass. Now you can take everything from him. No feeling like it in the world." Then the man looked at the Chevy Impala. He craned his head to stare into the interior.

"Hold on, RJ. I think this dude's a cop. He seen us both. You gotta do it now."

Now the crazy guy was using logic. And he wasn't wrong. I'd have been willing to forget about RJ, but I needed to check out his friend "Tight" regarding the homicide a block away.

That wasn't going to happen, though. I swallowed and had a quick thought of each of my children. When you have ten kids, you can't spend a lot of time on each one as your life flashes before your eyes.

RJ was ready. He used his left hand to steady the gun. He started to squeeze the trigger.

CHAPTER 5

AT A MOMENT like that, facing a gun, there's no telling what will go through your head. I was hoping for a miracle. And I said a quick prayer. It wasn't specific or particularly elegant. Just a *Please help me, God*. At least I think that's what I prayed.

Then it happened. A car coming from a side street onto this main road squealed its tires. It wasn't long or really loud. But it was enough. Just enough.

Both men looked over their shoulders to see what had caused the noise. Just a basic reaction, like an instinct. It was a gray Dodge racing away from us.

I took my chance. A movement I had done in training more than a thousand times. I shifted slightly. Reached back quickly with my right hand. Flipped my coat out of the way. Took a firm grip on my Glock semiautomatic pistol. Pressed the release on my holster and slid the pistol out. It felt natural because of all the practice. The idea that a human would be in my sights didn't really come into the equation.

Just as my barrel came to rest, pointing at the robber's chest, I shouted, "Police. Don't move."

I aimed at RJ because he had his pistol out, although I thought the other man was going to be the real problem. But RJ steadied his hands and brought the barrel of his pistol back toward my face. I squeezed the trigger of my own pistol. Once. Twice. I knew I'd hit him center mass.

The young man's arms lowered and the pistol dropped from his hand. It made a loud clank on the hood of my car, then slid down to the asphalt. RJ followed a similar path, staring at me the whole time as he tumbled to the ground.

My natural inclination was to follow the body to the ground with my pistol. I don't know why. It's not like cops are in so many shootings that we get used to them. Each one is traumatic and devastating in its own way.

As soon as RJ hit the asphalt, I realized he posed no more threat. Now I had to deal with Tight, who was already rushing backward, away from me. He fumbled for the pistol in his belt line, and I fired once. Then he spun and sprinted away. I didn't know if I'd hit him or if he'd dropped the pistol. The only thing I could think about was the young man bleeding on the street right in front of me.

I let the crazy man in the fur-trimmed jacket run away.

I dropped to one knee and immediately checked the pulse on the young man I'd been forced to shoot. Blood was already pumping from his chest and filling the indentation at the bottom of his throat. I opened his ratty coat all the way and ripped his Jets T-shirt right down the middle, then used part of the T-shirt to help stop the bleeding.

I quickly reached into my pocket and fumbled for my phone. I hit 911. As soon as the operator came on I almost shouted, "This is Detective Michael Bennett. I am on Third Avenue near 146th Street. I need immediate assistance. I have shots fired, a man down, and require an ambulance ASAP."

I ignored her other questions and went back to working on young RJ. I held the folded T-shirt rag directly on the bullet hole, hoping to stem the bleeding. Blood soaked the cuff of my shirt and speckled my chest. People started coming out of the bodega and some of the apartment buildings.

A young black woman kneeled down to help me. She said, "I'm in nursing school. Let me keep pressure on the wound." She wasn't panicked and kept a very calm tone.

That helped me focus. I kept saying to the young man, "Hang in there, RJ. Help is on the way." About a minute later, I heard the first in a storm of sirens heading our way.

It wasn't until paramedics stepped in and took over the first aid that it really hit me what had happened. I could have been killed. I *should* have been killed. And I had been forced to use my duty weapon. It was the last thing I'd wanted to do. It's the last thing *any* cop wants to do. But I didn't regret it. I couldn't. Not when I hugged my kids tonight.

And now all I could do was stare helplessly as paramedics did everything they could to save this young man's life.

CHAPTER 6

AS MORE PARAMEDICS and squad cars arrived, I simply walked down the street a short distance and plopped onto the curb. I had nothing left. I wasn't even ready to call Mary Catherine. I just stared straight ahead into the empty street. I noticed everything from the rough asphalt patches over potholes to the random Three Musketeers wrapper blowing in the light breeze. It felt as if the city had gone silent.

Even though the paramedics were still busy, I knew RJ was dead. My mind raced, but I couldn't settle on a single thought. I vaguely realized it was some sort of shock settling over me. It's a common occurrence after a police shooting.

It had all happened so fast. Virtually all police shootings do. I'd acted out of instinct. Now I had to let things take their course.

All I knew at the moment was that I couldn't leave the scene. I just wanted to sit here with my thoughts. Silently I prayed, *Dear*

God, have mercy on this young man's soul. I thought about calling my grandfather, Seamus.

Then I heard someone shout, "He did it." It didn't register immediately, then someone else said it. I looked up and over my shoulder to see a small group of people facing me.

A heavyset African American man of about thirty-five pointed at me and shouted, "That cop shot RJ for no reason. He murdered him."

I let him talk. It never did any good to speak up. People had to vent. This neighborhood had fought to shed its reputation from the 1980s. Crime, especially homicides, was down. Cops could only do so much. Neighborhoods and the people in them had to decide to change. And this one had. I could understand some misplaced anger over a shooting.

The vast majority of cops try to do the right thing. That's why they get into the business. A few go overboard. And like anything else, most groups are judged by the actions of a few. It's been like that since the dawn of time.

I recognized that prejudgment was contributing to this crowd's growing fury. They were pissed off. Right now they were pissed off at me. I just took it.

My heart fluttered and my hands shook.

This heavyset guy gathered more followers. He was like a singer energized by the crowd. He turned to face the crowd and yelled, "We're tired of cops treating us like criminals. Now this guy shot RJ for just standing there."

No one was speaking in my defense. Someone had to have seen what happened.

Someone tossed a bottle, which shattered on the sidewalk next to me. A young patrol officer who had been near the paramedics stepped toward the crowd with her hands up like she was trying to calm them down.

An older, lean woman scowled at the officer and said, "Keep your ass over there. This don't concern you."

Another bottle sailed through the air. Then a half eaten McDonald's hamburger smacked me right in the face.

I wiped some gooey cheese from my cheek with my bare hand.

The mob of fifteen or twenty people moved toward me now. I just sat there. Numb. I understood these people's anger. Every interaction with a cop was viewed with suspicion. Some cops' attitudes didn't help, treating everyone like a criminal. Forgetting that most people didn't cause any problems at all.

I cleaned the rest of the hamburger from my face and stood up. I faced the crowd. The young patrol officer and her partner started to move toward me, but I held up my hand to stop them. They would only make things worse.

I mumbled, "Let them vent for a minute. We don't want a riot." I'd been in riots, and they were no fun. This crowd could go either way. There didn't seem to be outside agitators, who could kick demonstrations up a notch to a riot. No one wanted to destroy their own neighborhood.

More garbage flew through the air. A few more steps and the mob would be right on top of me.

CHAPTER 7

I KNEW NOT to say something stupid, like "Let's all just calm down." That had never worked in the history of law enforcement. I couldn't explain that I had done everything I could to avoid shooting RJ. No one wanted to hear that. Not the crowd, not the news media, and certainly not RJ's family.

The crowd was close enough that I could see the heavyset man who was leading them had a cracked front tooth. That was too close for comfort. For the first time it started to sink in that I was in real danger.

Then I heard a voice—a booming, commanding voice. I recognized it immediately. It may not have been God, but it was the best I could hope for right now. It was just a simple "Everyone freeze."

And they did.

My lieutenant, Harry Grissom, stepped out of a black,

unmarked NYPD Suburban. The tall, lean, twenty-six-year veteran of the force looked like an Old West gunfighter, his mustache creeping along the sides of his mouth. He was toying with the NYPD grooming policy, but so far no one had the balls to say anything to him about it.

A gold badge dangled from a chain around his neck. His tan suit had some creases but gave him an air of authority. As if he needed something extra.

He kept marching toward the crowd without any hesitation. As he got closer, he said in a very even voice, "What's the problem here?"

The pudgy leader yelled, "He shot an unarmed man."

Someone in the back of the crowd added, "For no reason."

Other people started to crowd in around Harry to tell him why they were so angry.

And he listened. At least to the people not shouting obscenities. Harry was an old-school pragmatist. He'd been part of the enforcement effort that helped clean up New York City. He didn't need to knock heads. He could talk.

He engaged the heavyset guy. "Who is an actual eyewitness?"

No one answered.

Harry kept a calm tone. "What do you say I give you my card and we talk in a couple of days? That way you can see what we find out. The shooting will be investigated thoroughly. Just give it forty-eight hours. Is that too much to ask?"

The heavyset man had a hard time ignoring such a reasonable request. He tentatively accepted Harry's card.

The crowd wasn't nearly as discerning. That's how it always is. In sports and politics and real life. A rowdy crowd drives the conversation and clouds the issues.

Harry stood firm and gave them a look that had withered many detectives under his command. More police cars arrived, along with a crime-scene van.

The crowd could see things were happening, and they started to lose their initiative.

Harry turned to me without any more thought of the crowd behind him. It was that kind of confidence that had inspired countless cops and defused dozens of confrontations.

He said in a low tone, "You doing all right, Mike?"

"I'm not physically hurt if that's what you mean."

He led me toward his Suburban and simply said, "That'll do for now." It was a complex and touchy subject; he wouldn't be part of the investigative team and, by policy, couldn't ask me any probing questions.

It didn't matter. When I slid into his SUV, I realized he wasn't acting as Harry Grissom, lieutenant with the NYPD. He was just being my friend.

That's what I needed right now.

CHAPTER 8

HARRY DROPPED ME off at my apartment on West End Avenue a little after six. I had done all the procedural shit that overwhelms a cop after a shooting. I talked to a union rep, a Police Benevolent Association attorney, and a psychologist. Finally, I told them I had a tremendous headache and needed to lie down. Really all I needed was my family.

As I walked down the hallway to my apartment, my neighbor, Mr. Underhill, spoke to me for the first time in all the years we'd lived there.

He said, "You doing okay?"

I just shrugged and said, "Yeah, you?"

The older, corpulent man nodded and smiled. Then he disappeared back inside. It was the only conversation I had ever had with the man. It was unnerving.

People wondered how an NYPD detective could afford

such a great apartment on the Upper West Side. If they were bold enough to ask, I usually just said, "Bribes," and left it at that. In reality, the apartment had been left to my late wife, Maeve. She had cared for an elderly man here for years. In that time, her personality and warmth had brought the man from a dour, solitary existence to happiness. He felt such joy being around her that when he passed away he left her the apartment and a trust to help pay the taxes. He had wanted Maeve and her growing family to enjoy it. The apartment was a constant reminder of what a ray of sunshine Maeve had been to everyone she met.

Occasionally, when I was in a weird mood, the apartment could make me sad. The idea that my wonderful wife had meant so much to someone that he had changed our entire family's life was amazing. The fact that she had only gotten to live here a short while was tough to swallow.

The smell of pot roast hit me as soon as I opened the front door. So did two kids. Shawna, my second youngest daughter, and Trent, my youngest son, barreled into me like out-of-control race cars. I didn't mind one bit.

When I dropped to my knees, Shawna gave me a big hug and kissed me on the cheek. "I'm so glad you're home safe, Dad."

Trent chimed in, "Me too."

So much for my hope that I could ease everyone into what had happened to me. And now I understood Mr. Underhill's gross show of emotion. I had known word would leak out. Obviously I'd spoken to Mary Catherine about it. I'd told her not to make a fuss. Have something serious happen to you, then try to tell an Irish woman not to make a fuss. It would be easier to keep the sun in the sky an extra two hours.

Before I could even navigate into the kitchen, Mary Catherine found me and gave me a huge kiss.

"I appreciate the attention, but I'm fine."

Mary Catherine said, "And I thank God for it. But your name has already been on the news. The guy who has the cable access show, Reverend Caldwell, is already in the Bronx saying that you're a murderer walking free."

"I thought you'd learned by now that most people don't have any clue about the facts when they're spouting garbage like that." I half expected Mary Catherine to ask me if it was a good shooting. The only thing I had heard the news got right was that there were two men and a police officer involved.

Shootings were ratings monsters, so every news team covered them from start to finish. They always had the same elements: sobbing family members telling the world that their dead relative had been sweet and would have never hurt a fly. And in New York, no shooting was ever complete without the commentary of the Reverend Franklin Caldwell. The "people's voice."

To distract myself, I wandered back to the corner of the living room where my teenager Eddie had his face in a computer monitor. I needed something normal like this. Foolishly I said, "Need a hand with anything, Eddie?"

He didn't take his eyes off the screen. Another common occurrence. He said, "Thanks, Dad. I think I've got this. I'm writing an algorithm to find documents where references to *The Lord of the Rings* are made. Google just doesn't cut it for me anymore. Do you have any ideas where I should search?"

All I could do at this point was lean down and kiss the teenager on the top of his head. In his case, I'd never be the *smart dad*. The best I could be was a loving dad.

Even though all ten of my kids are adopted, I'm still at a loss to understand where they each got their unique skills. Eddie is a standout, with his phenomenal computer knowledge.

A few minutes later, my grandfather, Seamus, arrived. He was wearing his usual clerical collar, which identified him as a Catholic priest. Even though he'd joined the priesthood very late in life, he loved nothing more than walking around in his tab-collared clergy shirt.

He was the one man who knew not to coddle me. He was also the reason I didn't like being coddled. He said, "Hello, my boy. Will you share a glass of wine with me? Think of it as a way to laugh in the face of death. You can drink and none of it is going to leak out through holes in your stomach or chest."

Then he shocked me by giving me a hug. "Thank God the NYPD trained you well."

We all filed into the dining room. I heard the news come on the TV where Ricky had been watching a cooking show. All I heard was the first line: "The Reverend Franklin Caldwell says he will personally investigate the claims that NYPD detective Michael Bennett shot an unarmed man in cold blood today."

I cringed at the fact the kids had to hear something like that. My grandfather stomped to the TV and shut it off as he threw a quick scowl at Ricky for not turning it off after the show.

We all took our seats at the long table. One chair, as always, was left open for my son Brian. The other nine children, Mary Catherine, my grandfather, and I clasped hands for grace.

As always, Seamus said it. This time it was surprisingly short. "Dear Heavenly Father, all we can say today is thank you."

Silently I added, *Please have mercy on Ronald Timmons Junior's soul.*

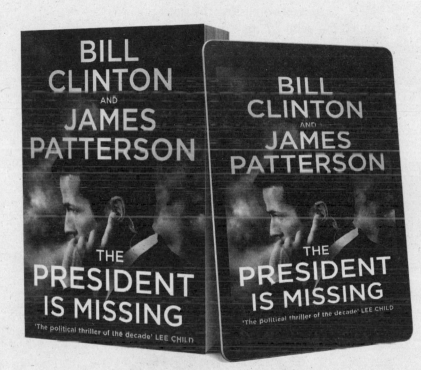

CRISS CROSS

James Patterson

Mere hours after witnessing the execution of a killer he helped put behind bars, Alex Cross is called to the scene of a copycat murder. A note signed 'M' rests on the corpse: 'You messed up big time, Dr. Cross.'

Was an innocent man just put to death? As the executed convict's family launch a vicious campaign against Cross, his abilities as a detective are called into question.

More murders follow, all marked with distressingly familiar details that conjure up decades-old cases and Cross family secrets. Details that make it clear the killer's main target is Alex Cross.

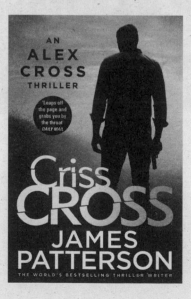

A HARRIET BLUE THRILLER

HUSH HUSH

James Patterson
& Candice Fox

Harriet Blue used to be a detective. Now she's inmate 3329.
Prison is a dangerous place for a former cop – as Harriet
Blue is learning on a daily basis. So, following a fight for
her life and a prison-wide lockdown, the last person she
wants to see is Deputy Police Commissioner Joe Woods.
The man who put her inside.

But Woods is not there to gloat. His daughter Tonya and
her two-year-old have gone missing. He's ready to offer
Harriet a deal: find his family to buy her freedom . . .

THE INN

James Patterson
& Candice Fox

The Inn at Gloucester stands alone on the rocky New England shoreline. Its seclusion suits former Boston police detective Bill Robinson, novice owner and innkeeper. Yet all too soon Robinson discovers that leaving the city is no escape from dangers he left behind. A new crew of deadly criminals move into the small town, bringing drugs and violence to the front door of the inn.

Robinson's sense of duty compels him to fight off the threat to his town. But he can't do it alone. Before time runs out, the residents of the inn will face a choice. Stand together? Or die alone.

UNSOLVED

James Patterson
& David Ellis

FBI analyst Emmy Dockery's unique ability to uncover the patterns that others miss has brought her an impressive string of arrests. But a new case – unfolding across the country – has left her looking for something which may not exist.

The victims all appear to have died by accident, and seemingly have nothing in common. But this many deaths can't be a coincidence. Can they?

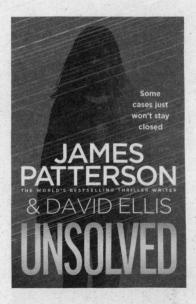

Also by James Patterson

ALEX CROSS NOVELS

Along Came a Spider • Kiss the Girls • Jack and Jill • Cat and Mouse • Pop Goes the Weasel • Roses are Red • Violets are Blue • Four Blind Mice • The Big Bad Wolf • London Bridges • Mary, Mary • Cross • Double Cross • Cross Country • Alex Cross's Trial (*with Richard DiLallo*) • I, Alex Cross • Cross Fire • Kill Alex Cross • Merry Christmas, Alex Cross • Alex Cross, Run • Cross My Heart • Hope to Die • Cross Justice • Cross the Line • The People vs. Alex Cross • Target: Alex Cross • Criss Cross

THE WOMEN'S MURDER CLUB SERIES

1st to Die • 2nd Chance (*with Andrew Gross*) • 3rd Degree (*with Andrew Gross*) • 4th of July (*with Maxine Paetro*) • The 5th Horseman (*with Maxine Paetro*) • The 6th Target (*with Maxine Paetro*) • 7th Heaven (*with Maxine Paetro*) • 8th Confession (*with Maxine Paetro*) • 9th Judgement (*with Maxine Paetro*) • 10th Anniversary (*with Maxine Paetro*) • 11th Hour (*with Maxine Paetro*) • 12th of Never (*with Maxine Paetro*) • Unlucky 13 (*with Maxine Paetro*) • 14th Deadly Sin (*with Maxine Paetro*) • 15th Affair (*with Maxine Paetro*) • 16th Seduction (*with Maxine Paetro*) • 17th Suspect (*with Maxine Paetro*) • 18th Abduction (*with Maxine Paetro*) • 19th Christmas (*with Maxine Paetro*) • 20th Victim (*with Maxine Paetro*)

DETECTIVE MICHAEL BENNETT SERIES

Step on a Crack (*with Michael Ledwidge*) • Run for Your Life (*with Michael Ledwidge*) • Worst Case (*with Michael Ledwidge*) • Tick Tock (*with Michael Ledwidge*) • I, Michael Bennett (*with Michael Ledwidge*) • Gone (*with Michael Ledwidge*) • Burn (*with Michael Ledwidge*) • Alert (*with Michael Ledwidge*) • Bullseye (*with Michael Ledwidge*) • Haunted (*with James O. Born*) • Ambush (*with James O. Born*) • Blindside (*with James O. Born*)

The
Laughing Hangman

An Elizabethan Mystery

Edward Marston

Allison & Busby Limited
12 Fitzroy Mews
London W1T 6DW
www.allisonandbusby.com

First published in 1996.
This paperback edition published by Allison & Busby in 2013.

A CIP catalogue record for this book is available from
the British Library.

10 9 8 7 6 5 4 3 2 1

ISBN 978-0-7490-1595-4

Typeset in 10.5/15.5 pt Sabon by
Allison & Busby Ltd.

The paper used for this Allison & Busby publication
has been produced from trees that have been legally sourced
from well-managed and credibly certified forests.

Printed and bound by
CPI Group (UK) Ltd, Croydon, CR0 4YY

To
VISCOUNT KRICHEVSKY
Laird of Dobbs Ferry
Lone survivor of the Stuart dynasty

Plays will never be suppressed, while her Majesty's unfledged minions flaunt it in silks and satins . . . Even in her Majesty's chapel do these pretty upstart youths profane the Lord's day by the lascivious writhing of their tender limbs and gorgeous decking of their apparel, in feigning bawdy fables gathered from the idolatrous heathen poets.

– Anonymous, *The Children of the Chapel Stripped and Whipped* (1569)

Chapter One

He missed her. Nicholas Bracewell felt a pang of regret so sharp and so unexpected that it made him catch his breath. He looked down involuntarily to see if the point of a knife had pricked his chest and drawn blood. Nicholas had not even been thinking about Anne Hendrik, still less talking about her, yet she was suddenly filling his mind, standing before his eyes and stroking his cheek with wistful fingers. It was at once reassuring and tantalising.

For several minutes, Nicholas was so enveloped by a flurry of wonderful memories that he paid no heed to the argument that was raging in front of him. Anne Hendrik whispered softly in his ear and kept out the violent discord. The book holder did not even hear the fist that banged the table like the blast of a cannon.

'I'll not be thwarted!' roared Lawrence Firethorn.

'Then leave off this madness!' argued Barnaby Gill.

'I put the good of the company first and foremost.'

'You have never done so before, Lawrence.'

'I have *always* done so! It is you who believe that Westfield's Men exists for the greater glory of one paltry individual.'

'And who might that be?'

'Look in any mirror, Barnaby. He will leer back at you.'

'That is a gross slander!'

'I speak but the truth.'

'Calumny!' said Gill, rising to his feet and inflating his chest to its full extent. 'But for me, there would *be* no company. I have oftentimes saved it from extinction and I am trying to do so again.'

'You are obstructing the path to triumph.'

'Yes, Lawrence. Triumph for our rivals. If we follow your lunatic advice, we hand the advantage to them.'

'My plan puts Westfield's Men in the seat of power.'

'It is a cucking-stool and we shall be drowned by ridicule if we place our buttocks anywhere near it.'

Firethorn gave a mock bow. 'I defer to your superior knowledge on the subject of buttocks.'

Barnaby Gill turned purple and slapped his thigh with a petulant palm. Turning on his heel, he tried to make a dramatic exit, but Edmund Hoode jumped up to restrain him.

'Hold, Barnaby. This is no way to settle a quarrel.'

'I'll not stay to be insulted.'

'Then scurry off,' said Firethorn, 'for the very sight of you calls up a hundred insults. We'll make the decision without you and inform you in due course.'

Gill stamped a foot. 'I demand to be part of that decision.'

'Take your seat once more and you will be,' soothed Hoode. 'Your voice is needed at this table, Barnaby, and you shall be heard. Is that not so, Nick?'

A nudge brought Nicholas out of his reverie and he adjusted quickly to the familiar scene. Lawrence Firethorn and Barnaby Gill were at each other's throats again. Two men who could combine brilliantly to lift the performance of any play were sworn enemies the moment that they quit the stage. Their mutual antagonism went deeper than mere professional jealousy. Firethorn, the company's actor-manager, felt that his remarkable talents were not properly acknowledged by his colleague; Gill, the resident clown with Westfield's Men, saw himself as the true leader of the troupe and resented any reminder that he occupied second place behind Firethorn.

Nicholas Bracewell helped to calm the quivering Gill and the latter eventually agreed to resume his seat. The four men were in the parlour of Firethorn's house in Old Street. Everyone in Shoreditch was aware of the fact because it intruded stridently on their eardrums and they were not sure if they found Firethorn's deep bellow or Gill's high-pitched wail the more tiresome. Regular acrimony in the parlour had one domestic compensation. It dusted the room so thoroughly that the servant did not need to brush the cobwebs from the beams or sweep the beetles out of corners. Every creature that could walk, crawl or fly vacated the premises at once. Even the mice in the thatch fled to a quieter refuge.

11

'I thought it might be a moment for more refreshment.'

Margery Firethorn came sailing into the room with a wooden tray in her hands and a benign smile on her handsome face. Her entry was perfectly timed to break the tension and allow the combatants to cool off. As she set a plate of warm cakes and a fresh pitcher of wine in front of them, she caught Nicholas's eye and gave him an affectionate wink. He replied with a quiet grin of thanks. Not for the first time, a woman who could rant and rail as loud as her husband on occasion had imposed a welcome stillness with a show of gentle hospitality.

While Gill reached for the wine, Firethorn grabbed a cake to pop into his mouth. He munched it happily and the crumbs found a temporary lodging in his black beard.

'Thank you, my dove,' he cooed.

'We are most grateful,' added Edmund Hoode, replenishing his own cup and taking a deep sip. 'Nectar!'

'Do you have need of anything else?' she said.

'No,' grunted Gill.

'We will call if we do, my angel,' said her husband, blowing her a fond kiss.

'I'll stay within earshot, Lawrence.'

Hoode nodded ruefully. 'All of London does that!'

Margery let out a rich cackle and went back into the kitchen. Her intervention had taken the sting out of the discussion. Anger subsided and reason slowly returned. Firethorn was soon ready to draw the others into the debate.

'What is your opinion, Nick?' he asked.

'It matters not,' said Gill, testily. 'This is a question to be

12

decided by we three sharers, not by one of the hired men. Nicholas is a competent book holder, I grant you, but he does not rank with us.'

'No,' said Hoode, coming to the defence. 'He ranks far higher. His wisdom and loyalty have rescued us from damnation more times than I can count. Lawrence seeks his counsel and so do I. Speak up, Nick.'

'Yours is the more important voice here, Edmund.'

'Mine?'

'Yes,' observed Nicholas. 'This touches you more directly than any of us. The argument thus far has simply been about a new play.'

'A masterpiece!' affirmed Firethorn.

'A monstrosity!' countered Gill.

'It is only right that players should dispute the merits of a drama,' continued Nicholas tactfully, 'but you may be more concerned with the character of the dramatist.'

Edmund Hoode winced slightly. He had been doing his best to separate the play from the playwright because the very name of Jonas Applegarth could set his teeth on edge. It was not a case of naked envy. Hood admired the other's work immensely and was the first to admit that Applegarth was the superior poet. In terms of literary talent, the latter could outshine anyone in London, but there were other aspects of Jonas Applegarth that were far less appealing. Edmund Hoode made an effort to draw a veil over them.

'The Misfortunes of Marriage is a fine play,' he said with unfeigned enthusiasm. 'It is comedy with a satirical edge and far exceeds anything that my wilting pen could

13

produce. The Queen's Head will not have seen a more riotous afternoon than Applegarth's play will offer.' He swallowed hard. 'I believe that we should put personal considerations aside and stage the play. There is pure genius in *The Misfortunes of Marriage*.'

'I love the piece,' said Firethorn.

'I hate it,' said Gill, 'yet I applaud the title. The misfortunes of marriage are far too many and varied to attract me into the connubial state.'

Margery Firethorn snorted with derision in the kitchen. Her husband chuckled and Nicholas traded an amused glance with him. Edmund Hoode tried hard to convince himself that it was in his own best interests to accept the new play for performance by Westfield's Men.

'Jonas Applegarth has his vices, I know,' he said with masterly understatement, 'but they are outweighed by his virtues. We must always embrace rare talent where we find it. For my own part, I will be happy to work alongside Master Applegarth. I look to learn much from him.'

Firethorn beamed. 'Nobly spoken, Edmund!'

'Indeed,' said Gill, 'but I would urge a little less nobility and a little more caution on your behalf. You are our poet, Edmund, and your art has served us well. Do you want to be eclipsed by this freak of nature? Do you wish to have your livelihood squashed flat beneath the hideous bulk of Jonas Applegarth?'

Hoode shifted uneasily on his chair. 'I must recognise a good play when I see one.'

'That is more than Applegarth does,' retorted Gill. 'He

pours scorn over everything you have written.'

'Only in his cups,' said Firethorn airily. 'What poet does not abuse his fellows when too much drink is taken?'

'Edmund Hoode does not,' noted Nicholas.

'He is far too trusting,' said Gill. 'Applegarth will tread all over him and unsettle the entire company.'

'That will not be tolerated!' said Firethorn firmly. 'You have my word on that. He works here on our terms or not at all. Nick will make him understand that.' He slipped another cake into his mouth and looked around contentedly. 'Well, Edmund and I agree that *The Misfortunes of Marriage* is a worthy addition to our repertoire.'

'I refuse to countenance the idea,' said Gill.

'Our two votes tip the scales against your one.'

'We have not heard Nick's opinion yet,' said Hoode.

'Nor need we,' muttered Gill.

'Unless it chimes with your own, Barnaby,' teased Firethorn. 'You'd elevate Nick Bracewell to sharer on the spot for that.' He turned to the book holder. 'Well? Cast your vote, Nick. Speak freely among friends.'

Hoode leant forward. 'How do you like *The Misfortunes of Marriage*?'

Nicholas sat up with a start, realising that it was the title and matter of the play which had conjured up Anne Hendrik's memory. When he had finally come to see how dearly he loved her, he proposed marriage on the confident assumption that she would accept his hand. Misfortune had struck. Anne Hendrik refused him and his emotional life had been adrift ever since.

'How do you like it?' pressed Firethorn. 'Tell us!'

'I like it well,' said Nicholas, shaking his head to evict its female ghost. 'The play will offer Westfield's Men a challenge but I am certain that we can rise to it. My only reservations concern the author.'

Firethorn flicked a dismissive hand. 'Jonas Applegarth cannot help being so ugly and ill-favoured.'

'I speak not of his appearance,' said Nicholas. 'It is his behaviour that troubles me. Quarrels, fights, drunkenness. Some companies refuse to let him near them.'

'So should we!' hissed Gill.

'Strict conditions need to be laid down at the outset. That is my advice. If he joins Westfield's Men, let Master Applegarth know that he must abide by our rules. We want no upheaval in the company.' Nicholas gave a shrug. 'In short, present the play for its sheer delight but keep a tight rein on the playwright.'

Barnaby Gill blustered but all to no avail. The die had been cast. *The Misfortunes of Marriage* would receive its first performance the following week. It would be left to Nicholas Bracewell to break the news to Jonas Applegarth and to make him aware of his contractual obligations. Edmund Hoode was sad and pensive. Honesty compelled him to praise the play but he sensed that he would suffer humiliation as a result. When Gill stalked out, therefore, Hoode also took his leave. Both men had grave misgivings, albeit of different kinds.

Lawrence Firethorn watched them through the window before turning to clap the book holder on the shoulder.

'Nick, dear heart!' he predicted. 'We have made one of

16

the most momentous decisions in the history of Westfield's Men. I dote on Edmund and on his plays, but Jonas Applegarth puts his work in the shade. My only complaint is that *The Misfortunes of Marriage* will spring to life in the mean surroundings of the inn yard at the Queen's Head under the gaze of that death's-head of a landlord. It calls for a truer playhouse. It deserves to be staged at The Curtain or at The Theatre.'

'The Rose would be a fitter place,' said Nicholas.

As the words came out of his mouth, Anne Hendrik stepped back into his thoughts. The Rose was a recently built theatre in Bankside. When the book holder lodged with Anne, sharing her life and basking in her love, he had been within easy walking distance of the playhouse. He would always associate The Rose with the happier times he spent on the south bank of the Thames.

Firethorn saw the faraway look on his friend's face. He knew the book holder well enough to guess at its meaning.

'Still brooding on her, Nick?'

'I must away. There is much work to do.'

'Go to her, man. Plead your case.'

'That is all past,' said Nicholas briskly. 'Pray excuse me. I must seek out Jonas Applegarth. He will be eager to know the fate of his play and I must explain clearly the conditions on which we accept it.'

Firethorn caught his arm. 'How long has it been?'

There was a brief pause. The pang of remorse was even sharper this time, the sense of loss more extreme.

'A year,' said Nicholas, as the truth dawned on him. 'A year to the day.'

He at last understood why he was missing Anne Hendrik so much. It was the first anniversary of their parting.

Jonas Applegarth lay back in the oak settle and rocked with mirth. Delighted that his play had been accepted by Westfield's Men, he was celebrating in the taproom of the Queen's Head with some of his new fellows. Applegarth was barely thirty but his vast girth, his thinning hair, his grey beard and his pockmarked skin added a decade and more. Whenever he moved, the hooks on his doublet threatened to snap and his huge thighs seemed on the point of bursting the banks of his breeches and flooding the settle.

The colossal body was matched by a colossal appetite and a seemingly insatiable thirst. Jonas Applegarth drank tankards of beer as fast as they could be filled, but it was no solitary indulgence. Generous with his money, he invited four of his new friends to join him in his revelry and they were soon cracking merry jests together.

Owen Elias laughed loudest of all. An ebullient Welsh actor with a love of life, he discerned a soulmate in Jonas Applegarth. The dramatist had not only provided Elias with an excellent role in his play, he was showing that he could roister with the wildest of them. In the short time he'd been with the troupe, Applegarth had taken the measure of Westfield's Men.

'What think you of Barnaby Gill?' asked Elias.

'Far less than he thinks of himself,' said Applegarth as he preened himself in an invisible mirror. 'Not a pretty boy in London is safe when Master Gill is strutting about the town in his finery. 'Tis well that he is not employed at Blackfriars or the Chapel Children would fear for their virtue every time they bent in prayer.'

Owen Elias led the crude laughter once again and two of his fellows joined in. The one exception was James Ingram, a tall, slender young man with the dashing good looks of an actor allied to the poise of courtier. As the others enlarged upon their theme, Ingram remained detached and watchful. The target of the general amusement was now fixed on the Children of Her Majesty's Chapel Royal, a theatre company of boys who performed at the reconstructed playhouse in Blackfriars. Westfield's Men competed for an audience with the Chapel Children so they had good reason to mock their rivals. James Ingram had equally good reason to stand apart from the ribaldry.

Jonas Applegarth told of his Blackfriars experience.

'He had the gall to ask me for a play.'

'Who?' said Elias.

'Cyril Fulbeck, the Master of the Chapel.' Applegarth emptied another tankard. 'He and his partner in the enterprise, Raphael Parsons, expected a full-grown poet like me to devise a drama for his dribbling pygmies. As if I'd turn punk and sell my art at so cheap a price!'

'What was its subject?'

'The stalest of all. Antony and Cleopatra.'

'Can a ten-year-old chorister with a piping voice wield power over the Roman Empire?'

'No, Owen. And think of my martial verse in the sweet mouths of those little eunuchs. I told Master Fulbeck as much. "Let me write another play for you,"

I suggested. "It is called *The Plague of Blackfriars* and tells of a verminous swarm of locusts, who devour the bread that belongs to their elders and betters. A wily beekeeper tricks them and every last parasite is drowned in the River Thames." When he realised that I was talking about his young charges, Cyril Fulbeck walked off in disgust and Raphael Parsons, Lord Foulmouth himself, used language that would have turned the black friars blue and set their cowls alight. In the whole history of Christianity, there cannot have been such irreligious cursing on consecrated ground. It was wondrous sport! I have not been so joyously abused by a vile tongue since my wedding night!'

Once again, James Ingram offered only a token smile.

Jonas Applegarth was in his element, carousing with his newfound companions as if they were his oldest friends and drawing from an apparently inexhaustible well of anecdote and jest. Seeing him in such a benevolent mood, it was difficult to believe that he had such a reputation for violence and wild behaviour. He seemed the epitome of amiability. Words gushed out of him in a happy torrent. Arresting phrases and clever conceits bubbled on the surface of the water. He positively exuded goodwill.

It vanished in a flash. When a figure came into the taproom and signalled with his hand, Jonas Applegarth stopped in mid-flow. The massive frame stiffened, the flabby cheeks shed their smile, and the teeth began to grind audibly. But it was his eyes which underwent the greatest change. Set close together beneath the bristling eyebrows, they had sparkled with such merriment that they almost redeemed his unsightly features. They now became black coals, glowing with a hatred which ignited the whole body and turned the face itself into a grotesque mask.

He grabbed the side of the settle to haul himself upright. His companions were shocked by the transformation.

'What ails you, Jonas?' said Owen.

'Spend this for me,' rumbled Applegarth, taking coins from his purse and tossing them onto the table. 'I'll return anon to share in your pleasure.'

Leaving the others still bemused, he waddled purposefully across the room and went out with the newcomer. Owen Elias was the first to recover. Scooping up the money, he called for more beer and grinned at his fellows.

'Let's raise our tankards to Jonas Applegarth!'

'Which one?' murmured Ingram. 'There are two of them.'

The genial dramatist from the Queen's Head was now a furious avenger with murder in his heart. As he swept along Gracechurch Street with his friend at his heels, Jonas Applegarth was cursing volubly and buffeting anyone foolish enough to stand in his way. He swung into a side street, then turned off that into a narrow lane. It was late evening and shadows were striping the buildings. When he reached a small courtyard, however, there was still enough light for him to recognise the two figures who lurked in a corner.

Applegarth glared at the bigger of the two men. Hugh Naismith was a stocky individual, in his twenties, with a handsome face set now in a scowl. His hand went straight to the hilt of his sword, but his companion, a much older and thinner man, held his wrist.

'Viper!' snarled Applegarth.

'Pig-face!' retorted Naismith.

'Rascal!'

'Knave!'

'Gentlemen, gentlemen,' said the older man, coming to stand between the two of them. 'There is no call for bloodshed here. Tempers were too hot when this tryst was arranged.' He turned to Naismith. 'Make but a simple apology and the matter is ended. You make shake hands again and part as friends.'

'He'll get no apology from me,' sneered Naismith.

'Nor would I hear one,' exclaimed Applegarth. 'I've come to separate this slave from his miserable existence. That is the only parting which will take place here.'

'Send for six horses!' yelled Naismith. 'You will need at least that number to drag away his fat carcass when I have cut the villainy out of it.'

'Gentlemen, gentlemen,' implored the peacemaker.

'Stand aside, old sir,' warned Applegarth, 'or I'll run you through as well. Honour must be satisfied.'

'Then let us not delay,' said Naismith.

Handing his cap to the old man, he drew his sword and took up his position. Jonas Applegarth reached for the rapier that his companion offered him and swished the blade through the air a few times. Duelling was illegal and both parties would be imprisoned if they were caught by the watch. The seconds were not there merely to ensure that the rules of fair combat were observed. They would also keep one eye out for any patrolling officers and be on hand to summon a surgeon in the event of a wounding. Jonas Applegarth and Hugh Naismith were both resolved that any wound they inflicted on their opponent would be fatal.

'I am ready for you, sir,' invited Applegarth.

Naismith smirked. 'Bid farewell to London.'

Steel touched steel in a brief greeting and the duel began. Jonas Applegarth held his ground while his opponent circled him. The seconds stood out of harm's way in the lane. Hugh Naismith sounded much more confident than he felt. Challenged to a duel during a fierce row, he had been forced to accept. Calm reflection had made him regret his decision and several cups of wine had been needed to lubricate his courage for the event itself. He still loathed Applegarth enough to want him dead but he was also aware of his adversary's strength and determination.

In theory, Applegarth's bulk made him an easy target. In practice, however, he was supremely well defended by a flashing rapier and a powerful wrist. When Naismith launched the first attack, it was parried with ease. A second assault was beaten away and a third met with such resistance that Naismith's sword arm was jarred. It was the younger and fitter man who was now breathing hard and perspiring freely. Jonas Applegarth moved in for the kill.

Swords clashed again. Thrust, parry and counter-thrust sent Naismith reeling back against a wall. Applegarth used his weight to imprison his opponent and his strength to finish the contest. Their rapiers were now locked together below the hilt and Applegarth was forcing the blade of

Naismith's sword slowly but inexorably towards the man's unguarded throat. Naismith's eyes filmed over with fear and his sweat dripped onto the weapon. Chuckling with triumph, Applegarth applied more pressure and the keen edge drew its first trickle of blood from the white neck.

Panic gave Naismith a fresh burst of energy and he contrived to push his adversary away, but he gained only momentary relief. Applegarth slashed the man's wrist and made him drop his sword with a howl of anguish. A second thrust opened up a wound in Naismith's other arm and sent him down on one knee in agony. Applegarth stepped back and drew back his arm for a final thrust, but the old man flung himself in front of his wounded friend.

'Hold there, sir!' he begged. 'You have won the day. Honour is satisfied and needs no more blood to assuage its thirst. Hugh kneels before you as a penitent. Show mercy!'

Applegarth was about to brush the old man aside when the other second saw someone coming along the lane.

'Officers of the watch!' he called.

The duel was over. Sighing with relief, the old man bent over his stricken friend. Jonas Applegarth was not yet done with Hugh Naismith. Kicking him to the ground, he used the toe of his shoe to flick offal into the man's face. He stood astride the body and hovered menacingly over it.

'Thus perish all actors who mangle my plays!' he said.

Then he fled nimbly into the shadows with his friend.

Chapter Two

Thames Street was his seventh home since leaving Bankside and he knew that he would not stay there long. Anne Hendrik's house had provided a secure mooring for Nicholas Bracewell in every way. Deprived of that, he drifted aimlessly through a succession of lodgings, never settling, never feeling at ease, never using the respective dwellings as anything more than a place to sleep. Loneliness kept him on the move.

Nicholas lived in a room at the top of a house on the corner of Thames Street and Cordwainer Street. Through its tiny window, he could watch the fishing smacks taking their catch into Queenhithe and larger vessels bringing foreign wines to the Vintry. Across the dark back of the river, he got a glimpse of Bankside with its tenements jostling each other for room around a haphazard collection of churches, brothels, taverns and ordinaries.

The Rose Theatre blossomed above the smaller buildings surrounding it.

He woke early that morning, as every morning, to the happy clamour of tradespeople below and the plaintive cries of the gulls wheeling hopefully above the wharves. After washing and dressing, Nicholas made his way out into Thames Street and paused to let its pungency strike his nostrils. The smell of fish dominated but the stink of the nearby breweries was also carried on the wind. A dozen other strong odours merged into the distinctive aroma of the riverside.

After throwing a nostalgic glance at Bankside, Nicholas headed east towards the subtler fragrances of the fruit market. He did not get very far.

'Good-morrow, Master Bracewell.'

'And to you, sir.'

'Are you bound for that den of iniquity?'

'If you mean the Queen's Head,' said Nicholas with a smile, 'then I fear that I am. It is not the ideal arena for our work but it is all that we may call our own.'

Caleb Hay put his head to one side and studied Nicholas carefully. The old man was short, neat and compact, and he carried his sixty years with surprising lightness. His sober apparel and intelligent face suggested a scholar while the ready grin and the glint in his eye hinted at a more worldly existence. Caleb Hay was one of Nicholas's neighbours and they had struck up a casual friendship. On the former's side, it consisted largely of jovial teasing.

'What made you do it?' said Hay.

'Do what?'

'Sell your soul to such a thankless profession.'

Nicholas shrugged. 'I like the theatre.'

'But how can such a patently good man work at such a manifestly bad trade?' The grin lit up his features. 'The theatre is the haunt of all the sweepings of the city. For every gallant in the gallery, there are three or four trulls and pickpockets and arrant knaves breathing garlic all over your inn yard. You play to plebeians, Master Bracewell.'

'Everyone who can buy entrance is welcome.'

'That is where the boys lord it over you,' said Hay. 'The Chapel Children and the Children of St Paul's charge higher prices at their indoor playhouses and keep out the commonalty. Sweeter breaths are met at Blackfriars. And finer plays may be set before a more discerning audience.'

'You'll not find a better comedy than the one that we next stage, Master Hay,' said Nicholas proudly. 'Its author is a scholar of repute with a wit to match any in the city. *The Misfortunes of Marriage* is a feast for standees and great minds alike. As for the children's companies,' he added with an indulgent smile, 'there is room for them as well as us. We serve the same Muse.'

Caleb Hay chuckled and patted him affectionately on the shoulder. He was carrying a leather satchel under his arm and Nicholas could see the scrolls of parchment poking out of it. Hay was a retired scrivener, who was devoting every waking hour to the writing of a history of London. Having been born and bred in the city, he knew it intimately and had witnessed extraordinary changes in the course of his long life. Those changes would all be listed scrupulously in his book, but research had first to be done into the earlier times of the capital, and Caleb trotted zealously about his task from dawn till dusk.

Nicholas was intrigued by the old man's obsessive interest in his native city. Caleb Hay was engaged in a labour of love that kept him glowing with contentment. It was impossible not to envy such a man.

'How does your book progress?' Nicholas asked.

'It grows, it grows. Slowly, perhaps, but we antiquarians may not rush. There is so much to sift and to weigh.'

'Then I will not keep you away from your studies.'

'Nor I you from your sinful occupation.'

'You do not fool me, Master Hay,' said Nicholas with a pleasant smile. 'Though you denigrate the theatre, I'll warrant that you have more than once rubbed shoulders with the lower sort in order to cheer a play in an inn yard.'

'I do not deny it,' admitted the other, 'but I did not venture there in search of pleasure. I forced myself to go in the spirit of enquiry. To know this city well enough to write about it, one must visit its most noisome quarters. How can a man describe a cesspool unless he has wallowed in it?'

They shared a laugh and exchanged farewells. Nicholas was about to move off when Caleb Hay plucked at his sleeve. 'Your author is a noted scholar, you say?'

'He can speak Greek and Latin like a schoolmaster.'

'What is his name?'

'Jonas Applegarth.'

Hay's cherubic face darkened. He walked abruptly away.

'No, no, no!' bellowed Jonas Applegarth. 'Speak the speech as it is set down, you dolt, and not as you half remember it. If you cannot learn my lines, do not pile insult on incompetence by inventing your own.'

Barnaby Gill spluttered with fury and waved his arms like a windmill out of control.

'I'll not be talked to like this!'

'Then play the part as it is written.'

'My art enhances any role that I undertake.'

'You are certainly proving a vile undertaker here, sir,' said Applegarth with heavy sarcasm. 'You have killed the character that I created and buried him in a wooden casket. Exhume him straight or I'll step up on that stage and aid the resurrection with my dagger.'

Barnaby Gill was so outraged by the criticism of his performance and so mortified by the threat of violence that he was struck dumb. His arms were now revolving with such speed that they seemed about to part company with his body.

'And do not saw the air so!' shouted Applegarth. 'If you wave your arms thus during my play, I'll tie them to your sides with rope and weight you down with an anchor. Gestures must match the verse, not slap it to death!'

Gill had heard enough. Jumping in the air like a startled rabbit, he bolted into the room which was used as a tiring-house. Torn between amusement and horror, the rest of the company either burst out laughing or slunk away from Jonas Applegarth in fear. Edmund Hoode did both. James Ingram did neither but simply watched Applegarth with a quiet disgust. The dramatist himself continued to berate the absent Gill in the most obscene language.

Nicholas Bracewell and Lawrence Firethorn came running to see what had caused the commotion. When trouble erupted in the yard of the Queen's Head, they had been having one of their regular quarrels with its erratic landlord, Alexander Marwood. A minor irritation was postponed as they raced to confront a major problem.

Nicholas read the situation at a glance. A predictable skirmish between player and playwright had occurred. He blamed himself for not being on hand to stop it and took instant steps to make sure that the skirmish did not turn into a battle, a certain result if Firethorn were drawn into it. Nicholas persuaded the actor-manager to go after Barnaby Gill and mollify him, then he announced a break in the rehearsal and cleared the yard of all but Edmund Hoode and Jonas Applegarth.

Hoode was still swinging to and fro between amusement and apprehension but he was able to give Nicholas a swift account of what had transpired. *The Misfortunes of Marriage* had claimed its first casualty. Unless firm action were taken, there would be many more. Nicholas let his friend join the others before crossing over to the playwright. Jonas Applegarth was sitting in the middle of the yard on an upturned barrel, chortling to himself.

'How now, Nick!' he greeted. 'You missed good sport!'

'Baiting Master Gill is not my idea of pleasure.'

'He asked for it!'

'But has it advantaged your play?'

'He will not be so rash as to forget my lines again. Players are all alike, Nick. Unless you hammer your wishes into their skulls, they will go their own sweet ways and destroy your work.'

'That has not been my experience,' said Nicholas, 'and it is not the way that Westfield's Men conduct their business. Master Gill is a most highly respected member of the company, and his contract as a sharer guarantees him an important role in everything we present.'

'He *has* an important role,' argued Applegarth. 'It is because of his significance in the piece that I taxed him about his shortcomings. Barnaby is one of the foundations of *The Misfortunes of Marriage*. If he falters, the whole edifice will come tumbling down.'

'Understand one thing, Jonas,' said Nicholas with polite reproach. 'Without Master Gill, there will *be* no edifice. Drive him away with your bullying and abuse and the whole enterprise crumbles. Your play will not reach the stage.'

Applegarth bristled and rose from his barrel. 'But you are contracted to present it.'

'Only if certain conditions are met, pertaining to your behaviour. That was made abundantly clear to you at the outset. I explained the terms myself.'

'My play has been advertised for performance tomorrow.'

'*The Misfortunes of Marriage* would not be the first

piece to be substituted at the eleventh hour. We have been on tour many times, Jonas, and are used to plucking a play from our repertoire at a moment's notice.'

'Cancel my masterpiece! It's a betrayal.'

'The play will have been betrayed by its author.'

'All I did was to box his ears with my tongue.'

'Then you will have to use that tongue to lick those ears better, Jonas, because Master Gill will not stir in the service of your play until you have apologised.'

'I'd sooner eat my night soil!'

'I'll convey that message to Master Firethorn.'

Nicholas turned away and headed for the tiring-house. Mastering his anger, Applegarth lumbered after him.

'Wait, Nick! Be not so hasty!'

'I must say the same to you,' said Nicholas, stopping to face him again. 'Hasty words from your mouth are the culprits here. Hasty jibes and hasty threats have put your play in jeopardy.'

'It *must* be staged!'

'Not if you grow quarrelsome.'

'I put my life's blood into that play.'

'Master Gill makes an equal commitment in his acting.'

Jonas Applegarth bit back the stinging retort he was about to make and stared deep into the book holder's eyes to see if he was bluffing. Nicholas met his gaze unwaveringly and the playwright was forced to reconsider his actions. His companion was making no idle threat. *The Misfortunes of Marriage* really did have an axe poised above its neck.

The playwright sounded a note of appeasement.

'Perhaps I was a little overbearing,' he conceded.

'That is patent.'

'It is my way, I fear.'

'Not when you work with Westfield's Men.'

'Barnaby Gill annoys me so!'

'You are not his favourite human being either, Jonas.'

'And must I kneel in supplication to him?'

'A sincere apology is the best balm for his wounds.'

'What about the scars he inflicts on my play?'

'They will not be there during the performance itself,' said Nicholas confidently. 'Master Gill has never let us down in front of an audience. Spectators bring the best out of him and he has a loyal following.'

Applegarth had to hold back another expletive. Heaving a sigh, he spread his arms wide and opened his palms.

'*The Misfortunes of Marriage* is my best play, Nick.'

'Its brilliance has been remarked upon by all of us.'

'Any company should be proud to present it.'

'So shall we be, Jonas, if you but stand aside and let us rehearse without interruption.'

'It was agreed. I have the right to offer advice.'

'Not in the form of abuse.'

'It is my play, Nick. I wish it to be played aright.'

'Then form a company on your own and act all the parts yourself,' said the book holder, 'for that is the only way you'll be satisfied. Give your play to us and you must allow for compromise. Theatre always falls short of perfection. Westfield's Men can simply offer to do their best for you.'

'Under my direction.'

'With your help,' corrected Nicholas.

There was a long pause as Applegarth reflected on the situation. It was not a new one. He had fallen out with other theatre companies in more spectacular ways and had found himself spurned as a result. Westfield's Men were a last resort. If they did not stage *The Misfortunes of Marriage*, it might never be seen by an audience. Applegarth weighed pride against practicality.

'Well,' said Nicholas finally. 'Am I to tell Master Firethorn that you are now ready to eat your own night soil?'

Applegarth guffawed. 'Tell him I am ready to drink a cesspool and eat every dead dog in Houndsditch if it will put my work upon the scaffold in this yard.'

'And Master Gill?'

'Send him out to me now and I'll cover him with so many kisses that his codpiece will burst with joy.'

'A less extreme demonstration of regret will suffice,' said Nicholas with a smile. He adopted a sterner tone. 'I will not caution you again, Jonas. Unless you mend your ways and give counsel instead of curses, there is no place for you here. Do you accept that?'

Applegarth nodded. 'I give you my word.'

'Hold to it.'

'I will, Nick.'

'Wait here while I see if Master Gill is in a fit state to speak with you.' Nicholas was about to move away when he remembered something. 'Rumour has it that you fought a duel in recent days.'

'That is a downright lie.'

'With an actor from Banbury's Men.'

'I have never crossed swords with anyone.'

'His offence, it seems, was damaging a play of yours.'

'Who is spreading this untruth about me? I am the most peaceable of men, Nick. I love nothing more than harmony.'

'It is so with us, Jonas. Bear that in mind.'

On that note of admonition, Nicholas went off to the tiring-house and left the playwright alone in the yard. Jonas Applegarth padded back to his barrel, flopped down onto it and stared at the makeshift stage in front of him. It was empty now but his quick imagination peopled it with the characters of his play and set them whirling into action. *The Misfortunes of Marriage* was an overwhelming success and he was soon luxuriating in thunderous applause from an invisible audience.

The lone spectator in the inn yard of the Queen's Head did not join in the acclamation. He stayed watching from the upper gallery. One wrist was heavily bandaged and his other arm was supported in a sling.

A long and arduous rehearsal produced a legacy of sore throats, aching limbs and frayed tempers. When their work was finally over, most of the members of the company adjourned to the taproom of the Queen's Head to slake their thirst and to compare notes about an eventful day. Opinion was divided about Jonas Applegarth's verbal assault on Barnaby Gill. Some praised it, some condemned it. Others felt that it was unfortunate but beneficial because, when Gill's ruffled feathers had been smoothed by an abject apology, he gave such an impressive performance of his role that he had the playwright gleaming with approbation.

Owen Elias belonged among Applegarth's supporters. Sharing a table with Edmund Hoode and James Ingram, he confided his feelings about the incident.

'Barnaby deserved it,' he said. 'He has grown lazy at conning lines. Jonas acquainted him with that truth.'

'Truth should have a softer edge,' said Hoode, with evident sympathy for the victim. 'Why belabour Barnaby so when you could request him with kind words?'

'Jonas Applegarth does not *know* any kind words,' said Ingram. 'Threat and insult are his only weapons.'

'You do him wrong,' defended Elias. 'He speaks his mind honestly and I admire any man who does that. Especially when he does so with such wit and humour.'

'I side with James,' said Hoode. 'Wit and humour should surprise and delight as they do in *The Misfortunes of Marriage*. They should not be used as stakes to drive through the heart of a fine actor in front of his fellows. Barnaby will never forgive him.'

'Nor will I,' thought Ingram.

'Jonas is a wizard of language,' asserted Elias. 'When I see a play such as his, I can forgive him everything.'

Hoode nodded. 'It is certainly a rare piece of work.'

Ingram made no comment. Elias nudged his elbow.

'Do you not agree, James?'

The other pondered. 'It has some wonderful scenes in it, Owen,' he declared. 'And the wit you spoke of is used to savage effect. But I do not think it the work of genius that you do. It has too many defects.'

'Not many,' said Hoode, reasonably. 'A few, perhaps, and they mostly concern the construction of the piece. But I find no major faults.'

'There speaks a fellow-writer!' noted Elias. 'Praise from Edmund is praise indeed. What are your objections, James?'

'Master Applegarth is too wild and reckless in his attacks. He puts everything to the sword. Take but the Induction . . .'

He broke off as Nicholas Bracewell came into the taproom to join them. Edmund Hoode moved along the bench to make room for his friend, but the book holder found only the briefest resting place. Alexander Marwood, the cadaverous landlord, came shuffling across to them with the few remaining tufts of his hair dancing like cobwebs in the breeze. The anxious look on Marwood's face made Nicholas ready himself for bad news, but the tidings were a joy.

'A lady awaits you, Master Bracewell.'

'A lady?'

'She has been here this past hour.'

'What is her name?'

'Mistress Anne Hendrik.'

Nicholas was on his feet with excitement. 'Where is she?'

'Follow me and I'll lead you to her.'

'Let's go at once.'

'Give her our love!' called Elias, pleased at his friend's sudden happiness. 'We'll not expect you back before morning.' He winked at Hoode, then turned to Ingram.

'Now, James. What is amiss with the Induction?'

Nicholas heard none of this. The mere fact of Anne's presence in the same building made him walk on air and forget all the irritations of a tiring day. Marwood conducted him along a corridor before indicating the door of a private room. Nicholas knocked and let himself in.

Anne Hendrik was there. When he saw her standing in the middle of the room with such a welcoming smile, he wanted to take her in his arms and kiss away a year's absence. She looked enchanting. Wearing a deep blue bodice with a blue gown of a lighter hue, she was as handsome and shapely as ever. Appropriately, it was the hat which really set off her features. Anne Hendrik was the English widow of a Dutch hatmaker and her late husband had taught her the finer points of headgear. She was now wearing a shallow brimmed, high crowned light blue hat with a twist of darker material around the crown.

'Nicholas!' she said with evident pleasure.

'By all, it's good to see you!'

She offered a hand for him to kiss and her fond smile showed just how delighted she was to see him. Nicholas felt an upsurge of love that had been suppressed for twelve long months. Before he could find words to express it, however, she turned to introduce her companion and Nicholas realised with a shudder that they were not, in fact, alone.

'This is Ambrose Robinson,' she said.

'I have heard so much about you, Master Bracewell,' said the visitor with an obsequious smile. 'All of it was

38

complimentary. Anne has the highest regard for you.'

Nicholas gave a polite smile and shook his hand, but there was no warmth in the greeting. He took an immediate dislike to the man, not merely because his presence had turned a reunion of lovers into a more formal meeting, but because there was a faintly proprietary tone in his voice. The way that he dwelt on the name of 'Anne,' rolling it in his mouth to savour its taste, made Nicholas cringe inwardly. He waved his visitors to seats and took a closer look at Ambrose Robinson.

Garbed like a tradesman, he was a plump man of middle height, with a rubicund face so devoid of hair that it had the sheen of a small child. His big red hands were clasped together in his lap and his shoulders hunched deferentially.

'Ambrose is a neighbour and a friend,' said Anne.

'A butcher by trade,' he explained. 'I am honoured to provide food for Anne's table. Only the freshest poultry and finest cuts of meat are saved for her.'

Nicholas lowered himself onto a stool opposite them but found no rest. The joy of seeing Anne again had been vitiated by the annoying presence of an interloper. She gave him an apologetic smile, then took a deep breath.

'We have come to ask for your help, Nick,' she began.

'It is yours to command,' he said gallantly.

'You are so kind, Master Bracewell,' said Robinson with an ingratiating grin. 'You do not even know me and yet you are ready to come to my assistance at Anne's behest.'

'*Your* assistance?'

'Let me explain,' said Anne. 'In brief, the situation is this. Ambrose has a son, barely ten years of age, as bright and gifted a child as you could wish to meet. His name is Philip. He is the apple of his father's eye, and rightly so.' She glanced at her companion, who nodded soulfully. 'Until this month, Philip was a chorister at the Church of St Mary Overy. He has a voice as clear as a bell and was chosen to take solo parts during evensong.'

'Philip sings like an angel,' said the doting father.

'Wherein lies the problem?' asked Nicholas.

Robinson glowered. 'He has been stolen away from me!'

'Kidnapped?'

'As good as, Master Bracewell.'

'He has been gathered into the Chapel Royal,' said Anne. 'Philip's beautiful voice was his own undoing. A writ of impressment was signed and he was spirited away.'

'Is that not a cause for celebration?' said Nicholas. 'They have a notable choir at the Church of St Mary Overy, but to sing before Her Majesty is the highest honour that any chorister can attain.'

'So it would be,' agreed Robinson, 'if that is all that Philip was enjoined to do. But it is not. The Master of the Chapel has made my son a member of a theatrical troupe that stages plays at Blackfriars. The boy is young and innocent. He should not be so cruelly exposed to wantonness.'

'That will not of necessity happen, Master Robinson,' said Nicholas with slight asperity. 'Playhouses are not the symbols of sin that they are painted. We have apprentices in our own company, little above your son's age, yet they have not been corrupted. The Chapel Children are far less likely to lead your son astray. Their repertoire is chosen with care and their audience more select than ours.'

'Ambrose did not mean to offend you, Nick,' said Anne when she heard the defensive note in his voice. 'He does not want to impugn your profession in any way. This is not a complaint about Westfield's Men or about any of the other companies. It relates only to the Chapel Children.'

'And the villain in charge of them,' said Robinson.

'Cyril Fulbeck?'

'He is the Master there, but the deadly spider who has caught my son in his web is called Raphael Parsons.'

'Why so?'

'Read Philip's letters and you would understand. He makes my son's life a misery. Raphael Parsons is a monster.'

Nicholas was still mystified. 'Why bring this problem to me? I can offer you little beyond sympathy.'

'We came for advice, sir,' said Robinson.

'Then take your story to a shrewd lawyer. Get a hearing for the case in the courts. Pursue it all the way to the Star Chamber, if need be. You have good cause.'

'We hoped there might be a quicker way,' said Anne.

'Quicker?'

'And less costly,' added Robinson. 'Lawyers' fees would eat hungrily through my purse.'

41

'It might take months to reach the Star Chamber,' said Anne. 'We need someone who can go to the Chapel Royal and speak directly to this ogre called Raphael Parsons.'

'His father is the proper person to do that.'

'I have tried,' said Robinson angrily, 'but they will not even hear me. Besides, I could not trust myself to be in Parsons's company and not throttle the life out of him with my bare hands.' He opened his palms to show thick and powerful fingers. 'That would gladden me but deprive Philip of a father. He has already lost his mother and could not bear to see me hanged upon the gallows.'

Everything about the man unsettled Nicholas and he wanted no part in the affairs of his family, especially now that he realised Robinson was widowed and in need of a stepmother for his hapless child. But Anne Hendrik looked at him with such trust and pleading that the book holder found it hard to refuse. He shrugged his shoulders.

'I have little hope of succeeding where you failed.'

'But you'll go?' begged Robinson.

'I have heard stories about Raphael Parsons, it is true, but I do not know the man.'

'He is the Devil Incarnate!'

'Philip must be rescued from his clutches,' said Anne.

'I will pay all I can,' promised her companion.

'I want no money,' said Nicholas. 'Furnish me with more detail and I will look into it. That is all I can promise. One thing I can assure you, Master Robinson. Chapel Children are not the wayward sinners you imagine. We have a young man in the company, one James Ingram, who learnt to sing, dance and act with the Chapel Children in the old Blackfriars playhouse. A more personable fellow you could not hope to encounter. I'll see what James can tell me of Raphael Parsons.'

'Let my son's letters speak their full as well,' insisted Robinson, pulling a bundle from his pocket and handing it over. 'I would like them back when you have done with them.'

'Linger a while and you shall have them anon.'

'Yes,' said Anne, rising to her feet. 'Nick will read and absorb them in no time. Wait for me outside, Ambrose, and I will join you in a moment.'

'I will,' he said, getting up. 'Thank you, sir.'

'Save your gratitude until I have earned it.'

'Listening to my tale was a kindness in itself.'

Ambrose Robinson walked heavily to the door and let himself out. Nicholas relaxed slightly and looked up at Anne. She put a hand on his shoulder and smiled.

'How are you?' he asked.

'Much as ever, Nick. And you?'

'I am kept as busy as usual here.'

'You thrive on work.' Her face puckered. 'I am sorry to burden you with this errand but it means so much to Ambrose. He is quite distracted with worry. You were the only person we could turn to, Nick.'

'We?'

'Ambrose has been kind to me. I owe him this favour. Do not blame me too much. Philip Robinson is suffering dreadfully, as you will see from his letters, and my heart

43

goes out to him. But he is not the only reason I came here today.'

'What else brought you here?'

Anne bent over to kiss him softly on the lips.

'You,' she said.

Then she let herself out of the room.

Chapter Three

Omens for *The Misfortunes of Marriage* were not propitious. The day began with torrential rain. It soaked the stage, blew into the galleries and turned the yard of the Queen's Head into a quagmire. Emotional tempests soon followed. Barnaby Gill awoke with a blazing headache, announced that he was too ill to move, and refused to appear in the play which he saw as responsible for his condition. Lawrence Firethorn experienced his own marital misfortune. Incautious enough to retain a letter from a female admirer because it flattered his vanity, he opened his eyes that morning to find his wife reading the telltale missive before turning on him like a berserk she-tiger.

Then there was Jonas Applegarth. Quiescent after the stern warning from Nicholas Bracewell, he worked through the night on emendations and additions which he wanted inserted into his play, and compiled a list of notes for individual actors whose performances, he felt on mature reflection, needed radical improvement if his work were to be given any hope of success. When his wife rose from her slumber and found him still poring over the foul papers of his play, Applegarth was like a powder keg in search of an excuse to explode. The sight of the downpour threatened to ignite rather than dampen.

Nicholas Bracewell looked out from his lodging to see Thames Street being turned into a replica of the river whose name it bore. Horses churned up the mud, wagon wheels dispersed it with indiscriminate force, and sodden figures waded to and fro with all the speed that they could muster. Nicholas gave a sigh of resignation. Inn yard theatre was at the mercy of the elements. In view of the religious satire which propelled *The Misfortunes of Marriage,* he was bound to wonder if the Almighty was inflicting the storm by way of a criticism of the play.

Though the performance dominated his thoughts, there was another vexation at the back of his mind. Anne Hendrik's request for help left him in a state of ambivalence. Willing to assist her in any way, he felt no such obligation towards Ambrose Robinson and still smarted at the memory of the man's unconcealed affection towards the woman whom Nicholas still loved deeply. It worried him that Anne's relationship with the Southwark butcher was so close that he felt able to entrust such a personal matter to her. Philip Robinson's letters were indeed heartbreaking in their description of the boy's ordeal, but Nicholas could not see why Anne Hendrik should be involved in his rescue, still less he himself.

Concentrating on the afternoon's performance, he braced himself for a tense morning at the Queen's Head and left his lodging. He had splashed his way no more than twenty yards along Thames Street when a small, bustling figure cannoned into him and bounced off. With his head bent forward and his cloak all but hiding him, Caleb Hay had not even seen his approaching neighbour.

'A thousand apologies, Master Bracewell!'

'The fault was as much mine,' said Nicholas.

'A deluge such as this makes the most nimble of us blind and clumsy. By the end of the day, we may need to return to our houses by boat.'

'The storm may yet blow over.'

Caleb Hay grinned. 'I admire your optimism but I do not share it. Nor can I offer you any sympathy with a clear conscience. If you serve such a filthy profession, you must expect the heavens to wash it for you out of sheer disgust.'

'We must agree to differ,' said Nicholas tolerantly.

'You are too honest a man for the world you serve.'

'It has brought me true friends and good fellowship.'

'Then I will leave you to join them so that you may all get down on your knees together and pray for a miracle. Without a couple of hours of sunshine, you will have to watch your play float off down the river.'

Adjusting his hat and pulling his cloak more tightly

around him, Caleb Hay bade farewell and moved away. Nicholas detained him by touching his shoulder.

'One thing puzzles me, Master Hay.'

'What might that be?'

'The way you behaved at our last encounter.'

'Was I rude or uncivil?' said Hay with genuine concern. 'Was I full of self-affairs? Pray, do not take offence, Master Bracewell. An antiquarian lives in the past. We sometimes forget the good manners we should display in the present.'

'You were not uncivil,' said Nicholas. 'We talked quite amicably. But you departed in a fit of anger.'

Hay's face clouded. 'I remember now. Jonas Applegarth.'

'You know the man?'

'I know of him, sir.'

'Enough to put you to flight in such a way?'

'I saw a play of his once at The Curtain.'

'So you *do* sink to our level from time to time,' teased Nicholas gently.

'What was the piece?'

'A vile concoction set in Ancient Rome.'

'You did not like Master Applegarth's work?'

'I detested it.'

'Too bawdy for your taste?'

'Too bawdy, too brutal and too full of bile. Only a person with a profound hatred of mankind could have penned such a malignant play. Clever, it certainly was. Laden with wit and scholarship of a high order. But, oh so cruel and so unkind. He even made jests in Latin and mocked a beautiful language until its face was covered

48

in ugly sores. That is Jonas Applegarth for you, Master Braccwell. I hope this rain washes his new play into the ditch where it belongs!'

The Queen's Head was a house of mourning. Drenched actors kept vigil around the slimy inn yard as if it were a mass grave containing the accumulated bodies of their departed relatives. Edmund Hoode watched a piece of straw being carried on a meandering journey by a tiny rivulet and saw his own life re-enacted in miniature. Peter Digby and his musicians played a dirge. Owen Elias sang in lugubrious Welsh. Lawrence Firethorn could still hear his wife, Margery, hammering nails into the coffin of their marriage as she tore the offending letter to shreds and pronounced a death sentence on their connubial delights. Jonas Applegarth was so grief-stricken that he simply stood in the rain and let it augment the tears that were coursing down his fat cheeks.

Alexander Marwood responded with his usual gleeful misery. Moaning like a wind trapped in a hollow tree, he sought out Nicholas Braccwell and rolled his eyes in despair.

'Your play is drowned,' he said in a hoarse whisper.

'Not yet,' replied Nicholas. 'It is but mid-morning and we have some hours to go.'

'This rain will last a week.'

'I doubt that, Master Marwood.'

'You'll be driven from the stage. No plays, no people to buy my ale. Disaster! How am I to sustain such a loss?'

'The same way as we do, Master Marwood. With patience.'

'But I rely on the income from Westfield's Men.'

'We pay our rent whether we play or no.'

'It is your spectators who give me my profit.'

'And so they will again as soon as the clouds move on. At the first sign of fine weather, they'll flock back to the Queen's Head to fill our seats and your coffers.'

'Causing affrays and damaging my property.'

Alexander Marwood was impossible to please. When a performance was abandoned because of inclement weather, he groaned at the resultant loss of income, yet he complained just as much when Westfield's Men were actually bringing customers into his inn yard. His relationship with the company was as joyless as that with his termagant wife. The landlord was the voice of doom in a beer-stained apron.

As Marwood oozed away into the building, James Ingram joined the book holder beneath the thatched roof that overhung the stables. A dozen small waterfalls provided a splashing descant to their conversation.

'What do you think, Nick?' asked Ingram.

'I have not given up hope yet.'

'Our playwright has. He is weeping his own rainstorm.'

'We all suffer in our different ways. But I am glad of a word alone with you, James,' said Nicholas, turning his back on the depressing scene in the inn yard. 'I seek advice.'

'On what subject?'

'The Children of the Chapel Royal.'

'I'll tell you all you wish to know about them,' said Ingram affably. 'I joined them as a boy of eleven and spent four happy years there. They so imbued me with a love of theatre that I sought my livelihood in the profession.'

'And you are set to rise swiftly in it, James.'

'Your praise is kind. There is nobody whose judgement I would trust more readily.'

Nicholas liked the young actor immensely and had been instrumental in getting Ingram taken on as a hired man. The latter's talent marked him out at once as a player of high calibre and he was now given more or less regular employment by the company. It was generally accepted that he would, in time, be invited to become a sharer with Westfield's Men and thus have a modicum of security in a wholly insecure trade.

'You must have many fond memories,' said Nicholas.

'I do, Nick. It was hard work, but the joy of performance is like no other. Whether you are thirteen or thirty, it sets fire to your blood. I am forever indebted to the Chapel Children and will never speak harshly of their work.' He flung a hostile glance at Jonas Applegarth. 'Unlike some.'

'Was Cyril Fulbeck the Master in your time?'

'Not at first. He was Master of the Children of the Chapel at Windsor. It was only in my last year that he took charge of the main choir here in London.'

'What manner of man is he?'

'A good and honest fellow. He began as chaplain at Windsor and rose to be choirmaster. He was also a noted composer and later wrote songs for our plays. I cannot speak too warmly of him, Nick. Why do you ask?'

'I have a friend whose son has been impressed by the Chapel Royal. Like you, he is being trained to act in the theatre. The boy does not follow in your footsteps, alas. Where you were happy, he is sorely oppressed and begs his father to release him in every letter he sends home.'

Ingram sighed. 'Things have changed at Blackfriars.'

'Has Cyril Fulbeck grown stricter with his charges?'

'No, Nick,' said the other sadly. 'He has grown older and is much hampered by sickness. It is an effort for him to fulfil his duties as choirmaster. The staging of plays has been handed over to another.'

'Raphael Parsons.'

'He is the manager of the Blackfriars Company of Boys.'

'A sterner taskmaster, by all account.'

'So I have heard.'

'How long has he been in charge?'

'Since the theatre was rebuilt and reopened. Raphael Parsons took a lease on it and paid for the new construction. It is a fine indoor playhouse, Nick, much improved since my time there. Blackfriars may not hold as many people as we do here in the Queen's Head but their plays are not plagued by this damnable bad weather of ours. In snow or rain, the Chapel Children can still perform.'

'They hold the whip-hand over us there,' agreed Nicholas with envy. 'You have never met this Master Parsons, then?'

'Only once, and that briefly. It was at their first performance at the new theatre. They played *Mariana's Revels* and did so exceeding well. Raphael Parsons may be a tyrant but he is a true man of the theatre.'

'A tyrant, you say?'

'So it is voiced abroad. He is a martinet. Striving for perfection, he makes the boys work long hours and punishes them severely if they dare fall short.'

'I have seen the letters I spoke of, James. They tell of harsh words and sound beatings.'

'It was never so in Cyril Fulbeck's day.'

'Where might I find this Raphael Parsons?'

'At the Blackfriars Theatre. He rehearses daily.'

'And Master Fulbeck?'

'There, too, as like as not. Master Parsons teaches the boys to be actors, but only Cyril Fulbeck can transform then into real choristers.' Ingram's curiosity was aroused. 'If you need to go there, Nick, I would gladly bear you company.'

'I accept that offer with thanks.'

'Cyril Fulbeck is always delighted to see his old choristers. My presence may open doors that would otherwise be closed to you.'

'It is settled, James. We'll go together.'

A rousing cheer interrupted their discussion. They turned to see that a small miracle had taken place behind them. The rain had stopped. The sun was wrestling with the clouds.

Westfield's Men shouted and clapped and stamped their feet with delight. Jonas Applegarth, soaked to the skin, was the happiest man in the yard. *The Misfortunes of Marriage* might after all be performed that afternoon.

The audience that streamed into the inn yard a few hours later had no notion of the frenetic activity which had

53

preceded their arrival. Under the supervision of Nicholas Bracewell, the assistant stagekeepers swept the water off the scaffold and strewed it with dry rushes so that an attenuated rehearsal could commence. While that was in progress, the mud was brushed into the corners of the yard and the benches in the galleries were rubbed with dry cloth. George Dart, the lowliest member of the company, was given the job of wringing the damp out of their flag. When it was hoisted at two o'clock to show that a play was being performed, they wanted it to unfurl proudly in the breeze.

Edmund Hoode was despatched to Barnaby Gill's lodging with the fictitious tale that the latter's role in the play had been assigned to Owen Elias instead. Professional pride was a shrewd surgeon. It effected a complete recovery in a matter of seconds and had Gill leaping from his bed of pain with a yell of indignation. Both men were soon taking their places on the stage at the Queen's Head.

Only a double blessing could have made the performance possible. Not only did the storm abate but a second wonder occurred. Jonas Applegarth behaved with impeccable restraint. Instead of cajoling the players, he watched the rehearsal in silence. Instead of unsettling the company with his fearsome presence, he was kept out of their way by Nicholas while the actors snatched refreshment before the performance.

By the time that Lord Westfield and his cronies took their places on the cushioned chairs in their privileged position in the lower gallery, all was in readiness. Bright sunshine turned the thatch into spun gold. Ladies and gallants filled the seating with a veritable riot of colour. The book holder made a final check behind the scenes, then signalled to Peter Digby. Music played and *The Misfortunes of Marriage* began.

The Induction had the spectators laughing within a matter of seconds. Four apprentices – Martin Yeo, John Tallis, Stephen Judd and Richard Honeydew – attired as choirboys, burst onto the stage in the middle of a fierce argument over who should take the leading roles in a play about Samson. They fought over Samson's club, each grabbing it in turns to strike at the others. Since all four of them were far too young and puny to convince in the Herculean role, the audience shook with mirth.

Competition for the part of Samson was matched by four-sided rejection of Delilah. None of the boys wished to don the long red wig of the betrayer, and they threw it at each other continually like a dead cat, hideous to the touch. In the space of a short scene, the stage had been filled with violent action, the audience's attention had been seized and they had been given, as they would later come to realise, the central theme of the comedy.

The interplay between marriage and religion fascinated Jonas Applegarth. It did not matter that Samson and Delilah were lovers rather than man and wife. The Biblical story was ingrained in the minds of all who watched. While the standees in the yard loved the wild antics of the boys, the sharper minds in the galleries also relished the satire on the children's theatre companies. When the scene ended with Richard Honeydew, the youngest of the apprentices, in the guise of Samson, and with lantern-jawed John Tallis, the fattest of them, as

Delilah, the deficiencies of the Chapel Children and the Children of St Paul's were writ large. Championing the adult company with whom he worked, Jonas Applegarth mocked their fledgling rivals mercilessly.

The Misfortunes of Marriage was a glorious romp with a serious undertone. Its plot revolved around Sir Marcus Coldbed, a wealthy landowner in search of a pretty young wife to satisfy his almost uncontrollable lust. When he marries the beauteous Araminta, he discovers that she is a strict Roman Catholic with a rooted objection to physical contact and an absolute horror of sexual intercourse. To keep her lecherous husband at bay, Araminta employs her Jesuit confessor, Father Monfredo, as a holy bodyguard, allowing him to sleep in the anteroom to her bedchamber in order to protect her virtue. Shuddering with comic frustration, Sir Marcus spends his wedding night in a freezing cold bed.

Out of sheer desperation, Sir Marcus turns for help to the weird Doctor Epididymis, a notorious mountebank who poses as astrologer, alchemist and necromancer, asking him to provide a potion that will send Father Monfredo to sleep and a powder that will arouse his wife's passion to such a point that she will demand uninhibited consummation. Potion and powder are given to the wrong victims, and it is Araminta who slumbers for twenty-four hours while her aged confessor chases every woman in sight like a mountain goat. Sir Marcus Coldbed returns to a cold bed yet again.

Lawrence Firethorn was at his supreme best as the luckless husband, bemoaning his fate with a range of comic gestures and facial expressions that kept the audience in a state of almost continual mirth.

> *Why, what is marriage if not a licence for a man*
> *to take his wife at will? To occupy her body with*
> *his largest proof of love and pluck the choicest*
> *fruit from out her orchard. To spurn a husband*
> *is to geld a stallion in his prime. Do Araminta's*
> *Popish thighs not feel the prick of high desire? Is*
> *Rome an icy region down below the waist? How,*
> *then, will this old religion last if it go forth not*
> *and multiply? And how reap a harvest of Jesuitical*
> *progeny except by the downright way of creation?*
> *Man above a woman is God's law. Man inside a*
> *woman is husband's right. Give me the due reward*
> *of marriage. Cover this Coldbed with the hottest*
> *sheets. Let me wallow in my wife's concupiscence.*
> *Throw off your holy garments, Araminta. Be naked*
> *in my arms. Be my slave, my mistress, my whore. Be*
> *the everlasting bride to my eternal lust. Oh, sweetest*
> *Araminta, hear my prayer. Be mine!*

As the grotesque Doctor Epididymis, Barnaby Gill was equally brilliant, trotting comically around the stage after his restless client and plying him with all kinds of bogus remedies. When all else fails, the crafty doctor tells Sir Marcus that the only way he will lie beside his wife is to disguise himself as a Cardinal and tell her that it is her solemn duty to serve the Church. The trick succeeds and Araminta submits with grace. In his eagerness, Sir Marcus throws off his disguise in order to ravish her and is left clutching the pillow as she flees in panic.

Abandoning all hope of carnal delight and unable to divorce his first wife, Sir Marcus secretly marries – at the suggestion of Doctor Epididymis – a second beauty, hoping to find a bigamous outlet for his lascivious appetite. Arabella, the new Lady Coldbed, is quite unaware of the existence of his first bride, and all kinds of stratagems are needed to keep the two wives from meeting each other. What Sir Marcus does not realise until his second wedding night approaches is that Arabella is a devout Puritan and will not even share the same bedchamber with him, let alone the same bed.

Sir Marcus spends the rest of the play trying to seduce the second wife while keeping her presence hidden from the first, professing Puritan values to Arabella while promising to convert to Roman Catholicism if Araminta will relent and embrace his manhood. The similarity in their names leads to all kinds of comic confusion. When the bigamy is finally exposed, the two wives join forces to wreak a revenge on their joint husband that deprives him of all wish to lie near a woman ever again.

The Misfortunes of Marriage was an uproarious success and the ovation which greeted it lasted several minutes. Lawrence Firethorn led out the troupe to receive the applause. He and Barnaby Gill had been the outstanding performers, playing off each other with dazzling brilliance, but there had been excellent support from Edmund Hoode as the moon-faced Father Monfredo, from Owen Elias as the drunken hedge-priest who was bribed to perform the second marriage, from James Ingram as Arabella's true love, from Martin Yeo as Arabella herself, and from Richard Honeydew as the Roman Catholic spouse.

Jonas Applegarth was suffused with delight. Potentially

the sternest critic of the performance, he was completely won over by it, and ignored the minor errors and examples of mistiming which inevitably crept in when such a complex piece was played at such breakneck speed. So thrilled was he with the outrageous Doctor Epididymis that he forgot all his earlier strictures of Barnaby Gill and resolved to make amends by showering him with acclaim. As he clapped his huge hands together, Applegarth was not just applauding his own play. He was expressing his profound gratitude to Westfield's Men. A playwright ousted by every other theatre company in London had finally found a home.

Approbation was still not universal. One spectator had detested every minute of what he saw. The spectre at the feast was in the upper gallery. Hugh Naismith had chosen a vantage point that allowed him to watch the dramatist rather than the drama. It was a painful afternoon for him. His wounded arm and bandaged wrist were constantly jostled by the excited spectators either side of him, but it was his pride which suffered the real agony. A man he loathed was being feted; a company he despised was being celebrated.

Hugh Naismith was an actor whose occupation had been stolen from him by the sharp sword of Jonas Applegarth. Dismissed from Banbury's Men because of his injuries, he would not rest until he had avenged himself on his enemy. Applegarth had to die.

'I have never known such a day as this,' said Nicholas Bracewell.

'Nor I,' agreed James Ingram.

'This morning, we were like to have our play drowned by rain. This afternoon, it sailed on a tide of triumph. Truly, we serve a profession of extremes.'

'Yes, Nick. Feast or famine, with nothing in between.'

'Today, we had a royal banquet.'

Joyful celebrations at the Queen's Head would go on all evening, but Nicholas and Ingram had only shared in them for an hour before slipping quietly away. It was a long walk to Blackfriars from Gracechurch Street and Nicholas needed a clear head for what he anticipated as a difficult confrontation. Ingram, too, had supped only a moderate amount of ale before quitting the taproom with his friend.

'There is one small consolation,' he said.

'What is that, James?'

'Neither of them will have seen *The Misfortunes of Marriage* today. Cyril Fulbeck is too unwell and Raphael Parsons is too involved in staging his own plays to pay close attention to the work of his rivals.'

'How is that a consolation?' wondered Nicholas.

'They will not have taken offence at the Induction. It pilloried the Chapel Children in particular. Word of the attack will surely reach them soon and my own welcome at Blackfriars will no longer be so cordial. Transact your business with them swiftly, Nick, before they realise that you were party to a scurrilous assault on their work.'

'Jonas merely turned his wit upon them.'

'He traduced them most shamefully.'

'You are bound to feel defensive to the Chapel, but do not overstate the case that Jonas Applegarth made against them. Mockery there was, certainly, but I hope it will not sour your own name at Blackfriars.'

'They'll hear about that callous Induction soon enough and find a means to answer it in kind.'

They were walking parallel with the river along Thames Street, retracing the steps that Nicholas himself took every night on his way back to his lodging. Even at that time of the evening, it was a busy thoroughfare with the sounds as noisy and the smells as pungent as ever. James Ingram was too fair-minded to let his reservations about the play obscure its finer points.

'Induction apart,' he said, 'it is a remarkable achievement. Only when I saw it performed did I realise how remarkable. How many of those who clapped its antics had any understanding of its true intent?'

'I cannot guess at that, James, but this I do know. The Master of the Revels was blind to its full import. He insisted on but few changes before he granted us a licence. Jonas Applegarth disguised his satire well on the page.'

'But not on the stage.'

'Indeed not. That is where any play is revealed in its true light. Those of discernment must have seen that Sir Marcus Coldbed was kin to our own dear Queen's father, King Henry. Sir Marcus changed the religion of his whole household in order to bed a woman, albeit with no success. Nor was King Henry happy with his change of wives.'

They discussed the deeper meaning of the play all the way along Thames Street. The spiritual upheaval of the reign of Henry VIII had been cunningly transposed into a sexual crisis in the life of a rich landowner. Nicholas was still trying to decide whether the indictment of Roman Catholicism was more searing than that of Puritanism when their destination came in sight.

Blackfriars Monastery had been built over three centuries earlier as the first London home of the Dominican Order.

Occupying a prime location near the river, it swiftly grew in size, wealth and influence until it reached the point where major affairs of state were occasionally decided within its walls. The monastery was dissolved and largely demolished in 1538 but it retained its privilege of sanctuary. Its vestigial remains included the Porter's Lodge, the Old Buttery and the Upper Frater, where the monks had taken their meals. Joined together, the resultant building contained the Blackfriars Theatre.

Nicholas had been past the edifice a hundred times but never across its threshold. He was curious to take full stock of the changes to the theatre and irritated that he was there on business which might preclude that. What he was going to say on behalf of Philip Robinson he did not know, but he could at least establish more facts about the boy's alleged ill-treatment. Ingram had warned him that a writ of impressment was rarely revoked and that Nicholas might well leave empty-handed, but he would at least have discharged his promise to Anne Hendrik, and that was paramount. James Ingram took him across the Great Yard.

'Good-eve, Geoffrey.'

'What? Who might you be, young sir?'

'Have you so soon forgot your favourite chorister?'

'By the Lord! 'Tis never Master Ingram.'

'The same.'

'Welcome, good sir. My old eyes delight to see you.'

The ancient porter was dozing when they rang the bell at his door. He clearly had a great affection for James Ingram, and Nicholas had to wait some minutes while the two men exchanged reminiscences.

'But what brings you here?' croaked Geoffrey.

'We have come to see Master Parsons about one of the choristers and hope to speak to the lad himself.'

'Then your journey has been wasted. Master Parsons is not here and the choir sing in a special service at the Chapel Royal.' He saw their disappointment and tried to lessen it. 'Master Fulbeck may still be here.'

Ingram was surprised. 'Not conducting the choir?'

'No, alas. Too old and too infirm, like me.'

'You seem as well as ever, Geoffrey.'

'I shall not look on seventy again, master.'

After more pleasantries between porter and former chorister, the visitors set off in search of the Master of the Chapel. They went up the stairs and into the playhouse. Nicholas paused to stare with admiration. It was an inspiring little auditorium with features that made the Queen's Head seem primitive. James Ingram was also struck by the major improvements made to the theatre he had known, but neither man was allowed to take a full inventory.

As soon as their eyes moved to the stage itself, they abandoned their appraisal of the building immediately for they were looking at the most dramatic event ever to take place upon its boards. Cyril Fulbeck was indeed there, but he was in no position to talk to either of them. Hanged by the neck, he was swaying slowly to and fro, his spindly legs some five feet above the stage.

The stunned silence was broken by the sound of eerie laughter that seemed to come from somewhere in the tiring-house. The Master of the Chapel was dead and someone was enjoying his demise to the full. Rising in volume, the laughter echoed around the theatre and took on a note of savage celebration.

Chapter four

Nicholas Bracewell reacted with speed. Running to the edge of the chest high stage, he put a hand on it and vaulted up in one easy movement. His first concern was for the victim and he checked to see if the man were still alive, but Cyril Fulbeck was palpably beyond help. James Ingram joined him to look up at the swollen tongue, the contorted expression on the face and the slack body. The last remaining ounces of life had been wrung out of the old man's emaciated frame. Having served his Maker with gentleness and dedication, he had gone to meet Him in the most excruciating way.

The weird laughter stopped, a door banged in the tiring-house and a key could be heard turning in a lock. Nicholas dashed through one of the exits at the rear of the stage and found himself in the tiring-house, which was divided into three main bays. Costumes were hanging from racks and an array of properties was piled up on a low table. A quick search of the whole area revealed a door in one corner, but when Nicholas tried to open it, he found it locked. There seemed to be no other rear exit from the tiring-house.

Leaping off the stage, he sprinted back down the auditorium and descended the winding staircase to the Porter's Lodge. Geoffrey had dozed off to sleep again but he came awake as the book holder went haring past him and out into the Great Yard. Nicholas dashed up to the southern end of the building and scoured it carefully, but he could see nobody. When he tried the door in the room immediately below the tiring-house, it was also locked, as were the doors on the side of the building which gave access to the parlour and the lower hall.

Nicholas called off the search. To reach the exterior of the tiring-house, he had run well over a hundred yards, giving his quarry far too much time to escape. He returned quickly to the theatre itself via the Porter's Lodge. Curious to know what was happening Geoffrey had staggered up the stairs and gone into the auditorium. The hideous sight halted him in his tracks. Nicholas was just in time to catch him as the porter's legs buckled beneath him. Ingram, who had been peering through one of the arched windows that looked out on Water Lane, hurried across to help him. They carried the porter to a bench and lowered him onto it, taking care to stand between him and the stage in order to block out the sight of the hanged man.

Geoffrey was wheezing heavily and trembling all over.

One hand clutched at his breast. Tears flowed freely. It was minutes before he was able to utter a word.

'Not Master Fulbeck!' he groaned.

'That is how we found him,' said Ingram softly.

'He was my dear friend.'

'Mine, too, Geoffrey.'

The porter tried to rise. 'Let me cut him down!'

'Rest,' said Nicholas, easing him back onto the bench.

'Cut him down!' insisted the old man. 'I'll not leave Master Fulbeck up there like that.'

'I'll do it straight,' agreed the book holder.

While Ingram remained to soothe the porter, Nicholas clambered back up onto the stage. The rope from which the Master of the Chapel was dangling went up through a trap-door in the ceiling. Nicholas could see the elaborate winding-gear above that enabled scenic devices and even actors themselves to be lowered onto the stage during the performance of a play. A facility of which Cyril Fulbeck would have been very proud had been used to engineer his death.

Nicholas ran into the tiring-house, went up the ladder to the storey above and found the windlass that controlled the apparatus. Slowly and with reverence, he lowered the dead body to the stage, then returned swiftly in order to examine it. Cyril Fulbeck's bulbous eyes seemed to be on the point of popping out of their sockets. His skin was a ghastly white, his neck encircled by an ugly red weal. But it was the trickle of blood on his shoulder that interested Nicholas. When he rolled the corpse gently onto its side, he saw an open wound in the man's scalp.

As he laid the man on his back again, Nicholas observed that the hem of his cassock was torn, that his black stockings were badly wrinkled and that one of his shoes had come off. He released the noose and lifted the rope clear of its victim. Slipping back into the tiring-house, he chose a large cloak from among the costumes and used it to cover the entire body.

'Let me see him!' sobbed Geoffrey. 'Let me see him!'

'Stay here, old friend,' advised Ingram, putting a hand on his shoulder. 'You have seen enough.'

'He was driven to it, Master Ingram.'

'Driven?'

'To take his own life. 'Tis shameful!'

'Suicide?' asked Nicholas, joining them again. 'Who or what might have driven him to that?'

'It is not my place to say, sir,' said Geoffrey, 'but this I can tell you. Master Fulbeck was very unhappy. It broke his heart, some of the things that went on here. He told me once that his spirits were so low that he was even thinking of putting an end to his misery.' He pointed to the prostrate figure on the stage. 'And now he has!'

'Calm down, calm down!' said Ingram, patting him on the back. 'Master Fulbeck may not have died by his own hand.'

'He did not,' confirmed Nicholas.

The porter flinched from this new intelligence.

'Murdered!' he gasped. 'Never! Who would lay a finger on Master Fulbeck? He was the gentlest soul alive.'

Nicholas sighed. 'Gentle but weak. Unable to defend himself against attack. Who else has been in the building today?'

'None but Master Parsons and the choristers. The boys all left this afternoon.'

'And Raphael Parsons?' said Nicholas.

'He stayed for a while with Master Fulbeck, then left.'

'You saw him go?'

'Not with my own eyes. He left by the other exit.'

'Through the door in the tiring-house?'

'He always comes and goes that way.'

'How, then, can you be certain that he quit the building? That door is a long way from the Porter's Lodge.'

'I spoke with Master Fulbeck not an hour since,' explained Geoffrey. 'He came to the Lodge to draw some water for refreshment. 'Twas he told me that Master Parsons had gone. I think that words had passed between them again. Master Fulbeck was very upset.'

'Did he say why?' probed Nicholas.

'No, sir. Nor was it my place to ask.'

'Did anyone else visit the theatre this evening?'

'Not a soul.'

'Is there no chance that somebody may have come here and escaped your notice?'

The porter was affronted. 'Nobody came, sir. I can vouch for that. Old I may be, but blind and deaf I am not. No man alive could sneak past Geoffrey Bless. Even when my eyes close in sleep, my ears stay wide open. Nobody passed me.'

'But they might have entered by another means.'

'Not into the theatre, sir. The main entrance is up the winding staircase. The only other way to reach the stage is

69

by the back stairs and the back door is kept locked.'

'Who has a key to that door?'

'Only three of us, sir. Myself, Master Parsons and Master Fulbeck. We are very careful to keep the building locked and guarded at all times. Thieves would else come in.'

Or murderers, thought Nicholas. 'I saw no keys upon Master Fulbeck. Where did he carry them?'

'Always at his belt.'

'Habitually?'

'He was never without them.'

'The keys are not at his belt now.'

'Then they have been stolen!' cried Geoffrey.

'And used to make an escape through the back door,' said Ingram, trying to think it through. 'That would explain how someone got out, but how did he get into the theatre in the first place?'

'Perhaps he was hiding in here all along,' suggested Nicholas, scanning the galleries. 'There are places where a patient assassin might lie in wait. The rooms above the stage itself would be an ideal refuge.'

'Nobody was here!' insisted the old man, defending himself against what he saw as a slur on his competence. 'I walk around the whole building first thing in the morning and I do the same at night when I secure it. A mouse could not sneak in without my knowing it.'

Indignation had helped to rally the porter and he had stopped wheezing. He was soon well enough to get up and walk. After a few last questions, Nicholas sent him off to fetch constables in order that he could have a word alone with James Ingram.

They knelt by the body in the middle of the stage. Nicholas drew back the cloak to reveal the staring eyes. Ingram blenched and lowered his own lids in a moment of silent prayer. Nicholas then indicated the bloodstains.

'He has a wound on the back of his head. I believe he was struck from behind by his assailant so that he was unconscious when the rope was placed around his neck. He may only have revived when it was too late.'

'Could he not have called out for help?'

'To whom?' said Nicholas. 'The porter was too far away and there was nobody else in the building. The murderer knew that. In case of interruption, he killed his prey sooner than the rope alone could have done.'

'How do you mean?'

'He grabbed Master Fulbeck by the legs and swung on him with his full weight.' He lifted the other end of the cloak. 'You see the tear in his cassock and the wrinkles in his stockings? A buckle snapped and one shoe was pulled off.'

Ingram was aghast. 'He helped to throttle him?'

'No question. It might otherwise have been a lingering death. Our only comfort is that it speeded up a dreadful execution and shortened the agony.'

'Who could *do* such a thing to sweet Master Fulbeck?'

'Someone who did not think him quite so sweet, James. I mean to track the villain down, however long it takes me. This is heinous work and the killer must answer for it.'

'How will you find him, Nick? Where will you start to look? You have no clues to guide you. The murderer vanished into thin air. I caught no glimpse of him when I ran to the window.' He shrugged his shoulders in despair. 'It is hopeless. You have no notion whom you seek.'

'Yes, I do. A laughing hangman.'

Anne Hendrik was not expecting any visitors to her Bankside house that evening, and she was consequently surprised when there was a knock on the front door. Her servant answered it and the sound of Nicholas Bracewell's voice filtered into the parlour. Putting her embroidery aside, Anne rose to greet him with spontaneous pleasure.

'Nick!'

'I am sorry to disturb you so late.'

'You are more than welcome.'

'Thank you, Anne.'

She offered both hands and he squeezed them gently. That moment alone redeemed in his mind an otherwise grim evening. For the first time in a year, he was back in the house he had shared with her, and it was both exciting and unnerving. Thrilled to be within those walls again, he was painfully aware of the parting that had taken place between the two of them in that same parlour. Nostalgia touched them both deeply and bathed their mutual wounds.

The silence and the mood were shattered by an urgent banging on the door. The servant opened it to admit an eager Ambrose Robinson. Blundering straight into the parlour, he grabbed Nicholas by the arm.

'Have you brought news of Philip?'

'Master Ambrose—'

'I saw you as you walked past my shop,' explained the butcher. 'Even in the shadows, I could not mistake you. Those broad shoulders and that long stride could belong only to our Nicholas Bracewell. Have you been to Blackfriars?'

'Yes.'

'I knew it! What transpired?'

'If you will calm down, I will tell you.'

'Did you see Philip? Have they agreed to release him?'

'Stop badgering him, Ambrose,' said Anne. 'Take a seat and let Nick explain in his own time.'

Robinson accepted the rebuke with his ingratiating smile and moved to a stool. Anne resumed her own seat and Nicholas remained standing to pass on his tidings. The note of oily familiarity in 'our Nicholas Bracewell' still grated on his ear. After one short meeting, Robinson was presuming a bond of friendship that would never exist between them. The book holder was brief.

'I went to Blackfriars this evening in the hope of speaking with Cyril Fulbeck, but that is no longer possible. Master Fulbeck is dead.'

'Dead?' repeated Anne. 'Was his illness that severe?'

'He was murdered.'

'God in Heaven!'

She was utterly shocked, but Ambrose Robinson took an almost perverse delight in the news. As Nicholas gave the two of them full details of what had happened, the butcher came close to smirking. Anne Hendrik offered wholehearted sympathy to the victim, but her

73

neighbour saw it only as a form of crude justice.

'Fulbeck deserved it,' he grunted.

'Ambrose!' exclaimed Anne in reproach.

'No man deserves such an end,' said Nicholas.

'He stole Philip away from me.'

'Cyril Fulbeck's death may make it far more difficult to gain your son's release. By common report, he was a gentle and well-loved Master of the Chapel. His assistant will now take over his duties, but the theatre will be entirely in the hands of Raphael Parsons. *He* is the one from whom we must wrest your son, and he will be far less amenable than the man whose murder brings you such cruel pleasure. Your joyful response is both premature and in poor taste.'

Robinson was far less abashed by Nicholas's strictures than by the glances of disapproval from Anne Hendrik. For her sake, he mumbled an apology, but his eye still had some truculence in it when it met the book holder's. Every time the name of Cyril Fulbeck was mentioned, the butcher sat there in quiet exaltation.

'What will happen next?' asked Anne.

'The law will take its course,' said Nicholas, 'though not with any great speed, I fear. Constables were summoned to the scene and they made examination of the corpse. James Ingram and I helped all we could, then gave sworn statements to the magistrate. The search for the killer has started.'

'I hope and pray that they catch him,' said Anne.

'We will,' vowed Nicholas.

'Are there sufficient clues that point to a murderer?'

'Not as yet, but they will emerge.'

'Poor man!' sighed Anne. 'Did he have a family?'

'Only the choir. All twenty of them will mourn him. Eight vicars choral and twelve choirboys.'

'Philip will not shed a tear,' promised Robinson.

'He may have more compassion than his father.'

'And more tact, Ambrose,' chided Anne. 'Show a proper respect for the deceased. Your attitude is unseemly.'

'Then you are right to tax me with it,' said the butcher with a surge of regret. 'I do not mean to upset you in any way, Anne, but you know my situation. If someone takes your son away, it is difficult to feel anything but hostility towards him. That is only natural but it is also unworthy, as you point out. I accept your correction. Forgive me.'

'It is Nick's forgiveness you should seek, Ambrose. Not mine. He would never have ventured into Blackfriars except on an errand from you.'

'True, true. I spoke out of turn. I crave his pardon.'

There was a bungling politeness about the man which made Nicholas wonder yet again how he had wormed his way into Anne's affections, but the book holder had given his word in front of her and could not go back on that now.

'This is bound to force a delay,' he explained, 'and it may be some time before I can secure an interview with Master Fulbeck's assistant or with Raphael Parsons. When they have a murder on their hands, we cannot expect them to put the future of one chorister to the forefront of their minds.'

'Philip is at the forefront of my mind always!' said the

father proudly. 'We must rescue him. If there is a killer stalking the Blackfriars playhouse, my son must be brought back to the safety of his own home as soon as possible. His own life may be at risk.'

'We must let Nick handle this,' said Anne.

'Of course, of course.'

'He will judge when the time is right to go back.'

'Meanwhile,' said Nicholas to the butcher, 'you must temper your anger with a little patience. Your son may not be as ill-used as you fear. While at Blackfriars Theatre, we took the opportunity to speak with the porter there, one Geoffrey Bless, who has been involved with the choristers for many a year. He knows them all by name and spoke well of young Philip Robinson.'

'What did he say?' demanded the father.

'Little beyond the fact that the lad always had a civil word for him and worked as hard as he was able. Your son is a diligent and talented chorister.'

'That much is not in doubt.'

'One thing still is,' said Nicholas. 'Philip is not the sole victim of Raphael Parsons. All the boys are swinged soundly if they do not attain the high standards which he sets them. Yet none of them is trying to leave the Chapel Children or writing home to entreat some intercession from a parent.'

Robinson's eyes narrowed. 'What are you saying?'

'Your son is the only apostate. Why is that?'

'You read his letters. You could see his terror.'

'His friends do not seem to share it.'

'I do not care a fig for the others!'

76

'Ambrose!' reprimanded Anne.

'My son is in pain. I must save him.'

'Nicholas is working to that end.'

'Yes,' agreed the book holder, 'and the more facts I have at my disposal, the better am I able to act on his behalf. That is why I would like to know why eleven choristers can tolerate a situation that one finds quite unendurable. I will look into it. Bear this in mind, however. Westfield's Men have first claim on my time and my energy.'

'I explained that,' said Anne.

'I want to hear that Master Robinson understands it.'

The butcher squirmed slightly in his seat before nodding his assent. His face moved slowly into a smile of appeasement, but Nicholas saw the muted resentment in his eyes. Ambrose Robinson was evidently a man who could shift from friendship to enmity with no intervening stages. He was no longer taking such obvious satisfaction from the demise of Cyril Fulbeck. He was dripping with envy. Accustomed to slaughtering animals with brutal efficiency, he felt cheated that the Master of the Chapel had escaped the even more horrific death that he would have inflicted upon him.

Nicholas also sensed danger of another kind, and it touched off his protective instinct again. Anne Hendrik had to be guarded from the man. The butcher would pursue his own ends with single-minded determination. Rescuing his son from the Chapel Children was the normal act of a concerned parent, but Nicholas now realised that it was only the first stage in Robinson's domestic plans. Marriage to Anne Hendrik was his next target. In confiding his problem to her, he had both flattered her by showing such trust and activated all her maternal impulses. Anne was wholly committed to the rescue of Philip Robinson.

Annoyed at first to be inveigled into the situation in which he found himself, Nicholas was now almost grateful. It would not only introduce him to the Chapel Children and give him an insight into the way that his young theatrical rivals operated, it would enable him to keep a watchful eye on the amorous butcher.

'When will you go back to Blackfriars?' asked Robinson.

'When time serves,' said Nicholas.

'Please inform me of everything that happens.'

'I will get in touch with Anne.'

Her smile of gratitude was a rich reward for his pains.

Success was an ephemeral pleasure in the theatre. It soon evaporated and could never be taken for granted. The day after the Queen's Head had reverberated to the cheers for *The Misfortunes of Marriage*, the troupe were back on the same makeshift stage to rehearse *The History of King John*. It was a staple drama from their repertoire and was beginning to look well worn. Edmund Hoode patched it assiduously each time it was played again, but even his art could not turn the piece into anything more than workmanlike chronicle. In the wake of Jonas Applegarth's play, it was bound to look dull and uninspiring. Westfield's Men would have to strive hard in order to lift *King John* to the level of a minor achievement. It could never emulate the triumph that was *The Misfortunes of Marriage*.

Lawrence Firethorn was all too conscious of this fact.

'From a mountain peak,' he said, striking a pose, 'down to the foothills. From cold Sir Marcus to Bad King John.'

'The play has served us well in the past,' reminded Edmund Hoode. 'You have *Magna Carta*-red your way through it fifty times without complaint.'

'That was before we had Jonas Applegarth.'

Hoode recoiled visibly. He was less hurt by the blow to his pride than by the implications of Firethorn's remark. The playwright had gritted his teeth to endure close proximity to Applegarth in the hope that the latter was a bird of passage. Was a more permanent relationship with the company now envisaged? Hoode was bound to wonder where that eventuality would leave its resident playwright.

'No offence meant to you,' said Firethorn hastily, when he saw the dismay on the other's face. 'And it will not affect your position among us in any way, Edmund.'

'I am relieved to hear that.'

'You will always be our leading author. You are the very foundation of Westfield's Men. Take but you away and we all tumble into a bottomless pit.'

He went off for a few minutes into such a fulsome paean of praise that Hoode lowered his guard. They were standing in the inn yard after the morning's rehearsal. Five yards away was the stage on which most of Hoode's plays had first come to life before an admiring audience. Firethorn's eulogy bolstered his self-esteem and made him feel deeply heartened. It did not last. Reassurance soon changed to dread.

'On the other hand,' warned Firethorn, 'we would be fools to spurn a dramatic jewel when it falls into our lap, and *The Misfortunes of Marriage* is unquestionably such a jewel. That is why we must stage it again.'

'Again?'

'Again and again and again.'

'It is to be our sole offering, then?'

'Of course not, Edmund. Every jewel needs a setting and we will surround it with baser material.'

'*My* plays!'

'No, not yours,' said Firethorn, trying to placate him. 'Well, not only yours. That does not mean your art is base or merely semi-precious. Far from it, man. You shower the stage with diamonds every time you pick up your pen and dazzle every eye. But Jonas has given us a much larger stone.'

'I feel the weight of it around my neck.'

'He has enriched us all beyond measure. Westfield's Men must respond accordingly.' Firethorn bestowed an affectionate smile on his friend before hitting him with his decision. 'That is why we play *The Misfortunes of Marriage* at The Rose.'

Hoode gulped. 'The Rose?'

'Ten days hence.'

'But my new play was to have graced The Rose!'

'And so it will, Edmund. In time, in time.'

'We so rarely seize upon the chance to work at the

theatre. It may be months before *The Faithful Shepherd* travels to Bankside.'

'A good play is like a good wine, old friend. It improves with age. Store it until a fitter time.'

'Why cannot Jonas do that with his play?'

'Because it has already been uncorked. It has already been tasted. You saw that audience yesterday. Drunk with joy at the play and doubly drunk with my performance as Sir Marcus Coldbed. They clamour for more. We must slake their thirst.'

'But not at The Rose, surely?'

'Where better?'

'Lawrence, you *promised.*'

And I will keep that promise – in due course.'

'*The Faithful Shepherd* stands first in line.'

'Jonas Applegarth leaps over it.'

'That is unjust.'

'Theatre mixes pain with its plaudits.'

'This is cruel in the extreme.'

'Is it not a greater cruelty to deny our patrons what they demand? We serve a fickle public, Edmund. Soon, they may cast *The Misfortunes of Marriage* away as worthless trash. At this moment, however, it is the talk of London. Lord Westfield himself was so entranced with the piece, he'll not rest until everyone at Court has been told about it. He insists that it take pride of place at The Rose.'

'Lord Westfield insists?'

'That was my understanding,' lied Firethorn, using the one argument that Hoode could not defeat. 'Who am I to flout the express wishes of our generous patron?'

Hoode sagged. 'Then am I truly lost.'

'Your day will come again.'

'Will I live to enjoy it, though?'

Firethorn chuckled. 'I knew that you would accept this unwonted check with fortitude. Be not afraid of Jonas Applegarth. He has not come to displace you in any way. Edmund Hoode is what he has always been to Westfield's Men. Our faithful shepherd.'

'Then why let a wolf into the fold?'

'We keep him well muzzled.'

'Look to your lambs. His claws can still kill.'

'It is decided.'

Lawrence Firethorn tossed his cloak over his shoulder and strode off towards the tiring-house, leaving Hoode speechless with indignation. A play over which he had laboured devotedly for months had been pushed contemptuously aside. It was an honour to have any work staged at a fine playhouse like The Rose, and *The Faithful Shepherd* was written specifically for that theatre. Jonas Applegarth had robbed him of that honour. Hoode had one more reason to resent the obese interloper.

He was distraught. He felt completely estranged from Westfield's Men. It was as if members of his own family had turned him out of the house in favour of a newcomer. Hoode contemplated suicide. Had he been standing on London Bridge, he would certainly have jumped off it, howling the name of Applegarth with defiance before hitting the cold water and drowning with alacrity.

While he was at the very nadir of his career, Fate stepped in to save him. It came in the shape of Rose Marwood, the landlord's daughter, a vivacious young woman with long dark hair and a readiness to please. How two parents as physically repellent as Alexander and Sybil Marwood could produce such an attractive creature between them he did not know, but it often exercised his mind. It was rather as if two gargoyles had copulated in order to produce a statute of a Madonna.

Hoode had once conceived a foolish passion for her that led only to humiliation, and so he tended to keep clear of the landlord's daughter. Rose's shining face was now an embarrassment to him.

'I have a message for you, Master Hoode,' she said.

'For me?'

'Put it into his hands, I was told.'

'By whom?'

'The lady who gave it to me.'

'Lady? What lady?'

'She would not tell me her name, sir.' Rose handed over the missive and gave a little curtsey.

'Can you describe this lady to me?' he said.

'I saw her for only a moment, sir. She said that I was to give the letter to you in person. It is a gift.'

'Gift?'

'From her mistress.'

Rose giggled, showed two exquisite dimples in her cheeks, and bounded off towards the taproom. Hoode was intrigued. He broke the seal on the letter and opened it to find a red rose pressed inside. Only three words had been written in an elegant hand, but they clutched at his very soul.

'To my love . . .'

Jonas Applegarth scratched his head as he quaffed his beer. The empty tankard was slammed back down on the table by way of a signal and it was soon filled by a servingman.

'Who could wish to kill Cyril Fulbeck?' he wondered.

'That is what we must find out,' said Nicholas.

'I'd happily have hanged his partner, Raphael Parsons. If ever a man invited a noose, it is that rogue. But not that shuffling Master of the Chapel. He was a harmless fellow.'

'Everyone speaks well of him.'

'He was a dear man and a gifted teacher,' said James Ingram. 'Cyril Fulbeck was the epitome of goodness.'

'Then why ally himself to such a villain as Parsons?'

'I do not know.'

'Nor I,' added Nicholas, 'but the talk is that the two men did not agree. Geoffrey, the porter, often heard arguments between them.'

'There is your murderer, then,' decided Applegarth. 'Look no further than Raphael Parsons. He stands to gain most from Fulbeck's death.'

'He must be suspect, assuredly,' said Nicholas, 'but I would not accuse him without further evidence. Indeed, one clue suggests he may be innocent of the crime.'

'What is that, Nick?' asked Ingram.

'The key to the back door of Blackfriars Theatre.'

'But Master Parsons has such a key. He, and only he, had the means to gain entrance privily. Unless you believe that old Geoffrey was involved in some way. His key fits that same lock.'

'We may exclude him straight,' said Nicholas. 'You saw the way he cried when he beheld the dead man. He was as shocked as we. The porter has no part in this.'

'You spoke of Parsons's innocence,' noted Applegarth.

'A suggestion of innocence,' corrected the book holder. 'If Raphael Parsons had a key that admitted him to the back door of the theatre, why did he steal Master Fulbeck's keys in order to get out again?'

'To prevent us from following him,' said Ingram.

'But we were unexpected visitors, and the keys had been stolen from the dead man's belt before we arrived.'

'I have it,' announced Applegarth. 'This Parsons is too devious and cowardly a man to do the deed himself. He hired a confederate, let him into the building and locked the door after him before quitting the scene. The killer stole the other keys to effect his escape.'

'This was no confederate,' affirmed Nicholas.

'How do you know?' said Ingram.

'You heard that man, James. He was no assassin, paid to kill a complete stranger. He *knew* Cyril Fulbeck and gloried in his death. The Laughing Hangman would never have delegated to another a task which gave him so much pleasure. He was connected in some way to the Master of the Chapel.'

'As his business partner,' asserted Applegarth.

'Master Parsons may be only one of many possibilities.'

'I'll help you to draw up a list,' offered Ingram.

'Thank you, James.'

It was early evening and they had moved to the taproom of the Queen's Head after the performance of *The History of King John*. The play had been a moderate success but seemed flat by comparison with *The Misfortunes of Marriage*. Jonas Applegarth had snored through the last two acts. Exhilarated at the thought that his own play would now be seen at The Rose, he was already working on refinements to the text. Considering himself now part of the troupe, he was ready to sit through their other work out of loyalty even if it bored him into slumber.

Nicholas emptied his tankard and rose from the table.

'I bid you farewell, my friends.'

'Hold,' said Applegarth, struggling to his feet. 'I'll walk part of the way with you. My house is close to Thames Street and there is something I would discuss as we walk.'

'Your company is most welcome.'

'What of Blackfriars?' said Ingram.

'We'll go again tomorrow, James. Meanwhile, gather what intelligence you can. You must have other old friends from the Chapel Children, choristers who stayed on when you left? Perhaps they can shed some light on this tragedy. I am certain that we look for someone who is, or once was, within Master Fulbeck's circle.'

'Leave it with me, Nick. I'll about it straight.'

They traded farewells, then Nicholas and Applegarth headed for the door, passing, as they did, Edmund Hoode. His feeling of betrayal had faded and a beatific smile now played around his lips. The rose from Rose Marwood had transformed him from a discarded playwright into a hopeful lover. Recognising the look on his friend's face, Nicholas glided past without comment and simply waved.

The book holder led Applegarth out into the fresh air.

'I have an idea for my play,' said the latter.

'It is already crammed full with ideas.'

'A scenic device. Something that we could lower from above with the winding gear they have at The Rose.'

'They have it at Blackfriars, too,' observed Nicholas as he recalled the hanging man. 'What do you wish to lower onto the stage?'

The question remained unanswered because Jonas Applegarth stumbled over the uneven surface of Gracechurch Street and pitched forward. Clumsiness saved his life. Something whistled through the air with vicious speed and sank with a thud into the door of the house directly behind them.

The dagger missed Applegarth by a matter of inches.

Chapter five

The suddenness of the attack took them both by surprise. By the time that Nicholas Bracewell swung round, there was no sign of the assailant. Several other people were walking peacefully along Gracechurch Street, and he called out to those nearest, but none of them had seen anyone throw a dagger. Fear of danger made them scurry quickly away. Nicholas went swiftly up and down the street in search of the assassin, but to no avail. For the second time in twenty-four hours, he was chasing shadows.

He went back to help Jonas Applegarth up from the ground. The latter was more concerned about the state of his apparel than about the ambush.

'Mud on my new breeches!' he complained bitterly. 'And a tear in my sleeve.'

'Someone just tried to kill you, Jonas.'

'Look at the state of my shoes.'

'Does it not concern you?' asked Nicholas.

'Mightily. My wife will take me to task for it.'

'I speak of the attack.'

'A mild annoyance, no more,' said Applegarth, dusting himself off. 'Why should I fear such a lame assassin? If he cannot hit a target as large as me, he must be blind. Besides, who says that *I* was his target? Perhaps the dagger was meant for you, Nick. Have you considered that?'

Nicholas had and dismissed the possibility. The weapon had been thrown directly at Applegarth and only the man's fall had helped him to evade it. Plucking the dagger from its resting place, Nicholas tried to work out from where it must have been thrown. A lane on the opposite side of the street turned out to be the vantage point. It would give the assailant good cover and an excellent view of anyone leaving the Queen's Head. He could have fled unseen while the dagger itself was still in flight.

After inspecting the weapon, Nicholas offered it to his companion. Applegarth showed scant interest.

'Do you recognise this?' said Nicholas.

'It is a dagger like any other.'

'Other daggers are not thrown at you, Jonas.'

'One or two have been in the past,' said the playwright with a grim chuckle. 'This one was as wayward as they were. No, Nick, I do not recognise it. A mean weapon, that is clear. Toss it away and forget all about it.'

'But it may lead us to your attacker.'

'Leave him to me.'

'You know who he is?'

'I have many enemies.'

'Match this dagger to one man and you have him.'

'Do not trouble yourself so. This is my battle.'

'And mine,' said Nicholas, slipping the dagger into his own belt. 'You are the property of Westfield's Men now. It is my duty to protect you as I would protect any other part of our property.'

Applegarth stiffened. 'I need no bodyguard.'

'You are in *danger*, Jonas.'

'I will live with that fear.'

They resumed their walk and the playwright returned to the subject of The Rose. His work would be seen by a larger and more perceptive audience at the Bankside theatre. He was anxious to improve the play in any way that he could. Applegarth was still explaining his ideas when they turned into Thames Street. The smell of the river invaded his nostrils and they could hear it lapping against the wharves down to their left.

Applegarth paused on the corner of the next street. 'Let me see it again, Nick,' he said.

'See what?'

'The dagger. Haply, I do recognise it.'

'Here,' said Nicholas, passing it to him. 'There are some marks upon the hilt that may be initials.'

'Ah yes. I see.'

After pretending to study the weapon, Jonas Applegarth turned round and pulled back his arm to propel the dagger with full force. It spun crazily through the air and landed with a loud splash in the river.

Nicholas was bewildered by his friend's action, but the latter chortled happily.

'There. 'Tis all past now. Think no more about it.'

'But that dagger was to have been a murder weapon.'

'I have blocked it out of my mind.'

'You have thrown away the one clue that we had.'

'There will be other nights, other daggers.'

'Next time, you may not have such good fortune.'

'Next time,' said Applegarth, 'I will not be taken unawares. This was a useful warning, but there's an end to it. I'll not lose sleep over the matter.'

Nicholas was convinced that the playwright knew the name of his attacker, but it could not be prised out of him. Jonas Applegarth lapsed into a kind of jocular bravado that was proof against all questioning. Even though it took him out of his way, Nicholas insisted on walking back to his friend's house to make sure that he got home safely. The journey passed without further incident.

Applegarth beamed hospitably at his colleague.

'Will you step in to continue our debate?'

'Not tonight, Jonas.'

'But I have much more to say about my play.'

'We will find time tomorrow,' said Nicholas. 'Stay alert and keep your doors locked. Your attacker may return during the night.'

Applegarth shrugged. 'What attacker?'

Nicholas could not understand his apparent unconcern. An attempt had been made on the man's life, yet he was choosing to ignore it. The book holder foresaw further trouble ahead and his anxiety was for the company as well as for its newest recruit. Westfield's Men might yet live to regret their association with the brilliant talent of Jonas Applegarth.

'Are you sure that you will not stay, Nick?'

'Unhappily, I may not.'

'There is plentiful wine within.'

'Thank you. But I have another call to make.'

The study was on the first floor of the house in Thames Street. Around all four walls were oak shelves heavily laden with books, documents, maps and manuscripts. Two long tables occupied most of the space and they were covered with more books and rolls of parchment. Quill pens lay sharpened in a little wooden box. Ink stood ready in a large well. The whole room smelt of musty scholarship.

Caleb Hay sat beneath the sagging beams and pored over a medieval document with intense concentration. He used a magnifying glass to help him translate the minuscule Latin script. His eyes sparkled with fascination as he took a privileged walk through the past of his beloved London. So absorbed was he in his research that he did not hear the respectful tap on the door of his study. His wife had to bang more loudly before she caught his attention.

Bristling with annoyance, he glared at the door.

'What is it?' he snapped.

'Can you spare a minute, Caleb?' she asked tentatively.

'No!'

'He said that it was important.'

'I've told you a hundred times, Joan. My work must not be interrupted. For any reason.'

'But you have a visitor.'

'Send him on his way.'

'He is too persistent, husband.'

'I'll see nobody.'

'He claims to be a friend of yours.'

'Friends know better than to disturb my studies. They only come to my house by invitation, and that rarely. Persistent, you say? Who is this rogue?'

'Nicholas Bracewell.'

'Give him a dusty answer and bid him farewell,' Caleb said abruptly. 'No, tarry a while,' he added, as curiosity began to grapple with irritation. 'Nicholas Bracewell, is it? What does he want with me? Did he state his business?'

'No, Caleb.'

'But he told you that it was important?'

'Yes,' she confirmed. 'He is a most polite and courteous gentleman, but resolved on talking to you.'

Caleb Hay glanced down at his work. Pursing his lips, he shook his head in mild anger before finally relenting.

'Ask him to stay. I'll come down anon.'

'Thank you!'

Waiting in the parlour below, Nicholas Bracewell heard the relief in her voice. Joan Hay was a submissive wife, eager to avoid her husband's displeasure. The mild-mannered historian whom Nicholas knew was evidently a more despotic creature within his own home.

She came clattering down the stairs to rejoin the visitor. A short, slim, timorous woman in a plain dress, she gave him a nervous smile of apology and relayed the message before bowing out again. Nicholas listened to the sound of a heavy bolt being drawn back in the study. A key turned in a stout lock and the door creaked open. It was immediately closed and locked. Feet padded down the wooden steps.

Caleb Hay shuffled in with an irritated politeness.

'Well met, Master Bracewell!'

'I am sorry to break in upon your studies.'

'A matter of some significance must have brought you.'

'Yes,' said Nicholas. 'It concerns Blackfriars.'

'Go on, sir.'

'I need you to tell me something of its recent past.'

'This is hardly the moment for a lesson in history,' said his host with quiet outrage. 'Have you dragged me away from my desk to purvey a few anecdotes about a friary?'

'With good reason, Master Hay.'

'And what may that be?'

'It touches on a murder lately carried out there.'

'A murder?'

'The victim was Cyril Fulbeck.'

'Cyril Fulbeck?' echoed Hay incredulously. 'The Master of the Chapel has been *murdered?* How? When?'

'He was hanged on the stage of the Blackfriars Theatre but yesterday.'

'Dear God! Can this be true? Cyril Fulbeck was a true Christian. The soul of kindness. Who could have wrought

94

such villainy upon him?' He grasped Nicholas by the arm. 'Have the rogues been caught? This heinous crime must be answered.'

'So it will be, Master Hay. With your help.'

'It is at your disposal, sir.'

His host waved Nicholas to a seat and sat beside him. Caleb Hay swung between agitation and sorrow. He pressed for more detail and Nicholas recounted the facts. The older man shook his head in disbelief.

'Cyril Fulbeck!' he sighed. 'I spoke with him not ten days ago. A gracious gentleman in every way.'

'You know him well, then?'

'Tolerably well. He gave me the kindest assistance in my work. The Master of the Chapel is a person of consequence. Through him, I gained access to many documents that would else have lain beyond my reach. He could not have been more helpful, nor I more grateful for that help.'

'How did you find him at that last meeting?'

'Not in the best of health, alas. Ailing badly.'

'I speak of his mood.'

'Sombre. Sombre and full of remorse. He seemed much oppressed by the cares of his office.'

'Did he confide the reasons?'

'No, no,' said Hay firmly. 'Nor did I seek them. It was not my place to meddle in his private affairs. I am a scholar and not a father confessor.'

'What dealings did you have with Raphael Parsons?'

'None whatsoever – thank heaven!'

'Why do you say that?'

'Common report has him a most unprepossessing fellow. I wonder that Cyril Fulbeck allowed the man near him. I had no call to make the acquaintance of Master Parsons. If you seek intelligence about him, look elsewhere for it.'

'Tell me about Blackfriars,' said Nicholas.

Hay brightened. 'Ah! Now, there, I am on firm ground. I can teach you all that may be taught on that subject. A Dominican House was first founded in London in 1221 at a site in Chancery Lane. Some fifty years or more later, Robert Fitzwalter gave them Baynard's Castle and Montfichet Tower on the river, enabling them to build a much larger monastery. King Edward I, of blessed memory, offered his patronage, and the House became rich and influential as a result.'

'I am more interested in recent events there.'

'They can only be judged aright if set against the ancient traditions of Blackfriars,' insisted Hay with a pedagogic zeal. 'Parliament first met there in 1311. It was later used as a repository for records relating to matters of state. Later still – in the years 1343, 1370, 1376 and 1378, to be exact – it was the meeting place of the Court of Chancery. Parliaments and Privy Councils were often convened there. Visiting dignitaries from foreign lands stayed there as honoured guests. In our own century,' he said, sniffing noisily in disapproval, 'a court sat in Blackfriars to hear the divorce case against that worthy lady, Catherine of Aragon. In that same fateful year of 1529, Parliament met there to bring a Bill of Attainder against Cardinal Wolsey.'

'All this is fascinating,' said Nicholas patiently, 'but not entirely relevant to my enquiry.'

'But you need to understand the greatness of the House in order to appreciate how ruinously it has dwindled. Before the suppression of the Religious, it was a major presence in the city. But now . . .'

'Largely demolished.'

'And the Dominicans expelled.' He gave an involuntary shudder. 'To make way for members of your profession.'

'The playhouse was not built until some years later.'

'In 1576, to be precise. Consecrated ground, used as a scaffold for lewd performance. By children, no less! Sweet choristers, whose voices should have been uplifted in praise of their Maker.' He became sharply self-critical. 'But I go beyond the bounds of my purpose here. An antiquarian must report the progress of events without making undue comment upon them. What is done is done. Who cares one way or the other what Caleb Hay may think about the Children of the Chapel?'

'I do,' said Nicholas.

'You are too indulgent, my friend,' said the other with a smile. 'When I fulminate against plays and players, you take the blows on your back with stoic resignation and never offer me a buffeting in return.'

'I admire plain speaking.'

'My guilt is unassuaged. You do not deserve to have my trenchant opinions thrust upon you. I console myself with the thought that a man of the theatre must hear harsher tongues than mine in the course of his working day.'

'That is certainly true,' said Nicholas, thinking of

Lawrence Firethorn's blistering tirades. 'But you forget that I sailed around the globe with Sir Francis Drake. Modest language has no place aboard a ship. Men speak in the roundest of terms. Your gibes are Holy Scripture beside the profanities of seafarers. Rail against the theatre as much as you wish, Master Hay. Simply give me the instruction that I seek.'

'In what particular?'

'Describe the first Blackfriars Theatre.'

'A species of Hell!'

Nicholas laughed. 'I wish to know something of its appearance and dimensions. Did it have secret passages leading to it or an underground vault beneath it? What changes were made when it was refurbished? Describe, if you will, all possible ways into the building.'

'You have first to get into the precinct.'

'Of course.'

'Five acres of land is all that is left of the original monastic community. They form the liberty of Blackfriars. It preserves its ancient right of sanctuary. Do you know what other privilege is bestowed upon them?'

'Only too well,' said Nicholas enviously. 'They are within the city walls yet free from city jurisdiction. We have no such freedom. While we at the Queen's Head must perforce observe the Sabbath and forego performance, the Blackfriars Theatre is able to stage its plays on the Lord's Day with impunity. That is a most important liberty.'

'The theatre is only a small part of the whole. It shares the precinct with the fine houses of respectable families.

The whole area is walled and its four gates are locked each night by the porter. Blackfriars is an address of note. You will know, I am sure, that many of its inhabitants fought hard to prevent a theatre from being reopened on the site.'

'I believe that a petition was drawn up.'

'Drawn up and willingly signed. It kept the boards clear of actors for an interval. Then Cyril Fulbeck made his shameful arrangement with Raphael Parsons.'

'Is that how the Master of the Chapel described it?' said Nicholas. 'As a shameful arrangement?'

'I intrude my own prejudices once more,' said Hay with a note of apology. 'That is not good, not right, not scholarly. Henceforth, I'll keep to particulars. What is it you seek? Dimensions and alterations? You will not lack for detail here, Master Bracewell. I will tell you all.'

Caleb Hay fulfilled his boast. He took his guest on a guided tour of Blackfriars, measuring out each wall, noting each doorway, indicating everything of even moderate significance and generally painting such a vivid picture in words that Nicholas saw the remains of the monastery rising before his eyes. It was uncanny. The older man tried to speak with deliberate calm but a more passionate note crept in from time to time. Here was someone who cared so deeply for the glorious past of London that he still lived in it.

Nicholas absorbed the salient details and thanked him.

'I will speak further, if you wish,' offered his host.

'You have told me all I need to know, Master Hay.'

'Pray God that it may help you! If I thought that my

99

knowledge of this flower of cities could somehow lead you to the devils who committed this unspeakable act, I would give you a different lecture on the history of Blackfriars every day of the week.'

'You have been most generous with your time.'

'Call on me again,' said Hay. 'I am desirous to know how well your enquiries go. Cyril Fulbeck was as decent a man as any in Christendom. Pursue his killers.'

'I will do so,' promised Nicholas, 'but I think that only one person is involved here. A perverse creature who takes delight in his villainy.'

He thought for a moment of the body swinging helplessly on the stage at the Blackfriars Theatre. The Master of the Chapel had been given no chance to resist as the breath of life was squeezed out of him inch by inch. It was a brutal death and it sent a chilling message. Nicholas would not easily forget the pallid horror on the face of the victim. Nor could he erase from his mind the glee of the murderer. That was what appalled him the most. The sound filled his ears so completely and so painfully that he had to shake his head to escape the callous mockery of the Laughing Hangman.

Too much drink and too little conversation had left Edmund Hoode in a state of maudlin confusion. Seated alone in a corner of the taproom at the Queen's Head, he was oblivious to the raucous jollity all around him. He sipped, he meditated, he sank ever deeper into bewilderment. Hoode was not sure whether he should be devastated by the tidings from Lawrence Firethorn or inspired by the message from Rose Marwood, and so he shifted with speed between despair and hope until they blended in his mind. A look of inebriated perplexity settled on his moonlike face.

A friendly arm descended upon his shoulder.

'Come, Edmund,' said a lilting voice. 'Time to leave.'

'What's that?' he murmured.

'You need help to get home. Lean on me.'

'Why?'

'Because those legs of yours would not take you more than seven yards towards Silver Street.'

To prove his point, Owen Elias hoisted him up, then let go of him. Hoode swayed violently, steadied himself on edge of the table, then felt a surge of confidence. He took three bold strides across the floor before losing his balance and pitching forward. The Welshman caught him just in time.

'Let's do it *my* way,' he said jovially. 'Otherwise, you must crawl back to your lodging on all fours.'

'You are a true friend, Owen.'

'I know that you would do the same for me.'

'Indeed, indeed,' mumbled the other.

It was an unlikely eventuality. Hoode was frequently overcome by alcohol, grief or unrequited love, and sometimes by a lethal combination of all three. Elias, by contrast, could carouse endlessly without lapsing into anything more than merriment or music, rarely gave way to sorrow, and led a career of cheerful lechery among the womenfolk of London. Half-carrying the drooping poet, he came out into the night and headed slowly towards Cripplegate Ward.

'What is her name, Edmund?' he asked.

'Name?'

'Your heart is heavy, my friend. I can feel the full weight pressing down on me. It is an all too familiar burden. Who is she this time?'

'I do not know, Owen.'

'A lady without a name?'

'Without a name, a face or substance of any kind.'

'An invisible creature?'

'To all intents.'

'Explain.'

To provide anything as logical as an explanation placed an enormous strain on Hoode's shattered senses, but he did his best. As he ambled along, supported by his friend, he tried to piece together the events of a day which had both destroyed and resurrected him. No sooner had his new play been evicted than an anonymous tenant moved into his heart. He pulled out the flower which he had slipped under his doublet. Crushed and forlorn, it yet retained the fragrance of its message. Elias noted the irony of the situation.

'You have lost one Rose and gained another,' he observed. 'Two, if we count the landlord's comely daughter. Rose Marwood is a rose in full bloom. It is a source of great regret to me that even my skilful hands have not been able to pluck her from the stem. Her parents are entwined around the girl like prickly thorns. They have drawn blood from my lustful fingers on more than one occasion.'

'Leave we Rose Marwood to her own devices,' said Hoode. 'She was only the messenger here, and my concern is with the message itself. Or rather, with the lady who sent it.'

'Your inamorata.'

'If such she be, Owen.'

'No question of that. You hold the certain testimony of her love in your grasp.'

'I hold a rose, it is true,' said Hoode gloomily.

'But was it sent by a female hand?'

Elias guffawed. 'A male admirer! Have you awakened some dark passion in a love-struck youth? Do not tell Barnaby of this conquest or he will roast on a spit of envy.'

'You misunderstand.'

'Then speak more clearly.'

'I fear me that this is some trick.'

'On whose behalf?'

'Some fellow in the company who means to buy a laugh or two at my expense. Luck has never attended my loving, Owen. Cupid has used my heart for some cruel archery practice over the years. Why should fortune favour me now?'

'Because you deserve it, Edmund.'

'Fate has never used me according to my desserts before,' said Hoode. 'No, this is some jest. The love token was sent to torment me. Someone in the company means to raise my hopes in order to dash them down upon the rocks of his derision.' He looked down at the rose. 'I would do well to cast it away and tread it under foot.'

'Stay!' said Elias, grabbing his wrist. 'Can you not see a rich prize when it stands before you? This is no jest, my friend. Westfield's Men love you too much to practise such villainy upon you. This message could not be more precise. You have made a conquest, Edmund. Take her.'

Hoode stopped in his tracks. 'Can this be true?'

'Incontestably.'

'I have at last won the heart of a lady?'

'Heart, mind and body.'

'Wonder of wonders,' Hoode said, sniffing the rose before concealing it in his doublet once more. 'I almost begin to believe it. It is such an unexpected bounty.'

'They are the choicest kind.'

'If this be love, indeed, it must be requited.'

'Enjoy her!'

'I will, Owen.'

'Go to your bed so that you may dream dreams of joy.'

'Press on.'

Still supported by the Welshman, Hoode lurched along the street with a new sense of purpose. Someone cared for him. He luxuriated in the thought for a whole glorious minute. A cold frost then attacked the petals of his happiness. The other Rose delivered a message of a different order.

'My occupation is gone,' he moaned.

'That is not so, Edmund.'

'I am pushed aside to make way for the ample girth of this Applegarth. There is not room enough in Westfield's Men for him and for me.'

'Indeed there is. Most companies lack one genius to fashion their plays. We have two. Our rivals are consumed with jealousy at our good fortune.'

'My talents have been eclipsed.'

'Never!'

'They have, Owen. *The Misfortunes of Marriage* is work of a higher order than I can produce. It ousts me from the Rose Theatre, and rightly so.'

'Your new piece will have its turn anon.'

'How will it fare in the shadow of Jonas's play? *The Faithful Shepherd* is a pigmy beside a giant. Why stage it and invite disgrace? I have suffered enough pain already.'

'You do yourself wrong,' said Elias earnestly. 'Jonas has one kind of talent, you have quite another. Both can dazzle an audience in equal measure. Jonas may invest more raw power in his verse, but you have a grace and subtlety that he can never match.'

'He is better.'

'Different, that is all.'

'Different in kind, superior in quality.'

'That is a matter of opinion.'

'It is Lawrence's view,' sighed Hoode, 'and his is the opinion that holds sway in Westfield's Men. He commissioned my new play for The Rose and could not have been more delighted with it. Until, that is, he espied this new star in the firmament. *The Faithful Shepherd* is then shunned like a leper and I become an outcast poet.'

'No more of this self-imposed melancholy!'

'I am finished, Owen. Dispatched into obscurity.'

'Enough!' howled the other, thrusting him against the wall of a house and holding him there with one hand. 'Jonas Applegarth will never displace Edmund Hoode.

You have given us an endless stream of fine plays, he has provided us with one. You are part of the fabric of the company, he is merely a colourful patch which has been sewn on.'

'His play is the talk of London.'

'How long will that last?'

'Until he produces a new one to shame me even more.'

'No!' yelled Elias.

'He has robbed me of my future.'

'Look to the past instead.'

'Why?'

'Because there you will read the true story of Jonas Applegarth,' said the Welshman persuasively. 'A huge talent fills those huge breeches of his, it is true, but Westfield's Men are not the first to perceive this. Jonas has been taken up and thrown back by every other troupe in London. He was too choleric for their taste.'

'What are you telling me, Owen?'

'He will not stay with us for long. His blaze of glory will be no more than that. A mere blaze that lights up the heavens before fading away entire. We must profit from his brilliance while we may. Jonas will not survive.' Owen patted his friend of the cheek. 'You will, Edmund.'

Nicholas Bracewell was almost invariably the first member of the company to arrive at the Queen's Head at the start of the day. On the next morning, however, the thud of a hammer told him that one of his colleagues had risen even earlier than he. Nathan Curtis, the master carpenter, was repairing a table for use in the performance that afternoon. Busy at his trade, he did not see the book holder striding across the inn yard towards him.

'Good-morrow, Nathan!' greeted Nicholas.

'Ah!' He looked up. 'Well met!'

'I wish that everyone was as diligent in their duties as you. You will have finished that table before some of our fellows have even dragged themselves out of bed.'

'There is much to do. When I have restored this, I must make some new scenic devices. And you spoke, I believe, about some properties that are in request.'

'One rock, one cage, one crosier's staff.'

'I'll need precise instructions.'

Nicholas passed them on at once and the carpenter nodded obediently. Curtis was a rough-looking man in working apparel, but his voice was soft and his manner almost diffident. His craftsmanship helped to put flesh on the bones of a play. Nicholas had another reason to be grateful of a moment alone with him. Curtis lived in Bankside. When the book holder lodged in Anne Hendrik's house, he and the carpenter were neighbours. The latter might well know one of the other denizens of the area.

'Are you acquainted with an Ambrose Robinson, by any chance?'

'Robinson the Butcher?'

'The same.'

'I know him as well as I wish to, Nick.'

'You do not like the man, I think.'

'I do not trust him,' admitted the other. 'He sells good

meat and is polite enough in his shop, but he hides his true feelings from you. I never know where I am with the fellow. His mouth may smile but his eyes are cold and watchful. My wife cannot abide him.'

'He is not an appealing man,' agreed Nicholas.

'How came you to meet him?'

'Through a mutual friend.'

'Ah, yes!' said Curtis. 'I should have linked their names.'

'Why do you say that?'

'We talk of Mistress Hendrik, do we not?'

'We do, Nathan.'

'Then *she* will have introduced him to you. The butcher is fast becoming a close companion of hers.'

Nicholas bridled slightly. 'Indeed?'

'My wife has often seen him visiting her house and both of us have taken note of them on Sundays.'

'Why so?'

'Because we worship at the same altar, Nick. It has been going on for a month or more now.'

'What has?'

'Mistress Hendrik and Ambrose Robinson. I was surprised at first, my wife even more so. We both have the highest respect for Mistress Hendrik. Her late husband was as decent a neighbour as we could choose. Not so this butcher. He is not worthy of her. But there is no gainsaying what we saw.'

'And what was that?'

'They come to church together.'

The information was deeply unsettling, and Nicholas took time to assimilate it. If Anne Hendrik was allowing Robinson to accompany her to her devotions, their relationship must be on a more serious footing than Nicholas realised. Before he could speak again, an ancient voice interrupted them. Thomas Skillen, the venerable stagekeeper, was talking to a stranger on the other side of the yard and pointing a bony finger at the book holder. The visitor thanked him and bore down on Nicholas, giving the latter only a second or two to appraise him.

He was a man of moderate height and square build, wearing a black doublet and hose which was offset by a lawn ruff and by the ostrich feather in his black soft-crowned hat. His black Spanish cape had a red lining. Neat, compact and dignified, he was in his late thirties. His voice was remarkably deep and had a slight Northern tang to it.

'May I have a word alone?' the visitor said, giving his request the force of a command. 'It is needful.'

'Let's stand aside.'

Nicholas moved him a few yards away so that Nathan Curtis could resume his work. The carpenter's hammer was deafening and the stink of fresh horse dung was pungent. Wrinkling his nose in disgust, the visitor waved a dismissive arm.

'I'll not stay here in the middle of the yard like some idle ostler complaining about the price of hay. I desire some private conference.'

Nicholas stood his ground. 'What is your business with me?'

'The deadliest kind.'

109

'Who are you, sir?'

'Raphael Parsons.'

Nicholas was at once surprised and curious. The name explained the histrionic air about the man. Parsons moved with grace and spoke in almost declamatory fashion. His black beard and moustache were well trimmed and there was a studied arrogance in his expression. He was accustomed to being obeyed.

'Come with me,' suggested Nicholas.

'This is indoor work.'

'We have a chamber at hand.'

The book holder led him to the room which was used as the wardrobe by Westfield's Men. Raphael Parsons ran an expert eye over the racks of costumes, feeling some of the material between his fingers and grunting his approval. Nicholas closed the door behind him.

'How did you know where to find me?' he asked.

'James Ingram advised me to call here.'

'You have spoken with James, then?'

'Briefly. Geoffrey, our porter, put me in touch with him. I wanted to see if your account confirms, in every particular, what Ingram alleges.'

'My account?'

'Of what you found at the Blackfriars Theatre. My dear friend and partner, Cyril Fulbeck, hanged by the neck.' Parsons relaxed slightly and even managed a thin smile. 'Besides,' he continued, 'I have long wanted an opportunity to meet Nicholas Bracewell. Your fame runs before you, sir.'

'Fame?'

'You have a reputation, sir.'

'I am merely a book holder, Master Parsons.'

'Your modesty is a credit to your character but it betrays your true worth. You talk to a man of the theatre. I know that a book holder must hold a whole company together and nobody does that better than you. I have sat in your galleries a dozen times and marvelled at your work.' His face hardened. 'Though it is perhaps as well that I was not at the Queen's Head when Applegarth's latest piece of vomit was spewed out on your stage.'

'*The Misfortunes of Marriage* is a fine play.'

'It swinged us soundly, I hear.'

'There was some gentle mockery of boy actors.'

'Jonas Applegarth could not be gentle if he tried,' said Parsons vehemently. 'He tore our work to shreds and questioned our right to exist. Boy actors were innocent lambs beneath his slashing knife. It was unforgivable. Applegarth will pay clearly for his attack.'

'In what way?'

'You will see, sir. You will see.'

'Do you make threats against our author?'

'Let him watch his back, that is all I say.'

'Take care,' warned Nicholas, looking him hard in the eye. 'Touch any member of this company and you will have to deal with me.'

'Proof positive!' said Parsons with a disarming smile. 'You are no mere book holder. You are the true guardian of Westfield's Men. Its very essence, some say.'

'I stand by my friends.'

'Why, so do I, sir. And that is why I came here this

111

morning. Away with that mound of offal known as Jonas Applegarth! Let's talk of a sweeter gentleman, and one whose death cries out for retribution. Cyril Fulbeck.'

'Ask what you will, Master Parsons.'

'Describe the scene in your own terms. When you and James Ingram entered the theatre, what exactly did you see?'

'I will tell you . . .'

Nicholas reconstructed the events with care, as much for his own benefit as for that of his visitor. He wanted to sift every detail in the hope that it might contain a clue that had so far eluded him. Raphael Parsons was a patient audience. When he had heard the full tale, he stroked his beard pensively. There was a long pause.

'Well?' said Nicholas.

'Your version accords with that given by Ingram.'

'And so it should.'

'There is a difference, however,' noted Parsons. 'Your account is longer and more accurate. You are the more reliable witness, but that was to be expected.'

'Why?'

'Because you never met Cyril Fulbeck until that grim moment. What you saw was an old man dangling from a rope. James Ingram, we must remember, was looking at someone he revered, and was thus too shocked to observe all the detail which you just listed.'

'That is understandable.'

'Also,' said Parsons dryly, 'you are older and wiser than Ingram, and far more closely acquainted with the horrors that man can afflict on man. You have looked on violent death before.'

'All too often, alas.'

'It has sharpened your judgement.' Parsons stroked his beard as he ruminated afresh. When he spoke again, his tone was pleasant. 'You have answered my enquiries willingly and honestly. I am most grateful to you for that. Allow me to return the compliment. I am sure that you have questions you wish to put to me.'

Astonished by the offer, Nicholas was nevertheless quick to take advantage of it. His interrogation was direct.

'Where were you at the time of the murder?' he said.

'At the house of a friend in Ireland Yard.'

'Close by the theatre, then?'

'Within a stone's throw.'

'When did you last see your partner?'

'An hour or so before his death, it seems,' said Parsons with a sad shake of his head. 'Had I known that Cyril was in such danger, I would never have stirred from his side. I blame myself for leaving him so defenceless.' He bit his lip. 'And the manner of my departure only serves to increase my guilt.'

'Your departure?'

'We had an argument. Strong words were exchanged.'

'On what subject?'

'What else but the Blackfriars Theatre? Cyril admired the plays I put upon the stage but criticised the means by which they got there. He thought I was too strict with my young charges.'

'How did you reply?'

'Roundly, I fear.'

'Was he upset by the altercation?'

'I did not stay to ask. I marched out of the building.' He clicked his tongue in self-reproach. 'Can you see what a weight on my conscience it now is? We parted in anger before but we soon became friends again. Not this time. A length of rope strangled any hope of reconciliation between us. Cyril went to his death with our quarrel unresolved. That cuts me to the quick.'

Nicholas was impressed by the readiness of his answers and by his apparent candour. Parsons seemed genuinely hurt by the demise of his friend and business partner. Here was a new and more compassionate side to the man. Others had spoken of a bully and a disciplinarian, and Nicholas had seen the odd glint of belligerence, but he had also discerned a sensitive streak. When Raphael Parsons offered his hand, he shook it without reservation.

'I must take my leave,' said the visitor.

'Let me teach you another way out.'

Nicholas took him through a second door and down a long passageway so that his visitor could step out into Gracechurch Street without having to go back through the yard. The book holder stopped him in the open doorway.

'There is another matter I would like to raise.'

'Be brief. I, too, have a rehearsal to attend.'

'One of your actors is a boy called Philip Robinson.'

'A gifted child in every way.'

'He was impressed against his will into the Chapel.'

'Who told you so?'

114

'The boy's father. He petitions for his son's return.'

'Then he does so in vain.'

'Why?'

'Because Philip is happy with us,' said Parsons bluntly. 'Extremely happy. Farewell, sir.'

With a brusque nod, he swept out into the street.

Chapter Six

For the rest of the morning, Nicholas Bracewell was so bound up in his duties that he had no time to reflect upon the unexpected visit of Raphael Parsons or to indulge in any speculation about the true feelings of Philip Robinson towards the Children of the Chapel Royal. Preparation for the afternoon's performance was his abiding concern, and *The Maids of Honour* gave him much to prepare. His first task was to prevent the stagekeeper from assaulting his smallest and lowliest assistant.

'No, no, no, George! You are an idiot!'

'If you say so.'

'I *do* say so because I know so!' shouted the irate Thomas Skillen. 'You have set out the wrong scenery and the wrong properties for the wrong play.'

'Have I?' George Dart scratched his head in disbelief. 'I thought *The Maids of Honour* called for a bench, a tree, a rock, a tomb, a well and three buckets.'

'You are thinking of *The Two Maids of Milchester*.'

'Am I?' he said, blushing with embarrassment. 'Why, so I am! We need no bench and buckets here. Our play demands a wooden canopy, a large bed, a stool, Mercury's wings and a rainbow. Tell me I am right.'

'You are even more wrong,' hissed the other, taking a first wild swipe at him. 'Dolt! Dunce! Imbecile! Mercury's wings and the rainbow belong in *Made to Marry*. Have I taught you nothing?'

Four decades in the theatre had made Thomas Skillen an essentially practical man. Actors might covet a striking role and authors might thrill to the music of their own verse, but the stagekeeper summarised character and language in terms of a few key items.

'Table, throne and executioner's block.'

'Yes, yes,' gabbled Dart.

'We play *The Maids of Honour*.'

'Table, throne and executioner's block. I'll fetch them straight.' He scampered off but came to a sudden halt. His face was puckered with concentration. '*The Maids of Honour?* There is no executioner's block in the piece. Why do you send for it?'

'So that I may strike off your useless head!'

The old stagekeeper lunged at his hapless assistant, but Nicholas stepped good-humouredly between them. Dart cowered gratefully behind his sturdy frame.

'Let me at the rogue!' shouted Skillen.

'Leave him be,' soothed Nicholas. 'George confused his maids of honour with his maids of Milchester. A natural

117

mistake for anyone to make. It is not a criminal offence.'

'It is to me!'

'Does it really merit execution?'

'Yes, Nick. Perfection is everything.'

'Then are we all due for the headsman's axe, Thomas, for each one of us falls short of perfection in some way. George is willing and well intentioned. Build on these virtues and educate him out of his vices.'

Skillen's anger abated and he chortled happily.

'I frightened him thoroughly. He will not misjudge *The Maids of Honour* again.' He gave a toothless grin. 'Will you, George?'

'Never. Table and throne. I'll find them presently.'

'No need.' said Nicholas, pointing to the makeshift stage. 'The table stands ready. Nathan Curtis was here at first light to repair it. And he is even now putting some blocks of wood beneath the throne to heighten its eminence.'

'What shall I do, then, Master Bracewell?'

'Fetch the rest of the properties.'

Skillen took his cue. 'Act One. First scene, table and four chairs. Second scene, a box-tree. Third scene, curtains and a truckle-bed within. Fourth scene, the aforesaid throne. Fifth scene . . .'

The rapid litany covered all seventeen scenes of the play and left Dart's head spinning. He raced off to gather what he could remember and to stay out of reach of the old man's temper. Nicholas looked fondly after him.

'You are too hard on the lad, Thomas.'

'Stern schoolmasters get the best results.'

118

'George has too much to learn in too short a time.'

'That is because of his stupidity and laziness.'

'No, it is not,' said Nicholas reasonably. 'We overload him, that is all. This season, Westfield's Men will stage all of thirty-six different plays, seventeen of them, like Jonas Applegarth's, entirely new. Asking George Dart to remember the plots and properties of thirty-six plays is to put an impossible strain on the lad.'

'I know what each play requires,' said Skillen proudly.

'You are a master of your craft, Thomas. He is not.'

The old man was mollified. He loved to feel that his age and experience were priceless assets to the company. After discussing the play at greater length with him, Nicholas went off to tackle the multifarious chores that awaited him before the rehearsal could begin. He could spare only a wave of greeting to each new member of the company who drifted into the yard.

Edmund Hoode came first, buoyed up by the thought that his admirer might send him another token of her love or perhaps even reveal her identity. Barnaby Gill shared his mood of elation, though for a more professional reason. *The Maids of Honour* was one of his favourite plays because it gave him an excellent role as a court jester, with no less than four songs and three comic jigs. Owen Elias and James Ingram arrived together, deep in animated conversation. Three of the boy apprentices came into the yard abreast, giggling at a coarse jest. The fourth, Richard Honeydew, strolled in with Peter Digby, the director of the musicians.

Lawrence Firethorn, predictably, timed his entrance for

maximum effect, clattering into the yard on his horse when everyone else was assembled there and raising his hat in salutation. From the broad grin on his face, his colleagues rightly surmised that he had tasted connubial delight that morning with his wife, the passionate Margery, a fact which was corroborated by the sniggers of the apprentices, who lived under the same roof as the actor-manager and who had heard every sigh of ecstasy and every creak of the bed. Silent pleasure was a denial of nature in the Firethorn household.

'Nick, dear heart!' he said, dismounting beside the book holder. 'Is all ready here?'

'Now that you have come, it is.'

'Then let us waste no more of a wonderful day.'

He tossed the reins to a waiting ostler, then strode off towards the tiring-house. Nicholas called the rest of the company to order and had the stage set for the first scene.

The Maids of Honour was a staple part of their repertoire, played for its reliability rather than for any intrinsic merits. A sprightly comedy with a political thrust, it was set in the French Court at some unspecified period in the past. The King of France is deeply troubled by rumours of a planned assassination. The Queen dismisses his fears until an attempt is made on his life but thwarted by the brave intercession of the Prince of Navarre, a guest at the Court.

Convinced that someone inside the palace is helping his enemies, the King lets his suspicions fall on the three maids of honour who attend the Queen. She is outraged by the suggestion that her most cherished friends could plot the overthrow of her husband, but the King follows his own intuition. Disguising himself as an Italian nobleman, he tests each maid of honour in turn to see if she can be corrupted by the promise of money. Two of them welcome his advances, proving that they have neither honour nor maidenhead; but the third, Marie, the plain girl matched with two Court beauties, vehemently rejects his blandishments.

The King removes his disguise and returns to his Queen. Presenting his evidence, he expects her to accept his word, but she flies into a rage and accuses him of trying to seduce her maids of honour. She flounces out of the Court and locks herself in her chamber. The Court Jester, acting as a mocking chorus throughout, takes especial pleasure in the marital discord. In his despair, the King confides in the handsome Prince.

Two of the maids of honour conspire with the exiled Duke of Brabant to overthrow the King. A second assassination attempt is planned, but it is foiled by Marie, who raises the alarm. The King is only wounded and the conspirators are captured by the Prince of Navarre. A contrite Queen tends her husband's wounds and promises that she will never misjudge him so cruelly again. As a reward for her loyalty, Marie, blossoming in victory, becomes the bride of the Prince. The play ends on a note of celebration with honour satisfied in every way.

The rehearsal was halting but free from major mishap. A large audience filled the yard of the Queen's Head for the performance itself. Jonas Applegarth sat in the upper gallery, paying for one seat but taking up almost three. Hugh Naismith sat where he could keep his mortal enemy in view. Lord Westfield and his cronies emerged from a private room behind the lower gallery to occupy their customary station and to whet their appetites for the play with brittle badinage over cups of Canary wine. Alexander Marwood circled his yard like a carrion crow.

Your pleasure and indulgence, dearest friends,
Is all we seek and to these worthy ends
We take you to the glittering court of France,
Where gorgeous costume, music, song and dance,
Affairs of state and matters of the heart,
Mirthful jests, a Barnabian art,
With pomp and ceremonial display
Enhance the scene for our most honourable play
About three Maids of Honour . . . .

Dressed in a black cloak, Owen Elias delivered the Prologue before bowing to applause and stealing away as a fanfare signalled the entry of the French Court. Lawrence Firethorn and Richard Honeydew made a magnificent entrance as King and Queen, respectively, in full regalia, and took their places at the head of a table set for a banquet. The solemnity of the occasion was soon shattered by the appearance of the Court Jester, who came somersaulting onto the stage to snatch a bowl of fruit and set it on his head like a crown. The Barnabian art of Barnaby Gill was in full flow and the spectators were enthralled.

Firethorn led the company with characteristic brio. James Ingram was a dashing Prince of Navarre, Owen Elias

122

a truly villainous Duke of Brabant, and Edmund Hoode, in a flame-coloured gown, was a resplendent Constable of France. What *The Maids of Honour* also did was to furnish the four apprentices with an opportunity to do more than simply decorate a scene in female attire. Richard Honeydew showed regal fury as the Queen while Martin Yeo and Stephen Judd were suitably devious and guileful as the two dishonourable maids.

But it was John Tallis who really came to the fore. The boy was a competent actor but his lantern jaw and unfortunate cast of feature ruled him out of romantic roles. The part of Marie was a signal exception. Overshadowed by the external beauty of the other maids, he evinced an inner radiance that finally shone through. Tactfully concealing his lantern jaw behind a fan, he knelt gratefully before his King as the latter joined his hand symbolically with that of the Prince of Aragon.

It was then that the crisis occurred. Until that point, John Tallis had given the performance of his young lifetime. Puberty then descended upon him with its full weight. When the King of France invited Marie to accept the hand of the Prince of Navarre in marriage, he tempted Providence with his choice of words:

> *Sing out your sweetest answer, soft-voiced Maid,*
> *And let your music captivate Navarre.*

John Tallis put all the sweetness that he could muster into his reply, but what emerged from his mouth was the croak of a giant frog. His voice had broken, and with it broke the spell which had so carefully been woven throughout the preceding two hours. A tender moment between lovers became a source of crude hilarity. The audience rocked with mirth. When John Tallis tried to retrieve the situation with a series of mellifluous rhyming couplets, they came out as gruff entreaties which only increased the general hysteria.

Lawrence Firethorn tried to limit the damage by cutting in with the final speech of the play, but he took Peter Digby and the consort completely by surprise. Instead of a dignified exit to music, the French Court shuffled off in grim silence, and it was only when the stage was virtually empty that the instruments spoke from above. Fresh peals of laughter rang out. Firethorn brought the cast on stage to enjoy the applause, but even his broad smile cracked when the entry of John Tallis was greeted with a loud cheer.

When he quit the stage, the actor-manager was seething.

'Where is that vile assassin!' he roared.

'Do not blame the boy,' advised Nicholas.

'Oh, I'll not *blame* him, Nick. I'll belabour him! I'll pull off those bulging balls of his and roast them like chestnuts in a fire! He killed my performance! He stabbed the play in the back!'

'It was not John's fault. His voice broke.'

'Then I'll break his arms, his legs and his foul neck to keep it company! You only *heard* the disaster, Nick. I had visible warning of its dire approach.'

'Warning?'

'Manhood reared its unlovely visage,' said Firethorn with a vivid gesture. 'When the Prince of Navarre stole that first kiss from Marie, the maid of honour's skirt twitched as if it had a flag-pole beneath it. Had John Tallis been wearing a codpiece, it would have burst asunder and displayed his wares to the whole world. I wonder that James Ingram kept his composure! What man wants to spend his wedding night in the arms of a frog maiden with a monstrous pizzle!' He glared around the tiring-house. 'Where is that freak of nature? I'll geld him!'

'Calm down,' said Nicholas. 'The play is done.'

'Done and done for!'

'It was well received by the audience.'

'Jeers of derision.'

'Even the best horse stumbles.'

'This one stumbled, fell and threw us all from the saddle.' He made an effort to bank down his fury. 'Nobody can accuse us of denying John Tallis his moment of triumph. Marie can steal every scene in which she appears. We did all we could to help the oaf. We covered his lantern jaw with a fan, we hid much of his ugliness under a wig, and we dressed him in such rich and jewelled apparel that it took the attention away from what remained of his charmless countenance. And how did he repay us?'

'John lost control of his voice, alas. It has been on the verge of breaking these past few months.'

'It was a humiliation!' recalled Firethorn with a shiver. 'He could not have ruined the play more thoroughly if he had sprouted a beard and grown hair all over his chest. God's buttocks!' he howled, as his anger burst out once more. 'He made Westfield's Men the laughing stock of London. Instead of a demure maid of honour, we have a hoarse-voiced youth afflicted with standing of the yard. Bring the rogue to me! I'll murder him with my bare hands!'

Nicholas diverted him by flattering him about his performance. When Barnaby Gill came up to complain that Firethorn had deliberately ruined one of his jigs by standing between him and the audience, the book holder saw his chance to slip away. John Tallis sat in the corner of the tiring-house, still wearing the costume of a maid of honour but weeping the tears of a young man. Richard Honeydew tried to console his colleague but his piping voice only reminded Tallis of his fatal loss.

'My hour on the stage is over!' he wailed.

'Do not talk so,' said Nicholas, crouching beside him. 'As one door closes, another one opens for you.'

'Yes! The door out of Master Firethorn's house. He will kick me through it most certainly. This morning, I was one of the apprentices; this afternoon, I am doomed.'

'You came of age, John. It happens to us all.'

'Not in the middle of the Court of France!'

He sobbed even louder and it took Nicholas several minutes to comfort him. Tallis eventually stepped out of a dress he would never be able to wear again and put on his own attire. The lantern jaw sagged with despair.

'What will become of me?' he sighed.

'We'll find occupation for you somewhere,' Nicholas reassured him. 'In the meantime, keep out of Master Firethorn's way and do not – this I beg you, John – do not let him hear your voice.'

The boy produced the deepest and harshest croak yet.

'Why not?' he said.

Even Nicholas had to suppress a smile.

She was there. He sensed it. Without knowing who she was or where she might be sitting, Edmund Hoode was certain only of her presence. It set his blood racing. Throughout the performance, he scanned the galleries whenever he came on stage, searching for that special face, waiting for that telltale smile, hoping for that significant gesture. When she chose not to reveal herself, he felt even more excited. In preserving her mystery, she became infinitely more appealing. Simply to know that she existed was an inspiration in itself.

Alone of the cast, the Constable of France was unmoved by the sudden transformation of a maid of honour into a husky youth. With a rose pressed to his heart beneath his costume, he was proof against all interruption. If John Tallis had turned into a three-headed dog and danced a galliard, he would not have distracted Hoode. She was there. That was all that mattered.

'What means this haste, Edmund?'

'I have somewhere to go.'

'Deserting your fellows so soon?'

'They will not miss me.'

'You have some tryst, I venture.'

'Venture all you wish, Jonas. My lips are sealed.'

Jonas Applegarth chuckled aloud and slapped Hoode on the back. The latter was just leaving the tiring-house after shedding the apparel of the Constable of France. Inspired by the hope that his admirer might make fresh contact with him, he was not pleased to find the massive Applegarth blocking his way.

'You have talent as a player, Edmund.'

'Thank you.'

'That is the finest performance I have seen you give.'

'Much thought went into it, Jonas.'

'To good effect. I could not fault you.'

'Praise, indeed.'

'The role was base, the play even baser, but you rose above those shortcomings. It is your true profession.'

'I am a poet. Writing plays is a labour of love.'

'But they show too much of the labour and too little of the love, Edmund. Abandon the pen. It leads you astray. Let sharper minds and larger imaginations create new plays. Your destiny is merely to act in them.'

The amiable contempt of his remarks did not wound Hoode. He was armoured against the jibes of a rival, even one as forthright as the corpulent Applegarth. Excusing himself with a pleasant smile, Hoode pushed past the portly frame and hurried along the passageway. Where he was going he did not know, but hope kept him on the move.

Chance dictated his footsteps, guiding him through the taproom, down another passageway, up one staircase, down a second, deep into a cellar, until he finally emerged in the yard once again. It was almost deserted. Most of the spectators had now dispersed, save for a few stragglers. Hoode halted with disappointment. There was no sign of his pining lover, no hint even of a female presence in the yard or up in the galleries.

Rose Marwood then materialised out of thin air and

came tripping across the yard towards him. He revived at once. Another rose? A different token of love? A longer missive? But all that she bore him was a shy smile. Wafting past him, she went back into the building and shut the door firmly behind her.

Hoode was abashed. Had his instincts betrayed him? Was his secret admirer absent from the afternoon's performance? Or had she taken a second and more critical look at her quondam beloved before deciding that he was unworthy of her affections? His quick brain conjured up a dozen reasons why she was not there, each one more disheartening than its predecessor.

He gave a hollow laugh at the depths of his own folly. While he walked the boards as the Constable of France, he was supremely aware of her attention. His vanity was breathtaking. Why should any woman swoon over *him*? Set against the imperious charm of Lawrence Firethorn, the sensual vitality of Owen Elias, or the striking good looks of James Ingram, his qualities were negligible. It was idiocy to pretend otherwise. The rose that had warmed his heart all afternoon was now a stake which pierced it. His hand clutched at his breast to hold in the searing pain.

And then she came. Not in person, that was too much to ask. An inn yard in the wake of a performance was not the ideal place for the first meeting of lovers. It was too public, too mundane, too covered in the litter of the departed audience. What she sent was an emissary. He was a tall, well-favoured youth in the attire of a servant. Walking briskly across to Hoode, he gave him a polite bow and thrust a scroll into his hand before leaving at speed.

The fragrance of the letter invaded Hoode's senses and confirmed the identity of the sender. He broke the seal and unrolled the parchment to read her purpose. His heart was whole again and pounding with joy. The elegant hand had written only one word, but it gave him a positive surge of elation.

'Tomorrow . . .'

'When did you speak with Raphael Parsons?'

'Yesterday evening.'

'You sought him out?'

'He came to me, Nick. The porter told him how he might track me down. He was waiting for me at my lodging when I returned from here.'

Nicholas Bracewell and James Ingram were sharing a drink and comparing opinions in the taproom. Both had been astounded by the unheralded arrival of Raphael Parsons, but each had learnt much from his visit.

'I found him at odds with expectation,' said Ingram. 'My first encounter with him was too fleeting for me to form a proper opinion. This time, I conversed alone with him. He did not seem at all like the ogre I had been led to expect. A strong-willed man, yes, and with strong passions. But he was too polite and reasonable to be a vile tyrant.'

'Tyranny can work in many ways,' observed Nicholas. 'A reasonable despot can sometimes be more difficult to resist. Master Parsons was civil with me but I sensed a capacity to be otherwise. We saw but one side of him.'

'A caring man, deeply shaken by the murder of a friend.'

'That was how he wanted to present himself, James.'

'It was a form of disguise?'

'I am not sure, but Raphael Parsons knew best how to engage our help. He was eager yet not overbearing, persistent but undemanding. He even invited me to question *him*. That was most enlightening. At the same time . . .'

'You had doubts about him?'

'I did.'

'He put mine to flight, Nick.'

'And most of mine, I must confess. He was very adept. Perhaps it was his ease in stilling my doubts which kept one or two of them alive. There is craft here. Deep cunning.'

'You saw qualities in him that eluded me.'

'I may be wrong, James. I hope that I am.'

'He spoke so warmly of Cyril Fulbeck,' said Ingram, 'and I can forgive a man most things if he does that. For what it is worth, my judgement is in his favour. I do not believe that Raphael Parsons was involved in this crime.'

'I delay my verdict on that.'

'He shook with grief when he talked of the murder.'

'It is a grief that is not allowed to interfere with his business affairs,' remarked Nicholas coolly. 'He may mourn his partner but he has not suspended performances at the Blackfriars as a mark of respect. His company are due to perform again tomorrow, young actors who must themselves be consumed with their own grief and beset by terror. Master Parsons tempers his sorrow with an instinct for gain.'

'That *is* strange behaviour.'

'Strange and unfeeling. What was his profession before he became a theatre manager?'

'He was a lawyer.'

'That explains much.'

They finished their drinks, then Nicholas took his leave. He crossed to the table at which Owen Elias was sitting with other members of the company, trading impersonations of the luckless John Tallis. Nicholas waited for the laughter to subside. Crouching beside the Welshman, he plucked his sleeve and kept his voice low.

'Will you undertake a special task for me?'

'Willingly, Nick.'

'Go about it privily.'

'A secretive assignment? You arouse my curiosity at once. What is it?'

'The rumour is that Jonas fought a duel.'

'More than a rumour. I know it to be a fact.'

'Find out who his opponent was.'

'Why?'

'Jonas was attacked last night as we walked home,' said Nicholas quietly. 'The ambush may be linked in some way to the duel. We need to recognise the face of the enemy so that we may safeguard Jonas from him.'

'He made no mention to me of any ambush.'

'He denies it happened in the same way as he refuses to admit that he was involved in a duel. But I was there when a dagger was thrown at him. Jonas is one of us now. Though he may spurn it, he needs our help.'

'This is work I'll readily accept, Nick,' said Elias with

concern. 'I am grateful you chose me for the task.'

'You can get closer to him than me.'

'That is because Jonas and I are birds of the same feather. Roisterers with red blood in our veins. Lovers of life and troubadours of the tavern. We were both born to carouse.' Elias grinned. 'I need him alive to buy his share of the ale. Besides, he's asked me to teach him some Welsh songs. I'll not let an assassin kill my fellow chorister.'

'Then we must find the man before he strikes again.'

'I'll about it straight.' He looked around the taproom. 'Jonas was here even now. Where is the fellow?'

'Returned home.'

'When danger lurks in the streets? He is too careless. Each time he goes abroad, he is at risk. Jonas needs protection.'

'I arranged it,' Nicholas assured him. 'Have no fear. He had a companion on his journey. By now, he will be safely bestowed in his house.'

The Maids of Honour had amused Jonas Applegarth for a couple of hours that afternoon, but it also fed his arrogance. He regarded the play as vastly inferior to anything he had written and voiced that opinion loudly in the taproom of the Queen's Head. Watching one comedy prompted him to work on another. After only one tankard of ale, therefore, he left the inn to waddle back to his house.

When Nathan Curtis fell in beside him, it never occurred to Applegarth that the carpenter had been assigned to act as his bodyguard. He was happy enough to have jocular company on the walk back home, not pausing to wonder for a moment why a man who lived in Bankside was walking in the opposite direction. The sturdy presence of Curtis kept any potential attacker at bay. Once Curtis saw the playwright enter his house, he turned his steps back towards the river. The duty which Nicholas Bracewell had given him was discharged.

Jonas Applegarth clambered up the stairs to the little room at the front of the house. He sat down before a table set under the window and covered in sheets of parchment. After sharpening his pen, he dipped it into the inkwell and wrote with a swift hand. The surge of creativity kept him bent over the table for an hour. Evening shadows obliged him to light a candle and he used its flame to read what he had written. Pleased with his progress, he took up his pen once more.

Hugh Naismith watched it all from the cover of a fetid lane opposite the house. While the actor stood in a stinking quagmire, the playwright sat in comfort in his window as he created a new theatrical gem to set before the playgoers of London. Naismith spat with disgust. The difference in their stations rankled. He was cast into the wilderness by a man whose career was now flourishing. It was unjust.

The sight of Jonas Applegarth made his rage smoulder. As he breathed in the foul air, he contemplated the various ways in which he could kill his enemy, dwelling longest on those which inflicted the greatest pain and humiliation.

Nicholas Bracewell approached the house from the far end of the street so that he did not have to walk past the premises owned by Ambrose Robinson. It irked him that since Anne Hendrik stepped back into his life, he had not yet managed to have a proper conversation alone with her.

When the servant opened the door to him, Nicholas heard voices within and feared that the truculent neighbour was already there, but the visitor was in fact a good friend.

'It is wonderful to see you again, Master Bracewell!'

'Thank you, Preben.'

'We have missed you in Bankside.'

'I lodge north of the river now.'

'That is our loss.'

Preben van Loew was the senior hatmaker in the business which Anne Hendrik had inherited from her late husband and which she managed in the adjoining building. A spectral figure in a black skull-cap, the old Dutchman embraced Nicholas warmly before quitting the house. Anne herself waited until they were alone in the parlour before she gave him her welcome.

'This is a lovely surprise, Nick!'

'Do I call at an inconvenient hour?'

Her answer came in the form of a light kiss on the cheek. He wanted to enfold her in his arms, but she moved to a seat and gestured for him to sit opposite her. There was a long pause as they simply luxuriated in the pleasure of being together again. Nicholas let a tidal wave of fond memories wash over him. When it passed, he was left with a profound sense of loss and of waste. Why had he walked away from a house which had given him so much happiness?

'What did you play this afternoon?' she asked.

'*The Maids of Honour.*'

'I have seen the piece more than once.'

'Not quite as it was performed today,' he said wryly. 'John Tallis came to grief at a most unfortunate moment. His voice broke as he was about to marry the Prince of Navarre.'

'Poor boy!'

'He is a man now.'

Nicholas recounted the incident in full and the two of them were soon sharing a chuckle. It was just like old times when the book holder would repair to his lodging and divert her with tales from the inn yard of the Queen's Head. Each day brought new adventures. A theatre company inhabited a world of extremes. Anne was a kind audience, interested and responsive, always rejoicing in the heady triumphs of Westfield's Men while sympathising with their numerous disasters. Her bright-eyed curiosity in his work was one of the things that he missed most.

'How goes it with you?' he asked softly.

'The business fares well.'

'Good.'

'We are to take on a new apprentice.'

'Preben will teach him his trade.'

'I have learnt much from him myself.'

Nicholas nodded. 'And the house?'

'What about it?'

'Do you have a lodger here?'

'That is my affair,' she said with a note of gentle reprimand. 'As it happens, there is nobody here at the moment, but that situation may change.' She looked at him with a cautious affection. 'Why did you come?'

'To see you.'

'For what purpose?'

'My own pleasure. Do I need a larger reason?'

'No,' she said. 'Not when that pleasure is mutual.'

She met his gaze and Nicholas thought of a dozen compliments he wished to pay. All of them had to be held back because there was now an obstacle between them. Until the intrusive figure of Ambrose Robinson were removed, he did not feel able to express his true feelings to her.

'A peculiar visitor called on me this morning,' he said.

'Who might that be?'

'Raphael Parsons.'

'Peculiar, indeed! Why did he come?'

'To ascertain the facts about the discovery of Cyril Fulbeck's corpse. Master Parsons had already questioned James Ingram on the matter. This morning, it was my turn.'

'Is he the beast that he is reputed to be?'

'Far from it, Anne.'

'Maligned by report, then?'

'Not entirely,' said Nicholas. 'He is a lawyer by training. He knows what to hide and what to show. Like most lawyers, he has the touch of an actor about him. I found him pleasant enough and remarkably candid. The Chapel Children no doubt see aspects of him that were concealed from me.'

'They loathe him.'

'So I am told.'

'You saw the letters written by Philip Robinson.'

'I did, Anne.'

'They speak of a cruel master, who makes them work hard and who beats them into submission if they try to disobey. Philip is more or less a prisoner there.'

'That is not what Master Parsons says.'

'Oh?'

'He claims that the boy is very happy at Blackfriars.'

'*Happy?* It is one long ordeal for Philip!'

'So his father alleges.'

'You read the boy's own testimony.'

'Yes,' agreed Nicholas. 'That is why I found Master Parsons's denial surprising. Why does it contradict the lad's version of events so completely?'

'The man must be lying.'

'That was not my impression.'

'What other explanation can there be?'

Nicholas let her question hang in the air for a moment.

'How well do you know Philip?' he said at length.

'Reasonably well. He lived but a step away from here.'

'Did you see much of him?'

'No,' she said. 'He was a quiet boy. Always polite but rather diffident. And very lonely after his mother's sad death. Philip was almost invisible. Until Sundays, that is.'

'Sundays?'

'When he sang in the choir. He came alive then. I have never seen a child take such a delight in singing the praises of God. His little face would light up with joy.'

'Does he not have that same joy in the Chapel Royal?'

'I fear not.'

138

'What chorister would not relish the opportunity of singing before Her Majesty?'

'His pleasure is marred by the misery he endures at the Blackfriars Theatre, where he is forced to be an actor.'

'By Raphael Parsons.'

'Even so. Philip's father has told you all.'

'Has he?'

She grew defensive. 'Of course. Do you doubt Ambrose?'

'Not if you can vouch for him.'

'I can, Nick.'

'I see.' He felt a flicker of jealousy. 'You and he seem well acquainted.'

'He is a neighbour and a friend.'

'Does he have no closer hold on you?'

'What do you mean?'

'Nathan Curtis has observed you in church together.'

'So that is it!' she said, stiffening. 'You have set your carpenter to spy on us.'

'Not at all, Anne. He vouchsafed the information.'

'In answer to your prompting.'

'I simply wondered if he knew Ambrose Robinson.'

'This is unworthy of you, Nick.'

'If I am engaged to help the man, I am entitled to know as much about him as I can. Nathan's opinion of your friend was helpful. It confirms my own impression.'

'You do not like Ambrose, I know that.'

'My concern is that you *do*, Anne. Sufficient to walk to church with him on a Sunday and to kneel beside him.'

'That is my choice.'

'Is it?'

'Yes!' she said, rising angrily from her seat. 'If you have come to turn me against Ambrose, you have come in vain. I live my own life, Nick, and you are no longer part of it. I am grateful to you for the help you have offered, but it does not give you the right to meddle in my private affairs.'

'I do it out of affection.'

'Then express that affection in a more seemly way.'

'Anne . . .'

He got up and reached out for her, but she moved away. There was an awkward pause. Before he could frame an apology into words, there was a loud knock on the door. The servant answered it and Ambrose Robinson came blundering in. His face was puce with indignation.

'Fresh tidings from Blackfriars? Why was I not called?'

'I came to speak with Anne,' explained Nicholas.

'Philip is my son. I have prior claim on any news.'

'How did you know that I was here?'

'I met with Preben van Loew in the street,' said the butcher. 'He told me that you were here. What has happened? I demand to know.'

'Can you not first offer my guest a polite greeting?' chided Anne. 'You burst in here with improper haste, Ambrose. Remember where you are.'

'I do, I do,' he whined, instantly repentant. 'Forgive my unmannerly behaviour, Anne. My anxiety over Philip robs me of my wits yet again.' He took a deep breath and turned back to Nicholas. 'Please allay my concern. What has happened?'

'I spoke with Raphael Parsons.'

'Did you insist on the release of my son?'

'I raised the topic with him.'

'What was his answer? How did that snake reply?'

'He told me that your son was content to perform on the stage at the Blackfriars Theatre. The boy has talent as an actor. He is keen to develop it.'

'Lies! Deception! Trickery!'

'That is all Master Parsons would say on the subject.'

'Falsehood!'

'Lower your voice!' urged Anne.

'Why did you not take hold of the rogue and beat the truth out of him?'

'He came to discuss the murder of Cyril Fulbeck,' said Nicholas firmly. 'It weighs heavily upon him. Set against the death of the Master of the Chapel, the fate of one chorister was an irrelevance.'

'It is not an irrelevance to me, sir!'

'I will try to pursue the matter with him.'

'Parsons is an arrant knave,' said Robinson. 'I should have done what a father's love told me to do at the very start. Attend a performance at Blackfriars and snatch Philip off the stage.'

'That would be madness,' argued Anne.

'I want my son back home with me.'

'Then achieve that end by peaceful means. Take him away by force and the law will descend on you with such severity that you'd lose both Philip and your own freedom.'

'Anne counsels well,' added Nicholas. 'What use are you to the boy if you're fretting away in prison? I'll speak with Master Parsons again and use what persuasion I may. In the meantime, you must learn patience.'

Robinson's fury seemed to drain away. Face ashen and

shoulders dropping, he stood there in silent bewilderment. He looked so wounded and defenceless that Anne lay a hand on his arm, like a mother comforting a hurt child. The gesture annoyed Nicholas but it had a different effect on the butcher.

It only served to ignite the spirit of vengeance until it glinted in his eyes. Taking her by the hand, Robinson led Anne gently out of the room and closed the door behind her so that he could speak to Nicholas alone. There was no ranting this time, no bluster and arm waving, only a quiet and quite eerie intensity.

'Very well,' he said. 'Try once more, Nick. Work within the law. Use reason and supplication to restore my son to me.' His jaw tightened. 'But if you fail, if they keep Philip locked up, if they continue to spread malicious lies about him wanting to stay there, I'll seek Raphael Parsons out and play a part for him myself.'

'A part?'

'The Laughing Hangman.'

'Keep well away from Blackfriars.'

'That is what Anne advises,' he said, 'and for her sake, I have stayed my hand. But not for much longer. Unless Philip comes home to me soon, I'll hang Raphael Parsons by the neck from the tallest building in London and I'll laugh until my sides burst.'

The threat was a serious one.

Chapter Seven

The Elephant was a large, low, sprawling inn, famed for its strong ale and unflagging hospitality. It stood near The Curtain, one of the two theatres in Shoreditch which brought the citizens of London streaming out through Bishopsgate in search of entertainment. Banbury's Men, the resident company at The Curtain, used the inn as a place to celebrate their frequent successes or to drown their sorrows in the wake of occasional abysmal failures. When Owen Elias arrived at the Elephant that evening, the boisterous atmosphere told him that celebration was in order. Banbury's Men were basking in the triumph of their new play, *The Fatal Dowry*, performed that afternoon to general acclaim.

Elias ducked below a beam and surveyed the taproom through a fug of tobacco smoke. Westfield's Men were deadly rivals of the company at The Curtain and relations between them went well beyond bitterness. The Welshman would not normally have sought out the other troupe, especially as he had once belonged to it for a brief and acrimonious period. Necessity compelled him to come, and he looked for the swiftest way to discharge his business and leave the enemy lair.

Selecting his man with care, he closed in on him.

'Why, how now, Ned!'

'Is that you, Owen?'

'As large and lovely as life itself.'

'What brings you to the Elephant?'

'Two strong legs and a devil of a thirst. Will you drink some ale with me, Ned?'

'I'll drink with any man who pays the bill, even if he belong to that hellish crew known as Westfield's Men.' He turned to his friends on the adjoining table. 'See here, lads. Look what the tide has washed up. Owen Elias!'

Jeers of disapproval went up and Owen had to endure some stinging insults before he could settle down beside his former colleague. Ale was brought and he drank deep. Ned Meares was a hired man, one of the many actors who scraped a precarious living at their trade and who made the most of their intermittent stretches of employment while they lasted. A stout man in his thirties, Meares was an able actor with a wide range. In the time since he had last seen the man, Elias noted, regular consumption of ale had filled out his paunch and deepened the florid complexion.

'A sharer now, I hear,' said Meares enviously.

'I have been lucky, Ned.'

'Spare a thought for we who toil on as hired men.'

'I do. I struggled along that same road myself.'

'It will never end for me, alas.' He nudged the visitor. 'Come, Owen, you crafty Welshman. Do not pretend that you are here to renew old acquaintance. Westfield's Men lurk in the Queen's Head. You have no place at the Elephant. What do you want?'

'To talk about a playwright you will know.'

'What is his name?' asked Meares, quaffing his ale.

'Jonas Applegarth.'

Elias had to move sharply to avoid the drink which was spat out again by his companion. Meares coughed and spluttered until his eyes watered. A few hearty slaps on the back were needed to help him recover.

Elias grinned. 'I see that you remember Jonas.'

'Remember him! Could I ever forget that monster? Jonas Applegarth was like a visitation of the plague.'

'Why?'

'Because he infected the whole company.'

'He wrote only one play for Banbury's Men.'

'One play too many!' groaned Meares. '*Friar Francis*. The name of that dread piece is scrawled on my soul for ever.' He sipped his ale before continuing. 'Most authors sell us a play, advise us how best to stage it, then stand aside while we do our work. Not Jonas. He was author, actor and book holder rolled into one. He stood over us from start to finish. We were no more than galley slaves, lashed to the oars while he whipped us unmercifully with his tongue and urged us to row harder.'

145

'He does have a warm turn of phrase,' conceded Elias.

'Threats and curses were all his conversation.'

'Did the company not resist?'

'Every inch of the way, Owen. Banbury's Men were to have played *Friar Francis* but that raging bull tried to turn us into Applegarth's Men. It could not be borne.'

Meares needed another fortifying drink of his ale before he could recount full details of the fierce battle against the arrogance of the author. Feigning sympathy, Elias took great satisfaction from the chaos which had been caused in the rival company while making a mental note to take precautions to stop the obstreperous playwright from wreaking the same havoc among Westfield's Men. Recrimination left Ned Meares shaking like an aspen. The visitor had to buy him another tankard of ale to restore his shattered nerves.

'Did anyone hate Jonas enough to kill him?'

'Yes,' said Meares. 'All of us!'

'Was there a special enemy of his in the company?'

'A dozen at least, Owen.'

'Who had most cause to loathe him?'

'Most cause?' The actor rubbed a hand ruminatively through his beard. 'Most cause? That would have to be Hugh Naismith.'

Nicholas Bracewell slept fitfully that night, dreaming of happier days at the Bankside home of Anne Hendrik and waking at intervals to scold himself for the way he had upset her during his visit. Both were strong-willed individuals and this had led to many arguments in the past, but they had usually been resolved in the most joyful and effective way in Anne's bed. That avenue of reconciliation had now been closed off to him, and he feared that as long as Ambrose Robinson stayed in her life, she would remain beyond his reach.

Jealousy of the butcher was not the only reason why he wanted to put the man to flight. Robinson had a temper which flared up all too easily and threatened to spill over into violence. Nicholas was worried that Anne might one day unwittingly become the victim of that choleric disposition. What mystified him was that she seemed to enjoy the man's friendship, enough to attend church in his company and to fret about his enforced estrangement from his son.

The plight of Philip Robinson had drawn the two of them together and placed Nicholas in a quandary. If he helped to secure the boy's release from the Chapel Children, would he be pushing Anne even closer to the Robinson family, and was it not in his interests to keep father and son apart? His sense of duty prevented his taking the latter course. Having promised assistance, he could not now go back on his word.

His mind was still in turmoil and his feelings still in a state of ambivalence as he left his lodging in Thames Street. The morning cacophony enveloped him and he did not hear the soft footsteps which came scurrying up behind him.

'Stay, sir!' said a voice. 'I would speak with you.'

Caleb Hay had to pluck at his sleeve to get Nicholas's attention. The book holder turned and exchanged greetings with him. Boyish enthusiasm lit up the older man's features.

'I hoped that I would catch you,' he said.

'Why?'

'Because I have something for you. Step this way, sir. Let us rid ourselves of this tumult.'

'I may not tarry long, Master Hay.'

'This will take but a few minutes and I think that you will consider them well spent.'

He led Nicholas back down the busy street to his house. Once they were inside, the noise subsided to a gentle hubbub. Joan Hay was sitting in the parlour with her embroidery as they entered. A glance from her husband made her jump to her feet and give the visitor a hesitant smile before moving off into the kitchen.

Caleb Hay went to a box on the table. Taking a large iron ring from his belt, he selected one of the keys and opened the box. Nicholas was first handed a sheet of parchment. His interest quickened as he studied the sketch of the Blackfriars Theatre.

'Forgive my crude handiwork,' said Hay. 'As you see, I am no artist, but it may give you some idea of the shape and size of the building. It is yours to scrutinise at will.'

'Thank you. This will be a great help.'

'Every exit is clearly marked.'

The sketch was simple but drawn roughly to scale. It enabled Nicholas to see exactly where he had been when he heard the Laughing Hangman and why it had taken him so long to reach the door at the rear of the building. Names of the adjacent streets had been added in a neat hand.

Caleb Hay produced a second item from the box.

'I can take more pride in this,' he said with a mild chuckle. 'You asked about the petition that was drawn up to prevent a theatre being reopened in Blackfriars. This is not the document itself but an exact copy. It must remain in my keeping but you are welcome to over-glance it, if you wish.'

'Please,' said Nicholas, taking the document from him. 'I am most grateful to you. Anything which pertains to Blackfriars is of interest to me.'

He read the petition with attention to its detail:

To the right honourable the Lords and others of her Majesties most honourable Privy Counsell – Humbly shewing and beseeching your honours, the inhabitants of the precinct of Blackfryers, London, that whereas one Burbage hath lately bought certaine roomes in the said precinct neere adjoyning unto the houses of the right honourable, the Lord Chamberlaine and the Lord of Hunsdon, which roomes the said Burbage is now altering and meaneth very shortly to convert and turne the same into a comon playhouse, which will grow to be a very great annoyance and trouble . . .

The complaints against public theatre were all too familiar to Nicholas. They were voiced every week by members of the City authorities and by outraged Puritans, who sought to curb the activities of Westfield's Men. The Blackfriars petition was signed by thirty-one prominent residents of the precinct, starting with Lord Hunsdon, who, ironically, was the patron of his own troupe – Lord Chamberlain's Men – but who drew the line at having a playhouse on his doorstep. Nicholas ran his eye down the other names, which included the dowager Lady Russell and a respected printer, Richard Field.

'Is it not strongly and carefully worded?' said Hay.

'Indeed, it is.'

'It represents my own view on the theatre. I was mightily relieved when the petition was accepted by the Privy Council.'

'With such names to sustain it, the plea could hardly be denied,' said Nicholas. 'But it was only a temporary measure. A public playhouse may have been kept out of Blackfriars, but a private theatre was reopened.'

'Alack the day!'

'The audiences who flock there will disagree.'

'No doubt,' said Hay, taking the document back and locking it in the box. 'This petition belongs to history.'

Nicholas moved to the door. 'You have been most kind. This drawing of Blackfriars will make a difficult task much easier.'

'Catch him! Catch this vile murderer.'

'I will bend all my efforts to do so.'

'Keep the name of Raphael Parsons firmly in mind.'

'You have evidence against him, Master Hay?'

'Nothing that would support his arrest,' confessed the other. 'But I have a feeling in my old bones that he is involved in this crime in some way. He is a man without scruple or remorse. Keep watch on him. From what I hear about this Master Parsons, he would be a ready hangman.'

* * *

Raphael Parsons endured the rehearsal for as long as he could but the lacklustre performance and the recurring errors were too much for him to bear.

'Stop!' he ordered. 'I'll stand no more of this ordeal! It is a disgrace to our reputation!'

The young actors on the stage at the Blackfriars Theatre came to an abrupt halt in the middle of the second act. Even a play as well tried as *Mariana's Revels* seemed to be beyond their scope. Their diction was muted, their gesture without conviction and their movement sluggish. A drama which required a lightness of touch was accorded a leaden treatment. Parsons was livid.

'This is shameful!' he snarled. 'I would not dare to put such a miserable account of the play before a crew of drunken sailors, let alone in front of a paying audience. Where is your art, sirs? Where is your self-respect? Where is your pride in our work? We laboured hard to make the Children of the Chapel Royal a company of distinction. Will you betray all that we have struggled to create?'

The cast stood there with heads bowed while the manager harangued them. Some shook with trepidation, others shed tears, all were plunged into the deepest melancholy. Parsons came striding down the hall to bang on the edge of the stage with his fist.

'Why are you *doing* this to me!' he demanded.

The youngest member of the company was its spokesman.

'We are grieving, sir,' said Philip Robinson meekly.

'That performance was enough to make anyone grieve!'

'Master Fulbeck is ever in our minds.'

Nods of agreement came from several of the cast and

more eyes moistened. Philip Robinson's own face was glistening with tears. Short, slim and pale, he wore the costume of Mariana as if it were a set of chains. Features which had a feminine prettiness when animated were now dull and plain. His body sagged. His voice was a pathetic bleat.

'We are too full of sadness, sir,' he said.

The manager's first impulse was to supplant the sadness with naked fear. It would not be the first time that he had instilled terror into his company in order to raise the level of their performance. Instinct held him back. These were unique circumstances, calling for a different approach. Instead of excoriating his juvenile players, therefore, he opted for a show of compassion.

Clambering upon the stage, he beckoned them closer.

'We all mourn him,' he said softly. 'And rightly so. The cruel manner of his death makes it an intolerable loss. Master Fulbeck was the only true begetter of this theatre. Though the Chapel Royal was his first love, he came to take an equal delight in your work here at Blackfriars. Hold to that thought. We do not play *Mariana's Revels* for our own benefit or even for the entertainment of our spectators. We stage it in remembrance of Cyril Fulbeck, late Master of the Chapel. Will you honour his name with a jaded performance?'

'No, Master Parsons,' said Philip boldly.

'Shall we close the theatre and turn people away? Is that what he would have wanted? Or shall we continue the noble work which he first started here? Cyril Fulbeck died in and for this theatre. The place to celebrate his memory is here on this very stage with a play which he held dear.'

'Yes!' called a voice at the back.

'We must play on!' added another.

'Under your instruction,' said Philip Robinson.

'So it will be,' decided Parsons, watching their spirits revive. 'But let us do it with no show of sadness or despair. *Mariana's Revels* is a joyful play. Speak its lines with passion. Dance its measures with vigour. Sing its songs with elation. Tell us why, Philip.'

'They were written by Master Fulbeck himself.'

'Even so. Most of them fall to Mariana to sing. Give them full voice, my boy. Treat them like hymns of praise!'

'Yes, sir!'

The rehearsal started again with a new gusto. For all his youth and inexperience, Philip Robinson led the Chapel Children like a boy on a mission, taking his first solo and offering it up to Heaven in the certainty that it would be heard and applauded by the man who had composed it for him.

Marriage to an actor as brilliant and virile as Lawrence Firethorn brought many pains but they were swamped beneath the compensating pleasures. Foremost among these for his redoubtable wife, Margery, was the never-ending delight of watching him ply his trade, strutting the stage with an imperious authority and carving an unforgettable performance in the minds of the onlookers. His talent and his sheer vitality were bound to make countless female hearts flutter and Firethorn revelled in the adulation. When

Margery visited the Queen's Head, she could not only share in the magic of his art, she could also keep his eye from roving and his eager body from straying outside the legitimate confines of the marital couch.

Vincentio's Revenge was a darker play in the repertoire of Westfield's Men, but one that gave its actor-manager a superb role as the eponymous hero. It never failed to wring her emotions and move Margery to tears. Since it was being played again that afternoon, she abandoned her household duties, dressed herself in her finery and made her way to Gracechurch Street with an almost girlish excitement. Good weather and high hopes brought a large audience converging on the Queen's Head. Pleased to see the throng, Margery was even more thrilled to identify two of its members.

'Anne!' she cried. 'This is blessed encounter.'

'You come to watch *Vincentio's Revenge?*'

'Watch it, wonder at it and wallow in it.'

'May we then sit together?' suggested Anne Hendrik.

'Indeed we may, though I must warn you that I will use all the womanly wiles at my command to steal that handsome gallant away from your side.'

Preben van Loew blushed deeply and made a gesture of self-deprecation. Margery's blunt speech and habit of teasing always unnerved him. When the three of them paid their entrance fee to the lower gallery, the old Dutchman made sure that Anne sat between him and the over-exuberant Margery. It allowed the two women to converse freely.

'I have not seen you this long while,' said Margery.

'My visits to the Queen's Head are less frequent.'

'You are bored with Westfield's Men?'

'Far from it,' said Anne. 'It is work that keeps me away and not boredom. I love the theatre as much as ever.'

'Does Nicholas know that you are here?'

'No, he does not.'

'Then it were a kindness to tell him. It would lift his spirits to know that you were in the audience.'

'I am not so sure.'

'He dotes on you, woman,' said Margery with a nudge. 'Are you blind? Are you insensible? If a man as fine and upright as Nick Bracewell loved me, I would never leave his side for a second. He *misses* you, Anne.'

'I miss him,' she said involuntarily.

'Then why keep him ignorant of your presence?'

'It is needful.'

'For whom? You or him?'

'I simply came to watch a play, Margery.'

'Then why not visit The Rose, which is closer to your home and far more commodious? Why not go to Shoreditch to choose between The Curtain and The Theatre? Deceive yourself, but do not try to deceive me. You came here for a purpose.'

'To see *Vincentio's Revenge*.' insisted Anne.

'I will not press the matter.'

'What happened between Nick and myself is . . . all past.'

'Not in his mind. Still less in his heart.'

Anne grew pensive. Margery's companionship gave her joy and discomfort in equal measure. Anne's feelings were so confused that she was not quite sure why she had decided to find the time to attend the play, and to release Preben van Loew from his work in order to chaperone her. She had responded to an urge which had yet to identify itself properly.

'Forgive me,' said Margery, squeezing her wrist in apology. 'My fondness for Nick makes me speak out of turn. You and he need no Cupid. I'll hold my peace.'

'A friend's advice is always welcome.'

'You know what mine would be. I say no more.'

Anne nodded soulfully and a surge of regret ran through her. It soon passed. *Vincentio's Revenge* began and the forthright woman beside her turned into a sobbing spectator. Anne herself was caught up in the emotion of the piece and whisked along for two harrowing but glorious hours by its poetry and its poignancy. It was only when the performance was over that she realised why she had come to it.

Having piloted another play safely into port, Nicholas Bracewell supervised the unloading of the cargo and the crew. It was not until the last of the properties and the costumes had been safely locked away that he was able to spare the time to listen to Owen Elias's report of his findings. The two of them were alone in the tiring-house.

'His name is Hugh Naismith.'

'Can you be certain, Owen?'

'As certain as it is possible to be. The fellow was a regular member of Banbury's Men, a promising actor, secure in the company's estimation and likely to rise to the rank of sharer.'

'What happened?' asked Nicholas.

'*Friar Francis*. By one Jonas Applegarth.'

'I remember seeing the playbills for it.'

'Hugh Naismith did not like the piece. *Friar Francis* was a most un-Christian play, by all account, as full of fury as *The Misfortunes of Marriage,* and with an even sharper bite. This foolish actor dared to rail against it in the hearing of the author and the two of them had to be held apart for they squawked at each other like fighting cocks.'

'Was this Naismith his opponent in the duel?'

'Ned Meares confirms it,' said Elias. 'The varlet was so badly injured that his arm was put in a sling for weeks. Banbury's Men expelled him straight. The fight with Jonas has cost Naismith both his pride and his occupation.'

'Two strong reasons for him to seek revenge.'

'One arm was in a sling but he still might throw a dagger with the other. It *must* be him, Nick.'

'Where does he dwell?'

'In Shoreditch. I called at his lodging.'

'You met him?'

'He was not there. Out stalking his prey, no doubt. That thought made me straight repair to Jonas's house, where I found our fat friend, sitting at his desk in the window of his chamber, writing away as if he did not have a care in the world.'

'You and he arrived here together, I saw.'

'Yes, Nick,' said Elias. 'I felt compelled to go back to his house again this morning. An assassin may strike on the journey to the Queen's Head just as well as on the walk back home. Four eyes offer better protection than two.'

'How did Jonas seem?'

'As loud and irreverent as ever.'

'Did you mention Hugh Naismith to him?'

'He affected not to know the man and would not discuss his time with Banbury's Men except to say that it was a species of torment.'

'For him or for them?' asked Nicholas with a wry smile.

'Both.'

The book holder checked that everything had been cleared out of the tiring-house before taking his friend through into the taproom. It was throbbing with noise. Players and playgoers alike were ready for drink and debate after the stirring performance of *Vincentio's Revenge*.

Jonas Applegarth was holding forth in the middle of the room, addressing his remarks to all who would listen. His lack of tact and restraint made the newcomers gasp.

'It is a miserable, meandering, worm-eaten play,' he argued.

'*Vincentio's Revenge* is a sterling piece,' countered James Ingram. 'You saw how the audience loved it.'

'Ignorant fools! What do they know of drama? If you put ten bare arses on the stage and farted at them for two hours, they would applaud you just as wildly. *The Maids of Honour* was base enough, but today's offering was putrid.'

'That is unkind! Unjust!'

'And untrue!' added Barnaby Gill, entering the fray.

'*Vincentio's Revenge* has been a loyal servant to the company. It fires my imagination each time we play it and raises the pitch of my performance.'

'Then is it time for you to retire,' said Applegarth with scorn. 'You were a walking abomination up on that stage. I have seen sheep with more talent and less confusion. Show some benevolence to mankind, Barnaby, and quit the theatre for good.'

'I was sublime!' howled Gill.

'Scurvy!'

'Unparalleled.'

'In absurdity!'

'Barnaby was at his best,' defended Ingram stoutly.

'Then I would hate to see his worst,' retorted Applegarth, 'for it would beggar belief. Why wave his hands so, and pull his face thus?' His grotesque mime turned Gill purple with rage. 'It was a barbarous performance, almost as bad as that of Vincentio himself.'

Lawrence Firethorn came sailing into the taproom.

'What's that you say, sir?' he growled.

'The play was ill-chosen.'

'Not as ill-chosen as your words, Jonas,' warned the other. 'Have a care, sir. We like *Vincentio's Revenge.*'

'Can any sane man admire such a botch of nature?'

'Yes!' challenged Firethorn. 'He stands before you.'

'Then I will list my complaints against the piece in order,' said Applegarth, quite unabashed. 'Firstly . . .'

'Save your strictures for another time,' insisted Nicholas, diving in quickly to take the heat out of the argument. 'Master Firethorn is entertaining his wife and does not wish

159

to be led astray by idle comment that smells too strongly of ale. Our play found favour this afternoon and there's an end to it.'

With the aid of Owen Elias, he shepherded Applegarth to a table in the corner and sat him down on a bench. Barnaby Gill was still pulsating with anger and James Ingram with disgust, but the quarrel was effectively over. Lawrence Firethorn mastered his fury. Reminded that Margery was still waiting for him in the adjoining chamber, he ordered wine and withdrew to the urgent solace of her embrace. An uneasy peace descended on the taproom.

Jonas Applegarth was still in a bellicose mood.

'I am entitled to my opinion,' he asserted.

'Not when it offends your fellows so,' said Nicholas.

'Can they not cope with honesty?'

'Honesty, yes, but this was random cruelty.'

'I will not praise where praise is not due, Nick.'

'Then hold your tongue,' counselled Elias, 'or you'll lose every friend you have made in Westfield's Men. Insult Master Firethorn again and your career with us is ended.'

'This play was lame stuff.'

'Why, then, did you force yourself to watch it?' said Nicholas. 'If *Vincentio's Revenge* is not to your taste, avoid it. That way, you will not have to suffer its shortcomings and your fellows will not have to bear your gibes. How can you expect actors to give of their best in *your* play when you mock their performances in every other piece?'

'Stop biting the hand that feeds you,' said Elias. 'You

have spat out enough fingers already. Respect our work and we might grow to respect yours.'

'My art demands reverence!' said Applegarth, slapping the table with a peremptory hand. '*The Misfortunes of Marriage* is an absolute masterpiece.'

'Only when it is played,' reminded Nicholas.

'Why, so it will be. At The Rose next week.'

'Not if you talk it off the stage.'

'Westfield's Men are contracted to perform it.'

'We were contracted to perform *The Faithful Shepherd* by Edmund Hoode until you came along. If one play can be ousted thus easily from The Rose, so can another.' Nicholas did not mince his words. 'And if Westfield's Men do not perform your work, it will remain as no more than words on a page. I gave you fair warning at the start, Jonas. You will be out of the company and we will cheer your departure.'

Applegarth was momentarily checked. 'But you saw my play, Nick. It blazed across the stage like a meteor. Owen will vouch for its quality. He tasted its true worth from the inside. Would any company be so prodigal as to cast aside a work of art?'

'Our doubts are not about *The Misfortunes of Marriage*,' said Nicholas. 'It is a rare phenomenon. We all agree on that. But the playwright obstructs our view of the play. In plain terms, you are making us regret the misfortunes of marriage between Westfield's Men and Jonas Applegarth. Divorce grows daily nearer.'

'Then let it come!' shouted the other.

'Listen to Nick,' said Elias. 'You need us.'

'Not if I must be bound and gagged. Fie on thee!'

161

'Sleep on what I have said,' suggested Nicholas. 'We would be friends. Why rush to make us mortal enemies?'

'God's blood!' exclaimed Applegarth. 'I'll not stand it!'

He rose to his feet and swayed over them. The smell of strong ale was on his breath. Applegarth had been drinking heavily before, during and after the performance. It made him even more pugnacious and fearless of consequence.

'A turd in your teeth!' he bawled. 'Oust me? I spurn you all like the knaves you are! There is a world elsewhere!'

Kicking the bench aside, he lurched towards the door. Owen Elias was outraged by his behaviour but his affection for the playwright won through.

'Wild words spoken in haste,' he said.

'That tongue of his will talk him out of employment.'

'I'll after him and see the rogue safe home.'

'Counsel moderation, Owen.'

'What I counsel is a bucket of cold water over his foolish head before I deign to speak to him. If Jonas will not see sense, he loses my esteem. I'll not sew another patch on the torn sleeve of our fellowship.'

As soon as the Welshman left, Nicholas was joined by James Ingram, still in a state of agitation.

'Applegarth is a menace to us all, Nick!'

'But chiefly to himself.'

'Do not ask me to show him sympathy.'

'Jonas has supped too much ale.'

'Sober, he is merely obnoxious; drunk, he is beyond excuse. He poured contempt on the whole company.'

'I heard him, James.'

162

'He is one big barrel of arrogance.'

'His time with us may be very short indeed.'

'It will be,' said Ingram with feeling. 'If he takes the cudgel to us, we will fight back. I tell you, Nick, I'd willingly strike the first blow.'

Nicholas was surprised. James Ingram was not given to fits of anger. With the exception of Edmund Hoode, he was the most mild-mannered person in the company. Yet he was now curling his lip in a sneer of animosity. It was several minutes before Nicholas could calm him down. When he finally did so, he slipped his hand inside his buff jerkin to take out the sketch which Caleb Hay had drawn for him.

'I have something to show you, James.'

'What is it?'

'Blackfriars. Given to me by a friend.'

Ingram examined the sketch with great interest and traced the outline of the theatre with his finger. There was a hint of nostalgia in his voice.

'It is very accurate.'

'The artist is a keen historian of the city.'

'Then here, in this small drawing, is history writ large. Castle and tower are turned into a monastery. Monastery becomes a theatre. And this very week, theatre becomes a place of execution. Master Fulbeck's death is one more violent change in Blackfriars. God rest his soul!'

'Amen.'

'When will you go back there, Nick?'

'This evening.'

'Take me with you.'

'Gladly.'

'I am ready,' said Ingram, handing the sketch back to him. 'Why do we tarry here?'

'Because I have to pay my respects first.'

'To whom?'

Nicholas glanced towards a door on the far side of the room and Ingram gave a smile of understanding. The book holder needed to exchange a greeting with Margery Firethorn.

'I'll be with you anon,' said Nicholas.

He crossed to the door and tapped lightly on it.

'Enter!' boomed the actor.

Husband and wife were seated at a table when he went in. Both rose to their feet instantly, Margery coming across to embrace the visitor and Firethorn seeing an opportunity to elude her matrimonial vigilance for a few minutes.

'Is that insolent braggart still here, Nick?'

'Jonas Applegarth has gone back home.'

'He is like to stay there if he rail against me. I was Vincentio to the life this afternoon. Was I not, my dove?'

'Beyond compare,' cooed Margery.

'Yet that wrangling malcontent denied my genius. I'll fetch him such a box on the ears, he'll not wake until Doomsday! Let me see that he has quit the premises or I'll not rest.'

Firethorn slipped out of the room and closed the door behind him. Margery was clearly delighted to be left alone with Nicholas. Taking him by the hand, she led him across to a small bench and they sat down together. She spoke in a conspiratorial whisper.

'Thank heaven that you came to me, Nick.'

'Why?'

'You'd else have missed the glad tidings.'

'Tidings?'

'She was here.'

'Who?'

'Who else, man?'

'Anne? Here at the performance?'

'Sitting as close to me as you are now. She loved the play as much as I did and wept almost as many tears. Anne sent a private message to you.'

'Did she?'

'I am to give you her warmest regards,' said Margery. 'What she really meant me to convey was her undying love but she could not put that into words.'

Nicholas was pleased that Anne had made contact through an intermediary, though disappointed that she had not delivered her message in person.

'Did Anne come to the Queen's Head alone?' he said.

'No,' replied Margery with a teasing grin. 'She was on the arm of the most striking young man I have seen for a long time. Were I not a contented wife, I would have fought her tooth and nail for the privilege of being escorted by so dashing a partner. An exquisite fellow.'

'What was his name?'

'Preben van Loew.'

Nicholas laughed with relief. There was no point in trying to hide his love for Anne Hendrik from her.

Margery had seen them together in earlier days and never ceased to tax him over their parting. Unwilling and unable to talk about Anne with anyone else, he was now with the one person who had some insight into the relationship.

'Go to her, Nick,' she advised.

'It is not the answer, I fear.'

'She wastes away without you.'

'That is not my impression.'

'I can tell when a woman is grieving.'

'It is not for me,' he said with a sigh. 'When I called on her yesterday, I only managed to upset her. We have lost the way of speaking to each other.'

'Use deeds instead of words. Embrace her with love.'

He shook his head. 'My suit is unwelcome.'

'Press it with more diligence.'

'I am too late. There is another man in her life.'

'Ambrose Robinson.'

He blinked in astonishment. 'She spoke of him?'

'Not a word.'

'Then how did you learn of his existence?'

'From her handsome escort.'

'Preben van Loew?'

'Yes,' she said airily. 'Anne would not talk of her personal affairs and so I bided my time until I could speak with the Dutchman alone. For some reason, the poor fellow is afraid of me. I cannot think why. I am mildness itself. Is any woman in London less frightening than me?'

'I think not,' said Nicholas tactfully.

'As we were leaving the gallery, Anne met a neighbour and

exchanged a few words with her. I seized my opportunity. Preben was most forthcoming.'

'What did he say?'

'He does not like this Ambrose Robinson, I know that.'

'No more do I.'

'Anne does, it seems. And with some reason.'

'What might it be?'

'Money,' she said. 'The Dutchman was too loyal to betray the full details, but he gave me hints and nudges enough for me to piece together the story. Earlier in the year, her business was in grave difficulty.'

'Anne told me that it was faring well.'

'Only because of the butcher. Thieves broke into the shop three times. Hats were destroyed, patterns stolen. They were unable to meet their orders and lost business. To make matters worse, the shop was damaged by fire and much of their material went up in smoke.'

'Why did not Anne turn to me?' Nick asked anxiously.

'Because you had drifted out of her life. What she needed was money to rebuild and restock her premises. That is when Ambrose Robinson came on the scene.'

'Now I understand her sense of obligation.'

'Understand something else, Nick. She came to *see you*.'

'But I was hidden from sight.'

'You were here, that was enough. Anne wanted to be close.'

'Is that what she told you?'

'She did not need to.'

Nicholas was touched. Margery had been active on his behalf, and for all her outspokenness, he knew that she could be discreet. What she had found out explained much that had been puzzling him. Though she did not feel able to speak with him directly, Anne Hendrik had taken a definite step towards him. It was something on which to build.

Edmund Hoode waited for well over an hour before disillusion set in. Standing alone in the empty inn yard, he began to feel decidedly conspicuous. He had been like a mettlesome horse at first, prancing on his toes and quivering with pent-up energy. His high expectation slowly trickled away and he was now as forlorn and motionless as a parish pump in a rainstorm.

Her message had been explicit. *Tomorrow.* Surely that was a firm promise? He was at the same spot, in the same yard at more or less the same time. Why did she not send word? A sleepless night in a fever of hope had been followed by a morning rehearsal. Knowing that she would be watching, he dedicated his performance in *Vincentio's Revenge* to her and invested it with every ounce of skill and commitment.

After changing out of his costume in the tiring-house and waiting for the yard to clear of spectators, he began his vigil with a light heart. It was now a huge boulder which weighed him down and which threatened to burst out of the inadequate lodging of his chest. Could any woman be capable of such wanton cruelty? A rose. A promise. Betrayal. Hoode was devastated.

There was no hint of Rose Marwood this time, no sign of a well-groomed servant with a secret missive. All he could see were a couple of ostlers, sniggering at him from the shadow of the stables and wondering why a man in his best doublet and hose should be standing in the middle of a filthy inn yard. Hoode gave up. With weary footsteps, he trudged towards the archway which led to Gracechurch Street.

When the horse and rider trotted into the yard, he stood swiftly to one side to let them pass, never suspecting that they had come in search of him. The young man in the saddle brought his mount in a tight circle and its flank brushed Hoode as it went past. About to protest, the playwright suddenly realised that he was holding something in his hand. Another missive had been delivered.

Spirits soaring once more, he tore the seal off and unrolled the sheet. Hoping for a letter, he was at first dumbfounded to find no words at all on the page. In their place was what appeared to be the head of a horse with a spike protruding from between its eyes. Was it a message or a piece of mockery? It was only when his brain cleared that he was able to read its import.

'The Unicorn!'

A rose. A promise. A tryst. Love was, after all, moving in ascending steps. She was waiting for him at the Unicorn. It was an inn no more than a hundred yards away. His first impulse was to run there as fast as his trembling legs could carry him, but a more sensible course of action recommended itself. Since she had kept him on tenterhooks, he would make her wait as well. It would only serve to heighten the pleasure of their encounter.

Adjusting his attire and straightening his hat, he left the Queen's Head and strolled along Gracechurch Street with dignity. He was no love-lorn rustic, rushing to answer the call of a capricious mistress. He was a conqueror about to enjoy the spoils of war. That illusion carried him all the way to the Unicorn and in through its main door. It was shattered the moment he was confronted by a smiling young woman with a fawnlike grace and beauty. His jaw dropped.

She gave him a curtsey, then indicated the stairs.

'My mistress awaits you, sir. Follow me.'

With uncertain steps, Edmund Hoode climbed towards Elysium.

Chapter Eight

When he reached the landing, he made an effort to compose his features and to straighten his back. It was as a man of the theatre that his admirer had first seen Edmund Hoode. She would lose all respect for him if he were to slink apologetically into her company and behave like a callow youth in a fumbling courtship. A dramatic entrance was called for and he did his best to supply it.

The maidservant tapped on a door, opened it in answer to a summons from within and then stepped back to admit the visitor. Pretending that he was about to face an audience in the inn yard, Hoode went into the chamber with a confident stride and doffed his hat to bow low. The door closed soundlessly behind him. When he raised his eyes to take a first long look at the mysterious lady in his life, he was quite bedazzled.

She was beautiful. Fair skinned and neat boned, she had an alabaster neck which supported an oval face of quiet loveliness. She wore a dark blue velvet dress but no jewellery of any kind. Well-groomed blond hair was brushed back under a blue cap. Gloved hands were folded in her lap as she sat on a chair, framed by the window.

Hoode was struck by her poise and elegance. Her voice was low and accompanied by a sweet smile of welcome.

'It is a pleasure to see you, Master Hoode,' she said.

'Thank you,' he replied politely, 'but I fear that you have the advantage over me.'

'My name is Cecily Gilbourne.'

A second bow. 'At your service, Mistress Gilbourne.'

'Pray take a seat, sir.'

She motioned him to a chair opposite her and he lowered himself gingerly onto it, his gaze never leaving her. Cecily Gilbourne was a trifle older than he had expected – in her late twenties, perhaps even thirty – but her maturity was to him a form of supreme ripeness. He would not have changed her age by a year or her appearance by the tiniest emendation. It was reassuring to learn that she was no impressionable child, no giggling girl, no shallow creature infatuated with the theatre, but a woman of experience with an intelligence that positively shone out of her.

'*The Merchant of Calais,*' she announced.

'A workmanlike piece,' he said modestly.

'I thought it brilliant. It was the first of your plays that I saw and it made me yearn to meet the author.'

'Indeed?'

'Such an understanding of the true price of love.'

'Your praise overwhelms me.'

'Not as much as your work overwhelms *me,*' she said with a sigh of admiration. 'You are a true poet of the soul. *The Corrupt Bargain.*'

'Another apple plucked from the orchard of my brain.'

'Delicious in the mouth. *Love's Sacrifice.* We have all made that in our time, alas. Your play on that theme was so profound.'

'Drawn from life.'

'That is what I guessed. Only those who have suffered the pangs of a broken heart can understand the nature of that suffering. *Love's Sacrifice* gave me untold pleasure and helped me to keep sorrow at bay during a most troubling time in my life. Your plays, Master Hoode – may I call you Edmund?'

'Please, please!' he encouraged.

'Your plays, Edmund, are a source of joy to me.'

'For that compliment alone, they were worth writing.'

'*Double Deceit.*'

'Juvenilia. When I was young and green.'

'Its humour bubbled like a mountain stream.'

'*Pompey the Great.* That is Edmund Hoode at his finest.'

'I regret that I have never seen it played.'

'You must, you must, Mistress Gilbourne.'

'Call me Cecily . . . if we are to be friends.'

'Thank you, Cecily,' he gushed. 'And we will.'

'Be friends?'

'I earnestly hope so.'

'No more than that?'

She gave him an enigmatic smile. Hoode was not sure if she was enticing him or merely appraising him. It did not matter. He was ready to surrender unconditionally to her will. A rose. A promise. A tryst. Cecily Gilbourne was a kindred spirit, a true romantic, someone removed from the sordid lusts of the world, a woman of perception who loved the way that he wrote about love.

'Well?' she said. 'Do I surprise you?'

'Surprise me and delight me, Cecily.'

'Am I as you imagined I might be?'

'Oh, no.'

'You are disappointed?'

'Overjoyed. The reality far exceeds my imaginings.'

She laughed softly. 'I knew that I had chosen well.'

'Did you?'

'Yes, Edmund. Your plays let me look into your heart.'

'What did you find there?'

The enigmatic smile played around her lips again. 'I found you.'

The words caressed his ears and he almost swooned. He could not believe that it was happening to him. Years of rejection by the fairer sex had sapped his self-esteem. Romantic disaster was his natural habitat. Women like Cecily Gilbourne did not exist in his life except as phantoms. There had been no chase, no agonising period of courtship, no sequence of sonnets to express his desire in honeyed phrases. She had come to him. It was the most natural and painless relationship he had ever enjoyed with a beautiful woman, intensified as it was by an element of mystery, and given a deeper resonance by the fact that she adored his work as much as his person.

'Will you come to me again, Edmund?' she whispered.

'Whenever you call.'

'It will be very soon.'

'I will be waiting.'

'Thank you.'

She offered her hand and he placed the lightest of kisses upon it, his lips burning with pleasure as they touched her glove. 'Farewell, my prince,' she said.

Cecily turned to stare out of the window, allowing him to see her in profile and to admire the marmoreal perfection of her neck and chin. Caught in the light, her skin was so white and silky that Hoode had to resist the urge to reach out and stroke it with the tips of his fingers. Instead, he gave her the lowest bow yet, mumbled his farewell and backed towards the door with his mouth still agape.

Their first meeting was over. He was ensnared.

When they reached the precinct of Blackfriars, they explored the surrounding streets and the church before going into the theatre itself. Geoffrey, the old porter, gave them a subdued welcome and told them that Raphael Parsons was still in the building. Nicholas Bracewell went briskly up the staircase with James Ingram at his side.

What met them in the theatre itself was a far less gruesome sight than the one which had greeted them on their earlier visit. Raphael Parsons was talking to a group of young actors, who were sitting on the edge of the stage in costume. Behind them was the setting for the final scene of *Mariana's Revels*. His voice was loud but unthreatening. None of the Chapel Children evinced any fear of the man.

Hearing their approach, Parsons swung round to face them.

'You trespass on private property,' he said crisply.

'The theatre is open to the public,' reminded Nicholas. 'You performed here this very afternoon, it seems. *Mariana's Revels*. Not that we come as spectators, Master Parsons. We would speak with you.'

'The time is not convenient.'

'Then we will wait.'

Nicholas and his companion folded their arms and stood there patiently. They would not easily be dismissed. The manager clicked his tongue in exasperation before snapping his fingers to dismiss the actors. They scampered off into the tiring-house. Nicholas looked after them.

'Was Philip Robinson in your cast?' he asked.

'He was,' said Parsons. 'He played Mariana herself.'

'The boy can carry a leading role?'

'Exceeding well. His plaintive songs moved all who heard him sing. But you did not come here to discuss the talents of my actors. I see that by your faces.'

'We are here on Master Fulbeck's behalf.' said Ingram.

'There is something you did not tell me?'

'It is the other way around,' explained Nicholas. 'We have questions to put to you.'

'To what end?'

176

'The arrest and conviction of a killer. A Laughing Hangman, who turned your stage into a gallows. You and I and James here, each working on his own, would never track him down. But if we pool our knowledge, if we share opinion and conjecture, we may perchance succeed.'

'I do not need your help,' said Parsons sharply.

'You know the murderer, then?'

'Not yet, Master Bracewell.'

'Then how do you propose to root him out?'

'By cunning, sir. Alone and unaided.'

'We came by Ireland Yard,' said Ingram, pointedly.

'So?'

'That was where you claimed to be when Master Fulbeck was dangling from a noose in here.'

'You doubt my word?'

'Not in the slightest.'

'We would simply like to know which house you visited,' said Nicholas reasonably. 'Your host would confirm the time of your arrival and departure.'

'Damn your impudence, sir!'

'What number in Ireland Yard?'

'I'll not be harried like this,' warned Parsons. 'Where I went that day was and will remain my business. I am not under scrutiny here. Do you dare to suggest that *I* was implicated in the crime in some way? Cyril Fulbeck was my partner. I worshipped the man.'

'Yet argued with him constantly.'

'That was in the nature of things.'

'Why did you open the theatre today?' said Ingram.

'Because a play had been advertised.'

'The murder of Master Fulbeck notwithstanding?'

'He would have sanctioned the performance.'

'I beg leave to question that.'

Parsons was blunt. 'Our beloved Master of the Chapel may have died but life goes on.'

'With no decent interval for mourning?'

'This theatre itself is his memorial.'

'And your source of income,' observed Nicholas.

'That, too.'

'Therein lies the true reason for performance.'

'I run this theatre the way that I choose!'

'No,' corrected Nicholas. 'The way that you *have* to run it, Master Parsons. By cramming in every performance that you possibly can and by working your actors like oxen in the field. That is why you staged *Mariana's Revels* today. Not by way of a memorial to Cyril Fulbeck. You wanted the money.'

'The theatre has expenses.'

'Is that why you wrangled with your partner?'

'Leave off this, sir!'

'Did you argue over profit?'

'I'll not account to you or anyone else for what I do within these four walls!' yelled Parsons, waving his arms. 'Blackfriars is my theatre. I live for this place.'

'Master Fulbeck died for it.'

Anger building, Parsons looked from one to the other. 'Envy drives you both on,' he sneered. 'I see that now. Blackfriars is without peer. We offer our patrons a real playhouse, not an inn yard smelling of dung and stale beer. Here they sit in comfort to watch the best plays in London, protected from the rain and wind, marvelling at our skill and our invention. Westfield's Men are vagabonds beside my Chapel Boys.'

'We pay our actors,' said Nicholas. 'Do you pay yours?'

'I'll hear no more of this!'

'Answer me but one thing.'

'Away with you both or I'll summon a constable!'

'Master Fulbeck's keys.'

'What of them?'

'Have they ever been found?'

Raphael Parsons made them wait for a reply, his eyes flicking around the theatre before finally settling on Nicholas with a defiant glare.

'They have not been found.'

'So they are still in the possession of the murderer?'

'We may presume as much.'

'Beware, Master Parsons,' said Nicholas. 'He can gain access to this theatre again by means of those keys.'

The manager was unperturbed. He walked to the door and opened it for them to leave. The visitors exchanged a nod. To remain any longer would be a waste of time. Nicholas felt that they had learnt far more from the manner of his answers than from anything that Raphael Parsons had said. When he questioned the two friends earlier, the theatre manager had been calm and plausible. Cornered by surprise on his own territory, he was resentful and uncooperative.

As they walked to the door, Parsons stopped them.

'Come tomorrow and pay to gain entrance,' he suggested.

'Why?' said Nicholas.

'Because you will not only see a fine play finely acted on a stage fit to bear it. You will witness our revenge.'

'Against whom?'

'Master Foulmouth himself. Jonas Applegarth.'

'What do you play tomorrow?'

'*Alexander the Great*. An old play on an old theme but with a Prologue newly minted to cut the monstrous Applegarth down to human size. Westfield's Men are soundly whipped as well. They who attack Blackfriars will suffer reprisals.' He wagged an admonitory finger. 'Deliver that message to your lewd playwright. We'll destroy his reputation entire. We'll hang him from the roof beam with a rope of rhyming couplets and strangle the life out of his disgusting carcass!'

Easing them through the door, he closed it firmly behind them. They heard a key turning in the lock. As they descended the stairs, Ingram glanced over his shoulder.

'Master Parsons has grown testy,' he said.

'We came unannounced into his domain and caught him on the raw. He has a malignant streak, no question of that. I would not care to be one of his young actors.'

'Nor I, Nick. It was never thus in my day.'

'You were trained as well as any of our apprentices.'

'And shown great kindness. Times have changed.'

The porter was waiting at the foot of the staircase to detain Ingram in conversation. Nicholas drifted out of the building and retraced the steps he had taken when in pursuit of the murderer on the earlier visit. Pausing at the rear of the theatre, he looked at the various avenues of escape which the man could have taken. If he had run fast, he might have been clear of the precinct before Nicholas reached the spot where he was now standing. Or he might have gone to ground in any one of the nearby streets and alleyways.

By way of experiment, Nicholas broke into a trot and dodged around a few corners. When he came to a halt, he saw that he was standing in Ireland Yard. He studied the houses with interest before he walked back towards the theatre. As he strolled past it, the rear door was unlocked and a dozen or more figures emerged. Wearing white surplices over black cassocks, they lined up in pairs and marched away in step, the choirboys at the front and the vicars choral behind them.

'Philip!' called Nicholas.

One of the boys turned in surprise to look at him. The resemblance to Ambrose Robinson was clear. His bright young face was puzzled by the salutation. The boy was pushed gently from behind by another chorister and the procession wended on its way. Nicholas was impressed by the sense of order and assurance about them. Philip Robinson was an integral part of the whole. He did not look like an unwilling prisoner. Nicholas watched him until the column vanished out of sight.

The journey took an eternity. Owen Elias was soon regretting his offer to safeguard the drunken Jonas Applegarth. The playwright kept stopping in the street to accuse innocent by-standers of unspeakable crimes, to hurl verbal thunderbolts at every church they passed, to kick at the stray dogs which yapped at his heels and to relieve himself unceremoniously against any available wall. When Elias tried to remonstrate with him, Applegarth either turned his vituperation on the Welshman or embraced him tearfully while vowing undying friendship.

Celtic patience finally snapped. Applegarth reviled him once too often and Elias expressed his displeasure in the most direct way. Grabbing the bigger man by the scruff of the neck, he dragged him towards a horse trough and threw him in head first. Applegarth hit the water with a fearsome splash. His face was submerged for a full minute as he emitted a hideous gurgling sound. Then he managed to haul himself out of the trough and fell to the ground.

He lay there twitching violently like a giant cod on the deck of a fishing vessel. His clothes were sodden, his hair and beard dripping and his hat floating in a puddle beside him. After expelling a pint of water from his mouth, he let out a bellow of anger and tried to get up. Elias put a foot in the middle of his chest to hold him down. Applegarth replied with an even louder bellow but it soon gave way to rumbling laughter. Instead of lambasting his colleague, he turned his derision upon himself.

'Look at me!' he said, wobbling with mirth. 'The most brilliant playwright in London, flat on his back in the mire! The greatest ale drinker in England, spewing out rank water. The fattest belly in Christendom, staring up at the sky! Is this not a pretty sight, Owen?'

'You deserved it.'

'Indeed, I did.'

'You went well beyond the bounds of fellowship.'

'I am the first to acknowledge it.'

'The horse trough was the best place for you.'

'No, my friend,' said Applegarth, as remorse wiped the grin from his wet face. 'It is too elevated a station for me. A swamp would be a fitter home. A ditch. A dunghill. Find me a hole big enough and I'll crawl into it with the other vermin. Why do I *do* it, Owen?'

'I'll tell you in the morning when you're sober.'

Reaching down, he took the other in a firm grip and heaved backwards. Jonas Applegarth swung slowly upright. He looked down at the state of his apparel with revulsion.

'My wife will assault me!' he moaned.

'There may be others keen to do that office for her.'

'My doublet is stained, my breeches torn, my stockings past repair. I am an insult to her tailoring.' He felt his head in a panic. 'Where's my hat? Where's my hat?'

'Here,' said Elias, retrieving it from the puddle.

'I dare not go home like this.'

'You will and you must, Jonas.'

'What will my wife say?'

'That is her privilege. But I marvel that you rail against religion so when you must be married to a saint. Who else would put up with you?'

'True, true, Owen,' agreed the other. 'She *is* a saint.'

'A martyr to her husband.'

Applegarth remained solemn and silent all the way home. He was a sorry sight as he was admitted to the house by a servant. Elias waited long enough to hear the first shriek of complaint from the resident saint before turning away. Movement in the shadows then alerted him. He was reminded why he had accompanied Applegarth in the first place.

Pulling out his dagger, he ran diagonally across the street to the lane on the opposite side but he was too slow. All he caught was the merest glimpse of a man, darting down the lane before disappearing into the rabbit warren of streets beyond it. Elias stabbed the air in his anger.

They had been followed.

Anne Hendrik counted out the coins and handed them over. 'There, Ambrose,' she said with relief. ''Tis done!'

'Thank you.'

'My debt is cleared at last.'

'There was no hurry to repay me,' he said, putting the coins into his purse. 'And I am far more in your debt than you in mine. No amount of money can ever discharge that obligation.'

'I have done nothing.'

'Is saving a man's life nothing? Is giving him fresh hope nothing? You did all that for me and more.'

'I think not.'

'Every penny I have is yours for the asking.'

'We can pay our own way again now.'

'You *must* know how much you mean to me, Anne.'

She turned away and resumed her seat in order to avoid what she sensed might be an embarrassing declaration. They were in the parlour of her house in Bankside. The butcher stood awkwardly in the middle of the room, peeved that the settlement of her debt had deprived him of an excuse to call on a regular basis and searching for a means to secure a more permanent mooring in her affections.

'I acted out of simple friendship,' she said.

'Is that all that it will remain?'

'For the moment, Ambrose.'

'And in time?'

'Who knows what the future will hold?'

'Who indeed?' he agreed, shaking his head ruefully. 'A year ago, I was the most contented of men. I had a happy marriage, a son I adored and a business that was thriving. What else could anyone ask? Then, suddenly . . .' He clapped his hands together. 'I lost it all. My dear wife died, my son was taken from me by deed of impressment, and I had no pleasure from my occupation. What was the point in struggling on?'

'There is always a point, Ambrose.'

'You taught me that.'

'I, too, lost my dearest partner.'

'But not your child as well.'

'No,' she conceded sadly. 'Not my child. The joys of motherhood were denied me and that is a grievous loss in itself. She brightened. 'Besides, your son has not left you for ever. Philip is still alive and likely to return to you before too long. Nick will see to that.'

'Will he?'

'Put your trust in him.'

'It is growing difficult to do so.'

'Ambrose!' she scolded.

'You saw the way he rounded on me. He is supposed to be helping Philip, not accusing the boy's father with such severity. I am sorry, Anne, but I begin to have serious doubts about Nick Bracewell.'

'Then you do not know him as well as I.'

'That is another cause of my discomfort.'

He moved away to hide the surly expression on his face. When he turned back to her, it was with a slow smile and a surge of ungainly affection.

'I have written to Philip again today,' he said.

'Your letters will be a comfort to him.'

'He is old enough to be told now. To understand.'

'Understand?'

'What an angel of mercy you have been. Without you to rescue me, I would have given in. Philip knows that. He always liked you, Anne. He always talked kindly of you. It will make such a difference to him. Philip was much closer to his mother than to me but that is only natural. It will make such a difference.'

'I do not follow.'

'A child needs a proper home, Anne.'

'He has one.'

'He has a house but something is missing from it.' Anne realised what he was trying to say to her and steeled herself. In paying off her debt she had hoped to lighten the weight of his friendship, but she had merely given him the cue to translate it into a deeper relationship.

'I know that I have little enough to offer,' he began, planting himself before her. 'Jacob Hendrik was a decent,

God-fearing, conscientious man and I could never be the husband to you that he was. But I swear to you—'

'That is enough,' she interrupted. 'I would prefer it if you said no more on that subject.'

Robinson was hurt. 'Have I offended you?'

'No, Ambrose.'

'Do you find me so revolting, then?'

'You are a good man with many qualities.'

'But not good enough for you?'

'That was not my meaning.'

'Then why do you spurn me?'

'I do not,' she said, standing and crossing to the window. 'I am just not ready to consider . . . what you wish to propose, that is all.'

'Not ready now?' he said, brightening. 'But one day . . .'

'I make no promises.'

'One day . . .'

'My life is happy enough as it is.'

'A husband and a son will make it even happier.'

'No,' she said, turning to face him. 'We are friends. I like to think that we are close friends. You helped me when others would not and I will always be grateful to you for that. It made me want to help you to bring Philip home.'

Robinson stared at her. A resentful note intruded.

'It is him, is it not?'

'Who?'

'Your precious Nick Bracewell. He is the canker here.'

'What do you mean?'

'It has all changed,' he said bitterly. 'Until he came back

187

into your world, you had time for me and interest in my affairs. We talked together, supped together, even walked to church together on a Sunday. All golden times for me. Then this friend, this Nick Bracewell, appears again and my chances go begging.'

'That is not true.'

'He changed everything.'

'No, Ambrose.'

'But for him, you would have been mine. I know it.'

'Nick changed *nothing*.'

The force of her rejection was like a slap in the face. His body tensed and his eyes blazed but he made no comment. Swinging on his heel, he went out of the house and slammed the door behind him.

Lawrence Firethorn was just about to climb into bed when he heard the thunderous knocking on his front door. Margery was already lying among the pillows in her nightgown with a smile of lustful anticipation on her face. *Vincentio's Revenge* had sent them early to their bedchamber and they knew that nobody in the house would dare to interrupt them.

When more knocking came, Firethorn stamped a bare foot on the floor to signal to the servant below.

'Whoever that is, send them on their way!' he yelled.

'Ignore them, Lawrence,' purred his wife.

'When you lie before me like that, my sweet, I would ignore the Last Judgement. Was ever a man so blessed in his wife? Was ever lover so well matched with lover?' He moved in to bestow a first tender kiss on her lips. 'Was ever an actor given such a fine role as this that I play now?'

He embraced her with fiery passion and buried his head between her generous breasts. Digging her fingers into his hair, she pulled him close and urged him on with cries of delight, groaning with even more pleasure when his hands slipped under her nightgown to explore her warm thighs. The bed soon began to creak rhythmically but a louder noise rose above it. Somebody was actually pounding on their door.

Ecstasy froze on the instant. Firethorn could not believe it. At a time when he and his wife most wanted to be alone, they were being rudely disturbed. It was unforgivable. Leaping from the bed half-naked, he stalked across the room, determined to castigate the servant in the roundest of terms before hurling her out into the street. When he snatched open the door, he fully expected the girl to be cowering in terror. Instead, he was met by the improbable sight of Edmund Hoode, hands on hips, standing there with his legs set firmly apart.

'I have come to speak with you, Lawrence,' he asserted.

'*Now?* Must it be now? Must it be here?' Firethorn stepped outside the bedchamber and pulled the door shut after him. 'Do you know what you have just interrupted?'

'I care not.'

'Margery is waiting for me within.'

'I will not keep you from your sleep much longer.'

'Sleep was the least of our concerns!'

'I had to see you.'

'Well, see me, you do. So turn tail and leave my house before I speed you on your way!' His eyes glowed in the half-dark. 'Come not between the dragon and his mate!'

'Who is it?' called Margery from within.

'Edmund!'

'At this hour?'

'Begone, sir!' snarled Firethorn. 'You hold up destiny.'

'That is why I am here,' said Hoode calmly. 'To discuss my own destiny. When I sensed danger in the person of a rival, my impulse was to shrink away and yield up my place. Not any more, Lawrence. I intend to fulfil my destiny. I am here to fight for my place in Westfield's Men.'

Firethorn exploded. 'If you tarry any longer, you will be fighting for your life! God's tits, man! The most wonderful woman in the world is waiting for me in that bed.'

'Not for ever,' cautioned Margery. 'I grow weary.'

'Come back tomorrow, Edmund!'

Firethorn tried to push him away, but Hoode held his ground with a determination that was unprecedented in so reserved a man. Five minutes alone with Cicely Gilbourne had transformed him. He was loved. His plays were admired. His life had purpose after all. What thrilled him most was her appreciation of his work. It was this which had restored his confidence in himself and made him reflect on the shabby treatment he had been accorded by Westfield's Men. With fire in his belly, he walked all the way to Shoreditch to beard Firethorn in his own den. Margery's presence was a minor disadvantage.

'Will *you* box his ear or will I?' she shouted.

'I will, my pretty one,' cooed Firethorn before glowering at the intruder. 'Leave now while your legs still carry you or I'll not be answerable for my actions!'

'If I leave now, Lawrence, I leave for good!'

'That will content us.'

'Who will pen your plays then, I wonder?'

'Still there?' wailed Margery. 'Throttle the idiot!'

'I talk of my place,' continued Hoode, unruffled. 'I talk of my destiny. Westfield's Men are contracted to perform *The Faithful Shepherd* at The Rose yet I am thrust aside to make way for Jonas Applegarth.'

Firethorn gasped. 'You have invaded my bedchamber in order to talk about a paltry *play*?'

'That paltry play means much to me. Thus it stands. Perform it at The Rose and I remain in the company. Supplant me with another playwright and I will henceforth offer my talent to Banbury's Men. Do you understand, Lawrence?'

The other was so stunned that all he could offer was a meek nod. Hoode's fearless manner and dire threat robbed him of the organs of speech. Panting on the bed, Margery Firethorn was more concerned with other organs.

'Lawrence!' she bawled. 'Get in here *now*! Your kettle is no longer boiling, sir. It needs more heat to make it sing. Light my fire again. Where are you, man?'

Hoode tapped politely on the door and inched it open.

'We are done now, Margery,' he said. 'I'll send him in.'

Unable to sleep for more than a few hours, Nicholas Bracewell rose before dawn and strolled down to the edge of the Thames. The river lapped noisily at the wharf and vessels bobbed in the gloom as they lay at anchor. Born and brought up in a seaport, Nicholas felt at home beside the dark water as it curled between its banks with lazy power.

When the first specks of light began to dapple the river, he inhaled the keen air and was at peace with himself. Gulls cried, a winch squealed into life, the plash of oars could be heard in the distance.

His eye then travelled across to Bankside and the demons returned to plague his mind. The Thames did not just snake through London on its way to the sea. Its broad back kept Anne Hendrik and him far apart. They would need more than a bridge to join themselves together again.

Nicholas was still brooding by the quayside when the river was teeming with boats and flanked by scores of people about their daily work. Kneeling down low, he cupped his hands to scoop up some water and let it run over his face. As he began the noisy walk to the Queen's Head, he felt refreshed and ready to begin his own day.

Blackfriars displaced Anne Hendrik from his thoughts. The second visit to the theatre had yielded much. Aided by Caleb Hay's sketch, he had been able to take his bearings with more accuracy and James Ingram had pointed out aspects of the precinct which had gone unremarked before. A most fashionable quarter of London had baulked at the notion of a public playhouse in their midst, yet the most successful private theatre in England stood in its place. He wondered how many of the residents who had signed the earlier petition were keen spectators at Blackfriars.

Raphael Parsons now came into the reckoning as a murder suspect. Their first meeting, Nicholas believed, had been deliberately engineered to throw suspicion off the victim's business partner. Pretending to investigate the crime on his own account, Parsons sought to put himself beyond any investigation. No stage management had been possible before their second encounter. He was taken unawares. His truculent manner, his wild threats and his refusal to account for his precise whereabouts at the time of the murder combined to make him a potential killer.

Nicholas was convinced that the man's vicious rows with his partner were as much over money as over the treatment of the young actors. Long service with Westfield's Men had given the book holder an insight into the perilous finances of a theatre company. Blackfriars might not be at the mercy of the elements in the same way as the Queen's Head, but there was still rent to pay, costumes to buy, scenery and properties to provide, expensive stage equipment to be installed, and the theatre itself to be cleaned and maintained.

When Nicholas added the fees for commissioning new plays with unceasing regularity, he could see how high the running costs must be. The Blackfriars audience might pay higher prices to view the entertainment, but it was much smaller in size than the public playhouses and the gatherers would take less at a performance even than at the Queen's Head. Raphael Parsons had to drive his actors hard to make a profit. He would not thank the soft-hearted Cyril Fulbeck for standing in his way.

Consideration of the theatre manager inevitably brought him around to the case of Philip Robinson and that let Anne Hendrik back into his mind. He brooded afresh on her until a voice hailed him. Nicholas looked up to see Nathan Curtis emerging from the crowd to join him as he turned into Gracechurch Street.

'Early again, Nathan. You put the rest to shame.'

'There are two benches to repair, a coffin to strengthen and a wooden leg to make.'

'A carpenter is always in request.'

'Until you go on tour. My trade falls asleep then.'

'Theatre is a cruel master.'

They were still chatting as they turned in through the archway of the Queen's Head and made for the rooms which they rented as storage areas. Costumes, properties and scenic devices were expensive items, kept under lock and key at all times. Nicholas was alarmed, therefore, when he tried the first door and found it already unlocked.

'Someone is here before us?' said Curtis.

'Not from the company. Only I have the key.'

'Who, then, can it be?'

Nicholas drew a cautionary dagger before opening the door. With Curtis behind him, he stepped into the room used as their wardrobe. Nothing seemed to be missing, but he was certain that someone had been in there. A creaking sound took his attention to the room beyond. It was the place where they stored their properties and scenery, and where the carpenter stowed his tools overnight. Nicholas crept over to the door and lifted the latch gently. The door was unlocked but it would only open a matter of inches before it met an obstruction.

Putting his shoulder to the timber, he applied more pressure and there was a scraping noise as a heavy object was pushed across the floorboards. The creaking sound continued throughout and the two of them froze in their tracks when they saw what was causing it.

Jonas Applegarth was hanging from the central beam by a thick rope. As he swayed to and fro, the stout timber creaked under his weight. His face was bloated, his eyes staring, his body twisted into an unnatural shape. His shoes were dangling only inches above the floor, but that short distance was enough to separate him from life. A man of enormous vitality and power had been reduced to an inert hulk.

The object which had impeded them was an open coffin jammed against the door. Reeling from the shock, Curtis bent over his handiwork and spewed uncontrollably into it. Nicholas recovered more quickly. He saw that the rope went over the beam and was tied off on a wooden cleat fixed to the wall. After unwinding it carefully, he took the full strain and lowered Applegarth's body to the ground with as much consideration as he could.

Nathan Curtis turned to help him but their examination of the body was cut short by another noise. It was a weird and maniacal cackle, which seemed to come from an adjoining room and which rose in volume and intensity until it filled the whole place. The carpenter was terrified by the sound but Nicholas had heard it once before. The Laughing Hangman had returned.

Diving to the other door in the room, Nicholas tried to open it but found it locked. He fumbled for his key and inserted into quickly into the lock. The adjoining chamber was the company's tiring-house. By the time that Nicholas burst into it, the laughter had stopped and the place was empty. He went through the door that led to the yard but could see no sign of a fleeing figure. Guests were departing, ostlers were going about their business, a servant wielded a broom. When he dashed back into the tiring-house, he tried a third door in the chamber. It opened on to the passageway that led all the way down to the taproom.

Nicholas raced along it, searching each room and alcove that he passed. When he reached the taproom, the door opened before him and he came face to face with Alexander Marwood.

'What's amiss?' demanded the landlord.

'Did anyone come through this door a moment ago?'

'I saw nobody.'

'Are you certain, sir?'

'My eyesight is sound.'

'Where, then, did he go?'

Nicholas went back along the passageway to see if he had missed anything. Scenting trouble, the landlord trotted at his heels with face aghast and hands clutching the air.

'What new calamity has befallen me?' he wailed.

'Send for the law, Master Marwood.'

'Thieves have got in? Property has been stolen?'

'It is a more serious crime than that.'

'Fire has been started on my premises?'

'Summon the constables.'

'Dear God!' howled Marwood, fearing that the worst had finally happened. 'My daughter, Rose, has been ravished by one of your goatish actors!'

Nicholas took him by the shoulders to calm him.

'Be still, sir,' he soothed. 'No theft, no arson and no assault upon your daughter. A greater affliction has struck us. There has been murder at the Queen's Head.'

'Murder!'

The word sent the landlord into a fresh paroxysm of apprehension. His body shuddered, his hands slapped his balding head and three nervous twitches united together to turn his eyebrows into a pair of mating caterpillars. Nicholas propelled him back towards the taproom.

'Fetch assistance!' he ordered. 'Raise the alarm!'

Marwood scuttled off like a chicken pursued by an axe.

'Murder! What, ho! Help!'

Abandoning the search, Nicholas made his way swiftly back to the room where Applegarth lay. It was important to look for clues and to guard the body from the invasion of ghoulish interest which the landlord's cries were bound to excite. Other members of the company would soon be arriving. They had to be shielded from the horror of viewing the corpse. Death would deprive them of the day's audience. There could be no performance that afternoon.

When Nicholas entered the room, the body lay in the exact position where he had left it. Nathan Curtis was still there but he had been joined by someone else. Nicholas was jolted. While the carpenter gazed down reverentially at Jonas Applegarth, his companion stared at the murder victim with a smile of quiet satisfaction.

James Ingram turned away to look across at Nicholas.

'Do not ask me to mourn him,' he said. 'I will not.'

Chapter Nine

Lawrence Firethorn was still bemused as his horse trotted in through the looming bulk of Bishopsgate that morning. A promised night of passion with an uninhibited lover had turned into an unseemly squabble with a disappointed wife. Thanks to the intercession of Edmund Hoode, the actor-manager spent the hours of darkness in a cold and cheerless bed. And yet he was not really angry with the playwright. Irritation was the most he could muster. Where he should have been thirsting for the man's blood, he was instead stupefied by his boldness.

Hoode entered the lion's den to deliver his ultimatum. He had to be admired for that. Even in the face of extreme conjugal frustration, he did not flinch. Firethorn could usually stifle him at will and his wife could vanquish Hoode with a glance, yet their combined powers had no impact on him this time. He had lain between them like a naked sword and kept two urgent bodies agonisingly chaste.

Who had changed a taciturn playwright into a brave knight? What had made him enter the lists so purposefully on behalf of his work? Why had he chosen to interrupt lawful copulation in a Shoreditch bedchamber at that particular moment? Only one explanation sufficed.

'A pox on his pizzle!' groaned Firethorn. 'He's in love.'

It posed a real problem for Westfield's Men. They could no longer take their resident playwright for granted. Hoode was forcing them to choose between his proven reliability and Jonas Applegarth's potential wizardry. What should they stage at The Rose – *The Faithful Shepherd* or *The Misfortunes of Marriage*? Hoode's romantic comedy would be an undoubted success, but it was Applegarth's trenchant satire which would reverberate throughout London.

Firethorn was in despair. To lose Hoode would cause him deep personal pain; to sacrifice Applegarth would be an act of professional folly. He was still weighing the two men in the balance as his horse picked its way through the crowd and turned into the yard of the Queen's Head.

Chaos awaited him. Bodies dashed hither and thither in wild confusion. Alexander Marwood charged around in ever decreasing circles, bewailing his lot to those who would listen and upbraiding those who would not. Thomas Skillen was shaking his head in disbelief, George Dart was pacing up and down in cold fear, and the four apprentices were weeping openly. Edmund Hoode sat on a barrel in a complete daze. Owen Elias strutted frenziedly around the edge of the yard with a sword in his hand.

Firethorn saw a large coffin being unloaded from a cart by two men. He kicked his horse to take him across to Hoode.

'Edmund!' he said. 'What means this commotion?'

'Jonas Applegarth has been murdered!'

'Here at the Queen's Head?'

'Hanged by the neck.'

The news hit Firethorn like a body blow. He quivered in the saddle. The implications would be horrendous and far-reaching. One problem had been solved: Hoode would now stay with the company which Applegarth had deserted for ever. But a hundred other problems had just been created. On top of a night of enforced celibacy, it was too much to endure.

Nicholas Bracewell worked as quickly as he could in the limited time at his disposal. To prevent any unnecessary intrusion, he stationed James Ingram and Nathan Curtis, respectively, outside each of the two doors. Ingram's reaction to the murder had been almost callous, but Nicholas could not spare a moment to reflect upon such an unexpected response from such a caring man. Jonas Applegarth pushed all else from the book holder's mind. Before examining the dead body, he first removed the rope and noted how carefully the noose had been tied. The playwright had not been dispatched from the world with the aid of a crude knot. The Laughing Hangman knew his craft.

Inspecting the body, Nicholas was surprised to find no sign of blood. Applegarth would not have gone willingly to the makeshift gallows. His killer would have had to disable him first or he would have fought and yelled. Nicholas eventually located the large swelling on the back of the victim's head. He had been knocked unconscious from behind. A sturdy mallet lay on the floor. The carpenter had unwittingly provided the weapon just as Westfield's Men had unwittingly provided the rope. The scene of the execution had been chosen with care.

When he turned the body on its side, Nicholas was puzzled by the sight of sawdust sticking to the doublet and breeches. Curtis was a tidy carpenter. Though he used the room as his workshop, he always swept the floor clean. Nicholas went over to the rough-hewn table in the corner. Pinches of sawdust still lay in the grooves and knot-holes of the carpenter's workbench. How had it found its way onto the victim's attire?

Bending over the prostrate Applegarth once more, he searched the man's pockets but found only one item that might be a clue. The brief note scribbled on a piece of paper went into Nicholas's own pocket. Mute and unprotesting, Applegarth lay on his back with his eyes searching the ceiling.

In his brief stay with Westfield's Men, he had made a forceful impact and he would be missed. Nicholas offered up a silent prayer for him, then reached down with delicate fingers to close his eyelids.

The sound of raised voices outside the door told him that he did not have much time left. He used it to search for parallels between this murder and that of Cyril Fulbeck. The similarities were too obvious to ignore. Both were rendered unconscious before the noose was fitted. Both were hanged by a man who celebrated his crime with mocking laughter. Both died in buildings from which the killer could make an easy escape. Nicholas was musing on the other common factors when there was a banging on the door.

Constables had arrived and the official investigation began. Nicholas and Curtis gave statements, the scene of the crime was thoroughly searched and the body was scrutinised. Unable to get it into their coffin, the two men had to perch it on top and cover it with a black cloth. More tears were shed in the yard as the corpse of Jonas Applegarth was carried solemnly out to the cart and driven away to the morgue. Westfield's Men were bereaved.

When Nicholas finally emerged, Lawrence Firethorn was standing outside the door. He took the book holder by the arm and led him aside for a hissed interrogation.

'Do you know what this will do to the company?'

'My thoughts are with his poor wife.'

'Mine, too,' said Firethorn defensively. 'Mine, too. The woman will be destroyed. But we suffer an act of destruction as well. Today's performance has been hanged by the neck and Marwood is in such a state of superstitious panic that he is talking of renouncing our contract. What are we to *do*, Nick?'

'Try to keep calm.'

'When one of our number has been murdered?'

'Reassure the rest of the company,' advised Nicholas. 'They need kindness and support at a time like this. I'll speak with the landlord and smooth his ruffled feathers.'

'Who did this, Nick?'

'I do not know.'

'And why did he have to do it *here*?'

'That question is easier to answer.'

'Why not stab Jonas in some dark alleyway?'

'Because the killer wanted to inflict the most damage on Westfield's Men. You see the disarray it has caused.'

'It was like Bedlam out in that yard,' said Firethorn. 'Marwood was prancing around like some lunatic at full moon. Why could not the hangman put *his* scrawny neck into a noose? If our landlord were swinging from the rafters, we'd have something to celebrate.' He pulled Nicholas close. 'Tell me what happened from the moment you arrived here.'

Nicholas was succinct. Firethorn frowned.

'What was Jonas doing here so early?' he wondered.

'Answering your summons.'

'My what?'

'You were the only person who could get him to the Queen's Head at the crack of dawn. The murderer knew that and set his trap accordingly.'

'Trap?'

'Here is the bait,' said Nicholas.

He handed over the letter which he had found in pocket of the dead man. His companion read the scribbled words.

If you would remain with Westfield's Men, meet me at the Queen's Head at dawn . . . Lawrence Firethorn.

'I never sent this!' protested the actor-manager.

'Jonas believed that you did.'

'This is not my summons.'

'I know,' said Nicholas. 'It is a death warrant.'

Anne Hendrik was at once saddened and relieved by her exchange with Ambrose Robinson on the previous evening. She was sorry to wound the feelings of someone who was already suffering a degree of emotional pain. A powerful man in a brutal profession, he was nevertheless remarkably sensitive and she had been touched that he felt able to reveal this side of his character to her. At the same time, however, she did not want her friendship to be misinterpreted. His unwelcome proposal had forced her to be more open with him about her own affections, and that brought a measure of relief. She may have hurt him but at least he would not pester her again.

'What time is he coming?'

'At noon, Preben.'

'Do you wish me to be there?'

'I shall insist,' she said, pleasantly. 'I would never dream of taking on a new apprentice without your full approval.'

'Where does the boy's family come from?'

'Amsterdam.'

'That is recommendation enough.'

Preben van Loew was, as usual, first to arrive at work. Anne came in from her adjacent house to discuss plans for the day. She took a full and active part in the running of the business. The old Dutchman and his colleagues might make the hats, but it was Anne who often designed them and she was solely responsible for gathering all the orders and for ensuring delivery. When demand was especially pressing, she had even been known to take up needle and thread herself.

By the time her other employees drifted in, the discussion with Preben van Loew had ended. Her first task was to buy some new material for the shop. She went back into her house and put on her own hat before she was ready to leave. A dull thud at her front door made her turn. A figure flitted past her window but far too quickly to be identified. She was mystified.

Anne crossed to the door and opened it tentatively. There was nobody there. Something then brushed against her dress. It was a large bunch of flowers in a wicker basket. She picked it up to inhale their fragrance. The scent was quite enchanting. Anne was moved by the unexpected present and she wondered who could have bestowed it on her.

The sender soon declared himself. Stepping around the corner of the street, Ambrose Robinson waved cheerily to her. His expression was apologetic and the flowers were clearly meant as some kind of peace offering. Accepting them as such, Anne replied with a grateful flick of her hand and a token smile. He grinned broadly before ducking out of sight again. She put the basket of flowers on a table without pausing to consider for a moment the real significance of the gift that she was taking into her house.

'That was nobly done, Nick. No man could have handled it better.'

'I wanted to be the one to break the sad tidings.'

'Thank heaven that you were!'

'Your presence was a help, Owen.'

'I said almost nothing.'

'You were there. That was enough. Mistress Applegarth drew strength from your sympathy.'

'It was your compassion which sustained her. You delivered the roughest news in the most gentle way. She will ever be grateful to you for that.'

Owen Elias and Nicholas Bracewell had just left the home of Jonas Applegarth. It had fallen to the book holder to inform her that she was now a widow, and he had done so by suppressing all the gruesome details of her husband's death. Neighbours had been brought in to sit with the woman until other members of the family could arrive to share the burden of the tragedy.

'She is a brave woman,' observed Owen. 'She bore up well throughout that ordeal. It was almost as if she were expecting something like this to happen.'

'I think she was. Jonas seemed to court destruction.'

'Yes, Nick. The wonder is not that he is dead but that he lived for so long.'

Nicholas looked back at the house with deep sadness. 'Jonas Applegarth was a playwright of distinction – we have not seen a finer at the Queen's Head – but his talent was marred by a perversity in his nature. His work won him friends, yet he thrived on making enemies.'

'One, in particular!'

'I fear so.'

'Let's after him straight,' urged Elias. 'Now that we have done our duty by his widow, we must seek revenge. We know who the murderer was.'

'Do we?'

'Hugh Naismith. Late of Banbury's Men.'

'I think not.'

'He has been stalking Jonas for days. You were there when Naismith hurled a dagger at him. And I dare swear that he followed us here last night.'

'That does not make him our man, Owen.'

'Why not?'

'Because he would not go to all the trouble of setting up a gallows at the Queen's Head when he could dispatch his victim more easily with sword or dagger. You forget something.'

'What is that?'

'Naismith was injured in his duel with Jonas. How could a man with his arm in a sling haul up so heavy a load over a beam? It is not possible.'

'It is if he had a confederate.'

'I heard one Laughing Hangman, Owen, not two.'

'Naismith had cause and means to kill Jonas.'

'Granted,' said Nicholas. 'But what cause and means did he have to murder Cyril Fulbeck at the Blackfriars Theatre?'

'The cause is plain enough, Nick.'

'Is it?'

'Fulbeck put those Chapel Children back on the stage to take the bread out of the mouths of honest actors. I am one with Hugh Naismith there. I'd happily wring the necks of those infant players myself and the man who put them there.'

'You are wrong, Owen.'

'It *has* to be Naismith.'

'Never!'

'Your reason?'

'He was too obvious an enemy,' argued Nicholas. 'Jonas would be on his guard as soon as he saw the man. Naismith might have forged a letter to lure him to the Queen's Head, but how did he entice him into our storeroom? The person who killed him was a man he did not fear. Remember the Master of the Chapel.'

'Cyril Fulbeck?'

'He also let someone get close enough to strike. A stranger would never have gained entry to Blackfriars.'

'Then Naismith was not a stranger to him.'

'He has no part in this, Owen.'

'But he does,' insisted the Welshman. 'You saw a dagger aimed at Jonas's back. Did that come out of thin air?'

'No, it was thrown by an enemy. But not by our hangman.'

'There are *two* villains here?'

'Most certainly,' said Nicholas, thinking it through. 'One of them haunts the shadows and strikes from behind. The other is a more calculating killer. Why was Master Fulbeck hanged on his own stage? Why did Jonas have to be enticed to the Queen's Head? There is method here, Owen. And it is way beyond anything that Hugh Naismith could devise.'

Elias nodded reluctantly. 'You begin to persuade me. Haply, he is not our man.' His ire stirred again. 'But that does not rule him out as the street assassin. Naismith trailed Jonas and hurled that dagger at him.'

'That may yet be true.'

'It is, Nick. Let's track him down and beat a confession out of him. Attempted murder must not go unpunished.'

'Nor shall it. But you must pursue Naismith alone.'

'And you?'

'I must to the Coroner to sign a sworn statement of how the body of Jonas Applegarth came to be discovered. Nathan Curtis waits for me there. Then I'll to the playhouse.'

'The Curtain? The Theatre? The Rose?'

'Blackfriars,' said Nicholas. 'That is where this riddle first started and where it will finally be solved.'

As the finger of guilt pointed at him once more, Edmund Hoode shut his eyes against its silent accusation. He only half-heard the argument that was raging nearby. Barnaby Gill and Lawrence Firethorn were sitting with him in the taproom of the Queen's Head. Inflamed with drink, they locked horns.

'Why was the performance cancelled?' demanded Gill.

'Out of respect for the dead,' said Firethorn.

'I was not consulted.'

'The decision was taken for us, Barnaby. Even you must see that. We could not stage a play in the yard while Jonas Applegarth was dangling from a beam in the storeroom.'

'He was cut down and carted away hours ago.'

'His memory remains.'

'I believe that you did this out of spite, Lawrence.'

'Spite?'

'Yes!' screamed Gill, working himself up into a full

tantrum. '*Cupid's Folly* should have been played today. A piece tailored to my genius. Audiences clamour for it time and again. You tore it off the stage to spite me.'

'That is madness!'

'You know how I rule the roost in *Cupid's Folly*. They adore me. They love to see my performance as Rigormortis.'

'Why, so do I!' said Firethorn with sarcasm. 'I would give anything to look upon your *rigor mortis*.'

'Spite!'

'Go rot!'

'The play was cancelled out of spite.'

'Is that why Jonas Applegarth got himself hanged? In order to spite you? "Pray, good Sir, put that noose around my neck so that I may aggravate Barnaby Gill." Think of someone else for a change, man. Sigh for the loss of a friend. That is what Edmund does.' He nudged the playwright hard. 'Do you not?'

Hoode opened his eyes. 'What's that you say?'

'You are in mourning for Jonas, are you not?'

'Yes, Lawrence. I mourn and I repent. As God is my witness, I must speak honestly. I writhe with guilt.'

'Why?'

'Because I wished the poor fellow dead.'

'So did I and so did every man,' said Gill. 'Why deny it? We hated him. Jonas Applegarth was an earthquake in our midst. See how we shake at his passing.'

'I would rather remember how the audience shook at his play,' said Firethorn proudly. 'They trembled with amazement at the sorcery of his imagination and shook with laughter at the sharpness of his wit. What use is theatre if it be not a two hour earthquake? Why do the spectators come if not to feel the ground move beneath their feet?'

'Lawrence is right,' admitted Hoode. 'Jonas Applegarth had the power to move mountains.'

'Yes,' snapped Gill. 'He did that every time he opened his bowels. His buttocks were mountains indeed.'

'Do not speak ill of the dead!' chided Firethorn.

'It is unjust,' said Hoode. 'In a moment of envy, I may have wished for his death, but I regret his passing now. He brought much to Westfield's Men. Mark it well. A great value has gone out of our lives.'

'He had whispers of genius,' said Gill grudgingly. 'I give him that. But he might have chosen another day to die. *Cupid's Folly* is an appalling loss. I have seventeen magical moments in the play and he has robbed me of every one of them!' He rose to his feet. '"Cruel death hath stolen my Rigormortis from me."'

Quoting his lines from the play, he flounced off. Hoode poured them both more wine from the jug. Alexander Marwood came buzzing around them with his woes.

'What am I to do? Where am I to go?'

'As far out of my sight as you can,' said Firethorn.

'Murder was committed on my premises. Guests have fled. Spectators have stayed away. My servingmen and ostlers are too frightened to do their offices. My wife is distraught. My daughter had taken to her bed. I am dead, sirs.'

'We'll sing lustily at your funeral.'

'I blame you, Master Firethorn.'

'For what?'

'Bringing that heathen among us,' said the landlord. 'His play all but caused an affray in my yard. Jonas Applegarth dared to mock God and the Almighty has given His reply. You should not have let that heathen befoul my yard with his irreverence!'

'Let him rest in peace,' said Hoode. 'He is gone.'

'And taken my livelihood with it!'

Marwood's twitch suddenly broke out around his mouth and both lips trembled so dramatically that they looked like a pair of fluttering wings. His words were distorted into grunts and whines. It rescued them from further persecution and the landlord stole away, holding his mouth in both hands lest it take flight.

'Which is worse?' asked Firethorn. 'Marwood with his twitch or Barnaby with his *rigor mortis?*' He lifted his cup of wine. 'Let's drink to Jonas!'

'I'll say Amen to that!' added Hoode.

'We have lost a playwright but his play lives on. *The Misfortunes of Marriage* must be staged again in tribute.'

'But not at The Rose next week.'

'Are we to have that argument all over again?'

'No, Lawrence,' said Hoode, becoming more assertive. 'The matter is settled. My new play will grace The Rose, as you promised. Choose another time for the tribute to Jonas Applegarth. I'll not forfeit my right.'

There was a glint in his eye which forbade any further debate. Hoode was reaffirming his position in the company. Firethorn gave a nod of agreement, then leant in close.

'What is her name, Edmund?'

'Whose name?'

212

'This fairy princess who has waved a wand over you.'

'I know of no fairies or wands.'

'Come, sir. You talk to a master of the sport. I am a denizen of dark bedchambers. I know how a woman can make your blood race. Love has put this vigour into you. Some enchantress has stroked your manhood upright at last.' He slipped an arm around Hoode. 'Who is she?'

'An invention of your mind.'

'Am I never to meet this goddess?'

'What goddess?'

'Share her wonder with me.'

'How can I?' said Hoode, coolly. 'She does not exist.'

'*Someone* has put this new spirit into you.'

But Edmund Hoode would not be drawn. Cecily Gilbourne was a secret he would share with no one. She had enlarged his mind and captured his soul. With her in his life, he felt, he could achieve anything. He recalled the one omission in her catalogue of his work.

'When do we play *Pompey* again?' he asked.

'It has fallen out of our repertoire.'

'Insert it back in, Lawrence.'

'Why?'

'Because I tell you. I, too, can make the earth quake on occasion, nowhere more so than in my tale of Pompey. See him put upon the stage once more. Those who remember him will welcome him back and he is sure to win fresh hearts.'

He thought of Cecily Gilbourne and smiled serenely.

* * *

Blackfriars Theatre brought a steady flow of spectators into the precinct. The reputation of the Chapel Children grew with each performance and the murder of their Master seemed to encourage interest rather than to deter it. Some came out of love for Cyril Fulbeck and others out of morbid curiosity, but the result was that the whole precinct was soon swarming with playgoers. Where the Dominican Order once held sway, *Alexander the Great* would now march in triumph.

Nicholas Bracewell arrived well before the performance was due to begin and loitered in the Great Yard to study the composition of the milling crowd. The audience differed markedly from that normally seen at the Queen's Head. Westfield's Men played to patrons drawn from every rank of society. Aristocrats, artisans and apprentices would share the same space as lawyers, landowners and local politicians. Merchants and mathematicians sat in the balcony while punks and pickpockets mingled with the standees in the pit.

Blackfriars had a more exclusive clientele. It was less a heterogeneous mix than a parade of sumptuary legislation. The laws designed to regulate the dress of men and women were strictly applied. Flashes of gold, silver and purple told Nicholas how many members of the hereditary peerage were present. Velvet denoted a large number of gentlemen and their ladies. Satin, damask, taffeta and grosgrain spoke of the eldest sons of knights and all above that rank, or of an income of at least one hundred pounds per annum. And so it went on.

Since costume was such an important element of

theatre and accuracy of detail vital, Nicholas had a close acquaintance with the regulations, and he took wry amusement from the fact that gifts of old clothing to actors were one of the few permitted exceptions to the rules. A deeper irony often impressed itself upon him. Actors who struggled to make ten pounds a year would appear on stage in apparel worth far more than that. Popes and princes at the Queen's Head were hired men who rubbed shoulders with poverty when they left it.

A face came out of the crowd to startle him. Nicholas had not expected to see James Ingram there. He was about to hail his colleague when he recalled the latter's strange behaviour beside the corpse of Jonas Applegarth. It had seemed so mean spirited. What, in any case, was Ingram doing at the Queen's Head so early? Was his sudden appearance in the storeroom coincidental? Nicholas stepped back out of sight as the actor went past, wondering if past loyalty had brought him to Blackfriars or if a more sinister motive was at work. Ingram would repay watching.

Waiting until the majority of the spectators had taken their places, he paid sixpence for a seat at the rear. Ingram was three rows in front of him but on a diagonal which allowed Nicholas a clear view of his profile. He did not dwell on it for long. His attention was captured by the splendour of the private playhouse. Shutters had been closed to block out the afternoon sun but the stage was ablaze with light. Candles burnt in branched candelabra, many of them hanging and operated by pulleys. The auditorium itself was illuminated by numerous small flames as well but full radiance was concentrated on the stage.

Musicians kept the audience entertained while they awaited the performance and Nicholas once again noted a stark contrast. Peter Digby and his consort inhabited a narrow balcony above the stage at the Queen's Head, a cramped and windswept arena in which to practice their art. Their music had to complete with the jostling hubbub of the inn yard, the strident yells of vendors selling refreshment and the relentless uproar of the adjacent Gracechurch Street.

Blackfriars was more benevolent to its musicians. Seated in complete comfort, they were given an attentive audience in a building that was designed to catch and amplify the beauty of their work. No raucous yells disturbed the concert, no violent quarrels broke out between onlookers. Music was able to create the perfect mood for the presentation of *Alexander the Great.*

Additional light flooded the acting area as fresh candelabra were brought in and set in position. All eyes were trained on the stage without distraction. Martial music played and the Prologue entered to a burst of applause. The attack began after only half a dozen lines:

> *Monstrous body with the Head of a Queen,*
> *A maggot-filled apple, so sour and so green,*
> *A running sewer of repulsive jest*
> *Besmearing grass in the field to the west.*

Nicholas was stung by the jibe at Westfield's Men, but it was the sustained assault on the character and work of Jonas Applegarth which really offended him. Tasteless

enough while the playwright was alive, it was disgusting when aimed at a victim of murder. Nicholas told himself that those who laughed at the vicious abuse were unaware of the fate of the man at whom it was aimed, but that did not ease his mind.

His acerbic mockery of child actors had set Applegarth up for a counter-blast. Nicholas accepted that. But while his had been a general satire on despised rivals, the playwright was now suffering a vindictive onslaught of the most personal kind. Every aspect of his appearance, his plays, his opinions and his alleged atheism was held up to ridicule. Nicholas could almost see the man, dangling from a rope in the middle of the stage while he was pelted with rotting fruit and sharp stones.

Alexander the Great stormed onto the stage with his entourage and the tale of heroism began. Military prowess and stirring poetry wiped out the Prologue for everyone else, but it wriggled like a tiny worm in Nicholas's brain. The play itself was a skillful drama, yet it lacked any of the sheer power that had made the work of Jonas Applegarth so compelling and controversial.

Ideal for Blackfriars, the piece would not have survived on the stage at the Queen's Head. Its language was too high-flown, its action too stylised and its moral judgements too oblique. Much of its political commentary would have been incomprehensible to the standees and there was none of the earthy humour with which even the most serious plays in the repertoire of Westfield's Men was liberally salted. The greatness of Alexander did not extend to a sense of humour.

At the same time, it was an instructive experience. As a member of one theatre troupe, Nicholas rarely had the opportunity to view the work of the others. Adult companies were scathing in their dismissal of juvenile actors, but he now saw how unfair that attitude was. The Chapel Children deserved to be taken seriously. They were worthy rivals to Westfield's Men and had one supreme advantage over them. While a typical season at the Queen's Head would last at most for five months, the Blackfriars Company could perform for twelve. In the interests of commercial gain, and regardless of the pressure on his actors, Raphael Parsons would keep the theatre open for the whole year.

Alexander the Great showed the strengths and exposed the weaknesses of the Chapel Children. They spoke the verse well, they sang superbly and they moved with the grace of dancers. What they lacked was physical presence and this was a failing in a play about recurring warfare. Battles were described in soaring language by children who did not look strong enough to carry spears, let alone to wear full armour. Older members of the company bore the principal roles with honour but there were occasional sniggers as the mighty Alexander entered with an army of boy soldiers.

Two things impressed Nicholas above all else. The first was the clear evidence of the manager's rich abilities. Whatever the defects of his character, Raphael Parsons had a flair for theatrical presentation. His cast was well drilled, his use of scenic devices was masterly and he brought off some stunning dramatic effects. Control of light was a feature

of the performance. Candles were whisked on in profusion to create the sun-baked deserts of Persia, then removed in a flash to leave Alexander's tent in virtual darkness for a dream sequence. As the play moved faultlessly on, one book holder admired the work of his counterpart behind the scenes.

The other striking feature was the performance given by Philip Robinson. Dressed as a Greek goddess, he wafted in and out of the action with ethereal charm. Three songs were allotted to him, each sung in the most sweet and affecting voice. Enjoyment shone out of the boy. Nicholas wondered if this Greek goddess really did wish to return to family life with a heavy-handed butcher in Bankside.

The final scene was the best. Having used all the stage equipment with consummate skill, Parsons saved the most arresting moment until the end. As life slowly ebbed away from the dying Alexander, a silver cloud descended from above with the goddess reclining in front of it. High above the stage, Philip Robinson declaimed a valedictory tribute to the great commander. Light slowly faded on his epic career.

While the audience was profoundly moved, Nicholas was shocked. The winch used to lower Philip Robinson was the one which had hauled Cyril Fulbeck up to his death.

An ovation greeted the cast as they came out to take their bows and several spectators rose to their feet in salute. When they began to file out of the theatre, nothing but praise was heard on every side. Nicholas waited until he reached the Great Yard before he accosted James Ingram.

'Nick!' Ingram said. 'I did not look to find you here.'

'It was a temptation too big to resist.'

'They acquitted themselves well, I feel, though they would fare better with a better play. Boys make wonderful goddesses but sorry soldiers.'

'Why did you come?' asked Nicholas.

'Out of interest.'

'Interest or envy?'

'Both, Nick.'

'There is certainly much to interest.'

'But even more to envy. Just think what we could do with that winding gear at the Queen's Head. And that scenery! Jonas was so wrong in his attack on the children's companies. So wrong and so vilely unfair.'

'What did you think of the reply?'

'In the Prologue?'

'Was not that vilely unfair?'

'No,' said Ingram evenly. 'Jonas deserved it.'

Before Nicholas could discuss it further, the actor wheeled away and was soon lost in the crowd. It was abrupt behaviour for a man who was unfailingly polite as a rule. The book holder was not left alone for long.

'I see that we have a spy in our midst.'

'Merely another spectator.'

'Our spectators do not come to sneer.'

'Nor more did I. There was much to admire.'

'I cannot say the same of Westfield's Men.'

Raphael Parsons was circling the Great Yard to garner praise and eavesdrop on opinion. He gazed around with a proprietary air and spoke to Nicholas over his shoulder.

'I wonder that you could spare the time, sir.'

'You advised me to come.'

'Not with any expectation of a response,' said Parsons. 'Should you not have been at the Queen's Head this afternoon to prop up that rabble of actors?'

'I should have been there, it is true.'

'Then why did you choose Blackfriars instead? And why did you not bring Jonas Applegarth with you so that we could throw his insults back in his teeth?'

'Jonas, I fear, is dead.'

Parsons turned to him in surprise. It quickly shaded into a pleasure that was fringed with disappointment.

'Then the rogue has escaped me, has he?'

'Not by design,' said Nicholas. 'Jonas was murdered at the Queen's Head early this morning. Hanged from a beam.'

'Hanged? Was there a rope strong enough?'

'A rope strong enough and a killer determined enough. We have seen his handiwork here at Blackfriars.'

Parsons blinked. 'You believe it to be the same man?'

'I am convinced of it.'

'Then he is enemy and friend in one.'

'How so?'

'I hate him for what he did to Cyril Fulbeck but I love him for the way he dealt with Jonas Applegarth.'

'You dealt cruelly enough with him yourself.'

'He invited it.'

'The dead invite respect.'

'True,' said Parsons. 'But when I commissioned that Prologue to *Alexander the Great*, I thought he would be alive to hear of it. How was I to know that he would be dead?'

'And if you *had* known?'

'What do you mean?'

'If you had been made aware of his death,' said Nicholas, 'would you have removed that offensive attack in your Prologue?'

Parsons grinned. 'By no means. I'd have called for a few more couplets to celebrate the happy event.'

Nicholas struggled to control a powerful urge to strike him. The manager stood his ground, almost inciting some form of violence so that he could bring an action for assault against the book holder. A former lawyer would assuredly win any legal battle and penalise him severely. Nicholas held back. Delight danced in the other man's eyes. He was taking such pleasure in the death of Jonas Applegarth that Nicholas began to wonder if he might not have been directly involved in it. The egregious manager certainly hated the playwright enough to kill him. Had the surprise he expressed at the news been real or feigned?

Still grinning broadly, Parsons moved away to collect more congratulations from members of the audience. There was a blend of arrogance and obsequiousness about him which was unpleasant to watch. He was alternately boasting and bowing with mock humility. When a generous compliment was paid to him by a lady, Parsons let out a high laugh of gratitude. It made Nicholas prick up his ears. He had an uncomfortable feeling that he might have heard that sound before.

Speculation was not enough. It was time to support it with evidence, and he was in the correct place to begin the search. The audience was fast dispersing and Ireland Yard was all but empty when he reached it. Starting at the first house on the left, he knocked hard and waited for the servant to open the door.

'Is Master Parsons at home?' he asked politely.

'There is no Master Parsons here, sir.'

'Does Raphael Parsons not live at this address?'

'I have never heard the name.'

It was a painstaking process, but Nicholas stuck to his task until he had been to every house. Several of the residents did not even know him. Of those who did, a number were resentful of the fact that he ran a theatre in the precinct and thus disturbed their peace. Nicholas found no close friends of Raphael Parsons. Where, then, had the man been at the time when Cyril Fulbeck was killed?

He was deep in meditation when a figure came around the corner towards him. He threw the woman a half-glance and let her go past before he realised that he knew her.

'Mistress Hay!' he called.

'Oh,' she said, turning around. 'Good-day, sir.'

He could see from her expression that she did not recognise him, largely because she was too shy to look at his face properly. He walked over to her.

'I am Nicholas Bracewell,' he said. 'I called at your house to speak to your husband.'

She gave a nervous laugh. 'I remember now.'

'Have you been to the play at the theatre?'

'God forbid, sir!'

'Then what are you doing in Blackfriars?' he asked.

'Visiting old friends. I was born and brought up here.'

'In the precinct?'

'Around the corner,' she explained, pointing a hand. 'My father was a bookseller. That is how Caleb and I . . . how my dear husband and I first met. He came into the shop to buy books and prints.' A timid enthusiasm flickered. 'He is such a learned man. Nobody in London knows as much about the history of the city as my husband. I am married to a genius. How many women can say that, sir?'

'Very few, Mistress Hay. Your husband has been kind and helpful to me. I am grateful.'

Anxiety pinched her. 'I must return home now. He will be expecting me back. I must be there for him.'

'Your father was a bookseller, you say?'

'Yes, sir.'

'What name?'

'Mompesson. Andrew Mompesson. I must go.'

'Adieu!'

Nicholas waved her off and watched her shuffle along with her shoulders hunched and her head down. Joan Hay was a woman whose whole purpose in life was to obey her husband's bidding. A bookseller's daughter was an ideal helpmeet for him.

'Mompesson,' repeated Nicholas. 'Andrew Mompesson.' He had a vague feeling that he knew the name.

Hugh Naismith used his free arm to lift the tankard and drain the last of his ale. It was good to be back in the Elephant again and to share in the banter with his old friends from

Banbury's Men, even though he was no longer a member of the company. His wounded arm would heal in time and he would be fit for employment again. Meanwhile, he could cadge a few drinks from Ned Meares and his other fellows.

When he got to his feet, he swayed slightly and bade his farewells. Meares and the others sent him on his way with shouts and laughs. It was early evening when Naismith came reeling out of the inn, adjusting the sling around his neck. His lodging was only a few streets away but he did not get much closer to it.

As soon he passed the lane beside the Elephant, a strong hand reached out to grab him by his jerkin and swing him hard against a wall. All the breath was taken out of him and his wounded arm was jarred. The point of a dagger pricked his throat and made him jerk back his head in terror.

'Leave me alone!' he begged. 'I have no money!'

'That's not what I want,' growled a voice.

'Who are you?'

'A friend of Jonas Applegarth's.'

'That rogue!'

'Yes,' said Owen Elias. 'That rogue.'

He let the blade of his weapon caress the man's neck.

'Tell me why you tried to kill him.'

Chapter Ten

An air of gloom hung over the Queen's Head like a pall. The murder of Jonas Applegarth changed a haven of conviviality into a murmuring tomb. There was desultory movement in the yard with few guests seeking a bed for the night once they heard about the crime on the premises. The atmosphere in the taproom was funereal. Westfield's Men sat over their ale with a sense of foreboding. Superstitious by nature, they were convinced that a curse had descended on their company and that a violent death presaged an even worse catastrophe.

Alexander Marwood was in his element. A man whose whole life was agitated by imaginary disasters now had a real one to make him truly despondent. Revelling in his misery, he circled his premises like a lost soul, chanting a monologue of black despair and pausing each time outside the storeroom where the horror had occurred to

226

wonder if it should be exorcised, boarded up or torn down completely. Partnership with a theatre company had visited many tribulations upon his undeserving head but this, he felt, was easily the worst. The ghost of Jonas Applegarth would haunt him for ever.

When Nicholas returned from Blackfriars, the landlord was still perambulating the yard with enthusiastic grief. He swooped on the book holder at once, bony fingers sinking into his arm like the talons of a bird of prey.

'Why have you done this to me?' he groaned.

'It was not deliberate.'

'My trade blighted, my womenfolk prostrated, my happiness snatched away! Ruination, sir!'

'A cruel twist of Fate,' said Nicholas. 'Westfield's Men cannot be blamed. You must see that.'

'Who brought that heretic to the Queen's Head? Who staged his blasphemy in my yard? Who permitted him to fetch the wrath of the Lord down on my inn?'

'Jonas Applegarth was a brilliant playwright.'

'His brilliance has destroyed me!'

'It cost him his own life, certainly,' admitted Nicholas. 'Had he not written *The Misfortunes of Marriage*, he would still be with us. It was too powerful a piece for its own good. Someone was deeply offended by it.'

'Yes!' howled Marwood. 'God Almighty!'

'Jonas was killed by a human hand. I can vouch for that.'

Another torrent of self-pity gushed from the landlord but it washed harmlessly over the book holder. He was diverted by the sight of the woman who had just come hurrying in through the archway of the yard. Detaching

227

himself from Marwood, he ran to greet Anne Hendrik. There was a spontaneous embrace. She hugged him with relief.

'I am so glad to see you safe, Nick!'

'What brought you here?'

'The grim tidings,' she explained. 'I met with Nathan Curtis as he was returning home to Bankside. He told me of the murder here this morning and I had to come. I feared for you.'

'But I am in no danger, Anne.'

'If you pursue a killer, you must be. He has two victims already. Do not become the third, I beg you. Nathan told me how determined you were to avenge this death. Why put yourself in such peril?'

Nicholas soothed her as best he could, then led her across to the tiring-house, unlocking it with his key to give them some privacy. As they stepped into the room, Nicholas felt a pang of remorse. Jonas Applegarth had been hanged in the adjoining chamber and his unquiet spirit hovered over the whole building.

'Nathan was still trembling at what he saw.'

'It was a grisly sight indeed. The mere thought of it has thrown the company into chaos. Jonas Applegarth was one of us.'

'Why was he murdered?'

'To silence his voice.'

'I do not understand.'

'He was a man of strong opinions, who used his art to express them and his wit to belabour his enemies. Jonas was killed for something that he wrote.'

'But what of Cyril Fulbeck?' she asked. 'Did you not tell Nathan that he was killed by the same fell hand? The Master of the Chapel was a gentle man with quiet opinions. He made no enemies. Why was his voice silenced?'

'I will find out in time,' he said confidently. 'But you are wrong about him. Meek as he was, Cyril Fulbeck did make enemies. You introduced me to one of them in this very inn.'

She gave a sigh. 'Ambrose Robinson.'

'He would cheerfully have practised his butchery on the Master of the Chapel.'

'That is not so.'

'Your friend has too much anger swilling inside him.'

'He has a temper but is learning to govern it.'

'The wonder is that he has not descended on Blackfriars in a fit of rage and seized his son by force. How have you prevented him from doing so?'

'I urged him to proceed by legal means. That is why I brought him to you, Nick. I hoped that you could help.'

'I have tried, Anne.'

'What have you found?'

Nicholas hesitated. Delighted to see her and touched by her concern for him, he was anxious not to provoke another quarrel. He took her hand and led her to a bench against the wall. They sat down together.

'We parted unhappily the last time we met,' he said.

'That was as much my fault as ours.'

'I was unmannerly with you, Anne.'

'You could never be that.'

'Too bold in my enquiries, then.'

'They carried the weight of accusation,' she explained. 'That was what distressed me. Your tone was possessive.'

'I can only beg forgiveness.'

'You harassed me, Nick. I am not bounden to you. In my own house, I am entitled to make my own decisions.'

'I accept that.'

'To choose my own friends without first seeking your approval. Is that so unreasonable a demand?'

'No, Anne,' he conceded. 'I am justly rebuked.'

'I deserve some censure myself for being so harsh.'

'The fault is mended.'

'You were only drawn into this business because of me. I should have borne that in mind. You did not choose this situation. I did, Nick, and I was wrong to foist another man's domestic problem on to you.'

'I embrace it willingly if it makes us friends again.'

She smiled and kissed him softly on the cheek.

'This you must know,' she said quietly, 'and then we may put it aside so that it does not come between us again. Ambrose Robinson is a kind and generous man. Thefts and damage to my property left me in difficulty. Many offered sympathy but he alone offered me the money I needed at that time. It saved me, Nick. It let me rebuild. I cannot forget that.'

'Nor should you.'

'It brought us close. When his son was taken into the Chapel Royal, he was distraught. I could not deny him my help. That brought us even closer. And yes, you were informed correctly, I *have* been to church with Ambrose – ·

but only to pray beside him on my knees and not for any deeper reason.'

Nicholas took both comfort and regret from her words.

'Why did you not confide your troubles in me, Anne?'

'You were not there.'

'And he was.'

'Yes.'

He lowered his head in dismay. The thought that she had been in dire financial straits was upsetting, all the more so because he was unaware of her predicament. It was a disturbing reminder of how far apart they had drifted. If the butcher had come to her aid, the man deserved gratitude. Nicholas felt slightly ashamed. He squeezed her hand in apology.

'My debt has been fully repaid,' she continued. 'I owe Ambrose nothing now. What I do for him, I do out of simple friendship for I would see him reunited with his son.'

'That may prove difficult.'

'You have looked further into it?'

'The deed of impressment has the might of the law behind it. Philip Robinson belongs to the Chapel Royal.'

'Can he not be released by any means?'

'It seems not.'

'Have you spoken again to Raphael Parsons?'

'He is not the stumbling block,' said Nicholas. 'Nor was he responsible for having the boy impressed. That was Cyril Fulbeck's doing. He is now dead and the lad is answerable to the Assistant Master of the Chapel.'

'But Master Parsons is the real tyrant here.'

'Not so.'

'He is the one who makes Philip's life such an ordeal. He shouts at the boy, beats him and forces him to act upon the stage. He makes the whole company work from dawn till dusk without respite. It is cruel. Complain to him. Exert pressure there. Raphael Parsons is the problem.'

'One problem, perhaps. But there is a bigger one.'

'What is that?'

'Philip Robinson himself.'

'In what way?'

'He enjoys being one of the Chapel Children.'

'There is nothing he loathes more.'

'I have seen the boy, Anne,' Nick argued. 'I watched him play in *Alexander the Great* this afternoon. He was a delight to behold. He acted well and sang beautifully, all with true zest. I tell you this. I would make Philip Robinson an apprentice with Westfield's Men without a qualm. We will need a replacement for John Tallis now his voice has deepened into manhood. If he were not already ensconced at Blackfriars, the lad would be ideal.'

'I find this hard to believe. Philip *enjoys* it?'

'He has found his true profession.'

'Then why are his letters so full of misery? Why does he rail at Raphael Parsons so? Why does Philip beg his father to come and rescue him from his imprisonment?'

'He does none of these things, Anne.'

'He does. I read his tales of woe and so did you.'

'What we read were letters given to us by the father,' said Nicholas. 'We only have his word that they were written by his son. Ambrose Robinson has been a good neighbour to you and I respect him for that, but I beg leave to doubt his honesty. I believe that we have been misled.'

It was an unsatisfactory confessional box. The lane beside the Elephant in Shoreditch was too public for Owen Elias's liking. Revellers kept arriving at the inn or tumbling out of it. Grabbing his quarry by the neck, therefore, Elias marched him through a maze of back streets until they found a small house which had collapsed in upon itself. The Welshman kicked Hugh Naismith into the ruins and made him sit on a pile of rubble.

'Peace at last!' said Elias. 'Now – talk!'

'I've done nothing to you,' bleated Naismith.

'You offend my sight. Apart from that, you have the stink of Banbury's Men about you and that's even more revolting. Tell me about Jonas Applegarth.'

A slow smile spread. 'He's dead. That's why I went to the Elephant. To drink to his departure.'

'Take care I do not drink to yours!' warned Elias, still brandishing his dagger. 'Jonas was a friend. Remember that if you wish to stay alive.'

'He was no friend of mine.'

'So I hear. You fought a duel. He bested you.'

'Only by chance.'

'He should have run you through like the dog you are.'

'He gave me this,' said Naismith, holding up the sling. 'Banbury's Men had no work for an actor with only one arm.'

'Is that why you sought to kill Jonas?'

'No!'

'Is that why you threw a dagger at his back?'

'I never did that!'

'Do not lie to me or I'll cut your mangy carcass to pieces and feed it to the crows. You stalked him, did you not?'

'That I do admit,' grunted Naismith.

'You followed him home last night and ran away when I saw you. Do you admit that as well?'

'Yes. It was me.'

'Hoping for a chance to throw another dagger.'

'No! That would have been too merciful a death. Jonas Applegarth deserved to be roasted slowly over a hot fire with an apple in his mouth like any other pig.'

'Enough!'

Elias slapped him hard across the face and the man keeled over onto the ground. The Welshman knelt beside him.

'Insult his memory again and you will join him.'

'Stay, sir!' pleaded Naismith.

'Then tell me the truth.'

'I have done so. I despised Jonas Applegarth. I wanted him dead but lacked the opportunity to kill him.'

'You mean, you hurled a dagger and it missed.'

'How *could* I?'

Naismith held up his free hand. The bandage was now removed but the hand was still badly swollen and a livid gash ran from the wrist to the back of the forefinger.

'I can hardly lift a tankard,' he said bitterly. 'How could I hope to throw a dagger? It was not me!'

Elias saw the truth of his denial. Naismith was not their

would-be assassin. He had been watching Applegarth in order to feed his hatred of the man, waiting until his wounds healed enough for him strike back at his enemy.

'Why did you fight the duel?' asked Elias.

'He challenged me.'

'Something you said?'

'And something I did not say,' explained Naismith. 'We played *Friar Francis* at The Curtain. It was a clever comedy but full of such sourness and savagery that it was not fit for the stage. I said as much and he took me to task. I hated the play. It bubbled like a witch's brew. He cursed the whole world in it. Then came the performance itself.'

'What happened?'

'We were all at odds with Applegarth by then. He made *Friar Francis* a descent into Hell for us. Everyone swore to hit back at him but I alone had the courage.'

'What did you do?'

'I changed his lines.'

'Jonas would not have liked that.'

'Why speak such slander against mankind when it stuck so in my throat? I wrote my own speeches instead. They had less wit but far more sweetness.'

'No wonder he wanted to cut your heart out!'

'Jonas Applegarth put words in my mouth I simply could not say. What else could I do?'

But Elias was not listening. Convinced that Naismith did not throw the dagger at his friend's back, he was already asking himself a question.

Who *did*?

* * *

Edmund Hoode ascended the staircase at the Unicorn with far more alacrity this time. Summoned that evening by another sketch of the fabled beast, he responded immediately. A day of mourning might yet be redeemed. Bereavement was dragging him down with his fellows. He had sighed enough for Jonas Applegarth. Sighs of a different order were now in prospect.

Only when he reached the landing did he stop to consider how little he really knew of Cecily Gilbourne. Was she married? A lady of her age and beauty was unlikely to have remained single. Was she widowed? Divorced even? And where did she live? In London or beyond? Alone or with her family? He winced slightly. Did she have *children?*

'My mistress is ready for you, sir.'

The maidservant was holding the door of the chamber open for him. All his doubts melted away. Cecily Gilbourne was sublime. Her age, her marital status, her place of abode and her familial situation were irrelevant. It mattered not if she had three husbands, four houses and five children. She was evidently a lady of wealth and social position. More to the point, she was a woman of keen discernment where drama was concerned. One feature set her above every other member of her sex. Cecily Gilbourne was his.

Hoode entered the room to take possession of his prize.

'You came!' she said with a measure of surprise.

'Nothing would have kept me away.'

'Not even the death of a friend? The performance at the Queen's Head was cancelled because of him. We were turned away. I feared that you would stay there to grieve for him.'

'I would rather celebrate with you.'

'That is what I hoped.'

There was nothing enigmatic about her smile now. It was frank and inviting. Cecily Gilbourne was dressed in a subtle shade of green which matched the colour of her eyes. Perched on a chair near the window, she wore no hat and no gloves. He noted that a single gold band encircled the third finger of her left hand. Seeing his interest, she glanced down at the ring with a wan smile.

'I was married at seventeen,' she explained sadly. 'My husband was a soldier and a statesman. He was killed in action at the Siege of Rouen. No children blessed our union. I have only this to keep his memory bright.'

'I see.'

'Have you been married, Edmund?'

'No. Not yet.'

'It is something which should happen when you are very young, as I was, or very old, as I will be before I consider a second marriage. A husband should provide either excitement for your youth or companionship for your dotage.'

'What may *I* provide for you, Cecily?'

'You give me all that I need.'

Another candid smile surfaced and she beckoned him over to sit close to her. Hoode was enraptured. The hideous murder at the Queen's Head that morning was not even a distant echo in his mind. The Laughing Hangman had been obliterated by the smiling inamorata.

'I spoke with Lawrence Firethorn,' he told her.

'About me?'

'Indirectly. I wanted to fill the one gap in your knowledge of me. You have not seen my *Pompey* and so I instructed him to put it back on the stage soon for your delectation. It is a work in which I take much pride. *Pompey the Great* has a true touch of greatness.'

'Then my delight is assured. And your new play?'

'*The Faithful Shepherd* will be seen at The Rose next week,' he said, beaming. 'I insisted that it was. With your permission, I will write a sonnet in praise of you, to be inserted cunningly in one of the longer speeches so that its true meaning may be disguised from the common herd.'

'Can this be done without corrupting your tale?'

'It will enhance it, Cecily. My play is partly set on the island of Sicily, allowing me to conjure endlessly with your magical name. I'll move the action from midsummer's night to St Cecilia's Day to give my fancy even more scope and pen you fourteen lines of the purest poetry ever heard on a stage. Will this content you?'

'Beyond measure.'

'Look for pretty conceits and clever rhymes.'

'I will savour the prettiness of the conceits but I do not look to find a rhyme that is half so clever as this before us.'

'What rhyme is that?'

'Why, Cecily and Edmund. Can two words fit more snugly together than that? Edmund and Cecily. They agree in every particular. Set them apart and neither can stand for much on its own. Put them together, seal them tight, lock them close in a loving embrace and they defy the laws of sound and language. Edmund and Cecily. Is that not the apotheosis of rhyme?'

'They blend together most perfectly into one.'

'Edmund!'

'Cecily!'

No more words were needed.

Nicholas Bracewell escorted her back over London Bridge and on to Bankside. It was pleasant to have Anne Hendrik on his arm again and it rekindled memories for both of them.

The long walk was far too short for them to exchange all the information they would have wished, but he now had a much clearer idea of the life she had been living since their separation, and she, for her part, filled in many blank pages of his own recent history.

Anne invited him into her home for some refreshment before he journeyed back. Over a glass of wine, they let nostalgia brush seductively against them.

'Have you missed me?' she asked.

'Painfully.'

'How did you cope with that pain?'

'I worked, Anne. There is a dignity in that.'

'That was also my escape.'

'Westfield's Men have kept me busier than ever. I was able to lose myself in my work and keep my mind from straying too often to you and to this house.'

'Did you never think of straying here in person?'

'Daily.'

She laughed lightly, then her face clouded over.

'I worried deeply about you, Nick.'

'Why?'

'Westfield's Men thrust too much upon you. The burden would break a lesser man. Yet still they ask for more from their book holder. It is unfair.'

'I do not complain.'

'That is your failing. They will overload you and you will not raise your voice in protest. You always put the company first.'

'Westfield's Men are my family. Without them, I would be an orphan. That is why I always seek to advance them. And why I rush to defend them, as I do in this instance.'

'What instance?'

'The murder of Jonas Applegarth,' he said. 'It was no random killing. Only one man died, but the whole company will suffer as a result. That was the intention. Victim and place were selected with deep guile.' He made to leave. 'Our Laughing Hangman wants to strangle Westfield's Men as well.'

'Why?'

'He keeps his reason private.'

'Take care,' she said, moving close. 'For my sake.'

'I will.'

After a brief kiss, he forced himself to leave. The temptation to linger was almost overwhelming, but Nicholas resisted it. A year's absence could not be repaired in a single evening. Anne's feelings towards him had changed slightly and he could no longer trust his own promptings. They needed time to find more common ground.

Other commitments took priority over Anne Hendrik. Only when two murders had been solved and the fate of a chorister had been decided could he feel free to renew his friendship with her, properly and at leisure.

Instead of crossing the bridge, he walked down to the river to hail a boat. It felt good to be back on the water again and he let a hand trail over the stern like a rudder. His boatman rowed hard. Thames Street drifted slowly towards them. When he landed, Nicholas went straight to the house of a friend.

'I will not take much of your time.'

'Come in, come in, sir,' said Caleb Hay.

'I feel guilty at dragging you away from your history.'

'It will wait, Master Bracewell.'

'How many hours a day do you spend working on it?'

'Not enough, not enough.'

Caleb Hay looked weary. He rubbed his eyes to dispel some of the fatigue and conducted Nicholas into his parlour. His wife had answered the door, but he had come down from his study when he heard the name of the visitor. Joan Hay crept nervously away to leave the two men alone.

'Well, sir,' said Hay. 'How may I help this time?'

'In a number of ways. You were, I believe, a scrivener.'

'That is so.'

'How did you discover your aptitude for history?'

'In the course of my work. A scrivener spends much of his time copying documents of various kinds. I was fortunate enough to be commissioned to make fair copies of ancient records in the Tower of London. It was an inspiration. From that moment on, I knew what my life's work would be.'

'Were you ever called upon to write letters?'

'Frequently.'

'Of what kind?'

'All kinds. Most of London is illiterate. If people need to send an important letter, they will often dictate it to a scrivener. We are like parish priests. We hear a man's most intimate thoughts.' He gave a chuckle. 'Letters of love were my special joy. You have no idea how many times I ravished beautiful women with my quill. I must have seduced a hundred or more on paper. I knew the tricks and the turn of phrase.'

'Could you always tell the hand of a scrivener?'

'Of course.'

'How?'

'By the neatness of his calligraphy,' he said. 'And by a dozen other smaller signs. Why do you ask?'

'I read some letters from a boy to his father on a matter of some consequence. I took them at face value and the father is eager for me to do so. But I now suspect that the lad did not write them at all.'

'Bring one to me and I'll tell you for sure.'

'If I can contrive it, I will.'

'How old is the boy?'

'Eleven.'

'Then we have a certain guide,' said Hay blithely. 'I've taught many lads of that age to hold a pen. I know what an eleven-year-old hand can do.' He cocked his head to one side to peer at Nicholas. 'But is this not a trivial affair for so serious as man as yourself? When my wife told me you were here, I thought you'd come for more advice to help you catch the man who murdered Cyril Fulbeck.'

'There is a connection.'

'I fail to see it.'

'The boy is a chorister in the Chapel Royal. Against the express wishes of his father, he was taken there by deed of impressment at the behest of Master Fulbeck.'

'I begin to understand.'

'What distresses him most is that his son spends much of his time at Blackfriars as a child actor. The father is demanding his release, but to no avail.'

Hay's face darkened. 'Then we have one suspect before us. What father would not feel ready to commit a murder in such a case? Might not this same parent be the fellow who killed Cyril Fulbeck?'

'He might well be,' agreed Nicholas, 'but I think that it is unlikely. And I am certain that he is not guilty of the other hanging.'

'There has been a *second?*' gasped the old man.

'This morning. At the Queen's Head.'

'What poor wretch has died this time?'

'Jonas Applegarth.'

'Ah!' His tone became neutral. 'The playwright. I will not speak harshly of any man on his way to the grave. But I cannot pity him so readily as I do the Master of the Chapel. And this Applegarth was hanged, you say?'

'In the same manner. By the same hand.'

'But why? What is the link between them?'

'It is there somewhere.'

'One was a saint, the other a sinner.'

'Our hangman treated them with equal savagery.'

'The animal must be caught!'

Hay moved away and rested a hand against the wall while he stared into the empty fireplace. He was lost in contemplation for a few minutes. Nicholas waited. His host eventually looked over at him.

'I am sorry, I am sorry. My mind wandered.'

'It is gruesome news. Anyone would be jolted.'

'How else may I help you, sir?'

'Does your history of London touch on its inns?'

'In full detail,' said Hay, brightening. 'They are one of the splendours of the city and I give them their due.'

'Will the Queen's Head be mentioned?'

'It would be a crime to omit it. The history of that inn would fill a book on its own. Such a landmark in Gracechurch Street. Do you know when it was first built?'

'No,' said Nicholas, 'but I would love to hear.'

Caleb Hay launched himself into another impromptu lecture, taking his guest on a tour through almost two hundred years. His account faltered when he reached the point where Westfield's Men entered the action, and Nicholas cut him short.

'That was astonishing,' he complimented. 'I have worked at the Queen's Head for years but you have revealed aspects of it which I have never even noticed.'

'The scholar's eye.'

'You certainly have that. It showed in your sketch of

Blackfriars. That has been a godsend to me.' Nicholas walked to the door and threw a casual remark over his shoulder. 'It is strange that you did not mention your personal interest in the precinct.'

'Personal interest?'

'Your wife grew up there, I believe.'

'Well, yes,' said Hay with a chuckle, 'that is true but hardly germane. Her father was a bookseller there, but he died years ago. How did you come by this intelligence?'

'From your wife herself. We met in Ireland Yard.'

'She was visiting old friends.'

'So she informed me.'

Caleb Hay opened the door to usher him out. He gave Nicholas an encouraging pat on his arm.

'Work hard to catch Cyril Fulbeck's killer.'

'He also murdered Jonas Applegarth.'

'You must sing the Requiem Mass for *him*. I will not. The Master of the Chapel is the loss I suffer. He was a dear friend. Do you know why?' He gave another chuckle. 'Here is something else that slipped my old mind. Cyril Fulbeck not only assisted my researches in Blackfriars. He rendered me a more important service than that.'

'Did he?'

'Yes,' said Hay, easing him out into the street. 'He once had me released from prison.'

Nicholas found the door closed politely in his face.

Anne Hendrik went through into the adjoining premises to check that all doors were securely locked. The shop was kept in meticulous condition because Preben van Loew believed that cleanliness was next to godliness and that an ordered workplace was a Christian virtue. He would certainly have closed the shutters and bolted the doors before leaving, but Anne still felt the need to see for herself. In the wake of the thefts from her property, she had become more conscious of the need to protect both house and shop.

When she went back through into her parlour, she saw that her servant had admitted a visitor. Ambrose Robinson was in his best apparel. His hands had been thoroughly scrubbed to rid of them of the smell of his trade. His expression was apologetic, his manner docile.

Anne was not pleased to see him but she suppressed her feelings behind a smile of welcome. She indicated the basket of flowers standing on a table.

'Thank you, Ambrose. A kind thought.'

'It was the least I could do.'

'Their fragrance fills the room.'

'And so does yours!' he said with heavy-handed gallantry. 'You are a flower among women.'

Anne shuddered inwardly. She hoped that she had heard the last of his clumsy compliments but he was back again with more. Robinson inclined his head penitentially.

'I have come from church,' he said.

'At this hour?'

'I went to pray for forgiveness. On my knees, I can think more clearly. I saw the error of my deeds. After the way I left this house, I have no right to be allowed back into it.

You should bar the door against me.'

'Let us forget what happened,' she suggested.

'I cannot do that, Anne. My disgrace is too heavy to be shrugged off so easily. I sought forgiveness in church but I also appealed for guidance. My ignorance is profound. I blunder through life. I revile myself for the way that I hurt those I cherish most. When my intentions are good, why are my actions often so bad?'

He sounded quite sincere but she remained on her guard.

'You will find me a changed man,' he promised.

'In what way?'

'I will be a true friend and not an angry suitor. I offer you my humblest apologies, Anne. Please accept them.'

'I do.' There was a pause. 'With thanks.'

'And I will say the same to Nick Bracewell.'

'Why?'

'For mistrusting him. For abusing the man behind his back when I should be overcome with gratitude. What does Ambrose Robinson mean to him? Nothing! Why should he care about my dear son, Philip? No reason! Yet he has undertaken to help me with a free heart. That is kindness indeed.'

'Nick responded to my entreaty.'

'There is my chief source of shame,' he said, lifting his eyes to look at her. 'You, Anne. You took me to him. You engaged Nick Bracewell on my behalf. You did all this, then had to suffer my foul abuse of your friend.'

'It was uncalled for, Ambrose.'

'You are right to chide me.'

'I will not tolerate another outburst like that,' she

warned him. 'Master your anger or my door *will* be barred to you. Wild accusation has no part in friendship.'

'I know, I know. My rudeness is only exceeded by my gross stupidity. I love my son and would move Heaven and Earth to get him back. Yet what do I do? Carp and cavil. Malign the one man who may help me.'

'The one man?'

'Let us be frank,' he said with rancour. 'The law fails me. Were Philip the son of a gentleman, the case could go to court with some chance of success. Since he is only the child of a butcher, he is beyond salvation. That deed of impressment is a set of chains.' He took a step towards her. 'That is why we must work by other means. We must trust Nick Bracewell to insinuate himself into Blackfriars and use persuasion to set Philip free. Why did I dare to censure him? Nick is our only hope.'

Anne was in a quandary. She wanted Philip Robinson released from the Chapel Royal, partly because she believed that father and son should be together and partly because she felt that the boy's return would liberate her from the now irksome attentions of the butcher. A new factor had come into her calculations. Should she remain silent or should she confront Ambrose Robinson with it?

His earnest enquiry forced her to make a decision.

'Has there been further word from Nick?' he asked.

'I spoke with him at length.'

'And?'

'He visited Blackfriars this afternoon,' she said, 'and watched a play there. Philip was in the cast.'

'Dressed up as a woman, no doubt! Wearing a wig and daubing his face with powder! Strutting around the stage like a Bankside harlot for any man to ogle!' He scowled at her. 'I want my son to grow into a man. They do him wrong to force him into female attire. Philip detests it.'

'That was not Nick's impression.'

'He despises every moment of it.'

'Yet he gave a fine performance, it seems.'

'Under duress.'

'Of his own volition.'

'Never!'

'Nick loves the theatre. He spends every waking moment in the company of actors. When he admires a performance, he knows what lies behind it. I trust his judgement.' She inhaled deeply before confronting him. 'Your son enjoys working in the theatre. Nick says he has decided flair.'

'Blackfriars is a torture chamber for Philip.'

'That may not be so.'

'It *is* so. I know my son.'

'Nick has seen him on the stage – you have not.'

'The shame would be too much for me!'

'Philip was a most willing actor this afternoon.'

'Then why does he beg me to rescue him!' said Robinson with mounting rage. 'Why does he plead so in every letter that he sends me? You saw his pain, Anne, you saw his misery. Were those the letters of a boy who is *happy*?'

'No, Ambrose.'

'Then why did he write them? Let Nick answer that.'

'He has,' she said levelly. 'He does not believe that Philip sent those letters at all. They were written by someone else. Is that not so?'

Ambrose Robinson fell silent. He looked deeply hurt and betrayed. His fists bunched, his body tensed, and he began to breathe stertorously through his nose. Eyes narrowing, he glared at her with a mixture of animosity and wounded affection. Anne took a step backwards. She was suddenly afraid of him.

Nicholas Bracewell returned to the Queen's Head once more. As he turned into the yard, he heard the familiar voice of Owen Elias.

'So I told Barnaby that I'd translate *Cupid's Folly* into Welsh for him so that he could take it on a tour of the Principality and play to an audience of sheep!'

Appreciative guffaws came from the knot of actors around the speaker. When Nicholas came up, he saw with a shock that it was not Elias at all. James Ingram had been diverting his fellows with an impersonation of their Welsh colleague. It was the accuracy of his mimicry which had produced the laughter.

The mirth faded when they saw Nicholas. Actors who should have been mourning the death of Jonas Applegarth looked a little shamefaced at being caught at their most raucous. They slunk quietly away, leaving Ingram alone to talk with the book holder.

'You are a cunning mimic,' said Nicholas.

'Harmless fun, Nick. Nothing more.'

'Does Owen know that he has a twin brother?'

'He'd slaughter me if he did,' said Ingram. 'It was an affectionate portrait of him, but Owen would not thank the artist.' He became remorseful. 'But I am glad that we meet again. I was brusque and unmannerly at Blackfriars. You deserved better from me. I have no excuse.'

'Let it pass, James.'

'It will not happen again.'

'I am pleased to hear it,' said Nicholas. 'But you have still not told me what brought you to the Queen's Head so early this morning.'

'Eagerness. Nothing more.'

'It does not often get you here ahead of your fellows.'

'It did today.'

'Why did you come into the storeroom?'

'The door of the tiring-house was open. I wondered who was here. Nathan Curtis was in the storeroom with the body. I got there only seconds before you returned.'

Ingram spoke with his usual open-faced honesty and Nicholas had no reason to doubt him. The tension between the two of them had gone completely. The book holder was glad. Fond of the actor, he did not want a rift between them.

'Let's into the taproom,' he suggested.

'Not me, Nick,' said the other pleasantly. 'It is too full of reminiscence about Jonas Applegarth for me. You know my feelings there. I would be out of place.'

They exchanged farewells and Ingram left the inn yard.

The atmosphere in the taproom had lightened considerably. Members of the company sat in a corner and traded maudlin memories of the dead man, but most of the customers were only there to drink and gamble. Laughter echoed around the room once more and the servingmen were kept busy. Alexander Marwood could never be expected to smile, but his despair was noticeably less fervent than before.

Nicholas joined the table at which Lawrence Firethorn and Owen Elias sat. Both had been drinking steadily. They called for an extra tankard and poured the newcomer some ale from their jug.

'Thank heaven you've come, Nick!' said Elias.

'Yes,' added Firethorn. 'We are in such a morass of self-pity that we need you to pull us out. Marwood still swears we have performed our last play in his yard.'

'He has done that often before,' said Nicholas, 'and we always return to confound his prediction. Tomorrow is Sunday and our stage would in any case stand empty. That will make our landlord think again. Two days without a penny taken in his yard! His purse will speak up for Westfield's Men.'

'I hope so,' said Firethorn. 'The last twenty-four hours have been a nightmare. One author turns my marital couch into a bed of nails, another gets himself hanged and my occupation rests on the whim of an imbecile landlord! I might as well become a holy anchorite and live on herbs. There's no future for me here.'

He drank deep. Elias saw the chance to impart his news.

'I found Naismith,' he said. 'The dog admitted that he had been shadowing Jonas through the streets.'

'Did he throw that dagger?' asked Nicholas.

'Unhappily, no. I'd have welcomed the excuse to carve

252

him up and send him back to Banbury's Men in a meat pie. Hugh Naismith is too weak to throw anything, Nick. He is not our man.'

'Then we must look elsewhere.'

'What have you learnt?'

'Much of interest but little that ties the name of the murderer to Jonas Applegarth.'

'Choose from any of a hundred names,' said Firethorn. 'Jonas spread his net widely. Enemies all over London.'

'That was not the case with Cyril Fulbeck,' reminded Nicholas. 'Few would pick a quarrel with him. That cuts our list right down. We look for a rare man, one with motive to kill both the Master of the Chapel *and* Jonas Applegarth.' A new thought made him sit up. 'Unless I am mistaken.'

'About what?' said Elias.

'The Laughing Hangman. Do I search for one murderer when there are really *two*?' He thought it through. 'Jonas was hanged in the same manner as Cyril Fulbeck, it is true. And I heard what I thought was the same laughter. But ears can play strange tricks sometimes. Sound can be distorted in chambers and passageways.'

'It *must* be the same man,' insisted Elias.

'Why?'

'Coincidence could not be that obliging.'

'We are not talking of coincidence, Owen, but of mimicry. Someone who saw the first man hanged could dispose of a second in the identical way. Someone who heard that peal of laughter at Blackfriars could bring the same mockery to the Queen's Head.'

'Why go to such elaborate lengths?' asked Firethorn.

'To evade suspicion,' said Nicholas. 'What better ruse than to use the method of one killer as your own and put the crime on his account?'

'Your reasoning breaks down,' decided Elias. 'Only someone who actually *saw* the first victim could know the necessary detail. Only a trained actor with a gift for mimicry could reproduce a laugh like that. Where on earth would you find such a man?'

Nicholas said nothing. He was preoccupied with the thought that he had just been talking with that very person in the inn yard. Motive, means and opportunity. A perfect cloak for his crime. James Ingram had them all.

'I give up!' moaned Elias.

'Why?'

'The villains multiply before my eyes. First, I thought our killer and our dagger thrower were one man. Then you separate them. Now you split the hangman into two as well to give us three in all. By tomorrow, it will have grown to four and so on until we are searching for a whole band of them!'

'I am lost,' admitted Firethorn. 'What is happening?'

'Confusion, Lawrence!'

'Do we have any idea at all who murdered Jonas?'

'Yes,' said Elias with irony. 'Nick pulls a new suspect out of the air every minute. Each one a possible killer. We'll get them all to sign a petition, then pick out the name that pleases us most and designate him as Laughing Hangman.'

'Mompesson!' muttered Nicholas.

'My God! He's added another suspect to the list.'

'Andrew Mompesson.'

Nicholas remembered where he had seen the name before.

Chapter Eleven

The miracle had happened at last. After a lifetime's fruitless search, Edmund Hoode finally found his way into the Garden of Eden and discovered Paradise. Cecily Gilbourne was a most alluring Eve, soft and supple, at once virginal and seasoned in all the arts of love. She was a true symbol of womanhood. Hoode's ardour matched her eager demands, his desire soared with her passion. Hearts, minds and bodies met in faultless rhyme. Their destinies mingled.

It was several minutes before he regained his breath. He used the back of his arm to wipe the perspiration from his brow, then gazed up at the ceiling. The Garden of Eden, he now learnt, was a bedchamber at the Unicorn. When he turned his head, he saw that his gorgeous and compliant Eve had freckles on her shoulder. She, too, was glistening with joy.

What thrilled him most was the ease with which it had all

happened. A rose. A promise. A tryst. Consummation. There had been no intervening pauses and no sudden obstacles. No inconvenient appearances by returning husbands. Everything proceeded with a graceful inevitability. It was an experience he had always coveted but never come within sight of before. In Hoode's lexicon, romance was a synonym for anguish. Cecily Gilbourne offered him a far more satisfactory definition.

Her voice rose up softly from the pillow beside him.

'Edmund?'

'My love?'

'Are you still awake?'

'Yes, Cecily.'

'Are you still happy?'

'Delirious.'

'Are you still *mine*?'

'Completely.'

She pulled him gently on top of her and kissed him.

'Take me, Edmund.'

'*Again?*'

'Again.'

He kicked open the gate with his naked foot and went into the Garden of Eden, not, as before, with halting gait and wide-eyed wonder but with a proprietary swagger. Edmund Hoode had found his true spiritual home.

The silence seemed interminable. Anne Hendrik was petrified. She stood there unable to move, unable to call out for her servant and incapable of defending herself in any way. The menacing figure of Ambrose Robinson loomed over her. She felt like one of the dumb animals whom he routinely slaughtered.

Cold fury coursed through the butcher. The veins on his forehead stood out like whipcord as he fought to contain his violent instincts. When he took a step towards her, Anne was so convinced that he was about to strike her that she shut her eyes and braced herself against the blow. It never came. Instead, she heard a quiet snivelling noise. When she dared to lift her lids again, she saw that Robinson was now sitting on a chair with his head in his hands.

Her fear slowly shaded into cautious sympathy.

'What ails you?' she asked.

'All is lost,' he murmured between sobs of remorse.

'Lost?'

'My son, my clearest friend, my hopes of happiness. All gone for ever.' He looked up with a tearful face. 'It was my only chance, Anne. I did it out of love.'

'Love?'

'The loan, those letters . . .'

'You are not making much sense, Ambrose.'

'It was wrong of me,' he said, lurching to his feet. 'I should not have deceived you so. You deserved better of me. I will get out of your life for ever and leave you in peace.'

Wiping his tears away, he lumbered towards the door.

'Stay!' she said, curiosity roused. 'Do not run away with the truth untold. What *is* going on, Ambrose?'

He stopped to face her and gave a hopeless shrug.

'You were right, Anne.'

'Philip did not send those letters?'

'No,' he confessed, 'but they are exactly the letters that he *would have* sent, had he the time and opportunity to write. I know my own son. Philip is in torment at Blackfriars. Those letters only said what he feels.'

'Did you write them yourself?'

'With these clumsy hands?' he said, spreading his huge palms. 'They are more used to holding an axe than a pen. No, Anne. I only wrote those letters in my own mind. A scrivener put them on paper at my direction.'

She was baffled. '*Why?*'

'To reassure me. To tell myself that my son really did love me and want to come home to me. When I'd read those letters enough times, I truly began to believe that Philip had indeed sent them.' His chin sank to his chest again. 'And there was another reason, Anne.'

'I see it only too clearly.'

'It was a mistake.'

'You used those letters to ensnare *me*,' she said angrily. 'To work on my feelings and draw me closer. And through me, you brought Nick Bracewell in to help.'

'You spoke so highly of him. Of how resourceful he was and what a persuasive advocate he would be. That was why I was so keen and willing to meet Nick.'

'And to deceive *him* with those false letters!'

'They are not false. Philip might have written them.'

'But he did not, Ambrose. You beguiled us!'

'How else could I secure your help?'

'By being honest with me.'

'Honesty would have put you straight to flight.'

'Why so?'

'Because of the person I am,' he said, beating his chest with a fist. 'Look at me. A big, ugly, shambling butcher. What hope had I of winning you with honesty? When you thought I lent that money out of friendship, you took it gladly. Had I told you I gave it because I cared, because I loved, because I wanted you as mine, you would have spurned it.' A pleading note reappeared. 'What I did was dishonest but from honest motives. I worship my son and so I inveigled you and Nick Bracewell into working for his release. Because I dote on you – and this is my worst offence – I used Philip as a means to get close to you. To make you think and feel like a mother to him. I was trying to *court you,* Anne.'

'There was a worse offence yet,' she said vehemently.

'That is not so.'

'I see it now and shudder at what I see. You dangled your own son in front of me like a carrot in front of a donkey. That was disgusting enough. To mislead Philip as well was despicable.'

'I did not mislead him.'

'Yes you did,' she accused. 'We were not the only dupes. He had his share of false letters. You wrote to him to tell him that he would come back to a happy home with a second mother. You used *me* to tempt Philip back.'

'No!'

'It was the one thing that might bring him home.'

'You don't know Philip.'

'I know him well enough to understand why he likes it in the Chapel Royal. He has escaped from his father. No wonder he enjoys it so at the Blackfriars Theatre.'

260

'I want him *home*!' shouted Robinson.

Anne walked to the front door and opened it wide.

'Do not expect me to help you, sir,' she said crisply. 'There lies your way. Do not let me detain you. I'll be no man's false hope to wave in front of an unwitting child. Farewell, Ambrose. You are no longer welcome here!'

He glared at her for a moment, then skulked out.

Sunday morning turned London into a gigantic bell-foundry. The whole city clanged to and fro. Bells rang, tolled, chimed or sang out in melodious peals to fill every ear within miles with the clarion call of Christianity and to send the multifarious congregations hurrying in all directions to Matins in church or cathedral. Bells summoned the faithful and accused the less devout, striking chords in the hearts of the one and putting guilt in the minds of the others. Only the dead and deaf remained beyond the monstrous din of the Sabbath.

Nicholas Bracewell left his lodging in Thames Street on his way to his own devotions. Recognising a figure ahead of him, he lengthened his stride to catch her up.

'Good-morrow!'

'Oh!'

'May I walk with you?'

'I am late, sir. I must hurry.'

'May I not keep your haste company?'

Joan Hay was not pleased to see him and even less happy about the way he fell in beside her. Keeping her head down and her hands clutched tight in front of her, she bustled along the street. Nicholas guessed the reason for her behaviour.

'I think that I must beg your pardon,' he said.

'Why?'

'For putting you in bad favour with your husband. I should not have told him that we met in Blackfriars. I fear he may have upbraided you for talking to me as you did.'

'No, no,' she lied.

'Master Hay is a private man, I know that.'

'He is a genius, sir. I am married to a genius.'

'Why is he not with you this morning?'

'He has gone ahead. I rush to catch up with him.'

'Then I will ask one simple question before I let you get on your way.'

'Please do not, sir. I know nothing.'

'This is no secret I ask you to divulge. Your husband talked openly of it yesterday.'

'Then speak with him again.'

'I would rather hear it from you.'

When they reached a corner, he put a gentle hand on her shoulder to stop her. Joan Hay looked up into his face with frightened eyes. Timorous at the best of times, she was now in a mild panic.

'Master Hay told me that he was once in prison.'

'Only for one day,' she said defensively.

'There must have been some error, surely? Your husband is the most law-abiding man I have ever met.'

'He is, he is.'

'What possible charge could be brought against him?'

'I do not know.'

'You must have some idea.'

'It was a mistake. He was soon released.'

'Thanks to the help of the Master of the Chapel.'

'Yes, I believe that he was involved.'

'So why was your husband arrested?' pressed Nicholas.

'Truly, sir, I do not know.'

'He could not have been taken without a warrant. Did they come to the house? Was he seized there?'

Joan Hay glanced nervously around, fearful of being late for church and anxious to shake off her interrogator. She was patently unaware of the full details of her husband's temporary incarceration, but Nicholas still felt that he might winkle some clue out of her.

'Let me go, sir,' she said. 'I implore you.'

'When the officers came for your husband . . .'

'Discuss the matter with him.'

'Did they take anything away with them?'

'Some documents, that is all.'

'Documents?'

'Do not ask me what they were for I know not.'

Nicholas stepped aside so that she could continue on her way. He felt guilty at harassing an already harassed woman but the conversation had yielded something of great interest. It gave him much to ponder as he headed for his own church in the neighbouring parish.

The jangling harmonies of London finally brought Edmund Hoode out of his protracted sleep. Expecting to wake up in the Garden of Eden, entwined in the arms of his beloved, he was disconcerted to find himself alone in a dishevelled bed at the Unicorn with a draught blowing in through an open window. As his brain slowly cleared, the full force of the bells hit his ears and he put his hands over them to block out the sound.

There was no trace of Cecily Gilbourne, not even the faintest whiff of the delicate perfume which had so intoxicated him the previous night. Had she fled in disappointment? Was their love shipwrecked on its maiden voyage? Hoode closed his eyes and tried to remember what had actually happened. Paradise had been recreated on the first floor of a London inn. He had been offered an apple from the Tree of Knowledge and had eaten it voraciously. It had been inexpressibly delicious.

The problem was that Eve had given him another apple. Then a third, a fourth, a fifth and possibly more. Before he collapsed in sheer exhaustion, he recalled looking around a Garden of Eden that was littered with apple cores. Eve, meanwhile, was straining to pluck another down from a higher branch. Her pursuit of knowledge was insatiable.

When Hoode struggled to sit up, he realised just how insatiable Cecily Gilbourne had been. She had left him for dead. His muscles ached, his stomach churned and his body seemed to have no intention of obeying any of its owner's commands. After long hours of sleep, he was still fatigued. His mouth was parched and he longed for some water to slake his thirst.

With a supreme effort, he rolled off the bed and got his feet onto the floor. They showed little enthusiasm for the notion of supporting him and he had to clutch at a bench to stay upright. Blown by the wind and buffeted by the bells, he staggered across to the door, using a variety of props and crutches on his way. What kept him going was the thought that Cecily might be in the adjoining chamber, waiting for him to join her before breakfast was served. But the door was locked.

Hoode leant against it while he gathered his strength. A question began to pound away at the back of his skull. Why did he feel so unhappy? After such a night of madness, he should be overwhelmed with joy. Having tasted the sweet delights of Cecily Gilbourne, his mouth should be tingling with pleasure. Yet his palate was jaded. What had gone wrong?

His body rebelled and threatened to cast him to the floor. Legs buckled, arms went slack and his neck tried to disassociate itself from his head. The bed was his only salvation but it now seemed to be a hundred yards away. Marshalling his forces for one desperate lunge, he flung himself across the room, kicked over a stool, a table and a chamber-pot on the way, then landed on the bed with a thud, resolving never to move from it again.

He was still lying there, moaning softly and idly composing his own obituary, when he saw something out of the corner of his eye. It was a letter, protruding from beneath the pillow, clearly left by Cecily Gilbourne. His heart lifted. He was not, after all, an abandoned lover in a draughty bedchamber. She had penned her gratitude in glowing terms before stealing away and affirmed her love. That thought made him open the letter with fumbling enthusiasm, only to drop it instantly in alarm.

Cecily was a laconic correspondent. One word

decorated the page and it struck an inexplicable terror into him:

'*Tonight.*'

Royal command had delayed the funeral of Cyril Fulbeck until that morning. It was no insignificant event. The Master of the Chapel was a loved and revered member of the royal household and the Queen insisted on paying her personal respects to him. Since she only returned from Greenwich Palace on Saturday evening, the obsequies could not take place until the following day.

It was a moving ceremony, conducted with due solemnity by the Bishop of London and held in the Chapel which Fulbeck had served with such exceptional dedication. The choir were in fine voice as they bade farewell to their mentor and Philip Robinson was allowed the privilege of a solo. The funeral oration paid tribute to the work and character of the deceased while tactfully omitting any reference to the manner of his death. Silent tears lubricated the whole service, and when the coffin was borne out, even Her Majesty was seen to lift a gloved hand to her cheek.

Yet still the murder remained unsolved. Pressure from above was strong and the official investigation was as thorough as it could be, but little evidence had been unearthed as yet and the Queen let it be known that she was displeased. Now that his body had been laid to rest, Cyril Fulbeck deserved to be avenged in the most prompt way. Additional men were assigned to help with the search for his killer.

Raphael Parsons kept his head bent and his thoughts

to himself throughout the funeral. When the burial had taken place, he waited until the congregation left in strict order of precedence before slipping away in the direction of Blackfriars. When he reached the theatre, he was annoyed to see a sturdy figure waiting for him.

'I am glad I have caught you,' said Nicholas Bracewell.

'Pray excuse me, sir. I am too busy to talk.'

'But there is no performance here today.'

'Sadly, no,' said Parsons.

'Even *you* would not expect to stage a play only hours after the funeral of the Master of the Chapel.'

'I most certainly would. Sentiment and commerce must be kept apart. We cannot let the former dictate the latter. I was sorry to see my old friend laid in his grave, but I would not, from choice, let it affect the entertainment here.'

'Is that not like dancing on a man's tomb?'

'Not in my opinion.'

'Do you take no account of your actors?'

'Actors exist to act.'

'They have feelings, Master Parsons,' argued Nicholas. 'Senses, emotions, loyalties. That is especially true of your young company. Their hearts were not hacked from the same flint as your own. I'll wager they did not want to tread the boards today.'

'I'd have *made* them!'

'They would have hated you for it. Westfield's Men did not think twice about performance yesterday. When we discovered the body of Jonas Applegarth, the play cancelled itself. Not a member of the company could have been forced upon that scaffold.'

'I'd have willingly taken their place,' volunteered the manager. 'Applegarth dead! I'd have danced a jig all afternoon to mark the occasion!'

Nicholas smarted. 'Where were you when he was killed?' he said. 'With your friend in Ireland Yard?'

'What is that to you?'

'I wondered if you would use the same lie twice.'

'I never used it once,' retorted the other. 'Yesterday morning, when that blessed hangman was testing Applegarth's weight, I was here at Blackfriars.'

'At dawn?'

'My day starts early.'

'Was anyone else here with you?'

'Not for an hour or so,' admitted Parsons. 'But then Geoffrey, the porter, arrived. He'll vouch for me.'

'I am only interested in the exact time when Jonas Applegarth was murdered,' said Nicholas. 'You have a story but no witness to its credence. It is so with the death of Cyril Fulbeck. You claim to be in Ireland Yard when that occurred. But nobody there will speak up for you.'

Parsons bridled. 'What do you mean?'

'I have asked them all.'

'The devil take you!'

'Most residents did not even know who Raphael Parsons was.'

'You had the gall to intrude on my privacy?'

'Most certainly.'

'By what right?'

'Simple curiosity,' said Nicholas easily, 'and the urge to catch a foul murderer. Whoever killed Cyril Fulbeck used the same villainy on Jonas Applegarth. If he was not in Ireland Yard when he claims, he may not have been at the Blackfriars Theatre when he alleges. Do you follow my reasoning?'

'Hell and damnation!'

Parsons lashed out a hand to strike Nicholas but the book holder was far too quick. He seized the manager's wrist, twisted his arm behind his back, then pushed him to the ground. Parsons cursed aloud. Rolling over, he got slowly and painfully to his feet, dusting himself off and regarding Nicholas with growling hostility.

'Let us begin again,' said Nicholas. 'Where were you when Cyril Fulbeck was hanged by the neck?'

'In Ireland Yard.'

'That lie will not serve.'

'Ireland Yard!' repeated Parsons through gritted teeth.

'Then why will nobody come forward?'

'Why do you *think*, man?'

'Tell me.'

Parsons looked around furtively to make sure that they were not overheard, then glared at Nicholas. After much agonising, he decided that the only way to get rid of his visitor was to tell him a measure of the truth.

'My dear friend in Ireland Yard is not in a position to acknowledge my friendship,' he said.

'Why not?'

'She is married.'

'Oh.'

'Do not ask me to give you her name and address, for that is too great a betrayal. Just accept that I was with the lady at the time when Cyril Fulbeck was hanged.' He glanced in the direction of Ireland Yard. 'She would also swear that I was with her at dawn yesterday morning. Her husband is a merchant and travelling to Holland. Do I need to say more?'

Nicholas shook his head. He knew the man was telling the truth now. It absolved him of both murders and took away the one obvious link between Fulbeck and Applegarth. Parsons argued with the one and fulminated against the other. He gave more detail of his relationship with both men.

'That was what we were quarrelling about only hours before he was killed,' he said. 'Cyril found out about her. He read me a sermon on the virtues of marriage and the evils of adultery. Was I a fit person to be put in charge of his choristers when I was committing a dreadful sin? Would not my mere presence corrupt their young minds? Arrant nonsense!'

'What did you say?' asked Nicholas.

'What any man would have said. In round terms, I told him not to meddle in my affairs. What I do between the sheets, when I do it, and with whom, is my affair. I called him a vestal virgin and stormed out of the theatre.'

'Before going straight to Ireland Yard?'

Parsons grinned. 'I felt in need of consolation.' The rancour returned. 'As for your second accusation, I can rebut that as well. I hated Jonas Applegarth but I did not hang him. I was enjoying other pleasures at the time.'

'Why did you detest him so?' asked Nicholas.

'Ask of him why he detested *me*? For that is how it

began. We admired his plays greatly and invited him to write one for the Chapel Children. And what did he do?'

'Reject the offer and rail at you.'

'Then continue that railing in *The Misfortunes of Marriage*. We work hard here in Blackfriars and have problems enough to contend with. Why should that bloated knave be allowed to sneer at everything we did? It was unjust. Applegarth simply had to be put down somehow.'

'With a knife in his back?'

'That was one way,' said the manager calmly. 'I prefer to stab him in the chest with a Prologue.'

Nicholas studied him for a moment with quiet contempt. There was nothing more to be gained from the confrontation, yet he found it difficult to walk away. The manager might have proved that he was not the Laughing Hangman, but Nicholas still felt that the man had some blood on his hands. Had he planned the murders and left a confederate to commit them? His work at Blackfriars was a testimony to his theatrical skills. Could not those same skills be used to stage two hangings?

Parsons taunted him. 'Have you done with me?' he said.

'For the moment.'

'Good. I must prepare for my rehearsal.'

'On the day of the funeral?'

'They've taken the performance from me. I'll not be robbed of a rehearsal as well. The boys are coming here after evensong.'

'Why are you making them do this?'

'I am not,' said Parsons. 'They requested it. Ask them, if you do not believe me. You are welcome to watch us, for we only rehearse a few scenes. The boys are rightly upset by the funeral. They want to push it out of their minds for a couple of hours.' He peered at Nicholas. 'Have *you* never lost yourself in work to escape your thoughts?'

Evensong filled the whole building with the most beauteous sound, climbing up into the vaulted roof and penetrating every corner of the chancel and the nave before seeping down into the dank crypt to swirl around the ears of the dead. Ambrose Robinson was oblivious to it all. He knew that Anne Hendrik would be in the congregation but he did not even try to catch a glimpse of her, still less attempt to sit beside her. She now belonged to his past.

When he looked at the choir, he did not see the upturned faces of the boys as they offered their praise up to God. What he noted was the absence of his son from his accustomed position in the stalls. Evensong had always been an occasion of great joy to him when Philip Robinson's voice was an essential part of it. Without him, the service had become an ordeal for his father.

Nor did the sermon offer any comfort or inspiration. The meaningless drone of the vicar's voice was a grim reminder of another service at the same place of worship. When Robinson's wife was buried there, the vicar had consoled him with the simple statement that it was the will of God. Philip Robinson's enforced departure to the Chapel Royal was also characterised by the vicar as the will of God, and the butcher was certain that he would describe the loss of Anne Hendrik in the same way.

One bereavement was enough to bear. Three were quite

insupportable. Wife, son and potential second wife. He had lost them all and was now left with an existence that was both empty and pointless. The vicar might counsel resignation but Robinson refused to accept that counsel any more. He would not simply lie down and let the stone wheels of Fate roll over him time and again. He would get up and fight.

With the service still in progress, therefore, he rose from his seat and marched up the aisle before the surprised eyes of the other parishioners. A gust of wind blew in as he opened the west door. Robinson did not hear the rustle of complaint that ran up and down the benches and pews. His mind was on more unholy matters than Evensong.

When he reached his shop, he let himself in and stood in front of his bench. He surveyed the weaponry which hung from the ceiling on iron hooks. Knives, skewers, cleavers and axes were kept clean and sharp at all times. It was a matter of pride with him. Everything was in readiness for the morrow, but some butchery was now called for on the Sabbath. Ambrose Robinson selected a cleaver and examined its blade with his thumb. It was honed to perfection.

He set off on the long walk towards redemption.

Nicholas Bracewell decided to avail himself of the chance to watch the evening rehearsal at Blackfriars and he timed his return to the theatre accordingly. He was halfway across the Great Yard before he noticed Caleb Hay. Tucked away in the far corner, the old man was scanning the buildings with a small telescope. Nicholas walked across to him.

'Good-even, good sir!' he called. 'Is your eyesight grown so bad that you need a telescope to see something that is right in front of you?'

'You mistake me,' said Hay with a chuckle. 'What I look at is the distant past. You see only the vestigial remains of Blackfriars. I was trying to map out, in my mind's eye, the full extent of the old monastery. Then I may draw my plan.'

'I would be most interested to see it.'

'In time, sir. All in good time.'

Nicholas remembered something. 'I am glad we have met,' he said. 'Andrew Mompesson. Was not he your father-in-law?'

'Indeed, he was. A sterling fellow and a bookseller of high repute. He taught me much.' His eyes twinkled. 'And he entrusted me with the best volume on his shelves when he gave me the hand of his daughter.'

Nicholas smiled, but he was not sure that Hay would make such a gallant remark about his wife in the woman's presence. Joan Hay had the look of someone who had been starved of compliments for a considerable time.

'It is an unusual name,' said Nicholas. 'That is why it stuck in my mind. Andrew Mompesson. He was among the signatories on that petition against the opening of a public theatre in Blackfriars.'

'Your memory serves you well. My father-in-law helped to draw up that petition. He allowed me to make a fair copy of it, which is what I was able to show you.'

'Did he live to see the present theatre opened?'

'Mercifully, no,' said Hay. 'It would have broken his heart. The precinct was still unsullied by a playhouse when he died. No sound of drums and trumpets disturbed his peace. No swarming crowds went past his front door seven days a week. No actors mocked the spirit of Blackfriars with their blasphemy and lewd behaviour. He died happy. How many of us will be able to say that?'

'Not many.'

'Not poor Cyril Fulbeck, certainly. God rest his soul!' Head to one side, he looked up at Nicholas. 'Is that what has brought you here once more? The hunt for his murderer?'

'Yes, Master Hay.'

'And are you any closer to catching him?'

'I believe so.'

'That is excellent news.'

'It is only a matter of time now.'

'You deserve great credit for taking this task upon yourself when the Master of the Chapel meant nothing to you.' He heaved a sigh of regret. 'If only *I* had strength enough for it. Cyril Fulbeck was kind to me. I have many reasons to avenge his death but lack the means to do so.'

'But for him, you might still be incarcerated.'

A hollow laugh. 'That is more than possible.'

'Which prison did they lock you in?'

'The Clink.'

The approach of feet deflected their attention to the other side of the yard. Choristers from the Chapel Royal were processing towards the theatre with their heads bowed in reverential silence. Philip Robinson was at the front of the column as it wended its way in through the main door. Caleb Hay was duly horrified.

'There surely cannot be a performance this evening!'

'A short rehearsal only.'

'On the Sabbath? In the wake of a funeral?'

'Raphael Parsons is allowing me to watch them.'

'Then I will take myself away,' said the old man as he put his telescope into his pocket. 'This is no place for me. Choristers making a foul spectacle of themselves upon a stage! Sanctity and sin are one under the instruction of Raphael Parsons. There's your killer, sir. That man will murder the Sabbath itself.'

Hay made a dignified exit from the Great Yard. Nicholas made his way across to the theatre and explained to the porter why he had come. Geoffrey Bless surprised him.

'Then you will have seen Master Ingram,' he said.

'When?'

'A few minutes ago when he left the theatre.'

'He was here?'

'Talking to me even as you are now.'

'I saw no sign of him.'

'You could not have missed him,' said the porter. 'If you came across the Great Yard, you would need to be blind to miss him. I wonder that Master Ingram did not hail you.'

Nicholas was wondering the same thing. He decided that Ingram must have seen him first and concealed himself in one of the angles of the building. It was strange behaviour for a friend. He went swiftly back through the main door and looked around, but Ingram was nowhere to be seen. Nicholas concluded that he might not yet have left the premises. He returned to the ancient porter.

'What was James doing here?'

'He called in to see me, sir,' said Geoffrey. 'To talk over

old times when Blackfriars was a happier place to be.'

'How long was he here?'

'Above an hour.'

'Did he know that there was a rehearsal this evening?'

'I told him so.'

'What was his reaction?'

'He thought it wrong, sir. On the day of the funeral.'

The porter's eyes moistened. He was old and tired. Murder in the Blackfriars Theatre had taken all the spirit out of him. Alert and watchful before, Geoffrey Bless was now a broken man. It would not be difficult for someone like James Ingram to slip unnoticed back into the building.

Nicholas went up the staircase and let himself into the theatre as quietly as he could. Raphael Parsons was standing on stage, clapping his hands to summon his actors. Having changed into costume for the rehearsal, they drifted out from the tiring-house. Philip Robinson was the last to come, wearing a dress and pulling on an auburn wig. Nicholas took a seat at the very back of the auditorium. Parsons and his young company seemed unaware of his presence.

'We'll rehearse the Trial Scene,' announced the manager. 'Philip Robinson?'

'Yes, sir?' said the boy.

'You must carry the action here. All depends on you.'

'Yes, sir.'

'Regal bearing, Philip. Remember that. You may be in chains but you are still a queen. Regal bearing even in the face of adversity. Clear the stage. Set the scene.'

Parsons jumped down into the auditorium and caught sight of Nicholas. He gave his visitor a non-committal nod before turning back to his work. The stagekeeper set a table and benches on stage, then vacated it quickly.

'Begin!' ordered the manager.

Three judges came on stage in procession and took their places behind the table. Two soldiers, wearing armour and holding pikes, stood either side of the commission in order to signal its importance and to enforce its decisions.

'Bring in the prisoner!' called Parsons.

The gaoler dragged in the hapless Queen with a rope. Philip Robinson did his best to suggest wounded dignity. He stood before his accusers without flinching. The charges were read out, then one of the judges addressed the prisoner.

JUDGE: What have you to say?

QUEEN: The charges against me are false.

JUDGE: That is for us to decide.

QUEEN: You have no power over me, Sir. I am a queen and answer to a higher authority than any you can muster here. I'll not be subject to this mean court like any common malefactor. Do you dare to sit in judgement on God's anointed? By what perverse and unnatural right do you presume to put the crown of England on trial here?

The speech was long and impassioned. Philip Robinson began slowly but soon hit his stride, delivering the prose with a clear voice that rang around the theatre. Nicholas was impressed. It was more than a mere recitation of the lines. The boy was a true actor. Of the apprentices with

Westfield's Men, only Richard Honeydew could have handled the trial speech with equal skill and righteous indignation.

Having cowed his accused with his majesty, the boy flung himself dramatically to the ground before the judicial bench and challenged them to strike off his royal head. Before the judges could reply, a voice roared out from the back of the theatre.

'Philip! What on earth have they *done* to you?'

Ambrose Robinson stood in the open doorway looking with horror at his son. The sight of the dress and the wig ignited him to fever pitch. He went storming towards the stage with his hand stretched out.

'Come away!' he shouted. 'Come with your father. I'm here to rescue you from this vile place. Come home!'

But the boy showed no inclination to return to Bankside. As his father bore down on him, Philip Robinson leapt to his feet and backed away. Snatching his wig off, he cried out in fear:

'I am happy here, Father! Leave me be!'

'Come with me!'

'No,' said the boy. 'I will not!'

He fled into the tiring-house and Robinson tried to clamber upon the stage to pursue him. The manager moved in quickly to restrain the angry parent.

'Stop, sir! There is no place for you here.'

'I want my son.'

'Philip is a lawful member of the Chapel Children. You may not touch him. I am Raphael Parsons and I manage this theatre. I must ask you to leave at—'

'Parsons!'

Robinson turned on the man he saw as the author of his misery. He went berserk. Shrugging Parsons off, he pulled the cleaver from beneath his coat and struck at him with all his force, catching him on the shoulder and opening up a fearful wound that sent blood cascading all over him. The manager fell to the floor in agony and the butcher stood over him to hack him into pieces.

The young actors were too frightened to move, but Nicholas Bracewell was already sprinting down the auditorium. Before the cleaver could strike again, he dived into Robinson with such force that the butcher was knocked flying. As the two of them hit the wooden floor with a thud, the weapon jerked out of Robinson's hand and spun crazily away. He now turned his manic anger upon Nicholas, rolling over to get a grip on his neck and trying to throttle the life out of him.

Rage lent the butcher extra power, but Nicholas was the more experienced fighter, twisting himself free to deliver a relay of punches to the contorted face, then grabbing the man by the hair to dash his head against the floor. As the two of them grappled once more, footsteps came running towards them and James Ingram hurled himself on top of Robinson to help Nicholas to subdue him. The assistance was not needed. The butcher stopped struggling.

Realising where he was and what he had done, Robinson seemed to come out of a trance. He began to wail piteously. The porter came panting into the hall with two constables.

'I tried to stop him,' he said, 'but he pushed past me. I ran for help.' He almost fainted at the sight of Parsons.

'Dear God! What new horror is here!'

Nicholas got to his feet. With Ingram's help, he pulled Robinson upright and handed him over to the constables. As they marched him out of the theatre, the butcher was still crying with remorse. Raphael Parsons lay on the floor in a widening pool of blood. Nicholas turned to the porter.

'Fetch a surgeon!' he ordered.

'I'll go,' volunteered Ingram. 'Faster legs than Geoffrey's are needed for this errand.'

The actor went running off towards the staircase, but his journey would be in vain. Nicholas could see that Parsons was well beyond the reach of medicine. Groaning with pain, the manager lay on his back with half his shoulder severed from his body. Nicholas tried to stem the flow of blood but it was a hopeless task. Parsons revived briefly. He looked up through bleary eyes

'Who is it?'

'Nicholas Bracewell.'

'I am fading. Beware, sir.'

'Of what?'

'The theatre. A dangerous profession. It killed Cyril Fulbeck and now it sends me after him.' He clutched at Nicholas. 'Will you do me a service?'

'Willingly.'

'Discreetly, too.'

'I understand,' said Nicholas. 'Ireland Yard.'

'Number fourteen. Commend me to the lady. Explain why I am kept away. Do it gently.'

'I will, Master Parsons.'

The manager was suddenly convulsed with pain.

Nicholas thought he had passed away, but then life flickered once more. Parsons's lips moved but only the faintest sound emerged. Nicholas put his ear close to the man's mouth.

'One favour . . . deserves another,' murmured Parsons.

'Speak on.'

'I did not . . . hang . . . Applegarth.'

'I know that now,' said Nicholas.

'But I . . . tried to . . . tried to . . .'

'Yes?'

'Tried to . . . kill . . .'

His breathing stopped and his mouth fell slack. Raphael Parsons took leave of the world with confession on his lips. One mystery was solved. He was the man who threw the dagger at Jonas Applegarth's unprotected back. The playwright had not been stalked that day by a discontented actor with a grudge against him but by a furious theatre manager with an injured pride.

Nicholas could never bring himself to like Raphael Parsons. The man was too malignant and devious. As he looked down at the corpse, however, he felt compassion for him. There was a crude symmetry about his death. Having attempted to commit murder, he had himself been cut down in the most brutal way. On the very day that he bade farewell to the Master of the Chapel, he was sent off in pursuit of him. While rehearsing a trial scene with a favoured son, he was arraigned by a father who appointed himself judge, jury and executioner.

By the time Ingram arrived with a surgeon, Nicholas had taken charge with cool efficiency. The dead body had been covered with a cloak, the weeping porter had been led away, and the actors had been taken to the tiring-house to be comforted. Nicholas did not forget his promise to call on a house in Ireland Yard, but sad tidings had first to be broken to someone else. He took Philip Robinson to a quiet corner backstage where they might speak alone.

'You must be brave, Philip,' he said.

'Who are you, sir?'

'Nicholas Bracewell. A friend of Mistress Hendrik.'

'She was kind to me when my mother died.'

'I know,' said Nicholas. 'But it is about your father that I must now talk, I fear.'

'What happened, sir? I heard a fearful yell.'

'He attacked Master Parsons with a meat cleaver.'

The boy burst into tears and it took some time to soothe him. Nicholas gave him a brief account of what had taken place. He did not conceal the truth from him.

'Your father will have to pay for his crime.'

'I know, sir. I know.'

'One death may be answered by another.'

'And the two can be laid at *my* door!'

'No, Philip.'

'I killed them both! If I had not been here, Master Parsons would still be alive and my father would not soon be facing the public hangman.'

'You were not to blame,' insisted Nicholas. 'You are the victim and not the cause of this crime.' He held the boy until his sobbing gradually eased off. 'You like it here in the theatre, do you not?'

'I do, sir.'

'You were happy out on that stage.'

'Very happy.'

'So you did not write to your father to say how much you hated Blackfriars?'

'I did not write at all.'

'Would you rather be in the Chapel Royal or at home?'

'In the Chapel!' affirmed the boy. 'Anywhere but home.'

'Why is that?'

The boy felt the pull of family loyalties. Unhappy with his father, he did not want to divulge the full details of that unhappiness. Ambrose Robinson would soon be tried for murder and removed for ever from his son's life. The boy wanted to cling to a positive memory.

'My father loved me, I am sure,' he said.

'No question of that.'

'But it was not the same after my mother died. He told me I was all that he had. It made him watch me every moment of the day. That came to weigh down on me, sir.'

Nicholas understood. Philip Robinson was oppressed at home. The Chapel Royal had been his sanctuary. The boy looked around him in despair.

'What will happen to me?' he wondered.

'You will remain where you are.'

'But will they still want me after this, sir? I am the son of a murderer. They will expel me straight.'

'I think not.'

'Master Fulbeck was my friend. He looked after me. Who will do that now that he has gone?' His face was pale and haunted. 'What will happen to the theatre with Master Parsons dead? Chapel and theatre were my life.'

'They may still be so again.'

'It will never be the same.'

Philip Robinson was right. Cyril Fulbeck had been a father to him, and notwithstanding his strictness, Raphael Parsons had been an excellent tutor. Having lost both along with his own father, the boy was truly floundering.

'Which did you prefer, Philip?' asked Nicholas.

'Prefer?'

'Singing in the Chapel Royal or acting at Blackfriars?'

'Acting, sir, without a doubt.'

'Why is that?'

'Because I may get better at that in time,' he said. 'In the Chapel, I can only sing. On the stage, I can sing, dance, declaim the finest verse ever written and move all who watch to tears or laughter. I long to be an actor. But how can I do that without a theatre?'

Nicholas thought of the broken voice of John Tallis.

'Let me see if I can find you one,' he said.

Chapter Twelve

The day of rest was the least restful day of the week for Margery Firethorn. Tolled out of bed by the sonorous bells of Shoreditch, she had to rouse the remainder of the household, see them washed and dressed, lead them off to Matins at the parish church of St Leonard's, and smack them awake again when any of them dozed off during the service. Apart from the four apprentices and the two servants, she had three actors staying at the house until they could find a more suitable lodging. Thirteen mouths, including the ever-open ones of her children, had thus to be fed throughout the day. Since the servants tended to bungle some of the chores and burn all the food, Margery ended up doing more cleaning and cooking than was good for her temper.

When she got back from evensong with her flock in tow, she was vexed by the irreligious thought that the Sabbath had been invented as a punishment for anyone foolish enough to embrace marriage and succumb to motherhood. Margery looked ahead grimly to an evening laden with even more tasks and groaned inwardly. It was not the most auspicious time to call on her. Edmund Hoode felt the full force of rumbling dissatisfaction.

'Avaunt! Begone! Take your leprous visage away!'

'I have come on an errand of mercy.'

'Take mercy on me and go as fast as you may!'

'This is no kind of welcome, Margery.'

'It is the warmest you will get, sir,' she said. 'Have you so soon forgot your last visit here when you sewed such discord between man and wife that Lawrence and I have barely exchanged a civil word since?'

'That is one reason I came.'

'To part us asunder even more! Saints in Heaven! You will depopulate the city at this rate. Who can engage in the lawful business of procreation with you standing outside their bedchamber? What woman will submit to her husband's pleasure if she sees your ghoulish face staring at her over his naked shoulder?'

'I am here to beg your apology,' he said.

'Do so from a further distance, sir. Stand off a mile or more and I'll let you grovel all you wish.'

She tried to close the front door but he stopped her.

'Please do not turn me away!'

'Be grateful I do not set the dogs on you!'

'I am desperate, Margery.'

'Shift your desperation to another place, for we'll have none of it. Though it be the Sabbath, I'll use some darker language to send you on your way, if you dare to linger.'

'I must come in!'

'Go ruin another marriage instead.'

'I implore you!'

'You do so in vain,' she said. 'Lawrence is not within. Since you made converse with his wife impossible, he has taken himself off with his fellows.'

'But it is *you* I wish to see.'

'Wait till I fetch a broom and you will see me at my best. For I can beat a man black and blue within a minute.'

Seizing his cue, Hoode flung himself to the ground in an attitude of contrition.

'Beat me all you wish!' he invited. 'I deserve it, I need it, I invite it. Belabour me at will.'

Margery was taken aback. She looked at him properly for the first time and saw the haggard face and the hollow eyes. Hoode was suffering. She bent down to help him up from her doorstep.

'What is wrong with you, man?'

'Admit me and I'll tell all.'

'Have you stared at yourself in a mirror today?'

'I dare not, Margery.'

'Plague victims look healthier.'

'Their symptoms are mild compared to mine.'

Concern pushed belligerence aside as Margery brought him into the house and closed the front door. He was shivering all over. She took him into the kitchen and sat him down.

'What has happened, Edmund?'

'Armageddon.'

'Where?'

'In a lady's chamber.'

'Did she reject you?'

'Worse. She accepted me. Time and again.'

A series of uncontrollable grunts came from outside the door as if a frog with a sense of humour were eavesdropping. Margery darted out to find John Tallis bent double with mirth. She clipped his ear, kicked him on his way, then closed the door firmly behind her. Edmund Hoode's anguish needed the balm of privacy. A sniggering apprentice would only intensify the playwright's already unbearable pain.

She sat on the bench beside him and enfolded him in a maternal arm. This was no bold interloper, pounding on the door of her bedchamber. It was the old Edmund Hoode.

'This tale is for your ears only,' he insisted.

'Then it must be worth the hearing.'

'Lawrence would only mock me cruelly.'

'He will learn nothing from me. Speak on.'

Hoode needed a minute to summon up his strength before he could embark on his narrative. He was honest. He held nothing back. Margery was attentive and sympathetic. She realised that instant help was needed.

'When must you see the lady again?' she asked.

'This evening at the Unicorn.'

'Do not go.'

'That would be ungentlemanly,' he said. 'I must go. I owe her that. But I will not submit to another night of seductive exhaustion. My flesh and blood cannot stand it.'

'Explain that to her.'

'She would not listen. I know what she would say.'

'What?'

'Again!' he moaned. 'Again, Edmund, again, again! As if my manhood is a water-wheel that turns and turns with the flow of her passion. Save me, Margery! I drown!'

'There is only one sure means of rescue, Edmund.'

'What is that?'

She smiled benignly. 'You will see.'

'You have still not told me what took you to Blackfriars. '

'My own folly.'

'Folly?'

'Yes, Nick,' said James Ingram. 'I thought I knew best. I was convinced that Raphael Parsons was our Laughing Hangman and sought to spy on him. While you were watching the rehearsal, I was hiding up in the gallery.'

'You sneaked back into the building?'

'Geoffrey has grown careless. He did not see me.'

Nicholas Bracewell was relieved to learn that Ingram's presence at Blackfriars had no darker significance. His doubts about his friend were groundless. While Nicholas had a personal reason for hunting the killer of Jonas Applegarth, the actor had a personal reason for catching the man who hanged Cyril Fulbeck. From differing motives, both were searching for the same man.

'Parsons will no longer bother us,' said Ingram.

'True.'

'Nor will the Chapel Children.'

'Do not be so sure, James.'

'Why not?'

'One manager may have died, but another will soon

290

come to take his place. A private playhouse with a resident company which can stage its work for twelve months of the year. What temptation! It will not be long before a new Raphael Parsons is installed there.'

'Competing for our audience.'

'We must take our chances there,' said Nicholas. 'We have rivals enough without the children's companies, but we cannot stop them. Westfield's Men must find new and more cunning ways to outwit these young thespians.'

They were walking briskly across London Bridge together. Having given sworn statements regarding the killing of Raphael Parsons, the two men were free to leave. They plunged into Bankside and picked their way through its labyrinthine streets. Nicholas stopped outside a house.

'Whom do we visit here?' asked Ingram.

'You go on to another port of call.'

'Do I?'

'Yes, James. The Clink.'

'You are sending me to prison?'

'Only to make an enquiry.'

'The place is full of debtors and brothel-owners.'

'Not entirely. The man in whom I am interested is neither. Do you have money about you?'

'Sufficient. Why?'

'You'll need to bribe the prison sergeant.' After arranging to meet him back in Gracechurch Street, Nicholas gave Ingram his instructions, then sent him on his way. The book holder then tapped on door of the house. When the servant showed him into the parlour, Anne Hendrik got up from her chair with alacrity and embraced him.

'I prayed that you might come, Nick!' she said.

'Why?'

'It has been such a trying time since we parted.'

'In what way?'

'Ambrose Robinson has been here.'

She took him through the events of the previous day and admitted how frightened she had been of the butcher. Nicholas was deeply upset that he had not been there to protect her.

'Did he bother you at all today?' he asked.

'No. The only time I saw him was at evensong, and that was not for long. Ambrose got up in the middle of the service and stalked out with his face aflame. It was as if he suddenly had an irresistible urge to go somewhere.'

'He did, Anne.'

'Where?'

'To Blackfriars. I was there when he arrived.'

'At the theatre?'

'He came looking for his son.'

'I feared that might happen. Was there a tussle?'

'Yes,' said Nicholas, 'but not with the boy. He ran away from his father. It was Raphael Parsons who tussled with your neighbour and who came off worst. The butcher had armed himself with a meat cleaver.'

'Oh, no!' said Anne in horror. 'Murder?'

'One blow was all it took.'

'What then?'

'We overpowered him and constables led him away. Master Parsons did not survive for long.'

'What of Philip? It must have been a terrible experience

292

for him. Such humiliation! His own father!'

'Fortunately, he did not witness the killing. I made a point of talking at length with him to explain precisely what had happened and to prepare him for what was to come.'

'Poor child! He has lost everything!'

'There are gains as well as losses here.'

'Ambrose is like to be tried and hanged.'

'Most certainly.'

'Philip will have to bear that stain.'

'He has already foreseen that.'

'Will there be a place in the Chapel Royal for him after this?' she asked anxiously. 'Where will he go if they turn him out? This could blight his young life.'

'There may be salvation yet for him,' said Nicholas, touching her arm. 'But I may not tarry. I came simply to give you the tidings before you heard them, from a less well informed source.'

'I am deeply grateful, Nick. And relieved.'

'Ambrose Robinson will never pester you again.'

'Thank heaven!' she said. 'And yet, it did not seem like that at first. He helped me. I must not forget that.' She glanced towards the adjoining premises. 'Without his loan, I would have struggled to keep the business afloat. That was an act of friendship, whatever else he hoped to gain by it. Was he a good man with a streak of evil in him? Or an evil man with a vein of goodness?' She shook her head. 'Had his dear wife lived, we would not even be asking that question.'

'Too true.' He moved to the door. 'But I must go.'

'Nick . . .'

'Yes?'

'Now that you have remembered where I live, do not pass my house again without calling.'

'We play at The Rose next week.'

She smiled. 'Then I will expect you.'

Alexander Marwood surveyed the yard of the Queen's Head with mixed feelings. Instinct told him to sever all connections with Westfield's Men and thereby liberate himself from the recurring crises which beset the company and the ever present threat of assault upon his nubile daughter by one of the lustful actors. Commonsense whispered a different message in his hairy ear. The troupe paid him a rent and brought in custom. Westfield's Men also gave his inn a status in the capital which was important to him, and, more decisively, to his wife. The Queen's Head was recognised as the home of one of the most celebrated theatre companies in London.

Commonsense was still wrestling with instinct when Lawrence Firethorn and Owen Elias sidled up to him. They beamed with delight at a man whom they found unrelievedly loathsome.

'We need a decision from you,' said Firethorn.

Marwood grunted, 'I am thinking, I am thinking.'

'Is there any way we may aid your thought?'

'By leaving me alone, Master Firethorn.'

'You must not delay the verdict any longer. Too much rests on it. Do we play here tomorrow or not?'

'I do not know, sir.'

'The company is waiting to be told,' said Elias. 'We have

lost one performance and would hate to lose another. That would empty your yard for two afternoons next week.'

'Two?'

'Yes,' explained Firethorn. 'We play at The Rose on Wednesday. There'll be no crowds thirsting for your ale.'

'And no ruffians pissing in my stables,' said the landlord. 'No lechers ogling my daughter.'

They could see that he was weakening. Firethorn felt that he could handle the negotiations more easily on his own and nudged Elias accordingly. The Welshman moved away and was in time to welcome Nicholas Bracewell as the latter came in through the archway.

'Nick!' he called. 'Where have you been?'

'I'll tell you anon,' said Nicholas, looking across at Marwood. 'Has our landlord relented yet?'

'Lawrence is slowly bringing him round.'

'He must not be rushed. That's the trick of it.'

'I tried to help but was shooed away.'

'Then I'll borrow you for a weightier purpose.'

'And what might that be?'

'I need to hang you, Owen.'

'Hang me!'

Nicholas laughed at his expression. 'Come. You'll find me a gentle executioner.'

He led the way to the storeroom where the dead body had been discovered the previous morning. The noose had been taken away as evidence by the constables, but Nicholas quickly fashioned another out of a length of rope. Elias watched his deft fingers at work.

'You have done this before, I see.'

'What you see is a sailor's hands at work. If you spent as much time at sea as I have, you learn to tie knots of all kinds in a rope.' He pointed to the floor. 'Now, Owen. Lie there.'

'Why?'

'To please my fancy.'

'What is this all about?' grumbled Elias, lowering himself to the floor. 'Am I the dupe in this little game?'

'It is no game,' said Nicholas, placing the noose around his neck. 'How heavy are you? Half the weight of Jonas?'

'A third at least. I carried that man home and he was like a ton of iron. A triple Owen Elias.'

'I'll make allowances for that. Put your hands inside the rope to stop it cutting into your flesh.' He flung one end of the rope over the central beam. 'Are you ready?'

'*Iesu Mawr*! He really means to hang me!'

'Hold on.'

Nicholas pulled on the rope until it tightened around the hands and neck of his friend. He applied what he judged to be the correct pressure but could not move the body from the floor. Even when he wound the rope around his waist to give himself a stronger purchase on it, he could not lift the supine Elias.

'Thanks, Owen. You may get up now.'

'Good,' said the other, tugging at the noose.

'No, leave that on,' ordered Nicholas. 'I want to find another way to kill you.'

'You've tortured me long enough.'

'One more minute. That's all it will take.'

'Be quick about it then.'

'Stand there and do not move.'

Owen Elias was in the middle of the room. Nicholas moved the workbench until it almost brushed his jerkin. Picking up the mallet from the floor, he mimed a blow to the back of the Welshman's head, then grabbed him by the collar.

'Fall gently back.'

'Are you mad?'

'Go on. The table will catch you.'

Elias did as he was told and Nicholas guided him so that his back was across the workbench. When he tested the other end of the rope this time, he got more response. By applying some real pressure, he lifted the body into a sitting position. Hands inside the noose, Owen Elias gave a dramatic gurgle and pretended to be choking. Nicholas tossed the rope back over the beam. He then brushed the grains of sawdust from his friend's buff jerkin.

'Am I dead?' asked Elias, removing the noose.

'Completely. And now I know how he did it.'

'Who?'

'The Laughing Hangman.'

'Do you mind if we get out of here, Nick? I'm starting to feel like his next victim.'

They returned to the yard and found Firethorn talking volubly to James Ingram. The actor-manager preened himself as the others approached.

'I have done it, sirs! We play here tomorrow.'

A concerted cheer went up from the others.

'Marwood was like wax in my hands. Soft and smelly.'

'But you moulded him into shape,' said Owen.

They congratulated him profusely. Firethorn wanted to take them all to the taproom to celebrate, but Nicholas was more interested to hear the news from Ingram.

'Did you find out what I asked?' he said.

'I did, Nick. At a price.'

'A prison sergeant will do nothing without garnish.'

'I paid up, then came straight back here.' He turned to Firethorn. 'Please give my deepest apologies to your wife.'

'You've been to a prison and seen my *wife*?'

'No,' said Ingram. 'It was on my way back. I did not recognise her until it was too late. She must have thought it rude of me to ignore her. Explain that I was in such a rush to get back here.'

Firethorn was perplexed. 'Margery is in Shoreditch.'

'Not this evening.'

'Where else can she be?'

'Five minutes away at another inn.'

'An inn? Here in the city?'

Elias cackled. 'I spy merriment here.'

'You must have been mistaken, James,' said Firethorn.

'When I passed as close to her as I am to you? It was her. I'd swear that on the Bible.'

'I'm sure that there is a simple explanation,' said Nicholas with easy tact. 'Perhaps she is visiting a friend.'

'What kind of friend?' nudged Elias.

'And why did she make no mention of this to me?' added Firethorn as his suspicions grew. 'Was she alone, James?'

'She was.'

'And how was she attired?'

'In her finest apparel.'

'What was the name of the inn?'

'I did not mean to put you to choler in this way.'

'What was the name?'

'I assumed that you knew Margery was there.'

'The *name*?' demanded Firethorn.

'It was the Unicorn.'

Cecily Gilbourne did not waste much time on the formalities. Romantic dalliance was cast ruthlessly aside in favour of more tangible pleasure. As soon as Edmund Hoode was conducted in to her, she gave him a kiss on the cheek and took him through into the next chamber. He looked down at the bed on which they spent their torrid night together and he blenched. There was no resemblance to the Garden of Eden now. It reminded him of the gruesome rack which he had once beheld in the house of Richard Topcliffe, the master torturer. The bed was an instrument of pain.

'Have you written that sonnet yet?' she asked.

'It is still forming in my mind, Cecily.'

'But you promised to quote it to me.'

'Did I?' He saw a way to delay her ardour. 'Step back into the next chamber and I'll try a line or two for you.'

'In *here*,' she insisted. 'You swore that you would stroke my body with your poetry.'

'Did I?' gulped Hoode.

'Have you so soon forgotten?'

She pushed him into a sitting position on the bed. He was terrified. Cecily Gilbourne's appetite was too great for him to satisfy. Making love to her had turned into an ordeal. The thought that he would have to quote a sonnet to her in the middle of the exercise made it even more unappealing. Hoode looked around for escape but she was already unhooking his doublet.

'Why make such haste?' he said, panic-stricken.

She forced him back. 'Do you need to ask?'

'Will you not take refreshment beforehand, Cecily?'

'*This* is my refreshment!'

She writhed about on top of him until she was panting, then she began to pluck at her clothing. He had no idea that a dress could be removed so easily. When Cecily switched her attentions to his hose, his panic gave way to hysteria.

'I feel the first line of my sonnet coming!'

'Hold still while I take these off.'

'"O hot Sicilian Cecily . . ." Stay your hand. Please!'

'I am in too hot and Sicilian a mood!'

'Cecily!' he protested.

'Edmund!' she purred. 'My rhyming couplet!'

And before he could move, she flung herself full upon him and fixed her lips ineluctably on his. Hoode felt the waters closing over his head. He was just about to abandon all hope and submit when he heard a thumping noise on the door. The maidservant called out the warning.

'Mistress! Mistress! Beware!'

'What is it?' snarled Cecily in mid-rhyme.

'Master Hoode's wife is without.'

'His *wife*?'

'Yes!'

'But he does not have a wife.'

'I do, I do,' said Hoode gratefully. 'Can she be here?'

'Asking to come in,' said the maidservant.

'*Demanding!*' thundered a voice on the other side of the door. 'Edmund! Are you there?'

'No, my dear.'

'Stand aside, girl,' ordered the unexpected visitor.

The maidservant gave a little scream, the door burst open and the redoubtable figure of Margery Firethorn came through it at speed. She bristled at the sight of betrayal. Cecily Gilbourne retreated to a corner of the room, snatching up a sheet to cover herself and trying to show what dignity she could muster. Hoode threshed about helplessly on the bed. Margery did not stand on ceremony. Bestowing a glare of contempt on Cecily, she grabbed Hoode by the arm, hauled him off the bed and dragged him behind her like a sack of grain.

Hoode gladly withstood the discomfort of his departure. Bouncing down the stairs of the Unicorn was infinitely preferable to being eaten alive by a rampant lover with only one word in her sexual vocabulary – 'Again!' Margery played her part to the hilt. It was only when she had brought him out into the street that she relaxed and permitted herself a chuckle. Hoode was so thankful that he threw his arms impulsively around her and gave her a resounding kiss.

Lawrence Firethorn chose that moment to steal upon them.

Nicholas Bracewell knew where to find him. When the man was not at home, there was only one place he could be. It did not take the book holder long to walk to the precinct. He made his way across the Great Yard and into the theatre. Geoffrey Bless, the old watchdog, was slumped in his chair fast asleep, his eyes closed to shut out the fearful sight he had seen at Blackfriars that evening. The porter did not even stir when Nicholas took the key ring gently from his gnarled hand.

Creeping quietly up the staircase, Nicholas came to the door of the theatre and searched for the key to unlock it. He stepped into the auditorium to find it in darkness, the shutters now firmly closed to block out the last of the day. The place seemed deserted but Nicholas was certain that he was not alone. As he felt his way along, one hand held his dagger at the ready. He halted close to the stage.

'Come forth, sir,' he said. 'I know that you are here.'

There was a long pause before flickering light slowly appeared. A branched candelabrum was carried on stage and set on the table, which had been used during the brief rehearsal. A figure lowered himself onto the bench behind the table and set out some rolls of parchment before him. He seemed as confident and relaxed as if sitting in his own study.

'I expected you,' said Caleb Hay with a smile.

'Did you?'

'Sooner or later.'

'Then you will know why I have come.'

'Put that dagger away, sir. I am not armed. I will not talk to a man who threatens me with a weapon.'

'It is for my defence.'

'Against what? An old man with a pile of documents?'

Nicholas nodded and sheathed his dagger. Candlelight now illumined the area immediately in front of the stage. He looked across to the place where Raphael Parsons had fallen. The body had been removed but the floor was still covered by a dark stain. Caleb Hay glanced down at it.

'Master Parsons held one rehearsal too many in here.'

'Was he your next victim?'

'Do not look to me. He was killed by a disgruntled father.'

'And spared a more lingering death at the end of a rope,' said Nicholas. 'Is that why you were lurking in the precinct this evening? Until you could come upon him alone here in the theatre? Until you could let yourself in with Master Fulbeck's keys and take him unawares?'

'Why should I wish to murder Raphael Parsons?'

'For the same reason that you murdered Cyril Fulbeck and Jonas Applegarth.'

'The Master of the Chapel was my trusted friend. As for your fat playwright, how could a weak fellow like myself hoist such a weight upon the gallows?'

'With the aid of a workbench,' said Nicholas. 'It was easier to lever him up from that. You used another lever to bring Jonas to the Queen's Head in the first place. That letter, purporting to be from Lawrence Firethorn. An able scrivener would have had no trouble in writing that.'

'Able scriveners are quiet, sedentary souls like me.'

'You are not as weak and harmless as you appear. That was the mistake that Cyril Fulbeck made. Thinking you safe, he let you close enough to strike.'

'He let me close enough a hundred times, yet lived.'

'The case was altered the last time you met.'

'Pray tell me why,' challenged Hay. 'Here I sit at a judicial

303

bench and yet I am accused of unspeakable crimes. A friend whom I cherished. A playwright whom I never met. What flight of folly makes you link my name with their fate?'

'Religion!' said Nicholas.

'Indeed?'

'The old religion.'

'All three of us were Dominican friars? Is that your argument?'

'No, sir', returned Nicholas. 'I thought at first the theatre was the common bond between them. Cyril Fulbeck was involved with the Chapel Children and Jonas Applegarth was engaged by Westfield's Men. One here at Blackfriars and the other at the Queen's Head, both places of antiquity in their different ways and therefore fit subjects of study for a historian of London. Only someone who knew each room, cellar and passageway at the Queen's Head could have evaded me.'

'I hear no sound of the old religion in all this.'

'The Clink.'

'What of it?'

'You spent a day imprisoned there.'

'Yes,' said Hay. 'I made no secret of that.'

'It is a place where religious dissidents are held,' said Nicholas. 'Even a short stay there is recorded by the prison sergeant in his ledger. I found a way to peep into its pages. Master Caleb Hay was taken to the Clink but three months ago, his name and offence duly entered in the ledger.' He took a step forward. 'Documents favouring the old religion were found in your possession. You were held there as a Roman Catholic dissident.'

'Held but soon discharged.'

'On the word of the Master of the Chapel.'

'Yes!' said Hay, rising to his feet. 'I am a historian. Those documents were at my house so that I might copy them. They are a legitimate part of my work. Go search my study. You will find papers relating to John Wycliffe and others touching on the Jewish settlements in London. Does that mean I am a Lollard or a member of the Chosen People?'

'Cyril Fulbeck was deceived.'

'And so are you, sir.'

'He later came to see that deception.'

'Wild surmise!'

'Blackfriars,' said Nicholas calmly. 'The wheel has come full circle, Master Hay. This is where it started and must perforce end. Blackfriars was a symbol of the old religion to you. I recall how lovingly you talked of its past. Your father-in-law, Andrew Mompesson, only fought to keep a public playhouse out of the precinct because its noise would offend his ears. You had a deeper objection still. To turn a monastery into a theatre was sacrilege to you!'

'It was!' admitted Hay, stung into honesty.

'Vulgar plays on consecrated ground.'

'Anathema!'

'The Children of the Chapel mocking the Pope.'

'I could never forgive Cyril for that!'

'And then came Jonas Applegarth,' continued Nicholas. 'The scourge of Rome. A man whose wit lacerated the old religion in every play.'

'I saw them all,' said Hay, bitterly. 'Each one more full of venom and blasphemy. I thought *Friar Francis* was his worst abomination until you staged *The Misfortunes of Marriage*. What a piece of desecration was that! He stabbed away at everything I hold dear.'

'You made him pay a terrible price for his impudence.'

'It was downright wickedness!'

Caleb Hay took a few moments to compose himself. When he looked down at Nicholas again, he gave an amused chuckle.

'You have done your research well.'

'It was needful.'

'You would make an astute historian.'

'My study was the life of Caleb Hay.'

'How will that story be written?'

'With sadness, sir.'

'But my whole existence has been a joy!'

'It was not a joy you shared with your wife,' reminded Nicholas. 'She knew nothing of your inner life. You kept her on the outer fringes as your drudge. It was she who first made me wonder about the genius to whom she was married.'

'Why was that?'

'The fear in her eyes. The terror with which she climbed those stairs to call you. What kind of man locks out his wife from his room? What does he keep hidden from her behind that bolted door?'

'You have divined the answer, Nicholas Bracewell.'

'I think that I was not the only one to do so.'

'No,' confessed Hay. 'Cyril Fulbeck got there before

you. That is why he had to die. Not only because of this abomination in which we stand. He threatened to denounce me, and my bones are far too old for a bed at the Clink.'

He picked up the candelabrum and held it high to light up a wider area of the stage. He shook his head ruefully.

'Centuries of worship wiped uncaringly away!' he mused. 'A religious house turned into a seat of devilry. Innocent children schooled in corruption. A heritage ruinously scorned.'

The elegiac mood faded as he began to chuckle quietly to himself. His mirth increased until he was almost shaking. Then it burst forth in a full-throated laugh that Nicholas recognised at once. He had heard it at Blackfriars before and also at the Queen's Head. The difference was that it now lacked a note of celebration. As the laughter built and raced around the whole theatre, it had a kind of valedictory joy as if it were some kind of manic farewell.

Nicholas was thrown off his guard. There was a calculation in Caleb Hay's mirth. The laughter came to a sudden end, the flames were blown out, and the candelabrum was hurled at the book holder by a strong arm. It came out of the gloom to strike him in the chest and knock him backwards. Nicholas recovered and pulled out his dagger. He felt for the edge of the stage and vaulted up onto it. All that he could pick out in the darkness were vague shapes. When he tried to move forward, he collided with a bench.

He was convinced that Hay would try to make his escape through the rear exit and groped his way towards

307

the tiring-house. A sound from above made him stop. Light feet were tapping on the rungs of a ladder. Hay was climbing high above the stage. When Nicholas tried to follow him, a missile came hurtling down to miss him by inches. It was a heavy iron weight which was used to counterbalance one of the ropes on the pulleys. Nicholas moved to safety and considered his choices.

As long as he was trapped in the dark, he was at a severe disadvantage. Caleb Hay knew where to hide and how to defend himself. With no means of igniting the candles, Nicholas sought the one alternative source of light. He felt his way downstage, jumped into the auditorium and made for the nearest casement. Sliding back the bolt, he flung back the shutters to admit the last dying rays of a summer evening. One window enabled him to see the others more clearly and he ran down one side of the theatre to open all the shutters. When he turned back, he could see the stage quite clearly. He approached it with his dagger still drawn.

'There is no way out, Master Hay!' he called.

The familiar chuckle could be heard high above him.

'Come down, sir.'

'I'll be with you directly,' said Hay.

'It is all over now.'

'I know it well.'

'Come down!'

'I do, sir. Adieu, Nicholas Bracewell!'

Caleb Hay tightened the noose and jumped into space. The long drop had been measured with care. The rope arrested his descent with such vicious force that there was an awesome crack as his neck snapped. Six feet above the stage that he despised, he spun lifelessly until Nicholas stood on the table to cut him down.

The Laughing Hangman had chosen his own gallows.

'I regard this as a noble act of self-sacrifice, Edmund.'

'It was the least I could do to assuage my guilt.'

'Guilt?'

'Yes, Lawrence. I was too envious of Jonas.'

'That is not crime.'

'I sought to oust his work from our repertoire.'

'Only because we gave him precedence over you.'

'That rankled with me.'

'The fault was mine for riding roughshod over you.'

'All faults are mended this afternoon.'

'Amen!'

Lawrence Firethorn and Edmund Hoode were putting on their costumes in the tiring-house at The Rose. In view of the circumstances, Hoode had insisted that the privilege of performance at a proper theatre should go to *The Misfortunes of Marriage*. It would act as a fitting epitaph to the rumbustious talent of Jonas Applegarth and meet the upsurge of interest in the play which the murder of its author had created. The Bankside playhouse was packed to capacity for the occasion. Hoode was the first to concede that *The Faithful Shepherd* would not have provoked the same curiosity.

Barnaby Gill bounced across to them in a teasing mood. 'Is all well between you now?' he asked.

'Why should it not be?' said Firethorn.

'Rumours, Lawrence. Scandalous rumours.'

'Ignore them.'

'They are far too delicious for that.'

'Edmund and I are the best of friends,' said Firethorn with an arm around Hoode's shoulder. 'We have too much in common to fall out.'

'Too much indeed. Including your dear wife, Margery.'

'That is slander, sir!'

'A hideous misunderstanding,' said Hoode.

'They speak otherwise at the Unicorn,' prodded Gill. 'There they talk of the bigamous Margery Firethorn. One woman with two husbands. So much for the misfortunes of marriage! I give thanks that I never dwindled into matrimony.'

'It is only because the Chapel Children rejected your proposal,' rejoined Firethorn. 'You'd be bigamously married to every boy's bum in the choir if you could!'

Gill flew into a rage and Firethorn threw fresh taunts at him. Hoode found himself back in his customary role as the peacemaker between the two. He was home again.

Nicholas Bracewell gave the warning and the company readied themselves for the start of the performance. Its actor-manager had a last whispered exchange with Hoode.

'Turn to me when you are next in that predicament.'

'To you, Lawrence?'

'I have a remedy even better than Margery's.'

'And what is that?'

'Why, man, to take a woman off your hands and into mine. If this Cecily Gilbourne was too hot for your unskilled fingers to hold, you should have given her to me. My palms are proof against the fires of Hell.'

'Margery's was the deftest way.'

'I would have been a sprightly unicorn to the lady.'

'Then why did she not choose you in the first place?' said Hoode. 'No, Lawrence. The matter is ended and my debt is paid off to you both.'

'What debt?'

'I inadvertently disturbed *your* nuptial pleasure. By way of reprisal, Margery pulled me from the delights of the bedchamber. An eye for an eye.'

'A testicle for a testicle!'

Firethorn's chortle was masked by the sound of the music as Peter Digby and the consort brought the play to life once more. Westfield's Men soared to the occasion.

The Misfortunes of Marriage blossomed at The Rose. Its plot was firmer, its characters enriched and its satire more biting and hilarious. The company took full advantage of the superior facilities at the theatre to make their play a more exciting experience. Many dazzling new effects were incorporated by Nicholas Bracewell into the action, including one he had borrowed from Raphael Parsons and adapted for their own purposes. Trapdoors allowed sudden appearances. Flying equipment permitted the dramatic descent of actors and scenic devices. With the book holder in control behind the scenes, the pace of the play never faltered and its thrusts never missed their targets.

The acclaim which greeted the cast as they were led out to take their bow by Firethorn was so loud and so sustained that they could have played the final scene through again before its last echoes died. When the actors plunged back into the tiring-house, they were inebriated with their success. Barnaby Gill was dancing, Richard Honeydew was singing, Edmund Hoode was quoting his favourite speech from the play and John Tallis was croaking happily. Firethorn himself went around hugging each member of the troupe in tearful gratitude.

Even James Ingram was infected by the mood of celebration. He confided his feelings to the book holder.

'It is a better play than I gave it credit, Nick.'

'The play is unchanged,' said Nicholas. 'What has altered is your perception of it.'

'True. It is so much easier to appreciate when its author is not here to obstruct my view of its virtues.'

'Jonas *was* here this afternoon.'

'In spirit, if not in body.'

'That was his voice I heard out there on the stage. Even your mimicry could not reproduce that sound. It was a distinctive voice, James. Too harsh for some, maybe. You have been among them. But impossible to ignore.'

'Westfield's Men have done him proud.'

'No playwright could ask for more,' said Hoode, joining them as he pulled off his costume. 'Jonas Applegarth was a true poet. He died for his art. It is a tragedy that we only have this one play of his to act as his headstone.'

'We may yet have a second,' suggested Nicholas.

'Has he bequeathed us another?'

'No, Edmund. But you could provide it.'

'I could never write with that surging brilliance. Only

Jonas could pen a Jonas Applegarth play.'

'Work with him as your co-author.'

'How can he, Nick?' said Ingram. 'Jonas is dead.'

'Yes,' added Hoode with a touch of envy. 'He outshines me there as well. Not only did he live with more of a flourish, he died in a way that made all London sit up and say his name. Edmund Hoode will just fade away, unsung, in some mean lodging. That is what I admire most about Jonas Applegarth. His own life was his most vivid and unforgettable drama.'

'Then there is your theme,' urged Nicholas.

'Theme?'

'Put him back up on the stage in full view.'

'Jonas?'

'Why not?' said Ingram, warming to the idea. 'Change his name, if you wish. But retain his character. Keep that humour. Keep that wit. Keep that belligerence. If ever a man belonged on the boards with a mouth-filling oath, it is Jonas Applegarth.'

'His death will certainly give me my final scene.'

'The play foments in your mind already, Edmund,' said Nicholas with a smile. 'Write it as an act of appreciation. Let him know that Westfield's Men cherish his memory. We loved him but did not have time to tell him so before he left us.'

It took Anne Hendrik a long time to make a comparatively short journey. The audience at The Rose was too large and too inclined to linger for her to make a swift exit from the theatre. She and Preben van Loew were forced to wait until the earnest discussions of the play gradually subsided and the press of bodies thinned out. The Dutchman escorted her home before going on to his own house in Bankside.

There was no hurry. Nicholas would be delayed even longer than she had been. First of the company to arrive, he would be the last to leave, having supervised the removal of their scenery and costumes, the cleaning of the tiring-house and the collection of the money from the gatherers. There would be a dozen other chores before he could begin to think of slipping away.

When Anne caught herself calculating the earliest possible time of his arrival, she tried to pull herself together and put him from her mind. There was no guarantee that Nicholas would come. When Westfield's Men had last played at The Rose, she had no visit from its book holder afterwards. Why should this time be different? They had no obligations towards each other. Ambrose Robinson may have eased them back together but his arrest would just as effectively push them apart. She soon persuaded herself that Nicholas would be too busy carousing with his fellows to remember her invitation. She sank into a chair with resignation.

It was an hour before she got out of it. The tap on the door made her leap up and rush to answer it, waving away the servant who came out from the kitchen. Adjusting her dress and modifying her broad grin to a smile, she opened the door to find Nicholas standing there. She dismissed his apology for being so late and took him into the parlour.

'Did you enjoy the play?' he asked.

'As much as anything I have seen in years.'

'It is a remarkable piece of theatre.'

'A little too remarkable for Preben, I fear.'

'Oh?'

'He laughed at its jests but shied at its irreverence.'

'It is strong meat for a timid palate.'

They talked at length about the play until they felt sufficiently relaxed with each other to move away from it. Nicholas had some news for her.

'I spoke with Master Firethorn today,' he said, 'and put the name of Philip Robinson in his ear.'

'Why?'

'We need a new apprentice.'

'And you would consider Philip?'

'He recommends himself.'

'He may,' she said cautiously, 'but his situation does not. Did you tell Master Firethorn the full facts?'

'Each and every one.'

'The boy carries a stigma. Did he not baulk at that?'

'The only stigma that Lawrence Firethorn recognises is bad acting. Show him a willing lad with a wealth of talent and he'll take him into Westfield's Men, though his mother be a witch and his father have cloven hooves and a tail.'

'Then Philip is apprenticed?'

'If the Chapel Royal agree to release him.'

'They'll embrace the opportunity, Nick. Thank you!'

'For what?'

'Your kindness and consideration.'

'Philip will be an asset to us. I am only being kind and considerate to Westfield's Men, believe me.'

'I fretted over him,' she said. 'My mind is put at rest by

this news. It is a relief to know that some good has come out of all of this upset. I am still wracked with guilt about it.'

'Why?'

'I caused you so much unnecessary trouble. But for me, you would never have met Ambrose Robinson.'

'But for him, I might never have met Anne Hendrik again.' He grinned at her. 'I call that a fair exchange.'

'Then I am content.'

They fell silent. Nicholas feasted his eyes on her and basked in the luxury of her company. He had not been able to enjoy it to the full before. The obstacles between them had now vanished and he could appraise her properly for the first time. Anne wallowed in his curiosity before being prompted by her own.

'Do you live alone?' she said.

'No. The house is full of people.'

'I was talking about your room,' she said, probing quietly. 'I wondered if you . . . shared it with anybody.'

'I am never there long enough to notice.'

'Still married to Westfield's Men?'

'With all its misfortunes.'

They laughed together.

'But what of you, Anne? Alone here still?'

'Not for much longer.'

'Why?'

'That passage with Ambrose taught me much. I felt the lack of a man around the house. I will take another lodger.'

'I see,' he said with obvious disappointment.

'I do it for my own protection, Nick,' she argued. 'He

would not need to be here night and day. His scent would be enough. It would keep danger away.'

'What sort of lodger would you seek?'

'One that suited me.'

'In what way?'

Her eyes searched his. Nicholas was the first to smile.

'Where do you live?' she asked, moving closer.

'In Thames Street.'

'How much do you pay your landlord?'

'Too much.'

He took her in his arms for a long and loving kiss.

'I am thinking of moving,' he said.

If you liked *The Laughing Hangman*,
try Edward Marston's other series...

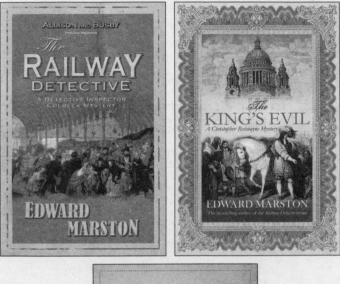

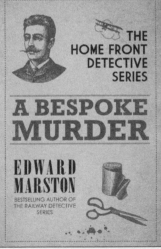

To discover more great books and to
place an order visit our website at
www.allisonandbusby.com

Don't forget to sign up to our free newsletter at
www. allisonandbusby.com/newsletter
for latest releases, events and exclusive offers

 Allison & Busby Books
 @AllisonandBusby

You can also call us on
020 7580 1080
for orders, queries
and reading recommendations